GIVING VOICE TO DAWN

BOOK ONE OF ELLIE'S STORY

Books by L. S. Gribko

Giving Voice to Dawn: Book One of Ellie's Story

The Lion's Apprentice: Book Two of Ellie's Story

GIVING VOICE TO DAWN

BOOK ONE OF ELLIE'S STORY

WRITTEN AND ILLUSTRATED

BY

L.S. GRIBKO

Milkweed Rising Publishing
Morgantown, WV

Giving Voice to Dawn
Copyright ©2016
Linda S. Gribko

Cover design, photograph of the sky on cover, and book design by Linda S. Gribko. Photograph of the hawk on cover by Paul Reeves Photography/ Shutterstock.com. Photographic portrait of General John Gibbon (pp. 82, 244) is courtesy of the Library of Congress. [Portrait of Brig. Gen. John Gibbon, officer of the Federal Army (Maj. Gen. from June 7, 1864)] http:// www.loc.gov/pictures/item/cwp2003000316/PP/

ISBN-10: 0-9978388-1-7
ISBN-13: 978-0-9978388-1-7

Published by Milkweed Rising Publishing, Morgantown, WV 26508
www.MilkweedRising.com

Dedicated to my brother

Michael R. Gribko (1965 - 2016)

who jumped free of gravity as I completed this book.

Adapt, Seeker, adapt!
Starve your appetite for dominion
And expel the bitter pill
That you might leap high enough
To snatch joy from the fleeting moments,
Reflect love back to your lover,
And leave your creative print upon the world.
Adapt, Seeker, adapt!
Leap high into the rising Sun.

I AM A NEOPHYTE MYSTIC...

"A neophyte, you say?" Mick looked doubtful. "I'd say you've moved well past the tenderfoot stage by now. At least I hope you have. I'm not entirely sure I'd have it in me to start over again with you."

"Hey, Mick, this is for my book. Remember? My story starts in 2013."

"Ahhh. Whereabouts in 2013?"

"At the beginning. In January."

"Ah, yes, January. When the winds began rattling your cage and calling you from your safe, dark perch. Such a relief when you finally started paying attention." Mick pushed forth a melodramatic sigh, which I chose to ignore.

"Yes. The winds. I'd almost forgotten. Thanks, Mick." I focused again on my computer monitor and poised my fingers over my keyboard.

I am a neophyte mystic...

"Mmm, pardon the additional interruption, but perhaps an invocation might be nice before we begin?"

I laughed. "An invocation, you say? You remember what happened last time we started with an invocation? How about a poem this time?"

"A poem? Yes, a poem would be quite nice."

"Okay, are you done now? Can I call you back in around page thirteen?"

"Oh, certainly. I'll be ready."

Mick slipped away and I turned back to my monitor. Before I began writing, however, I dug into my jeans pocket and pulled out the black, metallic stone that was my constant companion. As I rubbed my thumb over the smooth surface of the polished hematite crystal, I asked my guides for inspiration and protection.

And then I began.

Holding Back the Winds

Hold back your song
She was told.
Holding back my song
She said
Would be like holding back the winds.
Then the winds will not blow
He said.

Push away your glee
She was told.
Pushing away my glee
She said
Would be like pushing away the rains.
Then the rains will not fall
He said.

Pinch back your beauty
She was told.
Pinching back my beauty
She said
Would be like pinching the flower bud shut.
Then the flower will not bloom
He said.

Will away your passion
She was told.
Willing away my passion
She said
Would be like willing away the dawn.
Then the dawn will not come
He said.

She stepped back
Into the still, parched, gray darkness.

But holding back her song was like holding back the winds.

CHAPTER 1

THE TORMENTS OF THE WIND

The wind picked up, rattling the windows in their casings and inciting the branches of the white pine to riot against the side of the house. I hated nights like this — nights when the lights flashed several times and I held my breath to find out if I'd be plunged into cold darkness for the rest of the evening. I'd rather be left unchallenged with plenty of electronics to distract me, but on nights like this the wind dashed away my diversions and insisted on streaming memory past me like the debris of a hurricane…

"Why am I here?" I asked.

"What do you mean, why are you here? You're here to update me," said Steve. "You did bring the status report, didn't you?"

"Hmm?" I shifted on the couch to face Steve sitting across the office suite at his desk. "I'm sorry, I didn't mean to say that out loud." I grabbed a spiral bound report from the stack on the side table and held it up as evidence of my competence. "Right here."

Steve scowled at me and then glanced at his watch. Larry was late and the thirty minutes Steve had allotted for our meeting were draining away. He turned back to his computer monitor as my gaze settled on the view through the floor-to-ceiling windows that wrapped around the corner of Steve's office. What was happening in the sky as the sun slowly dropped behind the building was simply amazing. "Steve, look at the sunset. Isn't it gorgeous?"

Steve pushed an annoyed breath through his nose and looked at me, rather than the view. "You want a drink while we wait?"

I couldn't remember if I'd eaten lunch and didn't want to risk alcohol tonight, but Steve was already out of his chair and headed for the credenza. I heard a cabinet slide open behind me, followed by the clunk of two heavy tumblers on the thick glass that protected the walnut veneer of the credenza. A bottle bumped another with a gentle ting as Steve made a selection from his collection of offerings. There was the briefest pause in the auditory action while I envisioned Steve twisting the cap off the bottle, followed by three glugs of alcohol splashing into each glass. As was always the case, I was having what Steve was having and we were drinking it straight.

Steve came around the end of the couch and handed me a highball glass half full of Scotch. I steadied myself, hoping my eyes didn't reveal my dread, and accepted the drink with a smile. "Thanks." I took a sip and moved my reports aside to make room for my glass. Steve settled on the couch across from me and leaned forward to set his drink on the glass-topped coffee table between us.

"Larry will be walking in any minute, so I need to make this quick, but I've been a little worried about you lately. You've been off your game since the last RIF and I'm not feeling the same level of commitment from you. You need to take a few days? Get away? Timing's not great, but it could probably happen."

I studied Steve's face, suddenly aware of how much he'd aged in seven years. *Seven years. Had it already been that long?* "That's really nice of you, but..." I paused, knowing that I was now expected to decline Steve's generous offer and reconfirm my commitment. I had, after all, been spared in the recent layoff and shouldn't be thinking about time off. "...I think I'm ready to move on."

A look of disgust settled between Steve's eyebrows and lingered just long enough for me to notice. "Move on? As in leave the company? Is that what you just said to me?" Steve leaned back, stretched out his long legs, and crossed his ankles. He pressed his hands to his thighs and rolled his head, apparently trying to work a tight crick out of his neck.

"Yes, I guess I did. I wasn't really planning on having this conversation with you tonight, but I do believe the sunset has bewitched me." I laughed softly and took a long sip of Scotch.

Steve turned and looked over his shoulder at the fading red glow of the clouds. When he looked back at me, his face had softened into fatherly concern. He leaned forward again, but this time clasped his hands in front of him. "Just to confirm, you do understand the opportunity you've been offered, right? If you stay through the next merger? And, you understand that walking away now means walking away from everything, correct?"

A quick rush of fear coursed through me. The faint smile that played over Steve's lips indicated he'd noticed my flicker of doubt. He began carefully luring me back away from the edge of the cliff, using my personal commitment to him as bait. "That's right, the view is pretty scary when you're thinking more rationally, isn't it? A few more years. That's all. You can hold on for one more merger. For me."

"Well, I'm not..."

Steve's patience dissolved almost as quickly as it had coalesced. "Larry's going to be here any minute. I need you to make a commitment. Now. Are you in or out?"

I have to decide now? Well, that makes things easier. "I guess out. I want to do something else. Something that makes me feel alive. I ca..."

"Oh, holy shit. Why the hell are you still such a kid? Yeah, we all want to be doing something else. They call that retirement. Grow up! Put in your time and then do whatever the hell you want, but what I need from you now is a little more patience. One more merger."

"I don't think I have another merger in me. I'm afraid I won't find what's missing if I wait."

"What's missing? Is that what this is about? A mid-life crisis?"

"No, not a crisis. I just can't go another year feeling…numb." The last few golden rays of sunlight shot around the corner of the building and illuminated the silhouette of a large bird wheeling around against the iridescent clouds. *A hawk?* I tilted my head and stared hard, not completely trusting my eyes. *Yes, a hawk over downtown!* I imagined the bird screaming as it soared over the city, floating on the evening breeze. The hawk wheeled closer to the building, daring me to run to the window and press my nose against the glass to get a better look. I struggled against its appeal, afraid of the reaction I'd get, but allowed my fingertips to lift and spread as I imagined an invisible wind teasing my own wings.

Steve huffed in my direction, snapping my focus back to his face. He pushed himself off the couch, marched back to his desk, and hit the intercom. In spite of the late hour, his assistant's voice immediately came through the speaker.

"Yes, Steve."

"Martina, give Larry a call and let him know the meeting tonight is cancelled. Let's get it back on the schedule for early next week."

"Right away."

"Thanks, Martina."

Steve strode back across the office, retrieved his glass, and took a long swig of tolerance before settling back on the couch across from me. "Okay, I'm all ears. What's going on?"

If I got lucky, I might fall asleep in spite of the storm, but in addition to bringing me memories, the wind also had picked up a habit of swirling the same dream past me over and over again. I was used to dreaming, but my dreams had always been crazed and chaotic with no staying power. Those dreams were blotted away by the first rays of the sun. This new dream, though, the one carried by the wind, was careful and measured. I remembered it in excruciating detail even when I begged the sun to wash it out so my mind could relax from puzzling out its meaning. But the sun refused to bend to my will and, so, I tried instead to find release by sharing the dream…

"The valley is long and deep — much longer than it is wide. The sides start to slope up like a bowl, but halfway to the top go completely vertical. You know, like a valley you'd see out West — really rugged. Everything is really dry and inhospitable. Rock from the cliffs is jumbled on the floor of the valley, which is otherwise flat.

Umm, are you listening?"

"Um-hmm," Neil intoned without looking up from his phone.

"Do you want me to keep going?"

"Sure."

"Okay, because this is where things get interesting. I notice there are paths zigzagging up the valley walls. Not just a few paths, but a plethora of paths."

"Ahhh. A plethora. A plethora of paths."

I scowled at the top of Neil's head and kept going. "At this point in the dream, I always suddenly realize that I'm not sure where I could possibly be standing to see the entire valley. That valley must be hundreds of miles long, but I can see all of it. And then I always realize…"

"What time of day did you say it is in this dream?"

"Umm. I didn't. Why does it matter?"

"Hmm? I guess it doesn't. I'm just trying to engage with your story."

"Without really listening?"

"Uh, yeah, pretty much."

"Okay, I'm sorry, forget it. I clearly can't compete with your new phone app."

"No, no, no. I do want to hear."

"Then lift your head and put down your phone."

"Hold on, hold on…"

"Forget it."

"Hmm? Okay."

And although I struggled to find someone to listen, I began to feel sure that the storm would blow past and leave me be if only I got the dream out into the world. So, I kept trying…

"…I realize that I'm flying. I must be flying because I can move around and see the entire valley. At least I think I'm flying. Maybe soaring is a better way to describe it, because I'm not flapping my wings or struggling to stay in the air." My mind slipped back to the hawk I'd recently seen from Steve's office window. I held my hands out in front of me and spread my fingers.

"Cool. Let's call it soaring. Carry on."

The monotonous beep-beep-beep pulsing through my cellphone speaker indicated that Andy was on a job and was probably helping a delivery driver back his truck up. I picked up speed, desperate to plow through my story before he had to hang up.

"Okay, I'm soaring over the valley and I realize that I can't see where the paths end. I can see the entire valley in minute detail, but right at the lips of the bluffs, the landscape becomes all smeared and I can't see the paths once they leave the valley."

"Well, that sounds like a spiritual allusion. You know — all paths lead to God?"

"Huh? Oh!"

"Hey, I hate to completely change the subject, but I need to get back to it here and I really need you to do something for me. Can you do something for me?"

"Sure, I guess. What do you need me to do?"

"I need you, if you would be so kind, to stop by and see Carla. See if you can help me extract myself from the relationship."

"Oh, Andy, that puts me in such an awkward position. She's gotten so melodramatic since you started messing with her head and you know I don't do well with drama. And, besides, you do realize I'm at least somewhat sympathetic to her plight, right? I just might end up helping her hatch a plan that ultimately leads to your untimely demise."

"Don't worry, you'll do fine. Carla has always liked you and respects your advice. Just tell one of those stories you've got that's easy to relate to. Something with an animal in it — you know how soft she is on animals. And, don't mind me, I'm willing to overlook both your weakness for a sad story and your lack of…," Andy sniffed, "…loyalty." No doubt he'd be dabbing an eye with a crooked grin plastered across his face if we were together having this conversation.

"Oh, please spare me! I should refuse to help you, you know, seeing as you did this to yourself."

"Yes, you should, but you won't."

…and eventually…

"At first, the valley seems to be empty but then I notice the people — thousands of people with loads on their backs slowly moving around the valley. Well, actually, to be clear, only some of the people are moving around. At least half of them can't even stand up because they're so loaded down with boxes, suitcases, shopping bags — they're just buried." I rounded my back and crouched forward in my chair, illustrating the pathetic condition of my overloaded dream people. "Other people seem to have shrugged off their burdens, but they're not free — they're tethered to their piles like dogs chained to trees."

"Oh, I hate that. You know I hate that."

My dream dissolved from my mind's eye as my aunt's face swam back into focus. "Hate what?"

"When people tie their dogs out like that. I can't stand that level of neglect."

Oh, damn, I was losing her. "I'm sorry, Aunt Marge, maybe not the best visual to use, but you know what I mean, right? People are chained to piles of, well, stuff and…"

My aunt popped up from the kitchen table and bustled over to the fridge. "Would you like to stay for dinner?"

"Sure, I'd…"

"Oh, I heard from Aunt Liz last week." Marge pulled open the refrigerator and looked inside.

I opened my mouth to protest the change of subject, but my aunt was one step ahead of me. "Don't worry, this relates. She and Uncle Pete finally made a decision. They're selling the house and buying the condo at Myrtle Beach, after all." Marge leaned forward and disappeared behind the open fridge door. "Both of them finally agreed that it was time to downsize." Her head popped up again and I could see in her expression that she'd moved on from our conversation and now had a plan of attack. "Have you had chicken lately? Can I fix you some garlic chicken and a nice salad?"

…found someone eager to listen.

"Some of the tethered people seem content just sitting by their piles of boxes watching the world go by. But, others are straining against their chains, trying to get somewhere while dragging their massive loads. I get frustrated with this part of the dream because it feels like other dreams I've had where I'm trying to get ready to leave the house but everything is in slow motion." I looked up at the dispassionate face of the woman sitting in front of me and felt a sudden misguided need to make a personal connection. "Do you have those dreams, too?"

"Yes, actually I do. Usually when I'm feeling stuck in a situation that's not right for me any longer and I know deep down that I'm just forcing myself through the motions. Do you feel as if that rings true for you at this time in your life?"

"Uh." My right thumbnail became suddenly fascinating. I gently pushed the cuticle back and wondered if I should bother with a manicure this week, what with gardening season right around the corner.

"I'm sorry, I didn't mean to press. We can skip that for now. Would you like to continue?"

I looked up and made eye-contact again, wondering if my cheeks looked as flushed as they felt. "Sure. Uh. Well. So, I'm soaring around looking at all these struggling people when I notice movement on the bluffs surrounding the valley. But, I'm so far away at first that the movement looks like a mirage…like a shimmer on the horizon." I wiggled my fingers as I imagined a palm tree oasis shimmering in the distance. A wave of self-consciousness immediately washed over me and I dropped my hands back to my lap.

"Okay, go ahead."

"But, as I soar closer to the nearest bluff, I realize that the movement isn't a mirage. It's people. Thousands and thousands of people with daypacks are climbing the paths up out of the valley."

"Ah, so not everyone is chained down in a hopeless position."

"No. No, they're not. And the ones who are leaving seem to have left things behind because I notice unattended debris strewn all over the valley floor. Clothes, electronics, treadmills, status reports, boarding passes, shoes…there are shoes everywhere…I've never seen so many shoes. And, I'm wondering how all those people escaped their loads when *BAM!* — there's a flash of bright light and someone with a huge load on their back drops to the ground in a debris field of their belongings. And, then *BAM!*, *BAM!*, *BAM!* — more people go down…"

"Are they dead?"

"The people on the ground? No — just stunned. They recover pretty quickly."

"Ah, and how do they respond to their newfound freedom?"

"Their freedom? Oh. Well, some just sit on the ground, completely tapped out. But, others don't stay down for long. One guy, in particular, always jumps up immediately and starts gathering his loot. He gets frustrated every time because he can't get everything back the way it was. Some of his boxes seem to have disintegrated and others are burning. I always end up circling around this guy thinking, 'Uh, excuse me, you're not going to get your girlfriend back in that box…things have changed between you two forever.' But, he…"

"Wait. There was a woman in one of the boxes?"

"Yeah, apparently so, but she popped out and ran like hell."

"That's interesting. What does the man do next?"

"He bitches. He bitches about his girlfriend, bitches about his shitty job, his boss, his mother, his childhood. He's grasping to find someone to blame for his life flying apart."

"Ah, yes, pretty common response. So, everyone's either in shock or complaining…"

"Oh, no. Some are on their feet asking questions. I think of them as the seekers because they seem to be seeking answers."

"Interesting. What types of questions are they asking?"

"Mostly variations on 'what's next?'. They want some advice and want to know what's expected of them."

"Is anyone getting answers?"

"Well, I'm not sure, but about two-thirds of them plop down on the valley floor and get comfortable setting up house again. They start gathering up new piles of necessities."

The woman's eyes lifted to a point somewhere over my left shoulder. "And the others? What do they do?"

"Um, they're taking off." I twisted around in my chair and found a clock on the wall behind me. "I'm almost to the end. Do we have time to finish?"

"Sure, we have a few minutes left. Keep going."

"Okay, thanks, I'll make it quick. The rest of the seekers take off on their own. They pick up a few items, pack a small bag, and take off for the paths out of the valley. Some of them begin the climb alone but others pair up or go in groups."

"Ah! Well, how do the people climbing the paths seem? Confident?"

I paused, realizing that I hadn't paid much attention to the travelers' mindset. "No, more like hesitant, but they go anyway."

"Okay. How do you think they know which paths to take?"

"Well, it seems as if they just go. Like something on the path is pulling them and they just..." A bank of red clouds shot through with golden sunbeams intruded into my consciousness. I imagined myself back on the couch in Steve's office, but this time his voice droning on about my sudden lack of commitment was barely audible over the rush of wind in my ears and the screams of the hawks surrounding me. "...allow it. They allow it."

"They give up their free will?"

"No, it's not like that. They let what needs to happen, just...happen." I paused. "Without a fight."

"Interesting. So, the people pick a path and start climbing up out of the valley. What's next?"

"I don't know."

"You don't know?"

"No, the dream cuts away at that point and I'm in my house, but my house is empty except for a few pieces of furniture. All the windows are open and there's a strong breeze flowing through the house, which is filled with a strange light that's both clear and soft at the same time. Like it's morning, evening, and midday all at once. And something is expected."

"What's expected?"

"I don't know but there's an axe in the dining room table."

"An axe? Really?"

"Yeah, a red axe like one I used to own is stuck in the dining room table. And the axe is pinning a note to the table. I move over to read the note..." I paused and pinched my lower lip between my thumb and forefinger.

"Does it tell you what's expected?"

I let go of my lip. "Maybe, but I don't know."

"You don't know?"

"No, I see words on the note but wake up before I can read them."

"Interesting. Are you curious about what the note might say?"

"Well, no, not until right this moment. I'm usually just concerned about my table being ruined."

"Of course. Is that it, then?"

"Yes." I nodded slowly, allowing my head to just barely bob as I visualized blurry words scrawled on a piece of paper inexplicably pinned to a table with a red axe. *What did the note say?*

"Okay. Well, that's quite the interesting dream. I think we'll stop there for today. Next time we can start talking through what's going on in your life. Remember, I'll be out of town next week, so we'll have to schedule for the week of the 15th."

"Oh, no, that's okay. Thank you, but, I won't need to come back."

"You're not coming back? You don't want to explore the issues we discussed on the phone — your feelings of disconnection and…" The woman looked down at her notes. "…general anxiety around life purpose?"

I blushed again. "No, not coming back. But thanks for listening to the dream all the way through. I really needed someone to listen all the way through. I'm good now." I gathered my things and stood to leave, feeling suddenly ridiculous and in need of a daypack. "Have a great vacation."

And with that, the wind had done its job.

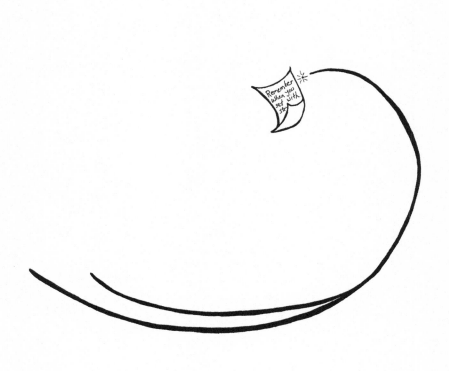

CHAPTER 2

SCENES FROM A METRO TRAIN I:
HEAVEN, HELL, AND KARMA

"Believing in reincarnation is so much kinder, you know."

I was pressed into a window seat on a DC Metro train screaming along the Red Line from Montgomery County to downtown when Mick dropped his bombshell in my ear. I shifted uncomfortably in my seat and glanced around. *Was anyone else hearing this conversation? Was anyone staring?* Fortunately, everyone within shouting distance appeared to be appropriately zoned out within his or her bubble of personal protection. My new fascination with spiritual matters wasn't going to be exposed, at least not this morning.

"It's so cruel to paint yourself into a corner, judging yourself good or bad, worthy of heaven or destined for hell. Why allow yourself only one lifetime to get everything right? Too much pressure to perform, I say," Mick continued.

Mick had only been part of my life for a few months, having invited himself to join me on my journey just a few days before I quit my job. He'd settled in quickly, wedging himself adeptly into my commute, and becoming immediately comfortable when it came to giving advice. "Go ahead and jump," he'd said when I'd mentioned my desire to leave the company. "Things will turn out mostly okay, you know." Nothing ever seemed alarming to Mick, not ending your career with nowhere to land and certainly not rejecting heaven and hell in favor of a trip through multiple lifetimes.

"Okay, so what about karma?" I said. "If you believe in reincarnation, don't you also have to believe in karma? Isn't karma the same as heaven or hell? You do good things, your karma is good and good things happen to you. You do bad things and karma kicks your ass. How is that at all different than heaven and hell?"

"Oh, karma," Mick murmured, clearly pleased that I'd brought it up. "Karma isn't good or bad. It's the sum total of your actions. Karma includes who you've been and what you've done, but karma isn't a tit for tat matter of cause and effect. Karma represents a seed you carry forward that contains within its shell all the ingredients you need for radical growth."

I paused and let Mick's explanation sink in and fill my head before responding. "So, hoping someone's karma takes them down when they've been particularly nasty is pointless?"

"Pointless, yes. Very much so."

"That's disappointing." My fantasies of Steve writhing in an acidic puddle of his own karma were suddenly dashed.

"Now, it is important to consider that karma does follow you from lifetime to lifetime and can emerge during your current tenure on Earth as thoughts and emotions that you might find difficult to explain; however, that's only because you've forgotten salient details from one lifetime to the next."

"Salient details? I think you just lost me."

"Hmmm. Perhaps I can illustrate my point with examples. Let's start with a phobia of arachnids completely out of proportion to your experience with spiders. Imagine a phobia so heightened that the mere thought of a spider causes you to become highly anxious, even though you've experienced not a single bite."

"Okay."

"Now, let's take a small peek into a previous lifetime where we find you imprisoned in a dark, damp dungeon in feudal England — a dungeon filled with spiders and the fear of execution. See how that changes things?"

"Yeah, I guess so."

"And what if you also routinely feel overwhelming responsibility for things out of your sphere of influence coupled with a nagging sense of failure no matter your accomplishments?" My ears perked up — this sounded like my friend, Neil.

"On top of the spider thing?"

"Yes, on top of the spider thing. What if that sense of responsibility originated during a stint as a French Army surgeon during the Great War?"

"Because I was responsible for saving people?"

"Yes. All those wounded soldiers placed their lives in your hands, but, being human, you were not able to save them all."

"Oh. So, our hang-ups? Karma is our hang-ups? And we carry them from lifetime to lifetime in a seed?"

Mick chuckled. "Yes, I guess you could put it that way. Karma is all your actions, though, so also included are all the gifts that you bring forward. What's important here, though, in terms of the point I want to make before we arrive at my stop, is that without a previous life, or many previous lives, we're always grasping back into our present childhoods for explanations of who we are and how we became injured. We ask ourselves, 'What happened to me when I was three years old to give me a fear of spiders, to compel me take responsibility for outcomes that aren't under my control, or...to saddle me with a burden of perpetual grief that I can't see to shake?' "

I winced, but Mick continued on, apparently unconcerned that he'd made me uncomfortable.

"Mostly the answers aren't back there in your three-year old world," he continued. "And mostly we might not need to search out those answers. Karma brought each of us to this present life based on what we need and want as a soul, which mostly boils down to living a life in the physical realm and, perhaps, allowing our seed to germinate."

"Oh." I sat and ruminated as the train slid up to the next station.

"Tenleytown. American University. Doors opening on the left," intoned a garbled human voice.

Mick stood and moved smoothly toward the doors, slipping away from the conversation just as it got good. "Wait!" I called out, "How do we get our seed to germinate?"

Mick turned to me and winked. "Live your truth, my friend. Relax, release your fear, and let yourself emerge. Oh, and don't worry if you screw it up, because you will screw it up." And with that, Mick stepped off the train and was gone.

FRIENDS AND FAMILY

Before we go too much further, I really should introduce you to my friends and family. You might be wondering about Mick right about now, too, but he doesn't really fall into either of those categories. Not really. But, he shows up in my life pretty regularly and, fair warning, he'll probably butt in during the introductions and turn the conversation a bit. Mick's just like that and you'll learn more about him as we go along, but right now I need you to meet a few other folks. They're all important to the story I'm about to tell you, and I don't want to turn you one way or the other on any of them, so I've decided to make introductions by sharing, to the best of my recollection, conversations I had with each of them shortly before the true depth of the commingling of our karma was revealed.

CHAPTER 3

INTRODUCTIONS: CARLA

It takes an extraordinary amount of energy to remain in a low orbit without burning up in the atmosphere. Andy's girlfriend, Carla, was continuously skimming the envelope of the mesosphere and probably had been for decades, although I'd only known her for the ten years that my brother and she had been together. I was sure, though, that when my beautiful, devoted, and achingly delicate almost-sister-in-law gazed at her reflection, she saw staring back the ugly burns and scars of a life lived just barely well enough. Lately I'd begun to worry that her orbit was rapidly decaying.

"Do you think I should give Andrew another chance? Alexa keeps telling me no, that he dulls my shine, but I really do love him." Carla took a sip of her coffee and looked at me with wide-eyed anticipation.

As I pondered whether I should participate in this conversation with Carla again or drop my coffee mug and run, a dragonfly paused on the deck rail and considered Carla with disturbing bulbous eyes. Staring at the metallic gold creature, I relaxed and allowed my mind to clear. To my surprise, a golden gift box tied with a red silk ribbon inexplicably swam into my awareness and stopped before me. I imagined reaching out and pulling the ribbon, which slipped from the box and released the shiny gold lid to rise up and free the contents of the box — a stream of golden light. Although I wasn't completely sure of what had just happened, I suddenly understood in totality what Carla needed to hear and leaned forward to deliver the message, which did, in fact, involve an animal story.

"Do you know about dragonflies, Carla?" I asked.

"Oh my god, that one's fabulous," Carla said, noticing the visitor on the rail. "It's freaking fabulous. I love dragonflies — they're so magical."

"Uh-huh, pretty on the outside, but do you know a dragonfly's heart?" I twisted my face into a sinister caricature, hoping I could get Carla to laugh.

"Does this have to do with Andrew? You know he moved out, don't you? Are you saying he still loves me?" Carla's eyes welled up.

Yes, of course, I knew that Andy had finally moved out but was still stopping by on Wednesdays and Saturdays to spend the night. And that the sex was still great. Dropping my coffee and flying up and out of the thickly cushioned deck chair that felt so deceivingly safe and welcoming suddenly seemed incredibly appealing. I wondered how Carla's cat would respond when I tore through the house, grabbed my shoes on the fly, and slammed out the front door. I imagined her as a cartoon cat with arched back, white fur standing straight up on end, eyes as big as silver dollars, and pink mouth held agape.

"Uh, no. Okay, yes, but not really. I'm hoping I can tell you about dragon-flies and you'll answer your own questions. Are you willing to play along?" I smiled at Carla and beamed love to her through my eyes.

"Sure, but remind me to tell you what he did last Tuesday. You will not believe it." I nodded vaguely as my smile became tight. Of course, I'd already heard about this most recent drama twice — once Tuesday night shortly after Andy had asked Carla for her friend, Nichole's, phone number and again Thursday morning as I balanced my phone and fumbled with my wallet while attempting to pay for groceries. My brother's inability to let go and his misguided attempt to incite one final fight to end the relationship were exactly why I was sitting here.

The gilded dragonfly remained on the rail, staring intently. I stared back into its unblinking eyes and attempted to read its mind. *Deception, yes. Start with the deception.* "So dragonflies are masters of deception," I started. "Most people don't realize what they have going on under that façade of cellophane wings and whimsical flitting, but they really make no secret of the fact that they're blood-thirsty predators with no qualms about eating their own kind."

Carla's eyebrows came together and her nostrils flared involuntarily. She squinted at me as if there were a blob of unidentifiable nastiness on my fore-head. Maybe this story was just the ticket. "That playful flitting and landing on the same perch over and over?" I cocked my head and paused, inviting Carla to respond. She nodded almost imperceptibly. I took that feeble affirmation as confirmation that I should continue. "It's all aggression and territorial maneuvering."

The dragonfly shifted on its perch, inviting me to glance back at it. I could feel the creature grin a crooked grin and could perceive, rather than see, an impish sparkle in its eye. "The dragonfly makes no excuses for its behavior," I added. "It embraces its dark side just as it embraces its light and has no use for the fairy tale illusions that humans nurture. A dragonfly lives its truth whether we accept it or not."

Carla looked perplexed. "So what does this have to do with Andrew?" she asked as she glanced over at the gold dragonfly still perched on the deck rail.

"Uh, think about it. Can you see where I'm going with this?"

Carla's eyes glazed slightly as she denied understanding. "No, you've really kind of lost me."

I breathed in and breathed out. And then breathed in and breathed out again. The dragonfly left its perch on the rail and came over to sit on the arm of my chaise. I imagined it at that moment in plaid boxers stretched out on Carla's spotless white couch with a beer in one hand and the remote in the other. My brother, Andy, reimagined as a glittering gold dragonfly. I snorted as I tried to stifle a laugh.

"Are you okay?" asked Carla.

"Yes. Andy is the dragonfly," I blurted quickly. "Does that help?"

"What do you mean?" Carla was tearing up again.

Breathe in and breathe out. Resist the urge to comfort her…and…go! "Andy is the dragonfly, Carla. He accepts his dark side as part of who he is and right now he's let his darkness out to play. I think he's hoping you'll respond with anger and kick him to the curb. He's had you tucked up under his wing for so long that he feels responsible for your happiness and is having a hard time letting go of that responsibility. But at the same time, it's obvious something's clicked in Andy. He's gotten some sort of cosmic call to action that has his outlook expanding so fast that the rest of us are struggling to keep up with what's next. He can't fight that off, Carla, but you seem to have created an incredibly needy persona recently in an attempt to rein him in as he pulls away. Andy can see right through what you're doing and he's not going to be manipulated, but he's also having trouble making a graceful exit. So, to answer your question, I'd say that even though you two will always love each other, Andy can't provide stability and security for you any longer and, for your own sake, it's probably time to cut things off yourself rather than wasting any more energy on his, uh, drama." I pushed all of that out into the atmosphere so quickly that I suddenly felt winded. I sucked in a big, greedy breath.

"What do you mean by his dark side?" Carla asked in a clipped tone that indicated she was hot on the trail of something she didn't know about my baby brother.

I was suddenly exhausted and exhaled my resignation. "Nothing that you haven't already seen, Carla. Think about all the parts of Andy's personality that drive you insane. All the things that you'd like to fix in him."

"Oh, he's always twenty minutes late, he's self-absorbed, he's so short-tempered when he's tired, he's manipulative when he doesn't get his way…" I zoned out as Carla continued. Rattling off Andy's offenses was always the easy part for her but the eyeholes of her new martyr mask were clearly too small — she was completely missing the bigger picture.

"…and I really wish he'd take life more seriously," Carla finished as she spread her hands beseechingly, suggesting that asking Andy to recast himself as an entirely new character in her play wasn't really all that unreasonable.

I paused for a moment before diving headlong into the deep end of Carla's emotional swimming pool. "Have you considered that it's really easy to be critical of Andy when you've given up so much of yourself to him that you can't help but feel resentful when you're not always the center of his attention?"

"Well, that's certainly something to say to me!"

"Yes, I guess it is and the last thing I want to do is cause you more pain. But…" I stopped, suddenly aware that I was mad at my brother and about to take it out on Carla. How could I help this fragile woman who had always been a friend to me and had meant the world to my brother for so many years? "It seems like it's time for you to grow, too, Carla," I started again more gently, "but in a way that's right for you. I think what's happening with Andy is painful but also an opportunity to get out of his shadow and reclaim yourself."

"Are you implying that I need to grow up?" Carla asked tersely.

Yes! Yes! Yes!, I wanted to scream. *Grow up and stop playing these games!* But, that wasn't completely fair and before I could actually speak the words, the dragonfly rose up a few inches and then settled again on the arm of my chair. Was it trying to get my attention? I gazed again into its bulging eyes, which seemed to stare right through the shadows that concealed Carla's secrets. *The illusion. Help Carla understand the illusion she's created.*

"No, that's not what I meant. It's just — Carla, you're a kind, gracious person, with so many wonderful traits and I think your friend, Alexa, is right. Your shine is dulled."

Carla took another sip of coffee and nodded appreciatively.

"But, Andy's not the one who dulls it — you do so you can stay dependent on him. For some reason, you're hiding under the mask of a clingy, emotional wreck. Peel off the mask and be yourself, Carla. And then stand toe to toe with Andy. If he sees himself reflected in you, he'll realize he still loves you, but make sure you see yourself reflected in him, too, or you've sold yourself short."

Carla looked at me through eyes that were about to explode. I'd clearly touched something that she thought was hidden from view. I exhaled and resolved that this would be my last conversation with Carla. "And if you don't want to do that, then detach emotionally and enjoy the sex while Andy scouts around for someone who truly does reflect his soul."

Before Carla could respond, her sleek white cat jumped smoothly into my lap and snatched the golden dragonfly from the arm of the chaise. The dragonfly buzzed once and then was still as the cat leapt down with the shiny insect clenched in her jaws. I watched in stunned silence as the cat spat bits of gold dragonfly out onto the deck boards, which now glittered in the late morning sun.

"Ohhhhhh, serves Andy right!" Carla exclaimed as she clapped her hands together in delight. "Did I tell you what he did last Tuesday?"

CHAPTER 4

SCENES FROM A METRO TRAIN II: LIVING YOUR TRUTH...OR NOT

The hollow whoosh of the Metro pushing air through the tunnel always reminded me of the soul-sucking Dementors from the Harry Potter movies. To kill time during this particular trip, I sat and imagined how many times the detached people lined up in the molded plastic seats around me rode this train before their souls were sucked away by the Dementors' kiss. *Once? Twice? Dozens of times? Did the obstinate ones, the dreamers, ride hundreds of times before their hearts sank to their shoes as they pursued a paycheck to keep them safe? What dreams had each of them given up to make their existence seem okay? How many novels, musical scores, art pieces, careers in the NBA, and business plans were stashed away in the past tense by the people on this train? And who sitting around me had the Dementors been unable to rob of their spark? How many were living their truths? And how many more were about to break free so they could?*

"It's not possible to heal your pain if you don't live your truth, is it Mick?"

"Your pain? No, I don't believe it is."

Carla's pinched features flickered in my mind's eye. "But so many people are detached from their truth."

"That's right," Mick confirmed, "they've pushed it away. It would be easy to say they'd numbed their true selves out of existence, but that's not true. Everything is still there, just buried and no longer easily accessible."

"Buried? Buried how? How can you bury your truth?"

"Oh, people are so creative when it comes to that. As soon as someone starts to live an inauthentic life, to become other than who they really are, a big hole opens. Their truth tumbles in and falls to the bottom. It's a gaping, greedy hole to fill with all the trappings of an ordinary life — routine, responsibility, employment, a two-hour commute, marriages, babies, friendships, obligations. Addictions...addictions, too. And possessions, we can't forget possessions. People pack the holes in their lives full of all kinds of baubles, both valuable and not. There's a gnawing lack, you see, when you deny your truth and most are quite diligent about covering up that lack."

I frowned, thinking back to my dream of the valley full of scattered possessions. "And then?"

"And then — what?"

"Well, what happens when people have all that they need? When they get the hole filled up — then what happens?"

"Oh, that's not possible. Filling the hole is not possible. No, no, not at all. The gnawing sense of incompletion is always there. The truth is still there.

Do you recall the recent story about the elderly gentleman who just earned the college degree he began in 1938?"

"Yes. He's ninety-seven years old. His education was interrupted by World War II. He was drafted."

"That's right. And he came back home and allowed his truth to drop to the bottom of a hole that he filled with life and love and family. But the gnawing lack was always there, wasn't it?"

"Sure, I guess it had to have been."

"And at ninety-seven he finally allowed it to rise to the top of the hole and stare him square in the eye."

I sat mutely visualizing a college diploma rising up gloriously as the sides of the hole that held it prisoner for so long fell in on themselves. The rolled parchment shuddered and swelled up from the earth as dirt, debris, and what looked to be an entire lifetime of mechanics tools, major appliances, and Lazy Boy recliners tumbled away.

The train screeched and slowed.

"Tenleytown. American University. Doors opening on the left."

"This is my stop, you know. See you next time?"

"When?" I asked, not wanting the conversation to end.

"Oh, just next time." Mick stepped onto the platform and disappeared into the sea of people pressing to get on the train or pressing to leave the station.

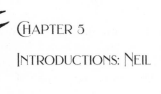

CHAPTER 5

INTRODUCTIONS: NEIL

"I read this parable on Facebook about a donkey stuck in a hole," I started breathlessly as I slid into the chair across the table from my friend, Neil. "Do you want to hear it?"

"Why would I want to hear that?" Neil snapped, not even looking up from his phone. "Aren't you going to order a drink? I've been waiting for fifteen minutes."

"Oh, sure, you're right," I demurred as I picked the drink list from the stack of leather-bound menus in front of me. I flipped carefully through pages of wines and cocktails, studying each description. *Bourbon? No. Skip the whiskeys entirely, thank you very much. Something fruity? A lightly sparkling wine?* I suddenly realized a waiter in a crisp white shirt was hovering a few feet away. I looked up at him. The same young guy with impeccable detachment who served us most Friday nights.

"Hi, Matt. I'll have something sweet. With vodka."

"A sweet martini, then?"

"Um, sure, sounds good," I answered, not exactly sure to what I'd just committed, but willing to risk it. "Thanks, Matt."

Matt disappeared toward the front of the house. I glanced across the table at Neil who was still staring at his phone. Scrolling and staring. Scrolling and staring. Ignoring me.

"Why so uptight tonight?" I poked. "I thought we were cool with 6:00, give a few minutes either way."

"Yeah, that works great," Neil replied as he scrolled through his email, "until I'm five minutes early and you're ten minutes late."

"Ah. Why so uptight tonight?"

Neil's head snapped up from his phone. His face was flushed red. "What about that donkey?" he said.

"The donkey? Oh, yeah, the donkey." I was relieved that we weren't going to start the evening with a rant about Neil's job — the incompetent project manager who picked his brain for two hours over lunch, the promotion Neil lost to the new Executive VP brought in from the outside, the maneuvering that resulted in Neil's office being moved two more floors down from the pinnacle of the corporate headquarters.

"Okay, so there's this donkey who falls in a hole. It's a really deep hole and when the farmer finds the donkey he realizes it's going to be impossible to pull it out by himself."

"What farmer?" asked Neil, whose head had dropped back down to his phone. "You didn't set that up very well. Where was the farm and what's the farmer's name?"

I rolled my eyes at the top of Neil's carefully groomed head and started again. "Imagine, if you will, the rolling Piedmont region of central Maryland… the red clay soils…the brushy green cedars dotting the long-abandoned farm fields that have yet to be touched by the developer's shovel."

"That's better," Neil encouraged without looking up. "Where are we, exactly? Howard County?"

"Sure. We're in Lisbon, just off I-70."

"Okay, keep going."

"We're visiting this afternoon with Farmer Brown who has just discovered his donkey, Pamela, trapped in a deep hole."

"What in hell is Farmer Brown thinking letting his beloved Pamela saunter around when there are deep holes about the place?" Neil asked. I could tell he was grinning even though his phone was still more engaging than my story.

"Farmer Brown curses himself as he becomes overwhelmed with guilt for allowing Pamela to saunter around the farm when deep holes were about. He'd assumed that Pamela was smarter than the average ass and wouldn't wander from the safety of the barn. But you know what happens when you assume and there's his ass at the bottom of a deep hole."

Matt slipped up silently and set a pink martini in front of me. I took a sip. Tasted like grenadine and hit me like vodka. "It's perfect. Thanks, Matt."

"Oh, that's clearly going to improve this story," Neil gestured with his phone toward my glass without looking up. "Please, please continue."

"So, Farmer Brown, grievously distraught, races to the Town Grill diner in the back of the Citgo station where he finds five of his brawny friends gathered for barbeque and sweet potato fries."

"I love that place," Neil commented. "Whenever I take Ava out to Heston Farms to pick up my CSA box, we stop there for ribs. Carry on."

"CSA as in Community Supported Agriculture? You eat vegetables, Neil? When did that start?"

Neil glanced up, finally making eye-contact. "When Ava became a teenager, Einstein. We juice together." He shrugged and dropped his head again. "Keep going with the donkey story — I was just getting into it."

I stared for a moment at the strange juicing man who had slipped unde-tected into Neil's body. *Looks the same to me. Kale probably hasn't fully kicked in yet.* "Yes, so Farmer Brown finds his friends at Town Grill and attempts to rouse them to the plight of poor Pamela, stuck at the bottom of the deep hole. But Farmer Brown's friends are not to be roused. They're just about to start a game of euchre and his good buddy, Tom, pulls up a chair for Farmer Brown. 'Surely the donkey will be fine for a spell,' Tom assures him. 'We're just about to deal a hand.' "

"Don't tell me this guy leaves his ass in the hole while he eats brisket and plays cards. Please don't tell me that."

I laughed. "Always the soft spot for animals, Neil. Must be why I still put up with you. Okay, let's say he doesn't eat, he's too distraught for that, but he does play cards and pretty soon he's forgotten all about Pamela."

"The rat bastard," Neil uttered in mock disdain.

"Yeah, but we all do that sometimes, you know — get distracted from what's important to us."

Neil looked up and made eye-contact for the second time this evening. I held his gaze. "Yeah, we do," he said. Neil dropped his head again and stared at his phone without bothering to feign interest in it. "Truth to that. Keep going with the story."

"Farmer Brown gets so engrossed in the card game that he completely forgets about Pamela, who's still at the bottom of the hole. The day fades away into evening, and when his friends ask if he wants to join them for a few drinks at Joe's in Mount Airy, Farmer Brown volunteers to drive and they all take off."

"What's he driving? You didn't mention make and model."

"An oh-one Subaru wagon."

"Geriatric, but practical. Continue."

"Well, they get to Joe's and there's beer and there's crab cakes. One thing leads to another and it's pushing closing time with Farmer Brown up front singing karaoke. Before you ask, he's singing "Love Me Tender" when all of a sudden he remembers — Pamela is stuck at the bottom of a deep hole! And now it's the middle of the night. Farmer Brown gathers his friends, stuffs them all back in his Subaru and they fly up the highway at eighty miles an hour. They arrive at the Brown Farm ten minutes later to find…"

"You're not killing off the donkey here, are you? I don't want to hear it if you kill off the donkey."

"Don't worry, she's still alive and Farmer Brown and his beer-sodden friends are now standing in a circle around the hole contemplating. They contemplate and discuss, discuss and contemplate, and finally decide that it's too late to do anything about the situation now. They'll come back in the morning and help their buddy retrieve his ass."

"Cute."

"Thank you. But as they begin to walk back to Farmer Brown's Subaru for a ride back to their vehicles, Pamela realizes she's going to be left behind and starts braying at the top of her lungs. 'Oh, shit,' Farmer Brown remarks, 'she's going to wake Tonya and the kids.' "

"Whoa, whoa, whoa…he's married with kids?" Neil put down his phone for the first time all evening. "Our hero just wandered off for most of a day and shows back up — what? — after midnight and he's not in fear for his life?"

"He texted. From Joe's. Even sent a few pictures of Betty Maxwell's husband singing karaoke with Tom. Tonya's cool. He'll be okay. Well, unless Pamela wakes up the baby."

I paused as Matt slipped back to our table through the crowded dining room. "Would you care to order?"

Neil looked across the table at me. "Just appetizers tonight?"

"Sure, that's fine."

Neil picked up the appetizer menu and studied the selection. "The oysters, for sure…the seared ahi…a plate of calamari…you like the pot-stickers, don't you?" He glanced up at me.

"Yes, the pot-stickers and the duck." I looked up at Matt. "And a house salad, please."

"Refresh your drinks, also?"

"Yes, please. Thanks, Matt," Neil answered for us.

"You're welcome," Matt said before gliding away.

"Tonya and the kids?" Neil prompted.

I was secretly thrilled that Neil was getting into my story but stayed steady. "Oh, yeah. So, Farmer Brown runs back to the hole in a panic. 'Shhhhhhh, Pamela,' he shushes the donkey, 'shhhhhhhhh.' Well, she's having none of that and continues to bray adamantly. Farmer Brown is completely melting down when Tom ambles over with an armload of branches. 'Let's jest cov-ah her up with sticks,' he slurs through a cloud of beer-breath. 'Thas a gud ideah, Tom,' Betty Maxwell's husband agrees as he stumbles over to Farmer Brown's apple tree and starts snapping off branches. The men set to work layering branches over Pamela and pretty quickly her brays become nothing more than a muffled protest."

"That's just wrong," Neil laughed as he slipped his phone into his jacket pocket.

"True, but there will be a point when I'm finished, I promise."

"I'm sure there will be. Your stories always have a point lately."

"Yes, they do. So, Farmer Brown runs his buddies back to Town Grill to pick up their vehicles and they part ways with promises to gather again around the hole the following morning. Farmer Brown drives back home, attempts drunken sex with Tonya, who orders him out of the bedroom and onto the couch, and the night passes. The next morning, Farmer Brown is relieved to see his buddies show up, as promised, to help him extract Pamela from the hole. The men retrieve the branches from the hole only to find that Pamela is slumped at the bottom, apparently deceased."

"What?!! You told me no animals would be injured in the telling of this story."

"The donkey's not dead — just exhausted from braying all night, but the men think she's dead so they gather up shovels and commence burying her."

"That's it? They just start burying her? No moment of silence or emotional send-off from Farmer Brown?" Neil exclaimed in mock dismay. "What's that all about?"

"Good point," I agreed, as he grinned wickedly. "Rewind back to the discovery of the apparently deceased donkey."

"Okay, I'm ready," Neil said as he settled back into the story.

"Pamela is slumped at the bottom of the hole, apparently deceased."

Neil nodded. "And Farmer Brown is so overcome with emotion that Tom is pressed into service to provide a tribute," he offered.

"Of course — how did you know? Tom leads off the proceedings with a moment of silence following by a heart-felt eulogy of 'She was a fine mare…a damn fine mare.' At which point, Betty Maxwell's husband loudly reminds Tom that it was a donkey, not a mare, who was dead in the hole, to which Tom replies, 'Go screw yerself, Rick,' thus concluding the service."

"That's better. I approve."

"Excellent. So the men grab shovels and start dumping dirt down on poor Pamela, who is shocked to consciousness when the first shovelful hits her back. She's too hoarse from braying all night, though, to get off a protest. All she can do is shake the dirt off her back. It falls to the bottom of the hole as Pamela glares up at the men. She's getting pissed."

"Damn straight she's getting pissed. First a lame-ass eulogy and now the nimrods are throwing dirt on her!"

"Exactly. The men keep dumping and Pamela keeps shaking and eventually there's a foot of dirt in the bottom of the hole. Standing in a foot of dirt really annoys Pamela, who pulls her hooves out of the accumulation and steps up on the pile. She's delighted to find herself a foot closer to the top of the hole. The men don't notice this new development — they keep shoveling and Pamela keeps stepping up."

"Smart donkey that she is. She really did deserve a better eulogy."

"Yes, she did, Neil, yes, she did," I agreed before continuing. "So, eventually Rick Maxwell, who appears to be more on top of things than the others, notices that instead of disappearing under the dirt, the donkey is eerily closer to the top of the hole than when they started. Rick's eyes widen and he suddenly drops his shovel in shock and exclaims, 'Holy shit, your donkey is rising up out of this hole, Bill!' The men gather shoulder-to-shoulder around the hole and peer in. 'Well, damn, yer donkey ain't dead, Bill,' proclaims Tom, 'and it's climbing up outta the hole.' "

"Tom is begging for a smack-down right about now — just suggesting."

"Not a bad idea at all," I allowed and paused, working through this unplanned twist before continuing. "Rick spins to face Tom with neck arteries bulging. 'Really, Tom,' he spits, 'like the rest of us can't see that?' Tom swings around to face Rick with fists balled. The pair's relationship has clearly dipped south since just the night before when they happily shared the karaoke stage. The rest of the men give Rick and Tom space as they square off at the edge of the hole. They glare through bloodshot eyes and each takes one step forward."

Neil leaned forward with blood-lust dripping from his eyes. Suddenly, the grizzled muzzle, intense gold eyes, and thick pointed ears of a wolf wavered in the space between us. I quickly blinked and the wolf was gone, replaced by Neil gripping his highball glass and waiting for the first punch to be landed. Too bad I was about to disappoint him.

"At this point," I continued, "Pamela really has had enough. She calmly pulls herself the rest of the way out of the hole, shakes the dirt out of her mane, and lets out a single hoarse bray. The men drop into stunned silence and stare vacantly at Pamela as she strides over to Farmer Brown and locks eyes with the man who muffled her with branches and then tried to bury her alive."

"Shake it off and step up. Right? The moral of the story is to shake off the shit that gets dumped on you and step up to the plate. Isn't it?" Neil looked smug.

I grinned. "Nope. Consider if you will, Neil, that so many of us have a lonely donkey that we were supposed to ride. We dropped here onto the face of the Earth destined to ride our donkey, aching to ride our donkey, almost desperate to ride our donkey, but then what happens?"

"Uh, we push her in a hole?" Neil looked dubious.

"Yes! We push her in a hole! Actually, we probably get ample help from so many people who tell us things like, 'That is so not your donkey, son — what are you doing trying to ride that thing? Your mother and I are counting on you to ride Uncle Rico's llama.' "

"Your mother and I are counting on you to attend Harvard Business School," Neil interjected with a snort. "That was my father's damn donkey, not mine."

"Right, but what does your donkey look like, Neil? Do you remember?"

"No. No, I don't. I know I'm not happy but...," he trailed off. "I know I'm not happy but I'm not sure why."

"Yes, you're not happy because a long, long time ago you started layering branches into the hole that held your true life purpose — the donkey that you wanted to ride. Those branches are all the things that make up a life — a decent life, even if not a happy life. Decent enough that you can't really isolate anything specific that's wrong, but you feel the little niggle of having left something behind. That's your donkey braying, Neil. Do you hear her? 'Neilllllllll…Neillllll…come back for me.' "

"Right," said Neil, who was now frustrated, "so how am I going to find a purpose that I don't remember? I mean, if we stick with your analogy, I've been riding other peoples' donkeys my entire life. I jump on and know almost immediately that I chose wrong but how do I find what's right? If I'm going to do another job search, I need to know what I'm searching for."

"If you were to start a job search tonight, Neil, what would get you excited? You know, little-kid-counting-down-the-days-to-Christmas excited — what would get you there?"

The color came up in Neil's face and he scowled at me. "I have no idea."

"Exactly. Because your donkey is still covered in branches. Expensive branches, that I'll give you, but still branches." I looked at Neil expectantly.

"Okay…," he prompted.

"Move the damn branches, Neil! You've already been given a head start."

"What do you mean by a head start?"

"The merger? The lay-offs? The dissolution of your department? All the young, low-priced managers who have been brought in for you to mentor?"

"It's the economy. That's happening everywhere."

"The promotion?"

"What promotion?" asked Neil sarcastically.

"Yes, that's the one," I nodded. "What if you thought of everything that's happened in the past two years as a process of excavation? A peeling back of your life so you can find the donkey you came to ride?"

"That could very well be the most perverse thing I've ever heard you say."

"Exactly, but you're still listening, right?"

"Yeah."

"So start cleaning house. What else needs to go from your life? Instead of straining and searching and trying to visualize an ideal life, start cleaning house. Evaluate everything — your job, your relationships, your house, your habits…"

"That's overwhelming."

"Yeah, it is, so just start someplace. Clean out a closet. Get at least two garbage bags of useless crap out of your house this weekend. And, as you do that, visualize Pamela looking up at you from the bottom of that hole. Invite her to tell you what needs to go and then listen for the answer."

"Are you fucking kidding me?"

"No. Do it. You'll thank me."

CHAPTER 6

SCENES FROM A METRO TRAIN III: FOG AND MIRRORS

Mick laughed as I finished relating my conversation with Neil. "Quite the creative twist on what we've been discussing the past several weeks. Did you think to tell your friend how to raise the donkey out of the hole once he uncovers it?"

"Well, no, the food came right about then and we ate. Talked about the weekend. Had a few more drinks. He really hates his job."

"Do you think he should quit?"

"Yeah, and before I met you I would have just gotten frustrated and told him that straight out. But, that would just make him retreat and pull his safety blanket tighter around himself. He's worked so hard and wants to believe that things will turn around."

"But they never do, do they?"

"No. Things are already decided behind Neil's back. He's looking into a foggy room full of mirrors. The truth is behind those mirrors, but he only sees reflected back what he hopes to see. He's holding onto the illusion that there's still something at the company for him."

"And that he's still needed?"

"Yeah. He went all in — let other opportunities pass. He's still trusting what his boss tells him, and I don't think he should. I think he's getting played. But Neil needs to come to that conclusion on his own, doesn't he, Mick?"

"Well, yes, but you can suggest different ways of seeing things if you'd like. You might give your friend glimpses around the illusions he has created. But when it comes down to it, he is the only one who can disperse the fog and smash the mirrors. Quite the evocative analogy, by the way. I'm quite pleased with your recent progress."

"I'm glad you approve, sensei. My teacher is truly masterful."

Mick tittered with joy as I mulled how much more I could explore with him without violating my loyalty to my best friend. I guessed just a little further down this path would be okay. "Neil thinks it's a temporary setback — that he just has to ride it out until things settle. Something new happens, he blows off steam privately, and then adapts to the new environment. He puts on a content, cooperative face at the office and keeps going. Neil doesn't want to burn bridges — doesn't want to leave anything on the table."

"But he's not happy, is he?" said Mick.

"No, he hasn't been happy in years."

"So, he's really already left it all on the table and walked away, hasn't he?"

I looked blankly at Mick as the train slid into his station.

CHAPTER 7

INTRODUCTIONS: TERRI

It had been preordained that Terri would be something beyond ordinary the moment she was born. I'm pretty sure of that. She shone like a thousand bright suns even as a very young child. Terri was an athlete, an artist, a poet, a scientist — she did so many things without struggle and excelled in so many ways. It was oddly right that I was sitting on a rustic wooden bench with her, swatting away an occasional mosquito, just days after my conversation with Carla. As much as Carla was skipping along the edge between a mediocre life and immolation, Terri was struggling along the interface between mediocre and unlimited greatness.

"God, I cannot believe the audacity of my department chair. He's pressuring me to add his name to my research pub. I busted my ass for three years on the lab work with no help, financial or otherwise, from him and he wants to swing in at the end and have his name tacked on. Can you believe it? The citation would be Martin and Gains. *Martin and Gains!* Equal billing on *my* work! Can you freaking believe that?"

"Have…," I started, but Terri was clearly not finished.

"He needs pubs to get full professor — that's what he's telling me! How is his promotion my problem? I'm trying to get tenure — he should be helping me! He should be supporting me!"

A crow suddenly flushed from the oak tree above us, cawed loudly three times, and took off. It seemed to barely skim the treetops as its image flickered through gaps in the heavy summer foliage. Crows were usually friends to me, but this one had just ditched me in the woods with my ranting friend. I wanted to call out to him — beg him to take me along on an adventure — but, instead, smiled benignly at my friend and nodded my head to confirm I was still listening.

"And I'm sick of his criticism of my teaching style! He's never once visited my classroom — not once! Other department chairs have taken the time to review me but he won't even come into my classroom. The students complain to him because my tests are too hard. They're seniors, for God's sake — I'm trying to get them to think and put information together. I don't freaking care if every other professor at the university gives them a list of facts to memorize and regurgitate — I want them to be better than that! I want to hear their ideas. I could care less about their ability to memorize someone else's ideas!"

"Do you think…," I began before I realized Terri was just pausing to take a breath.

"I have advocates at the university, just not in my department. What the hell?

Why is it that no matter where I work, I always end up getting held down? Why is that? Why can't Ralph Gains see my value?"

A mourning dove cooed from some distance away — "coo-COO-cooo-cooo-cooo." *Serenity. The messenger of peace and serenity.* I disengaged my attention from Terri's rant, dropping into the void between her words. The peace carried by the dove eased over me and grounded me into the solid heft of the bench. I felt completely at ease and could have remained sitting there in the silence of my own mind for the rest of the day. To be polite, though, I gently refocused on Terri's angry, golden-brown eyes.

"...and he supports Fred Jenkins! I simply cannot understand that. Why does Fred get the lion's share of the departmental research budget? He's not even doing anything original! And Ben is the golden child. I'm sick of hearing how great Ben is. I mean, okay, Ben is great — his research is fantastic, he brings in a ton of grant money, his students love him, but what about the rest of us?"

I didn't bother to attempt to interject this time as Terri took a quick swig from her water bottle and started in again.

"I want to do so many things and make an impact, but I just feel like my hands are tied. 'Slow down and focus' is all I hear from my faculty mentor. Slow down and focus? How am I going to get everything done if I slow down?!! And I can multi-task, damn it, I get bored if I don't have a lot on my plate. I don't get it."

I watched Terri's mouth quickly form each word of her tirade and imagined counterclockwise swirls of negative energy spinning past her lips and into the moist air that smelled of ferns and forest soil. Terri's face and head were quickly engulfed by energy swirls that bobbed in the air like soap bubbles. The bubbles muffled Terri's voice until all I could hear was one long string of static. I cocked my head and allowed my brows to knit together. *Is it possible to suffocate in your own negativity? If so, this might be Terri's last day on Earth. Hmmm, should I save my friend or allow her to drown in her own rant? Well, we've been friends since third grade and she hasn't always been like this — the humble shortstop who gracefully shone on the high school diamond has to still be there somewhere. Surely.*

I quickly conjured up two mourning doves to save Terri and stationed one on each of her shoulders. The soft brown birds gently plucked the bubbles from the air and swallowed them, clearing the air of negativity and cooing out peace and serenity for Terri to breathe in.

"Other junior faculty agree with me, you know, but they're not willing to speak up — not willing to buck the good ol' boy system. That's what's keeping me down, you know — the system."

I added a third dove to man the top of Terri's head.

"The system is completely stacked against me. I contribute so much but I never get the recognition that I deserve. Ben got the junior faculty award again this year! Can you believe that? I haven't been nominated in two years, while Ben just keeps on raking in the awards and grants. It's just not..."

A red-eyed vireo began singing somewhere high in the tree canopy. I lifted my face and smiled as the bird's short broken songs filtered down from the treetops. *Twenty thousand songs — this one bird will likely sing twenty thousand little songs before this day ends without collecting a single award or grant.* I looked back over at Terri, whose angry mouth continued to form the sharp words of her jealous rant. *Does she know of red-eyed vireos, who sing lead in the sound track of this moist green forest with no need of fame or recognition?* I opened my mouth intending to interrupt and ask Terri to listen for a minute, but then changed my mind. Instead, I gently bit my lower lip and silently wished for her the joy of singing as the vireo did — tirelessly and sweetly just because he had a song.

"…and Lacey Adams was the keynote speaker at the professional convention last month — Lacey Adams! I mean, okay, her research is really leading-edge, but keynote worthy? Seriously? And do you know what she did? She had a freaking baby! And took an entire semester off! An entire semester! Can you believe it? She's so damn lucky to have a supportive husband. Most men are just not that supportive. Tony's nowhere near that supportive. I can't even think of starting a family before tenure. No way. I don't get support at work and I sure don't get support at home."

Terri unzipped a pocket on her day pack and pulled out an energy bar. She ripped off the wrapper with vigor, pulled the bar into two pieces, and handed me a piece. She bit down so hard on her half that I imagined her molars shattering into millions of tiny white fragments and was almost surprised when she continued to chew rather than stopping to spit out shards of fractured tooth enamel.

"Do you want to start back?" I asked. "It'll take about half an hour to get back to the truck."

"Oh, shit, yes! I need to get back and grade midterms tonight. There's always something to do. I don't know why I don't get out and hike more often, though. It's always so peaceful here and I come back feeling so refreshed. Thanks for suggesting it today!" Terri popped up off the bench, shouldered her daypack, and set off down the trail.

"Sure, you're welcome," I murmured to Terri's retreating back. I carefully crumbled my half of the energy bar and sprinkled it under the bench for the birds and small rodents who might enjoy an exotic treat. It was the least I could offer in reparation for bringing Terri into their cathedral.

From a few yards up the trail I could still hear Terri ranting. "Oh, my god, did I tell you about the National Science Foundation grants? Remember how competitive I told you they were? I got my decision letter last week. I won a grant this year, but at only half my requested budget. What's that all about? The funding is down this year? Seriously?" Terri turned and called back to me, "Are you coming? I really do need to get back."

CHAPTER 8

THERE ARE A FEW MORE PEOPLE TO MEET, BUT FIRST A FIELD TRIP

"Perfect!" the woman sitting in front of me on the Metro exclaimed as she yanked out her ear buds and began winding the cord around her mp3 player. "Just perfect."

The garbled announcement had just come over the loudspeakers. "This train will not be continuing on to Gallery Place or stations to the east. All passengers must exit at Metro Center. Doors opening on the right."

"Dammit! Not again!" a young man standing near the front of the car in a fast food uniform swore as the doors slid open and the packed train began to empty. "Not again."

Mick and I filed out of the train and onto an already packed platform. The number of people backing up clearly signaled an issue farther up the tracks that could take quite some time to clear. We wouldn't be moving forward any time soon. *Perfect, just perfect, indeed!*

"Mick, would you like to visit the American Indian Museum today? I'd like to check it out."

"Ah, you mean take advantage of this unexpected deviation from routine to explore new territory?"

"Exactly. I'm pretty sure we both just received permission to have fun today."

"Fun, it is, then."

I turned from the rails and began slipping carefully through the crowd. Following protocol, I took care not to make eye contact or crash through anyone's invisible bubble of protection. I reached the escalator and climbed the ascending metal steps in pace with a crowd moving rapidly upward and away from the platforms. At the top, I stepped out of the flow and scanned the walls of the station until I located a large color-coded map of the Metro system. I cautiously picked my way over to the map, being mindful to avoid the surge headed toward the exit gates, and studied the crayon-colored lines representing the train routes under DC. For orientation, I found the green rectangle that represented the National Mall and a small symbol that looked like the Capitol Building. "Blue Line to L'Enfant Plaza?" I suggested. "I think it's near Air and Space — closer to the Capitol than to the Lincoln Memorial."

"I'm following you," Mick deferred. "Practicality is your ball of wax."

"Okay. I'm calling it as L'Enfant Plaza. Let's find us a train going that way."

I headed back to the escalators and followed the signs to the east-bound Blue Line on the lowest level of the station. A few minutes on the platform and the next train slid into place. This train was packed so I found a place to stand and hang on for the three stops it took to arrive at the L'Enfant Plaza station.

"L'Enfant Plaza. Doors opening on the left."

I bounded off the train and onto the platform like a giddy tourist. A tight press of bodies pulled me toward the escalators, but suddenly realizing that I had no idea where I was going, I stepped aside and paused in a little cranny near the wall of the station and pulled out my phone.

"Getting oriented, are we?"

"Mick! I'm glad you're still with me. Yeah, I'm trying to find the museum's web site. I need to figure out which exit we need out of the station. You know, to avoid stumbling around the block for half an hour."

Mick chuckled. "Ah, yes. No need to join the pack of wanderers circling the station."

I rolled my eyes at Mick's disdain for anything resembling a plan and clicked a link for the National Museum of the American Indian. The page that appeared kindly suggested that leaving the station through the Maryland Avenue exit would get us headed in the right direction. I pulled up a street map and planned my route from there, having learned from experience not to trust GPS when trying to navigate downtown on foot unless I really wanted to experience the path less traveled. A little nervous but confident in my preparations, I looked up from my strategic planning session and was relieved to find I was standing under a massive sign pointing up the escalators to Maryland Avenue and 7th Street. I slipped into the stream of humanity flowing up the nearest escalator and relaxed into the current. A few minutes later, I found myself deposited on the street, face to face with the largest bank of food trucks I'd ever seen. The scrappy entrepreneurs in their gaudy mobile kitchens had snagged every parking space on the block.

"Is it lunch time?"

"Not yet," offered Mick, "and I think we'll find something even better at the museum."

"You think?"

"Just a hunch."

I set off along Maryland Avenue with Mick in tow, checking out the food truck offerings. Greek, Mexican, Chinese, Korean, Turkish, Halal, more Mexican, Vietnamese, ice cream, nachos, barbeque, cupcakes, cookies, crab cakes, chicken and waffles, burgers, bubble tea, more Mediterranean, one last taco truck. It was a relief to hit 6th Street and break free from the carnival of brightly colored trucks. I joined a group to cross Maryland at 6th and noticed ahead of us, beyond a shady allée of willow oaks, the Smithsonian's Air and Space Museum. The building sat solidly at the end of the block, a massive arrangement of light gray granite squares and rectangles interrupted periodically by wide vertical panels of black glass. As I walked closer along 6th Street, I noticed a twisted metal sculpture in front of the building that seemed to be collapsing in on itself.

"It's not really moving," Mick said, "although it might appear to be. It is said to represent the continuum of space and it would be perfectly acceptable if you interpreted it as a black hole."

"Ah."

As I approached the crosswalk at Independence Avenue and the line of sight widened, banks of pink and white crepe myrtles were suddenly visible on both sides of the building's wide entry steps. Greenery was draped high in the sky over one of the massive cubes to the right of the steps. I looked more closely and could see there was a rooftop garden up there complete with several small trees. The sight of the lush organic greens dripping over the stark stone wall was wonderful and strangely disconcerting all at the same time — like brilliant moss growing on the surface of the moon. I couldn't take my eyes off the roof of the building as I crossed the street and then stood on the sidewalk in front of the museum gawking for a while. I finally hung a right across the front of the building and strolled along a sidewalk overhung by lush crepe myrtles decorated with dangling panicles of white and rose. As I walked and gawked, banks of golden black-eyed Susans smiled at me and twisted spikes of lavender liatris reached over the wall of a raised garden to brush my hair.

"I wasn't expecting a garden on the face of the moon."

Mick clucked like a happy hen. "Isn't it amazing what comes our way when we drop expectation and just enjoy the scenery?"

"Yeah, it is, actually. I've been to Air and Space I don't know how many times and never noticed the gardens. I guess I tend to come here with out of town guests more focused on what's playing at the IMAX."

I continued past the last of the walled gardens, not pausing to look ahead until I was almost at the end of the block. When I finally looked up, what I saw poking above the crepe myrtles was extraordinary.

"Mick, that tan building ahead of us looks like it was shaped by wind. It could have been lifted right out of Canyonlands National Park."

"Yes, I believe that is our destination."

I arrived at the signal across 4th Street and could barely contain myself as the light took its time changing. I looked up at the undulating lines of the building and the bright blue banner hanging down the wall that identified the museum. From what I could see from across the street, lush landscaping and sinuous paths flowed around the building. Over the traffic noise I could make out the sound of moving water. This was much more than I'd expected. The traffic light changed and I flowed across the street with the pack of tourists and office workers that had built up, but while most of them continued straight ahead on a curved garden path, I followed my ears and went left down the block past a service entrance and toward the sound of water. What I found on the other side of the building, which apparently had a roughly triangular footprint, was a cascading waterfall and a flowing man-made stream. Natural boulders were scattered everywhere as if tossed like gargantuan dice and allowed to lie where they fell. They protruded from the wide paved path, interrupted the stone edging along the walk, and also served as part of the water feature. I placed my hand on a cool, wet boulder the size of a grizzly bear at the foot of the waterfall. "Wind and water, Mick. These boulders were shaped by wind and water."

"Ah, so they were. Shaped by ethereal, formless wind and flowing water, which takes on the form of all things. These rocks hold the memory of past generations."

"You think so?"

"Know so."

As I stood with my hand on the boulder, I began to feel strongly grounded, as if my hand were growing roots and pulling sustenance from the energy bound up in the stone. I stayed there long enough for the high humidity at the waterfall to melt me just a little bit into the landscape. My hair went limp as an unbelievably sweet and familiar scent wafted over me from somewhere nearby. I turned around to find an entire bank of shell pink sweetspire shrubs blooming along the path behind me. After having stared so long into the sparkling waters, it took me a minute to recognize what else I was seeing — a deeply shaded natural woodland in the middle of downtown. The woodland drew me across the path and implored me to peer deeply into its depths. The layers of trees, shrubs, and small herbaceous plants that made up the wood felt balanced and self-sustaining. Humans felt welcome here, but the hand of the gardener wasn't immediately apparent.

"Earth," Mick said. "Deep, sensuous, luxurious Earth."

"It is luxurious, isn't it? And they're all native plants. Did you notice that? They belong together and they belong in this place."

"Yes."

I walked forward on the path between the woods on my left and the stream and building on my right, reading interpretive signs as I went. I gathered factoids like a sponge, learning that there were over thirty species of native trees planted in the woodland and the stream represented Tiber Creek, a real waterway that now flowed under the building but at one time sustained the wetland that preceded the National Mall. I kept wandering, soaking everything in, and became aware of the quacking of ducks. Navigating to the sound, I came to a large natural-looking wetland filling the space beyond the tip of the building. Rounded banks anchored in place by peeling birch trees and thick vegetation surrounded a shallow pond covered in waterlilies and edged by pickerelweed, grasses, and wildflowers. Several pairs of mallards paddled among the waterlilies, tipping up periodically to feed on some unseen bounty beneath the water's surface. I imagined the water spreading out and covering the adjacent streets and grass of the Mall. The many buildings and monuments elbowing each other for space slipped beneath the still waters as waterlilies spread over the surface. Hordes of ducks, wading birds, and muskrats spread like wild fire…*fire?*

"Mick, I think we're missing fire out here."

"Look to your left."

I leaned back to see beyond the group beside me at the wall overlooking the wetland and noticed the fire pit that I'd missed as I tracked the ducks.

"Fire, energy, passion animate all things," Mick said. "Without a bit of fire we might just end up floating aimlessly."

I laughed. "It's apropos, then, that I walked right past the fire pit. I've been living without passion and floating around for a long, long time."

"Yes. Perhaps our little field trip today will help shed a bit of light on that dilemma. Ready to go inside?"

"Sure."

I turned and found, across a wide round plaza, a bank of glass entrance doors tucked under layers of undulating stone overhangs that seemed to rise six or seven stories high. I felt as if I were entering a cave as I pulled open one of the heavy doors, but as soon as I stepped over the threshold I could see this was a cave like none I'd ever experienced before. The domed chamber I stood in was all of a hundred feet across and rose at least a hundred more in a series of concentric rings that ended in a round window to the sky. The entire interior was sparkling white and light-filled. On the far side of the chamber, a stacked pair of wide, open staircases was built into the side of the dome, allowing observation of the huge room as people climbed.

I stepped away from the security area at the entrance and looked up at the skylight so high above me. *What a tribute to the sun!* I wanted to lift my arms and rise up to the ceiling, but walked forward, instead, to a series of dark metal panels that suggested loosely woven basketry that screened the central area of the chamber from view. My eye was pulled to a sign, highlighted in red, which I walked over to read. "This says we should start on the fourth floor with an introductory film at the Lelawi Theater. The first showing is at 10:15. If we hurry, we can make it. If we don't hurry, there's another showing at 10:45. And another at 11:15. And another at 11:45. And another…well, they run every thirty minutes until 4:40."

"So, there's no hurry."

"Um, precisely. Let's take the stairs." Feeling a strong desire to experience the stairway to heaven, I skirted around the metal screen to the staircase and began climbing. As I slowly rose higher and higher, ascending to the sky and leaving the pull of the Earth behind, I could see that the screen on the first level had been concealing a large, round hardwood floor. The golden planks of the floor had been laid in a pattern that clearly delineated the four quarters of the circle. *The cardinal directions…the quarters must represent the cardinal directions.* A small circle of red stone was laid in the very center of the floor directly beneath the round skylight, which now brought to mind a smoke hole above a fire. I stopped to imagine people gathering from the four corners of the Earth to dance around the fire, allowing the passion of the flames to overtake them and lift them up through the smoke hole and into the cosmos beyond.

"I need to find a schedule of activities held on that floor. I'd like to come back when there's a dance."

"An excellent idea."

"I thought you might approve."

I continued climbing and although enticing exhibits vied for my attention from each floor, I adhered to the instructions on the sign downstairs, ignored all temptations to stop, and kept ascending until I'd reached the fourth floor. Once there, I followed the instructions on a sign that pointed the way to the theater and slipped left down a passageway between a bank of elevators and a wide display case of animal fetishes, masks, and other items, which I eyeballed longingly but resolutely resisted. There in front of me on the left side of the passageway was my target — the welcoming curved entrance to the theater. A neatly dressed young man with a ponytail stood smiling at the door, which he held ready to close, and beckoned me forward. I smiled back and picked up the pace. *I'm going to make the 10:15 showing after all.* With every intention of enjoying the museum in the correct order, I broke into a self-conscious half-jog and quickly covered the last few yards to the theater entrance. Right as the young man stepped aside to welcome me into the darkened theater, though, a streak of blue light shot out from somewhere to my left and gathered up between us into an amorphous glowing blob about the size of a baseball. I slammed to a halt as my immediate plans and, in retrospect, the entire course of my life, suddenly changed. "I'm sorry," I mumbled to the attendant as my head pivoted left to track the indigo blue light that was now dancing away from the theater entrance. "Don't wait for me, I'll catch the next showing."

As the theater door quietly closed, I stood transfixed, watching the blue light swirl and spin no more than a foot from my nose. *It's so beautiful.* I felt my jaw go slack and saw my hand reach out to touch the blue orb, which responded by dissolving with a loud pop into a scatter of tiny sparks that whizzed off into the darkened corners of the passageway. "Mick, what was that? It was so…oh, wow, look at *that*!" My eyes were now focused on the sculptural black and red head of a stylized bird emerging from shadow to glow against a light-washed, vivid yellow circle at least ten feet in diameter. I stepped closer. The bird was mostly all bill. His long, gently curved upper bill hooked to a sharp point and was paired with a slender, sharply pointed lower bill. The bill was matte black trimmed in red at the lips, should a bird have lips. A highly stylized eye and nostril had been expressed in geometric shapes by removing the matte black material to reveal vibrant red, also matte, layered beneath. Held securely, but almost loosely, in the bill was a shiny red marble that was lit in a way that made it glow hot and bright. "How Raven Stole the Sun," proclaimed the title posted below the bird.

"Look at the story here, Mick. The glowing marble is the sun. See? This raven stole it and hung it in the sky. He brought light to the dark world. And the sculpture is glass. Glass wrought by heat and fire to represent a story of creation." I stepped to the far side of the huge yellow sun and read a brief gallery description. "*Our Universes* — the exhibits in this galley share how native peoples understand their place in the Universe."

"Perfect for one who's feeling lost in the cosmos and might enjoy a little illumination. We should probably step in here and have a look around."

Stepping into the gallery space was like walking out onto the ledge of a windswept mountain at 2 a.m. under a moonless sky filled with stars. In spite of the other visitors to the gallery, the darkness made me feel alone on the curved path that arced around the looming mountaintop to my right. Artifacts and sacred objects set in transparent glass cases on the face of the mountain seemed to float in the night sky, giving the scene a sense of otherworldliness. I stepped to the side of the path and stared up into the constellations.

"Look at all the stars. So freaking beautiful. There's so much ambient light in the suburbs now that you're lucky if you see any stars at all. It didn't used to be that way. When I was a kid, I could still see the stars."

"That theft of the starlight makes one feel disconnected from the Universe, doesn't it?"

"Yes, it does. So disconnected." A sudden yearning for real starlight blew through me like a cool mountain breeze. "I need to find the stars again."

I dropped my gaze and allowed my attention to be drawn to a series of colorful grottos along the left side of the gallery space. Back-lit illustrations glowed on irregularly spaced black stanchions, identifying entrances into display areas where the traditions of specific nations were apparently presented. People were strolling past the stanchions into the grottos and disappearing behind curved panels. I wanted to join them but froze, inexplicably overwhelmed by a sudden need to choose the exact right grotto to explore.

"Start at the beginning and see them all or pick the first one that draws you in," Mick suggested. "It doesn't matter why it appeals. Let your curiosity lead you."

I glanced around, giving each the opportunity to catch my eye. "I like that one over there." I indicated one of the stanchions with a toss of my chin. "The illustration shows a guy standing up in a canoe. I'm wondering what that's all about."

"Lead the way, I'm right here with you."

I walked over and studied the illustration more carefully. There were two people in the canoe, one standing and one sitting. The person standing seemed to be poling the canoe through a wetland of emergent grasses, while the seated person bent a clump of grass into the boat with a pair of short sticks. They represented the Anishinaabe people, and I wanted to know more about them. I smiled as my overwhelm melted away. I stepped into the exhibit. The first thing I saw was a simple statement of what it was to be Anishinaabe — to understand your place in all creation, to acknowledge that you're a spiritual being on a human journey, and to recognize the aliveness, spiritual nature, and interconnectedness of all things. "Look at this, Mick. This really nails it, doesn't it?"

"Certainly addresses the disconnect, I'd say."

"Yes. Yes, it does."

A circle divided up like the dance floor into four distinct quadrants, but here colored yellow, black, red, and white, drew my attention next. It was a simple representation of the Anishinaabe universe. The quadrants represented each of the cardinal directions and concentric circles represented different attributes associated with each direction. "The four elements again...fire in the east, earth in the south, water to the west, wind in the north. And there are seasons of the year, seasons of life, plants and animals associated with each direction, too. This is really organized. It exposes my own personal universe as the chaotic free-for-all that it is." Studying the diagram, I was drawn to the animals, especially the wolf to the south. "I have a wolf thing going on lately. I was having dinner with Neil a few weeks ago and could have sworn he'd turned into a wolf. I was drinking, though."

"Ah."

An explanation below the representation of the Anishinaabe universe mentioned seven grandfathers who shared seven sacred teachings with the people that helped them live a harmonious and beneficial life based on honesty, love, courage, truth, wisdom, humility, and respect. The people learned about the four directions and the sacred teachings in a teaching lodge. Continuing on through the exhibit, I found the Seven Teachings explained in words and drawings on what looked like huge sheets of birch bark. Each teaching was represented by an animal. I read about Buffalo, Eagle, and Beaver, who taught respect, love, and wisdom, and then moved on to the next panel. Here was turtle who represented known truth — the things that never changed. Next to Turtle was Wolf…

"There is the animal as we know it on Earth and there is the spirit of the animal, which is larger than the Earth. Both teach us, but it is the Spirit Animals who instill their qualities in us."

I glanced to my right to see who had spoken. I found no one there. I turned around. There was no one else in the small exhibit space. Probably a recording. I'd triggered a sensor. I waved my hands in front of the display trying to trigger the recording again but couldn't find the sweet spot. *Well, it doesn't matter — I'll remember the point made.* I went back to reading about Wolf and how he teaches humility, or putting ourselves where we belong in the universe.

"The wolf always looks back when he leaves a place. He teaches us to look back on our lives and learn from them." The voice again, but this time I could barely make out from the corner of my eye the translucent figure of an older man with long snowy white hair swept back over his head and wire-rimmed aviator glasses. He seemed to be dressed casually in a red t-shirt and jeans. I shifted my head to see him more clearly and he was gone.

"Okay, that wasn't a recording. There was someone standing next to me." My comment was met with silence. Mick had wandered off while I was studying the exhibit and also was gone. *Alright, then.*

I moved past the panels to a life-size diorama depicting a teaching lodge. Behind a heavy pane of glass, people in dark clothing heavily embroidered with colorful flowers and leaves were shown conducting a ceremony in what looked like a domed tent stretched over cut saplings. The scene was dimly lit, mysterious, and full of artifacts. I leaned in to see the detail on a pipe bag near the front of the display and noticed flickering colors out of the corner of my left eye. Turning my head ever so slightly while willing my heart to slow down, I saw not the figure of a man this time but the changing scenes of a video reflected in the glass. I glanced to my right and spotted the small video screen that was the source of the reflection. As I walked toward it, the animated story being played out broke into static and then disappeared from the screen. I stood waiting for a few seconds but the screen remained dark.

"Guess I just missed the last show."

"Nah, they'll start it again. I wanted you to learn the story from the beginning." The man was back. I moved my eyes carefully to the right and there he was, dressed this time in elaborately embroidered dark clothing with a black covering on his head. The video screen in front of me sprang to life and the man began speaking in a deep, gentle voice.

"This is the story of Little Boy and the Seven Grandfathers," he began.

I stared wide-eyed at the screen as the man shared with me the story of a boy who went on a quest to find a way to improve his suffering people's way of life. The boy journeyed in the four directions, east, south, west, and north, aging as he went through childhood, youth, adulthood, and old age. When he got to the west, the animals and plants began speaking to him and educating him in the lessons of nature. By the time he was an old man, the boy understood how all things fit together and how his people could work together with nature to have a good life. When he finally got back to his camp, he was a very old man and very tired, so he lay down to rest. While resting, the man was spirited up to the home of seven spiritual grandfathers who completed his education and then sent him back to his people. He shared the teachings and the people returned to living a happy and healthy life. The screen went dark again.

"Do you understand this story?"

"Yes, I think so."

"The plants and animals and the people who have gone into the spirit world have lessons for you. They are waiting for you to begin your quest."

"They are?"

"Yes, they are waiting for you. And you will bring back their teachings."

The same sense of expectation that I felt upon finding the axe in my dining room table welled up in me. "The dream? Can you explain the dream? I'm not sure what it means."

The man didn't answer. I saw then in the screen a confused and unhappy face staring into my eyes. I stared back into the sad eyes and watched tears well up and slip down the reflection of my face in the glass. Overcome with an unexpected crush of grief, I suddenly wanted to run from the museum. I wiped my eyes with my fingertips and turned to go, but remembering the lesson of the wolf, looked back as I walked away. Staring back into my eyes now was the fierce face of a hawk.

hawk
drifting lazily above the Earth
take me
take me
take me with you.

CHAPTER 9

BACK TO THE INTRODUCTIONS: ANDY

"Andy, you're the most successful person I know and yet your life looks the most unsuccessful and disorganized from the outside," I said as I placed an African tribal mask in a cardboard box that already held a beat-up copy of *How to Cook Everything*, a framed pastel sketch of Jimi Hendrix in dark sunglasses, and a handful of bird feathers.

My brother's eyebrows came together and the right corner of his mouth lifted in a half-smirk as he shot me a sideways glance. "Reallllllly. The most successful person you know. I'll ignore the rest of what you just said." He laughed his rich, genuine laugh that started somewhere near his ankles as a small chuckle and built up sequentially until it rose out of his chest as an almost musical chortle. Andy's laugh attracted friends to his side and babes to his bedroom. It also defined his approach to life.

"Ha! The rest was the important part. You're unexpected. You don't follow the rules, you don't conform, and yet doors magically open for you."

"Well, most people around here don't consider me all that successful, you know. Here I am packing up my stuff and moving out of my girlfriend's place after a failed relationship. I'm scratching the seven-year itch yet again and ditching a perfectly good landscaping company to move to Jackson, Wyoming, where I might or might not make it as a nature photographer."

"Exactly what I'm talking about. You decide you want to spend six months shooting Yellowstone and the Grand Tetons and a resident artist gig falls in your lap right as an opportunity to sell your business pops up. I really admire how you do things until they're over and then move on. Some might call that a lack of loyalty or a lack of maturity. I call it success."

"Well, that's generous of you given my struggle leaving Carla, but I guess I do generally prefer to leave the party before the cops get called."

I rolled my eyes at my little brother. All the high school shenanigans he instigated never resulted in so much as a slap on his wrist. He always did have a knack for slipping out right as things soured, which left me perplexed by the way he'd dragged out his breakup. Choosing to waltz around that painful anomaly, I pulled Andy's battered cookbook out of the box and held it up. "And you travel light. Take this, for example. You love to cook and could afford a room full of cookbooks, but you own exactly one."

Andy laughed again. "Where one book will do, why buy dozens?"

"Right. You're a badass cook and no one's going to know it from your bookshelf."

"Yeah, I'll go along with that. I'm not too enamored with excess personal effects or keeping up with the neighbors. You know I've never aspired to own a television for every room or a cookie-cutter house complete with a homeowners association telling me what color I can paint my front door."

"Yep, that's success, as far as I'm concerned. You own just the stuff you have a real use for. Although, I'd really like to know the story behind this," I added as I lifted Jimi Hendrix's likeness from the box.

"Jimi? Are you implying that Jimi is excess baggage?" Andy's eyes went wide as he feigned shock, took the framed art reverently from my hands, and studied it. The picture depicted Jimi's face from chin to forehead. Dark sunglasses hid his eyes and a red bandanna was suggested across his forehead. Smudges and smears of thick oil pastel suggested features, a moustache and goatee. A faint smile danced across Jimi's lips. "I will have you know that Jimi Hendrix is the mastermind behind my success, as you call it. He's my guide… my muse," Andy said as he looked up from the picture. "Three years ago he told me to do what I love, that's all that matters."

I laughed, but Andy didn't laugh along with me. "Uh, Andy. The man is dead. He's been dead for forever."

"That is a true statement of fact and precisely why he had to talk to me through my intuitive artist friend who did this drawing. I can't see dead people, you know." I locked eyes with my brother, who was famously incapable of bluffing his way through a bad poker hand. His gaze was crystal clear and sincere. Apparently, Andy had an intuitive artist friend who talked to dead rock stars. That was good to know.

"Janice Joplin was there, too," Andy added. He cocked his head, checking my reaction before he continued. "See the flames here by Jimi's face?" I nodded as he pointed out the heavy lines of orange and red just barely kissing Jimi's right cheek. "Fire. Action. Passion. Don't over-think shit. Do what you love. Nothing else matters." Andy handed the picture back to me and returned to packing.

I opened my mouth to ask if that's how he made his life choices, but stopped and studied Jimi's likeness instead. My brother was hard-working and responsible, but also the happiest person I knew. Even the breakup drama of late was just a swirling tornado around Andy's steady, peaceful core. What I saw as success was really just another word for soul-deep happiness. Clearly, Andy was following Jimi's advice.

I set the picture back in the box and picked up the loose pile of feathers. "And the feathers?" I asked. "Why do you collect feathers?"

Andy paused from stuffing jeans and t-shirts into a cavernous black suitcase and smiled at me. His eyes lit up. "Well, I don't exactly collect those. They're more like gifts from the Universe. They seem to appear whenever I need to be reminded of something. See that big black and brown striped one?"

"This one?" I held up a feather that was all of twelve inches long and as wide as my palm at the tip. It was decorated with alternating bands of black and brown and finished at the tip with a faint band of buff.

"Yep, that's a wild turkey feather. I found it on a job near Germantown. I was feeling kind of down and a little bit at loose ends when that feather showed up. I wasn't really sure what was up with Carla at that point — just knew that the energy between us had changed and that I needed to figure out how to leave her." Andy took the feather from me and rolled the shaft back and forth between his thumb and forefinger. He gazed at the feather as he continued. "Turkeys are so alert, you know? You can't sneak anything past them. And they're so steady — two feet on the ground in perfect balance. This feather made me think. Reminded me to keep my eyes open and my feet on the ground. Helped me keep my mind from dashing here and there like a busy little sparrow so I could see that I was holding Carla back. I really did want her to break up with me, though." A faint smile brushed Andy's lips as he handed the feather back to me.

I replaced it with the rest of the feathers and lifted the last item from Andy's box. "And your tribal mask?"

"Ah, that one's obvious, isn't it?" A grin lit up all of Andy's features at once.

"Magic?" I said. "Because we all need a little magic in our lives?"

Andy's laugh rang out and he raised his hands to the sky in mock celebration. "We have a winner!"

Just One Box

If you had to walk away with only just one box,
What would you pack within it
To carry on your way?

Only just one box, you say?
Only just one box?
Where would, pray, I be going with only just one box?

Up into the mountains,
To walk among the clouds,
That hang below the treetops and make the edges vague.

Ah, I am the Traveler, then, about to hit the trail?
If that is the case, I'd pack my box with care,
Including all the things I'd need to live a placid life,
Shielded from the winds and rains,
And sheltered from all pain.

But, if you found that heavy?
Too benign to bear?

Well, then I guess I'd play the Fool,
And turn things on their head.

Turn things on their head, you say?
Turn things on their head?
How would you use just one box to turn things on their head?

Oh, I'd dump it out, you see,
Scatter all it holds,
Leaving me an empty shell to fill back up again.
But, this time, I'd raise my arms up to'ward the Sun,
And ask for only just those things
That make my box expand.

CHAPTER 10

THE LAST OF THE INTRODUCTIONS: ASHLEY AND ZOE

Zoe toddled over and handed me a large acorn cap. "Mine!"

"Always good to know," I told her as I accepted the offering and placed it on the growing pile of leaves, twigs, and acorn caps in my lap. Zoe smiled up at me and immediately went back to scavenging the small forest clearing for additional treasure.

I looked up at Zoe's mom, Ashley, who smiled from across the weathered picnic table where we sat rehydrating and sharing a bag of kale chips. "She's really determined to find them all, isn't she?" I said.

"Oh, yeah, and we'll be required to pack her haul out of here, too. Let no twig be left behind!"

I'd known Ashley since she was two or three years old and had never seen her happier. The joy she found in being mom to eighteen-month old Zoe shone out and brightened everyone around her. "Mine!" Zoe informed me as she dropped a small stone in my lap. "Explore and procure…it's the pirate's life for you, Zoe."

Ashley laughed. "That about sums it up." She took a kale chip from the bag between us and munched it slowly. "I really want to have another baby," she said as she swallowed the chip, "but I'm still not sure."

We'd been having this conversation since Zoe celebrated her first birthday. "Are you still torturing yourself with the idea that you have to start a career and have a second baby simultaneously?"

"Uh, yeah. Well, not exactly torturing myself. But, you know, I really should use my accounting degree. It's not fair that Paul's paying my student loans."

"What does Paul say about that? Has anything changed?"

"Oh, he still supports my staying home, if that's what I want to do. Both of us definitely want another baby and we're fine financially. We don't need the dual income — Grandma made sure of that when she left me the house. Paul always says, 'With a dowry like that, the least I can do is pay off your loans.' He's doing so well at NASA that we've even been able to start a college fund for Zoe."

"And you love being a full-time mom, so…"

"Dad would be so disappointed if I didn't use my degree. He's so proud that all of his kids graduated. Jess and Lauren have great jobs already and Ryan just started at the State Department. Dad's so proud of them."

"And he's not proud of you?"

"Oh, no, it's not that. He's thrilled to be a granddad and can't wait until Zoe is old enough to go fishing on the Bay with him. Dad's always telling me what a great mom I am and how proud he is. It's not that at all."

"Okay, so what's got you tied up in knots?"

Ashley considered for a minute before trying again. "Mom worked the entire time we were growing up. She loved being a mom and she loved her career at the non-profit."

"So your mom is pressuring you to start a career and a family at the same time because she did?"

"Well, no. She tells me how hard it was, even with Grandma's help. I just feel like…"

Say it, Ashley! Say it! Say it! I chanted silently as she searched for her answer. *Say it! For the love of God, put it all out there!*

"Well, like I'd be missing out if I didn't have a career."

Yes! She shoots! She scores!

"What if being a mom isn't my life purpose?" Ashley glanced over at Zoe, who was now happily playing in the dirt amongst the roots of the huge, old red oak that shaded our table. Zoe had forgotten about my lap and had busied herself piling a hefty collection of booty at the base of the tree. She was now chatting animatedly, not at all concerned whether the tree kept up its end of the conversation or not.

"What if you're over-thinking it, Ash? You know, for only some people is life purpose expressed through career. Many people happily work jobs to bankroll passions that have nothing to do with their professions. Some free spirits live loose on the Earth and don't identify at all with the idea of a career, a plan, or even a regular schedule. A certain number of people decide to suppress their individual identities and merge with others in monasteries. And some people, Ash, are here to learn how to live well on the Earth — how to make homes, grow food, take care of their health, raise kids. Look at the gift your grandmother gave you — she eliminated your need to work a job just to collect a paycheck. Remember the grief she got for showing you so much preference in her will?"

"Oh, yeah, for sure. Lauren was pissed. She still mentions it once in a while."

"And what did your grandma say to that?"

"That Lauren and Jess and Ryan and my cousins — that they were go-getters and would thrive out there in the career world. She said they needed that, but I didn't — it wasn't my arena."

"And you realize that doesn't mean you're less, don't you?" Ashley blushed red and dropped her gaze to her hands. She looked so sad as she carefully picked at her cuticles.

"Oh, baby. Don't give up your happiness because of something you think you have to do. There's nothing you need to chase, Ashley. Your grandma loved you and she loved that house. She knew you'd take care of it and fill it back up with happiness after she passed. Let things unfold — there's no hurry, there's no race to get everything lined out before you're thirty. Settle in and live your joy."

"That's really how Paul feels, too. He loves our life."

"And you? Do you love your life?"

Ashley looked up and smiled through her tears. "Yes, I do."

"Then you've nailed it, honey. Screw the guilt — settle in and enjoy."

The breeze rustled the oak leaves overhead and Zoe squealed as a small rain of early acorns pelted the ground. She reached her little hands out to catch the falling treasure. "Mine! Mine! Mine!"

CHAPTER 11

FINALLY A DREAM THAT BELONGS TO SOMEONE ELSE

It's night and I'm outside. I smell damp earthy decay, gold-enrod, ground ivy — the mixed perfume of my grandfather's overgrown farm. I see nothing at first. The night is pitch black. I open my eyes wide, straining to see. Mists rise up to engulf me, swirl and then part, revealing a dense tapestry of stars. The moon is absent from the sky, but the stars are bright. I feel relieved and oriented — at least I can tell now which way is up. A late summer symphony of tree frogs and katydids begins to play. There's an urgency to their opus. Trepidation settles at the base of my skull. Settles deeply and then wraps up behind my ears. The insect song becomes louder, filling my head. Expectation hangs in the damp night air. I focus beyond the urgency of the message that I cannot understand and find the sound of a stream flowing somewhere far down the hillside on which I stand. Water moving gently over rocks, lulling my mind into thinking everything is normal — everything is fine. It's just a late summer evening.

I start to move. I'm walking through a field. A fallow pasture. I see Queen Anne's lace glowing in the starlight. Thousands of luminous white flowers light my way forward. As I walk, the orbs of light dancing in the field become larger and brighter. They rise up higher and higher, illuminating thousands of men standing in the field. The insect song changes, becomes deeper and more hushed — becomes the murmur of ten thousand men all watching me. The trepidation is back. There's something I have to do, but I can't remember what it is. The orbs float higher and join the stars, which make the sky glow like the moment before dawn's breaking.

I notice a single man now ahead of me in the growing light. He's not standing still like the others. He's working hard at something. Grunting. Panting. I push my way through the stationary crowd to reach him. The man has a rope draped over his right shoulder and across his chest. His head is down and he's dug in with his feet. Straining against the rope. Attempting to drag something forward with the rope.

"What are you doing?" I ask.

The man looks up at me. Sweat from his forehead is running down his face and mixing with dirt and soot. He wipes the sweat and dirt out of his eyes. I recognize the man. It's Neil.

"We have to move," he says. "We have to move now! Help me with this! We have to move now!"

I see Neil's desperate — near tears. I step in behind him and grab the rope. I pull with Neil. I strain against the rope. We're not moving. Whatever the

55

rope is tied to is too heavy for Neil and me to move alone. Desperation and urgency overwhelm me. I start screaming, "Help! We need help! We need to move! We need to move *now!*"

The men stir and begin walking toward the rope, which stretches out behind me in a taut line. A face comes out of the half-light of gathering dawn. It's Andy. "I'm here," he says as he steps in behind me and grasps the rope. "I'm here now." Other men step in line and take up places on the rope. Thousands of men are now all pulling together.

"Heave!" shouts Neil over the grunts and curses of the men. "Heave!" Something gives with a start and we're moving forward. Slowly at first but then we gain momentum. "Heave! Heave! Heave! That's it, boys! Keep it coming! Keep it coming!" We're moving forward through the field. I look ahead over Neil's right shoulder and see we're climbing now. Climbing the hillside. Up, up, up. A mist rises from the damp ground. The mist swirls and dissolves. The soft swale of a low mountain pass appears in the faint light. "Heave! Heave! Heave!" We keep moving forward. Steadily forward. Neil's voice rings out again. "Heave, boys! That's it! Almost there!" We're climbing, still climbing.

I look up again. I can just make out a line of thunderheads above the pass before us. Lightning sizzles down through the thick damp air, strikes the ground, and throws dirt and rock into the sky. Thunder booms again and again as the earth explodes all around us. Neil drops the rope and turns to the rest of us. He raises his right arm into the air. "This is it, boys! This is it! Charge!" Neil sweeps his arm and points uphill at the mountain pass. A wave of adrenaline courses through the ranks. The men howl as one, drop the rope, and move forward through the storm.

I run toward the pass with Neil at my side as the lightning crashes down around us. Dirt and rock spray us with each lightning strike. Smoke rolls in from the left. The field is on fire. I hear a primal howl over the rage of the storm and turn to find Neil. My eyes sting and burn from the smoke as I strain to see him. The savage howl comes again, not two yards to my left. The smoke parts for an instant and I see the wolf running at my side. Stride for stride, the massive black animal is driving forward with me. I hear a wild piercing scream and realize that it's me screaming as I race forward through the storm.

I run and run until the lightning slows, the thunder fades, and the smoke begins to clear. The tempest is falling away. The black wolf leaps forward from the smoke as the sun finally breaks over the landscape. The animal lands in stride on its two hind legs as its body dissolves into the figure of a man. The man stops and turns back to face me.

"We took too long," Neil says. "Jackson has arrived."

Chapter 12

Scenes from a Metro Train IV: Animal Spirit Guides

The train slipped underground, inciting the howls of the Dementors. I was grateful that Mick had made an appearance this evening, as my soul had been feeling loose and susceptible to their kiss all day.

"Mick, what do you know about animal guides?"

"Animal guides? You mean animal spirit guides or, umm, service dogs?" Mick chuckled at his own lame joke.

"You are so not ready for late night," I said as I rolled my eyes and shook my head. "So not ready. animal spirit guides, then — what do you know about them?"

"Quite a lot. Have you researched them yourself?"

"Yeah, I have and I'm confused. There's too much information out there and most of it seems suspect. I've found lists of meanings to memorize for each animal and rules to follow for interpreting encounters with said animals. The lists go on and on until they become completely exhaustive and then contradictory. And the rules are, well, rules — black and white. You see a squirrel three times, it has a message for you. Look down the list of meanings for a squirrel encounter and pick a message, which could be just about anything."

"Ah, yes, that's a true dilemma. Have you done any independent investigation? Without reliance on a Google search?" Another giggle. *Sheesh.*

"Yes."

"Ahhh, good — good for you. And what did you come up with?"

"Well, I realized in those lists and explanations that I couldn't feel the spirits of the animals shining through. All that information was flat and academic, but I tried to memorize it. And when a squirrel showed up on my deck rail last night, my mind fell over itself trying to dredge up a list of squirrel attributes to explain the animal's appearance precisely at cocktail hour."

"Did you offer a beverage?"

"Certainly. You know I hate to drink alone."

Mick snorted back a laugh. "So, you've discovered a squirrel's taste in liquor. What else did you learn?"

"Well, to get my mind out of the way. I think I pulled that off with a dragonfly a few weeks ago without even realizing it."

"And did that dragonfly bring you a message?"

"Yes, I think it did. I'm sure it did. It appeared right at the moment when I needed it. I was talking with my brother's ex about seeing things for what they really are when a beautiful gold dragonfly appeared. That triggered me to describe the Earth-bound dragonfly's tastes as a cannibal, which he displays out in the open but so many people miss because they're caught up in a magical illusion of dragonflies as gentle dainties..."

"Ah, illusion again."

"Yes, illusion! The concept of illusion keeps coming up for me and this time I saw it explicitly linked to dragonfly behavior. But I don't think the dragonfly was just a handy symbol to help me explain illusion. I've been thinking a lot about our museum visit and how the Anishinaabe know the animal that shares the Earth with them, but also know the Spirit Animal. I think the dragonfly Spirit Animal is with me. Not the Earth-walking, marsh-loving, kin-eating dragonfly but the spirit of the Dragonfly. And I think it wants me to be an illusion-buster."

Mick giggled and I blushed to think he was imagining me in a gray jumpsuit with a proton pack on my back. "Ah, so you opened yourself to Dragonfly energy."

"Yes, and I wasn't sure how it happened until I had a conversation with Andy. He collects feathers — he says he feels their energy. He showed me a turkey feather that made him feel grounded and balanced. I couldn't feel that, just holding the feather, but I think it was important that he was feeling unbalanced and scattered when he found that feather."

"So you're thinking the spirit of the turkey presented itself to your brother at just the right moment in answer to his need?"

"Yes, that's it exactly. And I think the energy was there all along to tap but the feather drew Andy's attention to that energy and made him open to feel it. I think the dragonfly appeared right as I needed it, too. I was grasping for help and it just appeared."

"Ah, yes, you're learning so quickly." Mick's compliment carried a happy rush of accomplishment through me and I nodded enthusiastically as he continued his instruction. "You might also think of appearances or totems like Andy's feather as pause buttons. An animal might make a house call or you might find evidence of it also at times when your mind has been busy and needs to stop churning. Pause, retrieve the feather, and allow Turkey energy to fill you. Pause, watch the squirrel on your deck rail, and allow Squirrel energy to fill you. Preferably before said squirrel is too drunk to drive." Mick chuckled.

"And if you don't pause?"

"I think that's where folks may have gotten started with those rules you stumbled upon — 'carry on with your busy life and ignore the messenger until it appears three times.' " Mick clucked like a judgmental hen. "If there is a message and the message is important, perhaps the messenger will appear again and again until your cluttered mind clears, but think how much richer your life might become if you were constantly receptive — if you lived always within the circle of animals' spirit energies, allowing them to deepen your being."

"Oh, wow. I like that. I like the idea of being connected like that."

"Yes. The First People know that with Spirit Animals in our lives as guides, we remain on track. With their energies pushed away, we stumble and lose our way. Consider the current state of affairs that has species leaving us at such a rate that some are calling it the sixth mass extinction. The guides are being squeezed out of existence and memory."

I sat stunned. *The elephant tusks.* "I saw a live video feed from Times Square just yesterday, Mick. The government was destroying confiscated elephant tusks using a huge grinder. The tusks were on a conveyor belt that dropped them one by one into the machine to be ground into dust."

"What did you feel when you saw that?"

"Overwhelming sadness. Just overwhelming sadness."

"The sadness of the elephants," Mick confirmed. "That sadness is very real — it's the spirit attached to those tusks."

"It felt like a funeral, Mick" I said and paused. "Well, except that it was still Times Square. The people watching nearby were hushed, but the digital screens were still lit up and shouting. Still selling us electronics and hotel stays and fashion and lattes. How can the people living in the cities possibly connect with animal energy with all that going on? And how can they know the animals that they can't see except in a zoo?"

"Oh, it is harder to connect over all those distractions but you don't have to live with an animal to feel its energy. Animal energy knows no bounds. You can sit with a wolf at the zoo, you can contemplate its photograph, or you can conjure up its image in your imagination. Invite the wolf to sit with you and just ask — ask if it might reveal its gifts. Clear your mind of the perpetual digital screens, ask, and stay open for the response, which might not come immediately."

"Uh, interesting that you mention wolves."

"Oh?" Mick feigning innocence was like the ocean pretending to be orange.

"Remember I told you I, uh, saw Neil turn into a wolf?"

"Yes, I believe you mentioned a hallucination fueled by mixed drinks."

"I don't think that was a fluke. After that happened, I started having this recurring dream. There's a wolf in the dream. It has to do with Neil but I can't figure out what it means. I keep thinking 'wolf in sheep's clothing', but that's not right."

Mick sighed. "Stop thinking. Feel. What do you *feel* at the moment the wolf appears in your dream?"

"Feel? Um, well, let me get myself back into the moment…I'm running forward into a storm with the wolf at my side…"

Mick waited as I allowed myself to sink back into the dream and the feelings it conjured.

"I feel safe. I'm running into a horrific storm with lightning crashing down. There's smoke and I can't see well. I should be very afraid, but I'm not. I feel like

LUPUS (THE WOLF)

nothing can touch me because I have a guardian by my side who is always loyal and always with me. I feel like I can keep going through the storm — that I can persevere through anything. I don't usually feel like that." I stopped speaking and let the emotions surge through me.

"That's Wolf energy," Mick whispered. "Wolf is sharing himself with you. Cherish the gift and allow it to guide you."

The Dementors suddenly lost their grip on the train as we slowed and slid into my station.

"Shady Grove. Doors opening on the left."

I got up from my seat and took a few steps toward the door that was about to open, grasping one of the steel grab bars to keep from losing my balance as the train jerked to a stop. I was glad that Mick had deviated from usual routine and was still with me this evening as I stepped onto the platform. In contrast to the people dispersing across the nearly vacant platform, rushing to put space between themselves, Mick and I stuck tight as we navigated the station and emerged into the waning daylight.

"Hello, my friend! Can you spare any loose change today?"

"Excuse me?" I looked down in the direction of the question and found a handsome man looking hopefully up at me from the sidewalk just outside the station. I turned from Mick and focused my attention on my old friend seated comfortably today on a small blanket. A Styrofoam cup of silver coins and a carefully folded copy of the *Houston Chronicle* shared space on his blanket. He made friendly eye-contact and tried again.

"Loose change? Can you spare a quarter? You know, for a cup of coffee?"

"Oh, sure, I'm sorry. I saved my change for you." I pulled myself away from his beautiful gray eyes and dug around in the pockets of my jacket where I found two quarters, a dime, and four pennies. "Sorry about the pennies," I said as I bent slightly and handed the change to the man.

He closed his hand around the coins and grinned from beneath a reddish mustache badly in need of a trim. "Sorry? Don't need to be sorry 'bout nothin'. These pennies are a blessing to me. Thank you. I appreciate your kindness."

I smiled back. "You're welcome. Enjoy your coffee."

The guy tipped his head back and shared a cack-   CORVUS (THE CROW)
ling laugh. "I will," he said, "I will, for sure."

I stepped out onto the sidewalk and scanned the parking lot. A few dozen widely dispersed people were moving through the lot with purpose. A crow cawed loudly from the top of a small honeylocust tree growing between rows of parking spaces. The big bird flapped in the spindly branches of the tree and cawed some more — he seemed to be enjoying himself. As I headed towards Lot E and my waiting vehicle, I realized that Mick had evaporated into the rapidly advancing evening, leaving me alone to make my way home.

CHAPTER 13

Traveling Shoes: Grab the Comet's Tail

I sat perfectly still in my deck chair with my eyes closed as a bird spoke a broken song not far away. *Where exactly is this persistent songster, who has been muttering all morning as I've tried to enjoy the late summer breeze on my back deck?* I focused only on his song, allowing the chirps and calls from the other birds to fade into the background. "I am here. I am here. I'm just here. And nothing more. Just here. And nothing more today," the bird seemed to say in languid tones. "I'm not going anywhere. I'm just here today."

"But where is here?" I interjected. "And why are you messing with my pathetic attempts to relax?"

"Just here. Just here today."

I let my mind drop away from the bird's song and it quickly blended in with those of the other birds, the occasional engine noise from the lane on the other side of the house, and the more constant rustling of tree leaves in the breeze. I then tried to focus on the sound of the rustling leaves but my mind jumped from leaf to leaf, unable to find a resting place. The past few months of my life had been like that — jumping from place to place without a resting place until I felt just as fragmented and disorganized as the broken bird song. Conversations, ideas, and symbols swirled around in my head, bouncing off the bony interior of my cranium. There was a thread playing through the mess that would tie it all together if only I could grasp it, but that thread danced tantalizingly just out of reach. And the more I stretched my mind to reach for it, the more deftly the thread leapt and spun away from my comprehension. I was left with a nagging feeling of missing something important. *What's just out of reach that I need to know? What would Mick tell me right now?*

"I'm not going anywhere. I'm just here today," the bird broke in. "I am here. I am here." *Just be here.*

"Let the understanding come to you," Mick would say, "instead of trying to grab it out of the air." I sucked in a big breath and then let it all out, trying to will my head to clear. *Easier imagined than done today.*

Opening my eyes, I noticed that moisture had run down the glass of gingery lemon tea on the table next to my chair to collect in a puddle on the table top. I moved the glass over a few inches and dragged my index finger through the puddle of water, making wet swirls on the black metal table top. I idly pushed the water into the semblance of a loose puffy cloud as my thoughts wandered to Andy. I'd driven my brother over to BWI Airport two weeks ago yesterday for his flight to Jackson. His epic adventure in Wyoming had begun. I was somewhat patiently giving him space to drop into his experience and hadn't texted to see how things were going, even though his absence had me anxious, lonely, and more than a little off balance. I imagined him communing with the land and soaking up the energy of the Tetons — going out early for sunrise shoots, staying out late to catch the last rays of sunlight on the mountains, prowling the Yellowstone River and the Paint Pots for something unique that no one else had captured yet. I tried to work up some jealousy, but couldn't. I was happy for my brother and in awe of his ability to wring every bit of joy that he possibly could out of this experience called life. I couldn't help but make comparisons, though. *Why can't I break out of my holding pattern and do the same? What am I seeking?*

I added a shooting star to my impromptu doodle — a smeary asterisk trailing a gently arcing wake of star dust as it swept up and over my cloud. Then I drew a little stick figure standing on the cloud with a little stick hand reaching out to grab the comet's tail. Not that the little stick version of me was grasping, I rationalized, but if a comet happened past on its way to someplace fantastical it would be expedient to have your hand out ready to grab it. *Wouldn't it?*

I leaned back in my chair and let my energy drop out of my head and into my chest. I lifted my open right hand to the sky — reaching to the limit imposed by my flesh and bone shoulder, but imagining my hand ascending up, up, up into the atmosphere. Higher, higher — not grasping, not straining, just allowing my hand to come into position for the elusive comet's tail. I held my arm up in the heavens and dropped my energy deeper and deeper. The sounds of the birds became the sounds of amazing space creatures that floated past me in the darkness with little lights bobbing ahead of them on slender stalks. The gnats tapping my face became star dust gently pelting my skin. The sound of my neighbor's old pick-up passing in front of my house became the sound of an antiquated space ship puttering past on its way to Jupiter. And then my comet flew by. In a cotton housecoat and hair curlers.

"You need to go on a vision quest, fool!" an elderly woman's voice boomed in my head.

"A vision quest?"

"Isn't that what I just said? Don't get all obtuse on me now! Remember the boy? The Seven Grandfathers? Well, how 'bout you move your carcass up and about? It's time to meet a grandfather or two or three or five or seven of your own!"

Oh. Well, this seems like reasonable advice. "Okay, I'm hearing you. So, what do I do now?"

"Close your hand, you damned fool, and grab the comet's tail. The comet will carry you. Let yourself be carried!"

I closed my hand and heard a sharp *ding* from somewhere to my right. I turned toward the sound and was back on my deck. I shook my head to orient myself. *Ding!* The sun was now high in the sky above me. The sunlight was bright and disorienting. *Ding!* I squinted in the direction of the sound and recognized my phone on the side table next to my glass of tea. *Ding!* I sat up in the chair, grabbed the phone and looked at the alerts. Four texts from Andy.

Minute tween shoots
Headed yellerstone 2 wks
Amazing
AMAZING!!!!!!

Andy. Yellowstone. "I'm supposed to head out West, too?" I asked aloud.

No response.

"Lady?"

Still no response.

"Layyydeeee?"

Nothing.

Humph. I stood up to go inside and picked up my glass. The wet print left where the glass had been added a perfect crescent moon to my doodle. *Of course.* "Let the comet carry me," I said out loud. "Let it carry me to the Moon and beyond." *Ding!* I looked down at the phone still in my hand.

Litter bird told me u need get moving too. Let me no how it goes.

Your Name Here

Always be ready

In case a comet flies by

With your name on it.

Chapter 14

Traveling Shoes:
A Stroll Amongst Ancestors

I sat on the train waiting impatiently for Mick to join me. There was so much we needed to talk about; however, I'd ridden the entire length of the Red Line three times this morning and he still hadn't made an appearance. Finally frustrated, I pulled out my phone and composed a text to Neil. "Apps and drinks tonight?" I pressed "send" with a tiny bit of trepidation. I usually let Neil do the inviting, but he hadn't reached out for weeks and I missed him. Plus, he still didn't know how to get Pamela out of that damn hole. He needed me.

While waiting for a response, I flipped through my email. *Let's see…what important missives have landed in my box since I last checked? Any stimulating reading? Well, here's a confirmation from the electric company assuring me that my automatic payment has been received. Good to know. Lights and juice to power the coffeemaker are always appreciated.* I kept scrolling. *Hmmm, this looks interesting…"How to Turn 10 Minutes a Day into a 6-Figure Income!" Well, that certainly seems worthy of an open.* I tapped on the message, which opened to reveal the bright, smiling face of an attractive, twenty-something woman. *Ahhh, she wants to be my new business coach.* I sat contemplating the woman's beautiful smile, complete with a full set of gorgeous teeth, and felt the green gremlin of jealousy plop down in my lap. *I wonder how she feels out there amongst the thousands of young, energetic business and life coaches with little real business or life experience. How many webinars and training programs did she buy from other young, energetic coaches before feeling well enough prepared to launch her newsletter into my inbox? Was she living the entrepreneurial dream yet?* I clicked to unsubscribe, kicked myself just a little for being so catty, and went back to scrolling. *Ah, a celebratory note from LinkedIn — someone viewed my profile yesterday. Oh, my, yes, my career is back on track. Let's pop a cork.* My phone vibrated and buzzed as Neil's response scrolled slowly into view from the edge of the screen.

Nope. Working late. Lot going on. Remember?

Ouch, not friendly. I felt my cheeks burn as I remembered why I usually let Neil do the inviting. For some reason, though, I didn't let the conversation drop.

Next week?

I stared at the phone, waiting for Neil's response, as the train jerked to a stop at Judiciary Square. The wide man in khakis and a blue dress shirt, who smelled faintly of garlic and had been sitting next to me for three stops, got up and disappeared into the station. He was replaced by a young businesswoman, immaculately dressed save the slightly grungy pink sneakers on her feet. The train jerked again as we all began slowly accelerating out of the station. Right in sync, my phone buzzed and Neil's response crept onto my screen.

Maybe. Plenty of time soon. Will fill you in.

A little more friendly, but sounds like the wheels are coming off for Neil. I bet he's transitioning out. Wrapping things up and handing over any remaining responsibilities. Has to be tough. Not that he didn't see it coming, but still…

BTW, I can see the donkey. Appears to be wearing a tutu and support hose.

I laughed out loud and felt an urge to share the joke with the woman next to me. Fortunately, she'd dropped her head and had established a formidable bubble of isolation, which flung my energy right back in my face. I blushed again and bent my head to compose a response for Neil.

Your life purpose is wearing a tutu and support hose?

Neil's response came almost immediately this time.

Yeah. Don't think I'm supposed to take things so seriously.

The image of Neil in a dark field with his head down and a rope over his shoulder popped into my head. Without pausing to edit myself, I tapped out what I hoped was an engaging response.

Interesting. Been having a dream along those lines. You pulling a rope and trying to get others to help. But you the only one with urgency. Classic!

Feeling almost giddy that Neil and I were unexpectedly connecting, I waited for his next text with a big grin plastered across my face. When his response came, however, both my grin and my giddiness wilted.

What?!?!

He's pissed. What have I done? I quickly launched into damage control.

Just a dumb dream. You pulling a rope in middle of a field. Men standing around not helping. I jump in with the assist. Classic in a good way. Not criticism.

I tensed up, expecting a terse final send-off. *Stupid…stupid! He's busy. I should have just said hi with no pressure to get together...*

Holy shit. Is it night in the dream? Are there floating orbs of light?

I stared quizzically at my phone. *We must have already talked about this. He's being an asshole. He's mocking me. When had we last gotten together for dinner? Not last week. Not the week before, either...*

And we get all the guys to help?

Ha, ha, Neil. Early August. It was early August when we last had dinner — we tried that new place in Rockville and I had that really weird risotto. But that was before I started having the rope dream. He couldn't possibly know...

And we run together through a storm?

A chill raced up my spine and prickled over my scalp. *Oh, my god. Oh, my god.*

"Gallery Place. Doors opening on the right." *Screw Mick, I need off this train! I need air! Now!* I stood up from my seat by the window. The woman next to me pivoted and swung her pink sneakers into the aisle without standing, making room for me to pass. I glanced down to thank her, but was greeted by the back of her head, which was dropped over the iPod she held just inches from her nose. Taking care to avoid physical contact, I slipped past her and pressed into the crowd exiting the train. I patiently allowed myself to be carried out onto the platform like a fallen leaf on a meandering stream but then inexplicably broke protocol and began splashing through the river of bodies irreverently, not caring who I bumped or jostled. I was bombarded with glares and looks of disgust as I battled my way up the escalator to the mezzanine level. *Screw your isolation shields! Don't you know they don't work? Don't you know we're all in each other's heads? Don't you know we can't separate ourselves by refusing to look into each other's eyes! Wake up, people! Where's my fare card? Where's my damn fare card?* I fumbled in my pockets as I strode toward the fare gates. *No, sorry, no, I'm not waiting my turn. That's right, woman, I'm cutting you off. Throw all the shade you want!* I pulled my card from my pocket and waved it over the scanner. The gates parted. I strode to the exit escalator and bounded up the metal steps at a run. *Where the hell am I going? What am I doing downtown?*

I emerged from the ground at 7th and F Streets, walked out from under the building overhang, and was immediately overcome by an urge to run screaming down the sidewalk. Instead, I lifted my face upward. The sky above the busy downtown street was impossibly blue and filled with puffy white cumulus clouds. I pulled myself away from my emotions and joined the clouds — kicking back with my hands behind my head as I floated in the brilliant blue sky. As I bobbed in the breeze, I sucked up the perfect September morning in greedy gulps and blew out the stale air of the train. *Ahhhh.* Panic immediately released its grip, leaving me feeling playful. I tried a few frog kicks and imagined myself back-stroking through the clouds. Enjoying the sensation of being held hidden in the mists, I lingered in one particularly fluffy cloud and just floated. A rope hammock wove itself beneath me, providing gentle support. I melted into the ropes and closed my eyes.

"Caw!" My eyes flew open. A large black crow was flapping his way through my misty bedroom. "Caw!" He craned his head to consider me with shiny black eyes as he swept past on some mission known only to himself. "Caw!" *Wake-up call, I guess.*

Feeling refreshed and perfectly calm, I slid down to Earth and looked back out at the world through my eyes. Embarrassment rose up in my cheeks for a third time. A solid flow of business people in rumpled shirts and annoyed expressions was streaming around me on both sides. I mumbled an apology to no on in particular and stumbled out of the current toward a vibrant block of newspaper boxes lining the edge of the red brick sidewalk. The black pylon marking the location of the Metro station came out of nowhere and slammed into my right shoulder. Feeling too dazed to blush again, I leaned heavily into the metal pole and imagined the energy of the Earth coursing up it to catch me and pull me down. As my feet touched the ground again, roots grew from my soles to find the cracks between the bricks of the sidewalk. Down, down, down went my roots until I felt solid and grounded once again in my body. I focused my eyes and looked around. *I'm on a familiar city street with familiar sights and familiar sounds. Neil and I apparently share a brain, but you'll have that.* I pulled my phone out of my pocket, scrolled through our entire text exchange — Pamela in support hose, the rope, Neil mad at me, Neil not mad at me, the orbs, the men, the storm — and composed a casual message to Neil.

Yes to all that. You having the same dream?

My phone vibrated in my hand immediately, causing me to nearly fumble it into the street.

Where are you?

Downtown. 7th Street. Gallery Place. Chinatown.

Late lunch? Matchbox? 2:30ish?

Sure.

Great. We'll talk then.

"Caw!" I looked up from my phone to see a large crow staring down at me from the top of the pylon. I stared back. The crow turned and lifted his tail. I quickly stepped away from the pole as a stream of bird shit rained down onto the sidewalk and splashed my shoes. Evidently, I needed to get moving. Taking the ridiculously blatant hint, I walked the twenty or so feet to the light at the corner of 7th and F and surveyed the buildings in the immediate area. *Lunch at 2:30.* I looked at the phone in my hand. *Just past 11:30. What am I going to do for the next three hours?* The traffic light changed and the crowd that had gathered on the corner picked me up and deposited me on the other side of 7th. Ahead of me, a tour bus parked at the curb disgorged a steady stream of teen-aged boys in identical red polo shirts. With my path forward temporarily blocked and with nothing better to do, I walked the few hundred feet to the rear bumper of the bus and stopped to watch the boys. Like a line of red ants, they poured single-file from their bus, across the sidewalk, up a wide set of stone steps, and into a massive, colonnaded granite building. "DONALD W. REYNOLDS CENTER FOR AMERICAN ART AND PORTRAITURE" sat in foot-tall block letters above the row of entrance doors through which the boys, one by one, disappeared. The building was screaming at me with a megaphone to come on in and the ants were leading the way. Without hesitation, I followed the boys up the steps into the gallery's lobby, where they clustered to one side around a young woman standing ready with a stack of brochures.

Veering away from the group, I headed over to a large reception island manned by two white-haired women. The peppy woman who greeted me was clearly glad to make my acquaintance. "Welcome to the Smithsonian's Donald W. Reynolds Center for American Art and Portraiture. Have you been here before?"

"Actually, no, I haven't," I admitted. As many times as I'd been in Chinatown for lunch, I'd never once taken the time to check out the art gallery.

My guide popped open a map and immediately got to work orienting me. "This building was originally built to house the U.S. Patent Office and saw a number of uses, including service as a hospital during the Civil War. Clara Barton and Walt Whitman both served as nurses here."

"Oh, that's interesting." I leaned in closer to study the map as she continued.

"After a seven-year renovation that began in 2000, the building was reopened and is home to both the Smithsonian American Art Museum and the National Portrait Gallery. The museum collections include over two hundred thousand individual works, including the most complete collection of Presidential portraits outside of the White Hou..." The woman's voice was drowned out as the group of teenagers suddenly surged in a storm of loud banter and sneaker squeaks toward the arched hallway on my left.

"Are the Presidents down that way?" I yelled over the din as I pointed after the students.

"Yes, they are," the woman shouted.

"What's down there?" I mouthed as I pointed right down a long hall glowing lime green and neon pink.

"To the right we have *Eye Pop,* a special exhibition of contemporary portraiture, followed by the *American Origins* collection, which includes works from the Colonial Period through 1900," the woman shouted as the noise died away.

"Perfect, I think I'll go that direction. Thank you."

"You're so very welcome. Enjoy your visit."

I gathered a map and a few additional brochures and set off toward the shocking green hallway hung with photographs of celebrities. I stopped first at the neatly printed curator's statement, which described the elastic concept of celebrity and the subject's, artist's, and viewer's roles in controlling the personality that is perceived. "Who's in charge of shaping amorphous perceptions into a recognizable persona?" the anonymous curator implored me to consider. "And what happens during a fall from grace when that persona is found to be false?" *Illusion again!* I imagined myself with a magician's wand crafting a human form from a cloud of wispy vapors. As hard as I tried to create a static form, I couldn't get the swirling mists to hold still and cooperate. I flicked my wrist to scatter the mists. A woman's hushed voice drifted down the hall, inviting my attention. I tracked the voice easily to a side gallery on the opposite side of the hall and peeked through the doorway. A group of young adults was gathered around as an instructor walked them through interpretation of a Britney Spears portrait in an ornate gold frame. The small animated portrait appeared to be a mash-up of music videos that was cleverly produced to keep the singer's face stationary on the screen as the background scenes changed in a rush around her. The instructor was talking about the gold frame's ability to imply veneration of the subject. "You'd expect a frame like this around a revered subject — a religious figure, for example. The artist is suggesting through his choice of framing that the viewer admire and respect Ms. Spears." I was tempted to slip into the room and join the group but instead kept walking down the hall, willing something else to capture my interest. I had hours to kill before I'd see Neil and my stomach was tightening in anticipation of our conversation. I needed distraction. I studied a few of the photo portraits hung in the vivid green hall and peeked into a few more side galleries. Celebrities I recognized whispered greetings and peeked back at me from their frames, but no one called me into weighty conversation.

Continuing down the hall toward the corner of the building, I passed under a heavy arch and entered a different world. Men and women in ruffled collars, colonial neckerchiefs, and bonnets were now peering out at me from beige walls. The juxtaposition of modern day celebrities and dead builders of the American dream was at once jarring and so right. I stepped back into the neon bright hall of celebrities and came through the portal again. The sensation was very much like finding something solid and real just beneath the illusion of contemporary life. I immediately felt more grounded and steady as I surveyed the dead ancestors gathered around me. "American Origins 1600–1900," an oval sign mounted in the ceiling informed me. *Three hundred years of celebrities past — there has to be something here to occupy my mind.*

I moved forward into the exhibition hall and hit pay dirt immediately in the form of a large portrait of Benjamin Franklin in a dove gray colonial suit. I rushed over like the fan-girl that I was to greet my old friend. We shared a date of birth, Ben and I, and as a kid I'd always felt a special connection with the quirky man who wanted the wild turkey to be our national bird. We had everything in common in my eight-year old mind — we both liked writing funny stories, neither could focus on just one thing, and I loved flying kites surely as much as he did. I read the placard next to Franklin's portrait, which listed some of his accomplishments and lauded him as the single most famous American of his time. *Now, that's celebrity.*

The saturated teal walls of a vaulted side gallery caught my attention next and I wandered in to see who else was hanging around. I was greeted by a cast of colonial characters that included military leaders, framers of the Constitution, members of the Continental Congress, and a few men made infamous by their stubborn loyalty to Britain. I puttered around looking at art and reading placards long enough to learn that Lafayette was only nineteen when he came from France to earn military glory in America, that Henry Knox bombed the British out of Boston using artillery expertise gleaned from books, and that Andrew Oliver was hanged in effigy and forced to swear allegiance to America under the Liberty Tree in a pouring rain. Each of the men immortalized by paint on canvas in this room had a story and the passion they exuded was palpable. I couldn't help but feel jealous that they all seemed to have known who they were and hadn't been afraid to act in ways that demonstrated their true selves.

I moved on to the next gallery and found that time had progressed to the War of 1812 and beyond. Several military heroes vied for my attention here but I passed them up to stand before the portrait of a Native American man who had been painted in an elaborate red cape. According to the placard next to his portrait, this was Sagoyewatha, or Red Jacket, a Seneca chief who fought in the Revolution and War of 1812, but then washed his hands of Christianity and white civilization to spend the rest of his life as an impassioned orator in defense of native land claims and culture.

"Promises broken," a man whispered.

"Truth." I nodded in agreement as I turned, expecting to find someone standing behind me. No one was there. *That's strange — he sounded so close.* I stuck my head back through the doorway to the previous gallery. It was also empty except for my colonial friends staring out from their picture frames. I quickly stepped out into the main gallery and looked up the hall. I saw distinct movement — what appeared to be the sweep of a bright red cape disappearing behind a partition in a cloud of indigo blue sparks. *What the hell?*

I started up the hall in quick pursuit but slammed to a startled halt when a young woman popped around the partition and slipped down a side hall. As my heart raced, she strode calmly through a small collection of sculptures, pushed open a heavy glass door, and stepped out into a beautiful glass-covered courtyard that apparently filled the entire middle of the massive three-story building. Shuffling and a man's voice coming from the other side of the partition snapped my attention back to the main hall. Holding my breath, I quietly sidled up to the partition and pretended to study the portrait hanging there as I strained to hear what was being said.

"…and in his lifetime, over a thousand patents were registered in his name. Does anyone know what inventions Edison was famous for? Other than this phonograph?"

"Light bulbs," a bored adolescent voice responded.

"Yes, that's right. Edison invented the first long-lasting light bulb. What else? Does anyone know?"

Another school group. I sheepishly dove through a doorway on my right and found myself in a new set of adjoining galleries. Soft yellow replaced deep teal on the walls, which were hung with portraits of authors and artists, some of whom were familiar to me. *Okay, whoever that was behind me wasn't a threat. I'm fine and I need to calm the hell down and focus on something else.* I scanned the walls and recognized Nathaniel Hawthorne. Although his small, penetrating eyes weren't exactly friendly, at least they were familiar and seemed safe. I walked over to stand in front of Hawthorne's drab portrait and leaned in to read the biographical information posted next to its ornate gilded frame. As I read, I was reminded that Hawthorne had little use for those who yearned to live in the moment and had done his level best to point out the grave moral consequences inherent in every rebellious act. My mind immediately swung to my last conversation with Steve. I'd definitely staged a rebellion, at least as far as Steve had been concerned, and there'd been consequences, that was true. I hadn't yet been able to decide if those consequences were good or bad, but…

"Ahem, excuse me? I believe this belongs to you." Nathaniel Hawthorne lifted his right hand from his lap and reached through his picture frame. Dangling from the tips of his fingers was a bright red "Q" cut from what appeared to be wide wale corduroy.

"No, that's not mine," I protested as I stumbled backwards into the room.

"Not yours, eh? You claim, then, not to be a…quitter?"

I scowled hard at Hawthorne's smug face, shooting my best daggers into his forehead. Hawthorne laughed a small mirthless laugh and my imaginary scene faded away. I looked down at the front of my jacket and was relieved to find no incriminating corduroy. *Quitter, my ass! I moved on. I…well, shit.*

I moved left in a huff to stand in front of a more friendly face. I had to read the placard to identify the eager young subject as Edgar Allan Poe. "Oh! I love your work. I'm so sorry I didn't recognize you. You look so young and, uh, clear-eyed."

"We were all young once, were we not? Young and hopeful and brimming with enthusiasm? Alas, the chanticleer has crowed but once when Darkness comes a tapping at our chamber door. That ghastly caller takes our hand, enfolds us in his dank embrace, slips his card within our pocket; and thence commences our perpetual toil to deny our dark companion — to refute our fascination with the hard glow of his eyes, the mean grip of his talon, the wretched stench of his entrails. Ah, poor deluded drudges that we be! Ere the night bird of our mortal soul be concealed by light of day, he will never be banished — Darkness, our eternal consort, is forevermore tapping, tapping,

tapping at our chamber door. Where then is the mystery in the steady creep of a once young face into disrepair or the forlorn melancholy of once bright eyes? A man may live into infirmity or breathe but half a score and he has made acquaintance with the darkness…and his liaison with the darkness shows upon his face."

With wide horrified eyes I watched Poe lift a damp flat rock on the palm of his hand. As he thrust it toward me, a white spider emerged from between his fingers, climbed atop the rock like a conquistador planting a flag, and stared at me through shiny black eyes that looked all the world like Poe's. I leaned in to get a better look at the small spider and realized with revulsion that I could see its tiny beating heart through an almost transparent exoskeleton. Poe's dark eyes twinkled. "Go ahead. Lift the stone. Your truth lies beneath. Lift it." A single drop of blood and then another and another oozed from beneath the rock to drip from Poe's fingertips. *Drip…drip…drip…* I slowly stretched my fingers toward the stone held so provocatively on the flat of Poe's palm. The spider ran a tiny tongue over its fangs and dropped to a crouch, ready to spring on my outstretched hand. Poe's face sagged, his hair thinned, and his eyes became heavy with rheum. *What the hell is wrong with me today?* I stepped back from Poe's portrait, almost surprised there wasn't a puddle of blood at my feet or a spider embedded in my knuckle. *What can I look at in here that won't incite my imagination?*

I scanned the room and noticed I was standing behind a bronze bust on a simple pedestal painted the same soft yellow as the walls. I stepped around to the front of the sculpture and found myself gazing into the placid face of Ralph Waldo Emerson. Putting my imagination in timeout, I allowed myself to sink into Emerson's soft features. My eyes wandered down to the simple description of Emerson's philosophy posted on the pedestal. As I read, I was overcome by a gentle sense of coming home. One statement, in particular, felt so right that I read it again and again — "In Emerson's system, man approached God, embodied by nature, on his own, taking responsibility for his own salvation…in Emerson's system, man approached God, embodied by nature, on his own, taking responsibility for his own salvation…in Emerson's system, man approached God, embodied by nature, on his own, taking responsibility for his own salvation."

"God is in nature…I can find God in nature…I can find God in nature on my own," I mumbled out loud. "But how am I supposed to do that?"

"The little needle always knows the North, let it be your guide."

The voice was back and it was behind me again. I turned slowly, letting my eyes guide my head and then my shoulders and then my entire upper body while my feet remained rooted to the floor. The room was empty.

I carefully pulled my feet free of the floorboards and crept backwards toward the passage to the next gallery while continuing to scan the room. Backing slowly through the doorway and around the door jamb, I found myself in a second yellow-walled gallery. The theme here was unmistakably "westward expansion" and the strong independent energy of the frontiersmen on the walls absolutely filled the room. Promising myself that I'd revisit the invitation to find true north when I wasn't feeling so rattled, I scanned the faces surrounding me and felt compelled to walk over to a large painting of a man on horseback. It was future president Zachary Taylor in a blue military uniform sitting atop a majestic white steed. Reading the placard next to the painting, I learned that General Taylor had lived forty years as a warrior, becoming famous for his ability to overcome large enemy forces with only a handful of men. He'd ridden his success during the War with Mexico into the White House, where he'd struggled for a year to avoid addressing the issue of slavery and then, maybe mercifully for him, had died in office. I was immediately struck by the inability of a warrior, someone whose entire life had been characterized by direct action, to take an honest stand on slavery in America. *How could that have been?* Without trying to force an answer, I cocked my head and allowed my mind to empty. To my surprise, a golden set of old-fashioned scales materialized right behind my eyeballs. As I watched, the scales tipped ever so slightly to the right and then ever so slightly to the left. *Sure, of course. The country was in precarious balance in the 1850's and direct action would have tipped things into chaos. Diplomacy and partnership, not strong unilateral action, were required. No wonder Taylor was at a loss. It's too bad someone like Neil wasn't President at that point in history. He would have...*

I cut off my rumination and conjured Neil holding my little golden scales. He looked grumpy, so I put him in a Lady Liberty robe, planted a wreath of laurel leaves on his head, and painted a placid smile on his face. *Perfect. Neil's the most diplomatic person I know. He would have...* Before I could get my thought out, Neil scowled hard at me and threw the delicate scales to the floor in an explosion of little golden pieces. "Why the hell do I always have to be the diplomatic one? I have needs, too, you know." He ripped the wreath from his head, flung it hard in my direction, and marched out of my daydream with his skirts all aflutter. *Alright, then.*

I left Zachary Taylor on his horse, passing by portraits of Davy Crockett and Daniel Boone on my way to the final gallery in the set. As I walked through the door, a wall of intensely serious energy slammed me. It felt as if I'd left a spirited soccer match to interrupt a planning meeting of the visionary radicals who lined the room. Here were the abolitionists and suffragists of the decades leading up to the Civil War with their heads together around the conference table. I recognized many of their names — Elizabeth Cady Stanton, Susan B. Anthony, Frederick Douglass, Susan B. Anthony, Wendell Phillips, John Quincy Adams — but felt almost magnetically pulled to the man sitting at the head of the table, William Lloyd Garrison. Without even reading the placard next to his portrait, I knew that Garrison was the impatient, loud-mouth extremist who had raised the heat under more civilized discussions about slavery in America. Even when he stood alone in his unpopular conviction to abolish slavery immediately, still he stood. Eventually standing alongside William Lloyd Garrison were many disciples, including my great-great-great-grandfather, a passionate abolitionist in his own right.

As I studied Garrison's face, I wondered where the passion of my grandfather had gone that I lived such a constrained, almost invisible, life. *Why was it such a struggle for me to tap into my own fire and let the flames burn high enough to be seen? Had all that great DNA landed solely in Andy's hand-basket?* I sighed and pulled out my phone to check the time. Quarter to one and I was already hungry. *Wonder if this place has a café. Maybe I could get something light.*

"The soup is usually pretty good at the café." I froze as a chill raced up my spine. *A spirit who made lunch recommendations?*

"They have a good chicken sandwich, too."

I spun around to face the owner of the voice and found that I was finally not alone. A security guard in a white uniform shirt and black pants stood unobtrusively in the corner of the room. "I'm sorry," he said, "I didn't mean to startle you, just I could hear your stomach growling from across the gallery." He shared a genuine smile with me and blew a quick chuckle through his nose.

"Oh, thanks. Thank you. Soup sounds good." I turned to leave the gallery, a little embarrassed that my GI tract had been caught singing in public, but then turned back to the guard. "Have you been behind me for a while?"

"No, I just stepped in the room. Making some rounds."

"Oh. Okay. Okay, thanks."

Now feeling completely self-conscious, I stepped out into the main hall and found myself directly across from a rounded alcove guarded by an arched entryway. A huge painting was hung high up on the wall within the space but all I could see of it through the arch was a man in a blue uniform riding a chestnut colored horse surrounded by other horses of other colors that I assumed carried other men. In the center of the alcove was a solitary glowing pedestal topped with a placard and lit from above by multiple spotlights. *A beacon.* I took a single step forward. My stomach growled. I unobtrusively pressed the tips of my fingers under my ribs to cut off the protest. *Hush, I want to check this out. I'll feed you in a minute.*

I crossed the hall and stepped through the arch, finding myself in a beautiful stairwell with a curved back wall along which flowed a narrow staircase enclosed by a gorgeous balustrade of carved white spindles topped with a polished hardwood banister. Following the curve of the wall was an immense painting of Ulysses S. Grant and about thirty other uniformed men on horseback. "Grant and His Generals," the placard on the pedestal announced before meticulously identifying each man represented half a story above my head. I read the list carefully, finding only two familiar names — George Custer and William Tecumseh Sherman, although I'd always thought Sherman fought for the South. I tipped my head back to study the painting. It was amazing for its size but also for the fact that the horses appeared to be galloping full out while most of the men were paying not a whit of attention to where they were going. Only a few gazed in the direction of their captain — the rest were focused in myriad directions on unseen distractions. *Herding cats. Grant had a herd of cats to tend.* I swept the generals off their mounts with a wave of my hand and plunked a tabby in each saddle. The cats immediately flattened out and hung on for dear life as their eyes went wide with terror. *Oops, sorry!* I put up a hand and halted the bewildered horses. The petrified cats dove off their mounts and scattered in a confusion of dust and fur toward destinations beyond the confines of the picture frame. While I was busy giggling, the annoyed generals in their blue coats and high boots strode back onto the scene, remounted, and kicked their trusty steeds back into a gallop. I stepped back from the painting still giggling but suddenly interested in the distracted generals under Grant's command. I definitely wanted to know more about them, but it was going to have wait — I was now too hungry to think about anything but finding a snack.

I pulled out my map, finding a little knife and fork marking the Courtyard Café just around the corner from where I stood. *Perfect.* Folding my map and stepping out of the stairwell, I looked up and noticed the last exhibit in the *American Origins* collection — a display of paintings and artifacts in glass cases that had been hidden from view until now by the series of partitions breaking up the main hall. "Face of Discord: Civil War," proclaimed a red banner hanging from the ceiling. I was immediately struck by a weird vibe. The atmosphere felt different in this far corner of the building — heavier, maybe, although heavy didn't really describe what I was feeling. I glanced to my right and my mouth dropped open. *Oh my god, who is that guy?*

I strode diagonally across the hall to stand in front of a large portrait of a man who appeared to be in his sixties. His head was covered in thick gray hair that stood on end. Shaggy brows hung above his eyes and a heavy gray beard covered his upper chest. Deep-set, mean eyes glared out of a hard face bisected by an aquiline nose. His expression was absolutely terrifying — edging toward insanity. "John Brown: 1800–1859," announced the placard before going on to discuss Harpers Ferry and Brown's failed attempt to arm a slave rebellion. *Oh. That John Brown. If I want to learn about passion, maybe this man can teach me.* I leaned in to study his eyes. *Can I see here the edge between passion and fanaticism? Fanaticism and insanity? In life, were John Brown's eyes really tinged with insanity or did the artist take liberty to paint it there with his magic wand?* I stepped back from the painting and imagined John Brown standing shoulder-to-shoulder with William Lloyd Garrison. *Their objectives were comparable and they were both considered radicals, but their approaches were so different — violent, physical action that flared up and played out quickly versus the persistent use of persuasive prose over a period of decades. Where, then, did their passions lie? In the abolition of slavery? Or in the approach they each chose in pursuit of that common objective? Was it a combination of both?*

Not able to answer my own questions, I checked the time again — almost one o'clock. If I was going to grab a snack, I needed to get on it, but instead of turning around and heading for the café, I glanced around and realized I was standing in a small vaulted alcove — a small vaulted alcove filled with portraits of men with fascinating eyes and, with one exception, hair that stood straight on end just like John Brown's. *Screw the soup, I want to meet this hair on end posse.* I scanned the faces. The man glaring out into the main hall from the back of the alcove demanded my attention first, so I walked over to him. "Liberty and Union, Now and Forever, One and Inseparable! — Daniel Webster, U.S. Senate, January 27, 1830," was printed on the wall above the portrait of a fit man in the prime of his life. A messy ruff of black hair framed his balding head and punched his ticket as a member of the posse. His exceptionally heavy brow sat above a pair of intense dark eyes that looked right through me with something akin to abject scorn. The set of his jaw and the flush of his cheeks indicated that this man had no problem pushing his opinions out into the atmosphere. The placard next to the portrait discussed Webster's power as an orator and his devotion as a senator to the cause of the national union over the interests of individual states. He died in 1852 — almost a decade before the Civil War began. *If he'd outlived the war, would he have applied his voice to a new cause or would he have continued to beat the same drum even after the parade had passed? Maybe he would have retired to happy obscurity once the union had been recemented.* I tried to imagine Webster in a fly fishing get-up, about to wade into a pristine stream to enjoy retirement, but the image wouldn't come.

"Fishing's not your gig, eh?"

"No," Webster barked as he lifted a pair of drumsticks in his right hand and jabbed them at the tip of my nose. "I've work yet to do!"

"Ahh, so you have."

I left Daniel Webster to continue beating his drum and moved to a portrait of a man with a bushy mane of gray hair almost to rival John Brown's and a pair of startling eyes of indeterminate color that glowed like headlights and were just as round. Leaning in to read the placard next to the portrait, I learned that the eyes belonged to Daniel Webster's number one adversary, John C. Calhoun, who was as passionate about the rights of the states, particularly the rights of the Southern states to practice slavery, as Webster was about the importance of the union. I turned back to Calhoun's portrait. He'd been painted in a somewhat unique pose — leaning to his right while staring down the full length of his left shoulder with his head pulled back and his eyes wide like…like a snake about to strike.

"Probably a good thing you've got your back to Webster or your incisors might be embedded in his neck." Before I could imagine Calhoun's response, a bright red spark zipped around my left shoulder, paused momentarily between my nose and his, shot to my right, and slammed to a stop in front of what looked like a framed black and white print. As I stared at the spark with my mouth all agape and my eyes as round as headlights, it morphed into something that more closely resembled the filament of a light bulb. An electric crackle instantly filled the alcove, lifting my hair straight on end. My hands shot to my head. *I'm a freaking dandelion puff!* Quicker than I could fathom how I'd possibly be able to meet Neil looking like this, much less ride the Metro home, the filament disappeared with a sizzling pop and my hair slumped back to its typical style. Through the fringe of my bangs, I saw a monochrome etching of men in Victorian suits sitting behind curved rows of hinged desks arranged in a half moon under a high domed ceiling. *The Senate Chamber.* I pushed my hair out of my eyes to get a better look. The chamber was calm, almost serene. *This isn't right.* I twisted my hair into a protective ponytail and held it tightly against the nape of my neck as I added Webster and Calhoun to the arena and locked them in impassioned debate. I imagined flames rising up from the parquet floor to lick the walls and red sparks filling the thick air as the two men attacked and counterattacked in streams of words and rhetoric. *They were so sure…they let what was in them flow out without…without apology…they lived their truths…not someone else's illusion of who they should be…this is exactly what Mick has been trying to explain to me…but I can feel it now…I can feel it!*

I stumbled to my right and stood before the alcove's final resident — a thin man with mild eyes, an impossibly long neck and fine hair that hung flat against his head to cover his ears. He was Henry Clay, called the "Great Pacificator of the Senate" for preventing armed conflict between the North and South in 1850. *He was the water that cooled the flames.* I imagined a spent fire hose draped over Henry Clay's narrow shoulders. A single sparkling drop of water escaped the nozzle and disappeared into the fabric of his coat. In spite of his flat hair, I could see the resolve on Clay's face and could feel the power of this slight man, who was able to fashion a temporary compromise for the country. *He had passion, too, but it was for bringing people together… for balancing the golden scales.* I stepped forward to examine more closely Henry Clay's crystal blue eyes, but jumped back when they pivoted to meet mine. *Oh, shit, I didn't do that.* As I held my breath, Clay's jaw loosened, his pursed lips parted, and his voice boomed forth. "Let him who elevates himself above humanity, above its weaknesses, its infirmities, its wants, its necessities, say, if he pleases, 'I will never compromise,' but let no one who is not above the frailties of our common nature disdain compromises."

"I didn't…I…Mr. Clay?" The energy in the alcove had drained away. Henry Clay's jaw was again set, his lips were again pursed, and I was again looking at nothing more than an oil painting of a long-dead politician. I backed away, released my grip on my hair, and stumbled into the Civil War exhibit. My heart pounded as my brain strained to wrap itself around the gift I'd just been given. I needed a calm place to sort things out, but the scene around me was anything but calm. The walls were a disturbing bloody red and the exhibit was hopping — knots of people chatted and studied framed photographs lining the walls while a couple sat in loud personal conversation on an upholstered bench in the middle of the small space. Directly in front of me, a mass of elementary students pressed down the narrow hallway leading to the café. Feeling overwhelmed, I slipped through an open doorway to my right.

As I stepped into a dimly lit gallery also awash in blood-red, the noise from the hall snuffed out. My eyes opened wider to take everything in — the polished hardwood floors, the gold frames blazing against the red walls, several cases of artifacts mounted on matching red pedestals, five tall windows trimmed in a neutral grayish green that started at the floor and reached all the way to the base of the vaulted ceiling, and a pair of stark white busts that sat in front of two of the windows. I stepped forward. It was strangely quiet in here but the energy was anxious, as if the engines of a jet were revving in preparation for takeoff. I stepped farther into the room and was drawn forward to the portrait of a Union officer hanging directly in front of me. My eyes locked on the man's face.

"Uppity little peacock."

"He is, but cautious as a girl."

"Yep, he should have brung up the damned reserves when things got hot and let us end it. We could have driven them damned Rebs right into the river."

"You reckon that's why Lincoln's here?"

"Yep, I think Little Mac is gonna get sacked for good this time. Mark my words, he's gonna get sacked for good. Shame the colonel didn't live to see it."

I moved closer to the portrait or, rather, it appeared to zoom forward toward me, stopping inches from my nose. I could see the individual brush strokes and layers of oil paint that made up this image of a powerful dark-haired man who stood for his portrait with one gloved hand on his hip and the other on the hilt of his sword. He was all spit and polish in a crisp blue uniform buttoned tightly against his chest, and although his legs weren't visible, I could tell they were spread wide to create a sturdy, unyielding base. I knew this man — recognized the stubborn set of his jaw and the piercing eyes that did not welcome debate. Frustration swept up and crashed over me like a wave. *Son of a bitch. Let us finish it.* My heart began pounding in my ears and I felt an overwhelming need to rip the paint off the man's obstinate face. A blue spark zipped across my line of vision and broke my lock on the portrait just as I was about to raise my arms to tear it from the wall. I pulled my eyes away from the painting and stepped back, shaking my head to clear the anger that didn't seem to belong to me. *Who is this guy?*

The dispassionate red placard next to the portrait answered my question — "George B. McClellan, 1826–1885." A general appointed by Lincoln early in the Civil War to organize the Union Army after its defeat at Manassas, Virginia. He'd molded disorganized volunteers into a formidable fighting machine, but did lose his job soon after when he failed to pursue the retreating Confederate army after the Battle of Antietam.

I looked over my left shoulder and whispered to the empty room, "You were right, our boy got sacked and..." I stopped in midstream, shocked that the room now looked strangely soft and out of focus. As I glanced cautiously around, I could see that the light on the remaining portraits had dimmed and the faces in the frames had faded until they were indistinct. The two white busts were now weirdly translucent, almost as if they were composed of swirling mist. I froze, too scared to move. And then from somewhere outside the gallery door came the persistent, impatient tapping of a foot. I moved my head slowly to the left while peering out the corner of my eye, afraid of who might appear in my peripheral vision. What I saw was the full-length portrait of a man regarding me from the gallery across the hallway. I turned completely to face him.

"Get over here."

It was the portrait of another Union officer. Like George McClellan, this man was also standing, but his blue coat, which fell almost to his knees, was unbuttoned entirely to reveal a white vest opened to the middle of his chest. His white shirt collar was held closed with a tied blue cravat. He was ever so slightly slouched and his stance could almost be called casual, however, his hands expressed his authority and determination. Both were held in tight fists — the right was planted on his hip and the left clutched his brimmed hat in a white-knuckled death grip.

"Get. Over. Here."

I stepped into the hallway and found everyone gone. *How long had I been examining McClellan's portrait? Was it getting late?* I fumbled for my phone to check the time.

"Now."

"Okay, okay, I'm coming." I entered the gallery and cautiously shuffled over to stand in front of the general with the open coat. His brow was furrowed and his gaze was fierce. Here was a man who was clearly used to getting things done. He lived loosely and defiantly in his uniform, which didn't seem to define him as a man. Instead, he seemed to define the uniform, wearing it as he pleased. I glanced over at the placard — "William T. Sherman, 1820–1891." Rather than fighting for the South, this man had marched troops across Georgia and the Carolinas, burning and destroying anything of value in his path. And he apparently didn't care that the people of the South hated him because, as he'd said, "War is war and not a popularity contest." I suddenly realized how very little I knew about the Civil War.

"My apologies to you, sir," I said as I searched the man's face for any sign of softness, any twinge of compassion that might make him appear approachable. General Sherman continued to glare. I saw the movement of dark clothing out of the corner of my right eye and blushed with embarrassment. Someone had just caught me talking to Sherman's portrait. I turned with what I hoped was a friendly smile. "I'd always thought Sherman fought for the South," I said to the slight bald man studying the portrait to my right.

"No," he replied without looking at me, "Sherman was second in command to Grant in the last years of the war. He's been credited as the first modern general for his scorched earth policies, which he continued to employ even after the war in suppressing the Plains Indians. It was Sherman who engineered the decimation of the bison herds." The man paused and turned his head slowly to consider me. His intense, dark eyes peered past his hooked nose and straight through me. I sensed death around this man. The blush moved from my cheeks and seemed to envelope my entire head. A buzzing like a thousand angry hornets filled my ears. A trickle of sweat zigzagged down from my temple, tracing a route off the edge of my jaw that took it just in front of my right ear.

"Actually, you already know that," the man continued. "You need to remember. You need to remember A. P. Hill, too." He tilted his head slightly to the left, raised his eyebrows, and with his chin indicated a framed photograph to the left of Sherman's portrait. I followed his gaze to the sepia-toned image of a gaunt man with a full heavy beard and dark hair that hung almost to his shoulders. He was dressed in a bulky light-colored overcoat that was precisely buttoned. His lapels were carefully folded back and adorned with stars. This man looked tired and he appeared to be staring vacantly into the far corner of the room. "Meet Lieutenant General Ambrose Powell Hill, Confederate Army of Northern Virginia. He might look a bit spent here but he commanded one of the most dangerous light divisions on either side of the conflict. You should remember his name. He still haunts you, you know. Got you expecting a long time ago that things would always go sour for you right as you were about to taste victory."

A shudder ran through me. My sweat turned cold and my hands began to tremble. "How...how...," I croaked.

"How did I know that? Hit too close to home, did I? You could have really been part of something big that day. Instead you ended up trapped in that damned valley with all the rest as the Rebels slipped away. A good bit of you is still in that valley, isn't it?"

The room was rapidly turning yellow and indistinct. The buzzing in my ears intensified.

"Step over here."

I stared at the man, transfixed and unable to move.

"Now," he hissed.

I took two steps toward him. He reached out, placed his left hand behind my right shoulder blade and turned me around to face the portrait in front of him as he swept his right arm forward with his palm outstretched in a grand gesture of introduction. "This is who you're really here to remember. You need to start here. You need to start with Stonewall Jackson."

I caught a glimpse of a stern, determined face in full profile. Trimmed beard. Neat hair. Resplendent gray uniform. Gold buttons. Gold braid. This new face swam in front of me as yellow light obliterated the bloody walls. My knees buckled. I realized with dread that I was passing out. The buzzing in my head amped up another notch. I dropped to my hands and knees, still feeling the hand on my shoulder. The hardwood floor swam in front of me. Just as I was about to surrender and allow my head to hit the floor, the yellow light in my left eye softened and was replaced by a single, clear blue eye. It was not the caricature of an eye, not an animation — it was organic and real with an awareness behind it. It was regarding me. Just regarding me. *How strangely curious.* I blinked. The eye remained, softly observing me as I slipped into darkness.

CHAPTER 15

TRAVELING SHOES:
DON'T FEAR THE SHADOW

I felt the floor pressing into my left cheek and ear as I struggled back up to consciousness. I seemed to be lying on my stomach with my arms crossed at the wrist under my chest. *Where am I? Oh, yeah, the portrait gallery. I need to get up off the floor before the guard finds me lying here like a corpse. But I'm so comfortable — I didn't realize how tired I was. Maybe I'll rest just a little longer.* A hand on my right shoulder gently shook me. *Oh, shit, that weird guy is still here.* I kept my eyes closed and tried to will him away, dropping into a silent mantra of "go away, go away, go away." My muddled mind cleared just enough to remember the blue eye. It was gone, but my right ear was still buzzing. The hand on my shoulder became rougher and more insistent.

"Wake up. Sergeant Carson just came through. We need to form up and get ready to advance."

The buzzing in my ear ramped up to an insect-like shrill. *Boom!* An explosion from somewhere to my right jolted me wide awake. My eyes flew open as I rolled onto my left shoulder in a panic and used my right hand to push myself partially up. I swiveled my head from side to side to get my bearings but the gallery was strangely dark—not pitch black but dark enough that it seemed I was looking through a soft gray shroud at indistinct shapes and shadows.

"Hahahahahaha! Nothing like artillery to get a man going in the morning!"

The happy laughter peeling through the gray shroud melted my panic. I took a deep breath to slow my heart. My entire body felt stiff and damp and the right side of my face itched intolerably. I pressed down through my right hand, intending to push myself up to sitting, but found the floor beneath my palm strangely soft and spongy. I paused and closed my fingers, expecting to feel the nap of a carpet but instead came away with a fistful of the flooring. I lifted my hand to my chin and spread my fingers. A cascade of loose soil tumbled between my fingers.

"Shoo them skeeters away, they have your face all bit up."

I waved a small flock of mosquitoes away from my right ear and looked up into the happy face of a young man in his early twenties sitting cross-legged in the dirt next to me. His dirty blond hair was irregularly cut and small clumps of it stuck up off his head at strange angles. Dead grass and dirt adhered to the left side of his face. He squeezed his hazel eyes shut, tipped his face up to capture the first rays of early morning sunlight, and happily scratched the stubble on his cheeks. *Andy.* But a slightly different version of Andy than I knew in my waking life. I rubbed the sleep out of my eyes and sat up.

With unsettling clarity, I knew that Andy and I were in the plowed cornfield where we'd lain down with our rifles last night to sleep. We were still high up above the wide valley across which hundreds of cannons had dueled late into the previous evening as we watched awestruck and apprehensive over what the next morning might bring. That morning had come and men were stirring awake around us. Subdued voices created a hum that was period-ically interrupted by a shouted order or a shell whistling overhead. Mules brayed and horses stamped their feet. Metal clanked gently on metal. From farther away, the morning breeze carried the sound of continuous cannon and musket fire. I heard the faint sound of men hollering in unison way off in the distance and knew that the Ball had begun somewhere in the valley and the ladies were dancing without us.

Just as I was getting comfortable with my situation, a shell came whistling right over my head from the other side of the valley. I dove back into the dirt on my stomach and listened for an explosion, but instead heard a thump and a loud clattering just a short distance behind me. I peeked over my right shoulder to see a stack of rifles scattered not far from a young mail carrier who dumped his sack of letters on the ground and took off toward our rear at a dead run.

"Mail's here!" Andy said as he got up and ran in a crouch to the mailbag.

Oh, hell, what's he doing? I watched over my shoulder as Andy torn into the bag and dug through the contents, emerging with an envelope in his hand just as another man arrived to shoo him away. Andy came racing flat out back to me and slid headfirst back in line with the envelope clutched in his left fist.

"You got a letter!" He rolled to his right and presented the envelope to me with a flourish and a wild, goofy grin.

I laughed, propped myself up on my elbows and took the letter. I turned it over in my hands to see the name and address but a roar immediately rose in my ears as the envelope became smaller and smaller at a dizzying pace. I was rapidly sucked backwards out of my body, away from the letter, away from my brother, away from the line of men below me, away from the treetops. *No! Let me read it! I need to see the name. I need...*

The wind catches my outstretched arms and I wheel away from the line of men stretched out across the plowed field. The individual men become indistinct and merge into a dark blue line as I rise up and over a wide misty creek flowing lazily through a rolling patchwork of corn, wheat, pasture, raw earth, woods all stitched at the seams by wooden rail and stone fences. *This really is a beautiful place.*

My attention is pulled away from the beauty by muzzle flashes from big guns high up on the other side of the valley. I float in that direction and see a small town laid out in a neat rectangle behind a row of old-fash-ioned cannons on wooden carriages. There is a wide dark river, much larger than the creek, flowing behind the town. A column of men in gray and brown and tan is splashing across the river south of the town and joining other men who are streaming north.

I float lazily to the north to see where they're headed. I first come upon men massed within a high-banked country lane. They seem to be lying in wait behind piles of fence rails for other men whom they expect to arrive from across a field. The energy is uncomfortably anxious. The continuous boom of cannons and pop of musket fire has become deafening and uncomfortable. I feel agitated but circle higher and swing farther north, following the columns of men that are moving quickly from the south. Something is burning here. Buildings are burning. A barn. A farmhouse. Flames race up the walls and consume the roofs. I make wide sweeping circles above masses of men, wagons, horses. The smoke becomes thick and obscures my view.

I circle even farther north. Ahead of me now, I see other scattered farms and lines of men with colorful flags streaming across rolling pastures and a large cornfield. Huge banks of cannons pour fire into the men from all directions. Soldiers fire rifles, most topped with shiny bayonets, into each other at short range. Men fly up into the air or simply drop to the ground. Some become still on the field while others writhe in agony or attempt to crawl away. Other men, some dripping blood and hobbling, turn and run, pursued by gunmen who fire into their backs. Flags drop to the ground and are picked up, only to drop again. The cornfield becomes dark with blood as shards of green leaves scatter into the breeze and the corn stalks disappear.

I circle higher. Clouds of acrid white smoke now float over the landscape, fracturing the scene into small vignettes. Individual men and small knots lurk in the smoke, waiting to ambush their prey. Lines of men in dark blue uniforms storm out of woods behind the cornfield to be met by howling lines in gray and tan who are charging north. Scattered men on both sides with red sashes around their waists raise swords in outstretched hands and gesture forcefully. Others wheel on horses as they shout and swing their swords. This is where the column of men from the river is headed in a rush. I see them gathering behind the wood to the left — preparing to meet their enemy. I am sickened and have seen enough. *I want to leave this place.*

A shadow passes over me from above and I look up. Another passes and another. Vultures. Turkey vultures with ugly pink heads. Massing above the cornfield that is running red with blood. One swoops at my head and I see close-up the wrinkled skin and cluster of warts around its beady black eye and gaping earhole. I am repulsed by its appearance and its hunger for death. I cringe as another passes over me, blocking the sun momentarily before swinging around and dropping to face me. It opens its hooked yellow beak and glares straight into my eyes as it brushes past me on the left, close enough that I smell the stench of rotted carcasses on its hot breath.

"Don't fear the shadow, Seeker," it hisses inches from my face. "Do you remember General Jackson now?"

I stare at the creature in stunned silence as it swoops past and wheels around again in front of me. This time it's facing away. I see the ugly pink head crane back to look at me over the outstretched left wing. The shiny black eye strips me bare. My secrets tumble out around me and form up as little blackbirds that catch the wind and scatter with a thousand sighs.

"Follow me," the vulture hisses. "Follow me. Now."

The hideous bird dips down and traces a shallow arc to the left. I follow in its path. A small white building with shingled roof appears out of the smoke and fog of the morning. It's tucked into the corner of the wood behind which the men in gray and tan are massing. Other men are milling about the building on foot and on horseback. Fire blazes almost continuously from a long row of cannons stretched across a green field in front of the building.

The vulture swings behind the row of cannons and over the shingled roof to settle near the top of a tall tree behind the building. I settle next to it, surprised that the branch can take my weight. I hear terrifying asthmatic hissing and look up through the smoke and fog to see the black shapes of dozens of vultures circling high out of range of the artillery. *They are ready for their opportunity.*

"Yesssssss, we are opportunistic. We use all our senses and our past experiences together so that no opportunity goes to waste. We remember."

Four men sit on horses below us conferring. The vulture stares down at them with piercing eyes. "Look at the man on the small red horse below. The one sitting staunchly upright with braid on his sleeves. Do you know who he is?"

I immediately recognize Stonewall Jackson from his portrait and nod yes.

"You need to remember this place and you need to remember this man. They will give you the insight you require to leave the valley."

The vulture unfolds its wings and jumps from its perch. The black wings flap gracefully and silently as the vulture rises into the air to join its tribe. I follow suit, jumping off the branch and willing myself up into the sky and away from this terrible place.

I head back to the south, noticing that the roofs of the burning buildings have collapsed. Only the brick and stone of the walls and the chimneys still stand. I soar past the fire and over the heads of the men in the high-banked lane, many of whom are now leaving their positions and streaming north into the bloody fight. *I need to find Andy.* I follow the creek back to the south. The cannons still boom from both sides of the valley, sending shells whistling above an arched stone bridge and into the opposing hillsides. I swing to my left before reaching the bridge, heading east into the brightening dawn and toward the plowed field at the toe of the long ridge. I circle the field calling for Andy.

"Screeeeeeee! Screeeeeeeee!"

I see a head pop up from the line of men far below me. *Andy.* He pushes up on one elbow and smiles at me with wonderment in his eyes.

"Screeeeeeee!"

I look back to the sky and find the rising sun, which is now a full golden disk low over the horizon. Its rays paint the undersides of the clouds pink and gold. They glow against the brilliant blue sky. I notice for the first time how dark the tops of the clouds appear at sunrise. They are trapped in the shadow, untouched by the sun. I flap my arms and rise higher into the sky until I become part of the sunrise. I imagine the sunbeams warming my stomach and chest. I am spectacular in the growing light. I glow pink and gold like the clouds. I wheel around, circling in the magical light and moving farther and farther from the horror below me. I feel a chill between my shoulder blades and realize that, like the clouds, half of me is in the dark. But still I fly. Still I am beautiful.

"Screeeeeeee!"

As I continue to soar and scream my joy, my vision slowly goes dark from the outside in until I'm viewing the blazing sun and the ethereal clouds through a tiny peephole. And then the peephole closes.

CHAPTER 16

OF DREAMS, GENERALS, AND MINIATURE HAMBURGERS

The hand was back on my shoulder. Shaking gently.

"Hey, you okay? You okay?"

I again felt my left cheek and ear pressed against a hard surface but this time there was pain in my forehead. *Thump, thump, thump.* I could feel blood throbbing through the left side of my head. I opened my eyes to see shiny black shoes and the cuffs of a pair of black pants. Beyond them, a blur of hardwood floor stretched out to meet smeary, blood-red baseboards and walls. I blinked rapidly and my vision cleared. *How do they keep these floors so damn immaculate?*

"You awake now?"

My whole face began to throb as I blushed red. What I'd most feared had occurred — the security guard had found me sprawled on the gallery floor. With a rush of déjà vu, I realized I was lying on my stomach with my arms crossed at the wrist under my chest. I pulled my hands out, pressed them to the floor under my shoulders and pushed myself up to my knees. I shook my head a few times and slid back on my heels so I could gently rub my forehead. I found a knot about the size of a large acorn right at my hairline. I brought my hand down and inspected at my fingers. No blood.

"You need me to call EMS?"

I looked up into the security guard's dark worried eyes. "No, I think I just bumped my head a bit when I fell. I feel fine. Where's the bald guy? Did he come get you?" I'd forced an energetic perkiness into my voice that I didn't necessarily feel.

"No, didn't see anyone else in here with you. One minute you're looking at Stonewall Jackson and the next minute you're on the floor. Wham, bam, thank you, ma'am."

Oh, great, this guy didn't just find me on the floor, he watched me hit it.

"I knew you needed some soup."

Soup. Lunch! Lunch with Neil. Oh, no. I scrambled to my feet so quickly that the guard didn't even have a chance to offer me a hand.

"Do you know what time it is?" I asked.

The guard glanced at his watch. "Ten to two."

"Oh. Well that didn't take long."

"What didn't take long?"

I caught myself before I could blurt out the truth — the reframing of my entire Universe. "Looking through the Civil War exhibit. Although I haven't seen everything," I said as I noticed a huge portrait of Ulysses S. Grant over the guard's shoulder. He turned and followed my gaze to Grant's portrait, which presented the general in a casual pose with his right hand in his pants pocket and a cigar in his left. The portrait was intriguing but the massive black and gold frame around it screamed for my attention.

"Well, if you're okay, I'll leave you to it. Have a good afternoon and here's a little sugar to keep you going." The guard fished a yellow Starburst out of his shirt pocket and handed it to me.

"Thank you." I smiled into his eyes and he smiled right back.

"Just be cool about it. You're not supposed to eat in the gallery." The guard turned and slipped quietly from the room.

I walked over to stand before Grant's portrait as I absently unwrapped the Starburst and put it in my mouth. I guessed from the map and binoculars by his side that this was Grant at work on the battlefield. *Was he at the battle where I saw Andy?* I chewed the candy and my mouth filled with lemon. *The battle that I need to remember?* I leaned in and saw a bank of dirt represented behind Grant. There was a shovel propped near the map. Grant was in a ditch. I hadn't seen anything like a ditchworks on the battlefield I'd visited. My attention went to the map, which appeared to be spread out over a wicker basket of sorts filled with dirt. I leaned in even closer to read the labels on the map — "Vicksburg" and "Mississippi River". *That wasn't the Mississippi River I saw those Confederate soldiers wading across. How many battles were there during the Civil War, anyway?*

I swallowed the candy and turned my attention to the massive carved frame around the portrait. The frame was staggering in both size and design. It was so large and so ornate that it looked like a frame within a frame within a frame — a frame that didn't know where to stop framing. There was a large stylized eagle with gilded wings, a shield, and flags carved at the top. The rest of the frame consisted of a simple gold foundation onto which a rectangular wreath of black oak leaves had been carved. Golden acorns were placed regularly throughout the leaves. The wreath appeared to be tied down at the corners by four carefully carved gold ribbons. The two sides of the wreath were wrapped diagonally with additional ribbon. On each turn of the ribbon was carved the name of a battle — Vicksburg, Fort Donelson, Lookout Mountain, Appomattox, Fort Henry, Shiloh, Chattanooga, Battle of the Wilderness. All of this was surrounded by a wide filigree of stylized black and gold leaves. Frustration rose up into my chest. Beyond knowing that some of my ancestors had been soldiers for the Union, I'd never been particularly interested in the Civil War. *Here are ten new battles that I've never heard of before on top of others I've seen mention of today. How am I supposed to unravel this?*

Without even a cautious glance over my shoulder for witnesses, I leaned forward, grasped the ribbons on either side of the frame, and pulled hard. I stood watching with a gold ribbon in each hand as the blackened oak leaves slumped to the floor and a riot of golden acorns bounced around the gallery like ping-pong balls.

"Mine! Mine! Mine!" I laughed and my eyes refocused on the intact frame

still surrounding General Grant's portrait. *Zoe and her acorns. That day under the oak tree with Ashley. Ashley. Do I need to talk with Ashley? Maybe, but first I need to meet Neil.*

I turned and walked toward the door of the gallery, giving Stonewall Jackson one last glance as I passed his portrait. With a start I realized I was forgetting something. There was someone else here who I was supposed to remember. I walked to the corner of the room and looked again at the sepia-toned photograph hanging next to William Tecumseh Sherman's grumpy portrait. I read the name on the placard — "General A.P. Hill". I needed to remember that name. I pulled out my phone and typed in an email — *Note to self...remember Stonewall Jackson and A.P. Hill...and George McClellan...and...Webster, Calhoun, and Clay...and the abolitionists and the artists...and something about acorns.* I hit "send" and saw the message pop immediately into my inbox. My job at the gallery was done and I was well past pleasantly hungry.

I stepped out of the room and did an immediate U-turn to head down the back hall of the building toward an exit onto G Street that I'd noticed while searching my map for the café. The red glowing exit sign near the ceiling and the reception desk way off in the distance told me I was on the right track. I took one last look at my phone. It was exactly 2:15 and I was going to be on time to meet Neil. I locked in on the reception desk and took a half dozen quick steps down the hall before realizing what I was passing on the walls — photos of men in Civil War uniforms. I looked to my left in mid-stride and recognized George McClellan. I slowed and skimmed a few of the placards on each side of the hall. They all seemed to be Union generals. I felt as if I were on review and woefully underdressed. I stopped and stood in the hall contemplating. There was something here that I needed to see but there were twenty photos here, ten on each wall. I didn't have time to record their names, much less read about each man. *I wonder if Neil might want to come back and look after we eat. Or maybe I can come back down another day or find these online. Or shoot a video! Maybe I should shoot a video.* I was getting overwhelmed again.

As I stood frozen in indecision, a pair of blue streaks swept down each side of the hall as a clear male voice with a strong Southern twang boomed in my head. *"Who draws you in, kid? Who piques your curry-os-city?"*

Not even bothering to question what I'd just seen and heard, I decided to play along. *"Uh, okay, one from each wall?"*

"Shur-nuff! Who's it gonna be?"

I walked back to the beginning of the exhibit and started down the hall skimming faces, not stopping until near the end of the lineup. A bald, buttoned-up general stood before me. I leaned in to see the details of his face, which included exaggerated mutton-chop sideburns that met a thick mustache to segregate his lower jaw from the rest of his face. I pulled out my phone and snapped a quick picture of the photo and the placard next to it. *One down.*

I crossed the hall to start back up the other side using the same process but was stopped immediately by a clean-cut blond general who had chosen to sit for his photo. He stood out for his willingness to stare directly into the camera with icy eyes and for his clean-shaven face bobbing in a sea of hairy mugs. I hurriedly snapped his picture and information and then resumed my quick march to the exit, striding down the hall past knots of people enjoying a hodgepodge of portraits in a hodgepodge of media. "Recent Acquisitions" loomed past me on the wall to explain the variety here. The café streamed by — *should have had some soup* — followed by restrooms — *can go at the restaurant* — and a pair of elevators — *will check out the other floors next time.* Finally popping out of the hall and into the back lobby of the building felt like being reborn. I smiled and nodded at the white-haired gentleman manning the desk and bounced into the revolving door that led out to the street. For a split second I imagined with horror the possibility that there was no exit and I'd be deposited back into the gallery, but my glass cell lined up precisely with an opening back into the world and I was magically back out in the sunshine.

I stopped for a minute on the marble stairs leading down to the sidewalk and looked up at the gloriously puffy white clouds still hanging in a brilliant blue sky. The sun was high in the sky now, illuminating the tops of the clouds while leaving the undersides in shadow. The male voice with the touch of pecan pie and magnolia flowers rippled through my mind again, "What was dark is light. What was light is dark. It's all a matter of timing and perspective." *Timing. Time. I need to roll!*

From where I stood on the staircase leading to G Street, I had a clear view down 8th, which t-boned G at the back of the gallery and ended at the Renaissance Hotel two blocks up on I Street. The restaurant Neil had chosen was only one block up on H. I glanced at my phone one last time and saw that I could still make it on time. I bounded down the stairs, darted across G Street, and strode up 8th like I meant to get someplace, passing low office buildings and the Gothic red-brick Calvary Baptist Church at the corner of H. I pressed the button to get a crosswalk signal and looked up to consider the brick clock belfry and cast-iron spire looming over me as I waited at the corner for the light to change. *Gothic Revival. Reminds me of the original Smithsonian buildings built mid-19th Century. Wonder what this part of DC looked like when this church was built. How hard had it been to get that spire up there without a modern crane?* As I was pondering and conjuring up a team of horses and some sort of massive block and tackle apparatus, a resplendent indigo blue dragonfly zipped over from the small street tree in front of the church and hovered inches from my face. The creature locked its bulbous maroon eyeballs on the tip of my nose for just a moment, made a sudden hairpin turn, and zoomed up in the direction of the spire. *Illusion? What illusion? What are you showing me?*

Hands clamped down on my shoulders and shook me assertively. "It is so freaking rude to stop traffic and then forget to cross the street. What 'cha dreaming about, dreamer?"

I broke loose and spun around to face Neil with my eyes bugging an inch or so out of their sockets. "You scared the shit out of me!"

"That's my job." Neil laughed. Joy twinkled from his eyes. "It's fiberglass, you know."

"What?"

"The church spire. It's fiberglass. It was replaced maybe ten years ago. Was covered in *The Post*. The original was ripped off by a tornado in the early nineteen hundreds. Can you imagine a tornado ripping through downtown today? The light's changed again — let's go! Unless you're working this corner, that is. Which would be fine." Neil raised his hands in a conciliatory posture. An understanding expression flooded over his features. "No judgment…no judgment." The gaze of kind concern was almost instantly replaced by a wagging index finger and knitted brow. "But, seriously, right out in front of the church? In broad daylight?"

"Fiberglass? It's fiberglass?"

"Yep, fiberglass. Let's go." Neil darted into the crosswalk and shot across H Street with me in his wake. The back of his white dress shirt was a mess of imbedded wrinkles, indicating that he'd been sitting in meetings all day. It was going to be an interesting afternoon as he burned through his pent-up energy.

We walked the few doors down to the three-story brick building that at one time was a row house but now held Neil's favorite place for lunch in Chinatown. As Neil pulled the front door open and held it for me to enter, I wondered if kids had lived here and if their parents had brought them to Calvary Baptist Church on Sundays. I imagined three little kids all polished up and propped on a hard pew near the back of the sanctuary, legs dangling as they waited for the end of the sermon and their release back out into the world. *Had their father bribed them with candy to keep them still?*

Neil nudged me in the ribs with his elbow. A young woman in a blue t-shirt stood in front of us with menus in hand. She was looking at me expectantly.

"Yes, two of us, and a booth upstairs would be great," Neil said.

We followed the hostess past the bar and down the long, narrow space that was the first floor of the restaurant to the bright red industrial-style staircase toward the back. The hostess led the way to the second floor and brought us to a red-upholstered booth in the corner of the room. "Is this okay?"

"Perfect," Neil assured her with a big smile.

We slid in and I quickly scanned the room. Four other tables were occupied by a mix of business people and brightly colored tourists. There was enough space between us and enough privacy here to have a weird conversation.

"What can I get you two to drink?" the hostess asked as she handed us menus.

"A Dogfish IPA," Neil said. He glanced at me, signaling that I was up.

"The watermelon vodka lemonade."

"A Patio Pounder?"

"Yes, please. And could you bring me a water, too?"

"And you might as well just put in an order of nine sliders and a crab and avocado tower," Neil broke in. "You want spring rolls, too?" he asked me.

"Sure, yes, spring rolls would be great."

"That'll get us started," Neil said. He flashed his charming smile at the hostess again and the color went up in her cheeks.

"Jeremy will be your server and he'll be by in just a few minutes with your drinks. I'll put your appetizer order in right away. Is there anything else I can get for you now?"

"Nope, that'll do it," said Neil. "What did you say your name was?"

The hostess blushed even brighter. "Um, Katie."

"Thank you, Katie. I really appreciate you looking out for us."

"You're so welcome. Your drinks will be right out." Katie stumbled back downstairs with stars in her eyes.

I rolled my eyes and shook my head at Neil. "You realize, of course, that as we sit here idly contemplating miniature hamburgers and a pile of crabmeat, Katie is making plans to quit college, dump her boyfriend, and run away with you."

Neil's eyes went wide in mock astonishment. "Quit college? Say it isn't so! I'm going to need her to support me in my old age."

"You're so bad. What's going on back at the company? How many days you have left?"

A wicked grin shot across Neil's face. "Two, and I couldn't be more pleased."

"Two? Really? Your last day is Friday?"

"You got that right." Neil's eyes lit up with delight.

"I see you're all busted up about it."

"Oh, yeah. Almost as busted up as you were eight months ago. Have I told you how impressed I was that you leapt instead of being pushed?"

"No, but thanks. It wasn't too hard, though. I never did fit in. Couldn't get my head around who I was supposed to be there. And then one day realized I didn't want to get my head around it."

"I still maintain they would have kept you. Steve was sincerely shocked that you'd resigned."

"I know. He called me in when he got the official news. Wanted me to withdraw my resignation."

"Really? Why didn't you tell me that before?"

"Um, it felt bad. Like I was being pulled onto the island to survive so I could watch friends go down one by one."

"Hi, I'm Jeremy and I'll be your server today! I've got a Dogfish here..."

"That'll be mine," said Neil.

The enthusiastic young waiter set the beer down in front of Neil and the spiked lemonade in front of me. Fortunately, he remembered the waters. I wanted to grab one in each hand, tip my head back, and dump both glasses down my throat. Next time I was planning a freak-out on the Metro, I'd have to bring a water bottle.

"Katie put an app order in for you — are you interested in a pizza or entrees today?"

"Oh, we might be later on," Neil answered. "Why don't you leave the menus with us for now and we'll see how we do."

"Will do! Your apps will be out shortly." Jeremy zipped over to a table occupied by a family of four in screen-printed t-shirts, plaid shorts, strappy sandals, and other assorted summer wear.

"Aren't the kids back in school yet?" I asked Neil.

"Mine are." He glanced over this shoulder. "Maybe they're homeschooled or something." Neil took a long sip of beer as I drained my water glass. He pushed his water over to me. "Here, have mine, too. You do look kind of dry. And pale. Did you forget to eat again?"

"Uh, yeah, sort of. It's been a strange day. But, what about you? I knew something was up when you disappeared. How did everything go down?"

Neil laughed a small, sad laugh and looked down into his beer. "Well, you know how it goes. My role got smaller and smaller until it disappeared. They kept me around long enough to pull off some semblance of transition. Until three weeks ago, I really did expect to be reassigned. I was ready to move wherever they needed me. Had my entire life on hold waiting for the word to come down. It seems ridiculous now, but I was still invested — so concerned about there being a lack of continuity once my department was disbanded. The young kids HR sent me to mentor in were so arrogant and shallow. The substance wasn't there...the talent wasn't there. I still felt responsible and then I started to panic."

Neil looked up to make eye contact and continued. "I tried to get in to see Steve. I couldn't believe he knew what was going on and I had to warn him."

"How'd that go?"

"He wouldn't see me. Steve wouldn't see me. Martina didn't even bother with the pretense of putting me on the schedule and cancelling...just told me Steve didn't have time. And then I realized it was me, not Steve, who didn't know what was going on. It turned out that one of those kids was my replacement."

"Oh. I'm so sorry."

"Nothing really to be sorry about. I know it had more to do with the merger and with consolidation than it had to do with me, but I still felt responsible — like I hadn't taken care of my people and hadn't finished the job. When Steve refused to see me, though, I knew none of it was mine anymore. I realized I'd been taken out before the job was done and had no more control over what I'd built. I also realized that my sense of responsibility had been used for all it was worth — it kept me blind and it made me a valuable tool in the transition. I was pissed when I realized what was going on, but kept it quiet. I didn't want to talk to anyone about it. I imagined all the conversations that went on behind my back and got obsessed with wanting to know if Steve fought for me. Was his hand forced or was he complicit? I couldn't get past that. And I couldn't get past the fact that I didn't get to finish — I didn't take the team across the line. But then I woke up last Tuesday and was tired of feeling like shit. I decided I didn't have to carry the weight any further. I accepted that and said it out loud. 'I'm no longer responsible. I'm putting this down. Anything that happens going forward isn't my problem. My job is done.' It was amazing. I felt the relief rush in — I mean, I literally felt it rush in."

Neil took another sip of beer before finishing. "That very same day HR called me in and presented my separation package. The deal was fine and

I accepted it without negotiation. Only required two more weeks from me and that's done Friday. All the stress belongs to someone else now. And I'm in no hurry to find another executive position. Actually, I'm not interested in another corporate position, period. It's one of the things I've decided to let go. You know…to get the damn donkey out of the hole." Neil's grin was back.

"Ah, our friend, Pamela."

"Yes, Pamela. Do you realize how much that helped me?"

"I hoped it would."

Jeremy reappeared in our lives right at that moment with a tray full of food. "Hope you two are hungry!" He filled the table with a platter of sliders piled high with a tangle of fried onions, a plate holding a cylinder of crab surrounded by sliced crostini, and a plate of deep-fried spring rolls that had been split open to reveal the filling. Jeremy dropped a clean plate in front of each of us. "Is there anything else I can get you?"

"No, this will do it for now. Thanks, Jeremy," said Neil.

"No problem!" Jeremy darted across the room and disappeared down the stairs.

A small pile of greens and carrot shards shared the plate with the spring rolls. Neil spun the plate around so the vegetables faced me and pushed the plate my way. "There's your salad. Don't ever say I don't take care of you." Neil pulled the plate of sliders toward himself, pushed aside the onion straws, and grabbed two burgers. I scraped the salad and most of the spring rolls onto my plate. We both dug in and ate in silence for at least ten minutes. Apparently, Neil had forgotten to eat again, as well.

Eventually, Neil looked up and lifted his glass. "Okay, you're not so pale now. Pick up that drink. To moving on."

I lifted my lemonade and repeated the toast. "To moving on." We both drank. The vodka cut through the fruit juice and hit me immediately. I felt my shoulders relax. *Ahhhh, that's better.* I took another long sip and then dove headlong into the reason for our meeting. "So, Neil, about the dream…"

Neil leaned forward. "The dream is related to this, uh, transition of mine, isn't it?" Neil's intensity and excitement filled the booth and flooded over me. Whereas I was freaked out by the fact that we shared a dream, Neil was clearly pleased.

"I think it might be. Did you feel like you were on your own in the dream? Like you were the only one who understood the mission?"

"Exactly! I was completely surrounded by people but very much alone at the same time. I knew what had to get done but I was isolated and no one was listening to me."

"Like you've been feeling at work?"

"Yes, like I've been feeling for most of my career, but the people in the dream were wrong for that."

"Wrong in what way?"

"They didn't work for the company. They shouldn't have been there in a work dream."

"Uh, was my brother, Andy, in your dream?"

"Yes! He helped pull the rope after you showed up. So did that girl you set me up with a few years ago...that friend of yours...the professor at the university. What was her name?"

"Terri Martin? Terri Martin was in your dream?"

"Yes, Terri...that was her name. She was there. You didn't see her?"

"No. What was Terri doing in the dream?"

"She was the first person I saw that I recognized. She walked out of the field of orbs with her own rope over her shoulder and stood staring at me. She was mad, oh, man, was she mad."

"She was? Did she help you?"

"No, she just stood there and then you showed up."

"And I helped you?"

"Yes, you jumped right in and then your brother jumped in behind you."

"That's how I keep dreaming it, too, but what's the rope, Neil? Do you know what the rope is?"

"I don't know, but I do know we needed to hurry. We needed to pull that rope and we needed to do it quickly. But no one was hearing me and I couldn't do it by myself. I knew that terrible things were going to happen to the men if we didn't hurry, but they were content to stand in the field."

"But then I came and helped you and Andy helped you and the others fell in. And we pulled something up a hill, is that right? Toward a mountain pass?"

"Yes! And we dropped the rope just as a violent thunderstorm started."

"Yes, we dropped the rope and charged up the hill. We raced through the storm and you turned into a wolf!"

Neil's eyebrows flew up. "A wolf? I turned into a wolf? Well, that's interesting. You turned into a hawk."

Oh, crap. I grabbed my glass and poured the sweet drink down my throat in two gulps. I set the glass down and signaled to Jeremy who was delivering drinks to a nearby table. "Do you want another beer?"

"Uh, that was impressive and, yes, I think I'll need one to keep up with you."

I raised my empty glass to Jeremy who looked over and nodded. I turned back to Neil. "I was a hawk? Are you sure?"

"Yes, positive. You were some sort of hawk and you were flying along beside me. You even screamed like a hawk. Screeeeeeee!"

My mouth dropped open. "Okay, so that's interesting first because you just made a hawk noise in the middle of a restaurant in Chinatown and second because I've had a hawk thing going on recently. Hawks keep showing up for me and I've had this other recurrent dream where I'm flying — soaring around over a valley."

"Well, just so you know, it was good having you there as a hawk. I knew you could see the big picture and all our options. I felt secure with you there. You were locked in and focused."

"Really? Most people, uh, wouldn't describe me that way."

"Oh, don't sell yourself short — you have incredible flashes of complete clarity when you get out of your own way. The stuff you come up with sometimes is amazing. You really should let yourself go more. Drop your guard, you know, and don't worry so much about how others are going to react."

I flushed and fiddled with my glass, wiping the condensation down the sides. That sounded like something Mick would say to me. Neil laughed gently. "We can talk about me if I'm making you too self-conscious. How did you feel with a wolf by your side?"

"I felt protected with you there. You exuded this intense sense of loyalty. You were the guardian. I knew you'd take care of us…no matter what happened, you'd be right there. Do you remember what you said once we got through the storm, though?"

"Yes. I said we were too late. I said that Jackson had arrived. Jackson who? The only Jackson I know is Sheila Jackson in Accounting."

"Stonewall Jackson, Neil. You were talking about Stonewall Jackson."

"From the Civil War? Why would I be talking about the Civil War?"

"Um, I think we were there."

The color dropped out of Neil's face as he stared at me in shock.

"Another Dogfish IPA for you and here's your Patio Pounder. Happy hour started at three so I'm going to leave this happy hour menu with you. If you see anything there you'd like to try, just let me know." Jeremy held the menu out for Neil who looked over at him in a fog. I took the menu and thanked Jeremy, who gathered up our empties and the spring roll plate before dashing back downstairs.

Neil was still staring at me. "Neil…Neil…are you still with me? Are you dumbstruck by how plausible that sounds or by the sheer stupidity of the concept? Or do you just think I've lost it?"

"All of those. Can I pick all of those?"

"Sure. Do you need to process for a minute?"

"Yeah. I just realized the enormity of all of this. I mean, we're sharing a freaking dream. We're in each other's heads. That's what we're saying, right?"

"Yeah."

Neil sipped his beer while I broke into the crab and avocado tower. The crab tasted perfectly of the ocean and the avocado was creamy and ripe. I tasted mango and something herbal. *Wonder what…*

"So, the Civil War…"

"Yeah, I think we were Union soldiers. And Andy was, too. Maybe Terri, too, since you saw her in the field. I went to the National Portrait Gallery, Neil, to kill time until you could leave the office and I had a, uh, vision there. It was like I passed out sort of and had a dream, but more like I left my body and went somewhere else for a while. I went to a battlefield during the Civil War. I didn't see you there, but Andy was there. Andy and I were Union soldiers together. We were lying together in a plowed field waiting to go into battle. But the battle was far away up this valley with a creek at the bottom. I started flying in the vision and saw Confederate soldiers crossing a river and marching north. I wanted to see where they were going so I flew north and found the battle in a cornfield. There was a house and barn on fire and there was a small white building and a vulture took me to sit in a tree behind the building. The vulture told me…"

"Whoa, whoa, whoa…slow it down, slow it down. You were at the National Portrait Gallery. The gallery down the street?"

"Yes."

"And you just…passed out?" Neil looked at me with real concern in his eyes.

"Well, no, not really. I was actually fine until I met this bald guy who I'm pretty sure was the vulture. I mean, he looked like a vulture…bald head, long hooked nose, dark clothes. I think he did something to make me leave my body and go back to the Civil War. It felt real, Neil. Not like a dream. I really think we were there."

Neil dropped his chin just a bit and peered down at me. "Okay. Go ahead."

"So, the vulture and I were sitting behind the building and there were four men on horses below us. The vulture pointed one out. It was Stonewall Jackson. I knew it was Stonewall Jackson because the vulture had me look at his portrait in the gallery before he took me back to the Civil War."

"You know how crazy this sounds, don't you?"

"Yes. Does that bother you?"

Neil sipped on his beer and pondered my question. "No, not really. Continue."

I wrapped both hands around my wet glass and leaned forward. "We were in the tree looking at Stonewall Jackson on his horse and the vulture told me that I needed to remember him and I needed to remember the place…the battlefield. That it would help me understand how to leave the valley. I wasn't sure what that meant, but remember that other dream I had? The one about the people in the valley with all their baggage? And the lightning bolts that would hit them?"

"Oh, yeah, sort of. That was a while ago. You were still with the company then. We were sitting in my office eating lunch with that conference call on mute. You never finished telling me about that dream."

"Uh, yeah, because you were too distracted to listen. I finally paid Andy's ex-girlfriend's counselor to listen just so I could get it out."

"Why did you do that?"

"I had to tell it and no one would listen. I became completely obsessed with it. And as soon as I explained it to someone else, I understood what it meant."

"So, I'm listening now. How'd it go?"

I took a long swallow of watermelon lemonade and let the vodka settle in somewhere behind my left ear. I wondered if it was possible for only your left ear to get drunk on a Wednesday afternoon when all you'd had to eat all day was four spring rolls and a tiny salad.

"I'm listeninggggggg…"

"Right, sorry. The valley in that dream was different. It was dry and looked to be out West. I worked one summer in a place called Paradox Valley in Colorado. It was a paradox because the river didn't follow the valley. Instead, it cut straight across at a ninety-degree angle. That was the paradox. But there was a secret to it — the stream was there a lot longer than the valley and had dissolved and carried away this huge underground salt deposit that used to sit where the valley is now. I think the valley in the dream was Paradox Valley."

"That's pretty cool. That was the summer during college when you studied elk?"

"Yep, but there were no elk in the dream. There were people in the valley and most of them were struggling with all this stuff piled around them. Some had a lot and some had a little. It was a hodge-podge of possessions and what seemed to be relationships. I guess anything could have been in the boxes and suitcases that were piled up. Some people were trying to drag all their stuff around. Then these lightning bolts started raining down…"

"Lightning bolts again, huh? What's with the lightning bolts?"

"In this dream the lightning either destroyed people's stuff entirely or separated them from it. As the dream went on, the entire valley became littered with debris and scattered baggage." I took another long swig of my drink and grabbed a few onion straws while Neil processed what I'd shared.

"Oh. Oh! Like my marriage."

"Yes. And our careers."

"Well, yours wasn't exactly taken away."

"The lightning still hit it and changed it into something else. My career as I knew it was gone."

"Ah, okay that's true. What happened next in the dream?"

"Some people were completely cool with what had happened to them and seemed happy. They left almost all of their stuff behind and started up these paths out of the valley. Others were in a panic and tried to gather everything back together. They were trying to get their lives back."

"That sounds reasonable."

"Maybe or maybe not. The rest of the people didn't know quite what to do but they were asking questions and looking for answers. Some of them eventually filled daypacks and also took off up paths out of the valley. Others stayed in the valley and began to gather baggage again."

"New baggage or old?"

"I'm not sure. I don't think it matters. It just felt like they were gathering up things they didn't need — things that kept them tied to situations that weren't right for them."

"Like child support keeps you tied to a job that you've fallen out of love with…"

"Yes. Well. Maybe. No. I don't think the child support is the baggage — the belief that it takes away your choices is the baggage. The belief that it's a burden is the baggage. Any resentment towards your ex-wife because of it is baggage. Memories of feeling screwed over by the judge is baggage. Grief or guilt around the break-up of your marriage that's triggered when you transfer the money or write the check each month is baggage."

"Oh." Neil picked up another burger and munched thoughtfully. I took advantage of the pause to continue demolishing the crab tower, while watching

Neil out of the corner of my eye. He finished his burger, wiped his mouth, and crumpled his napkin into a tight little wad before flattening it against the table with his palm. "So, if all of this baggage makes you feel like shit, why gather it back up?" he asked.

"Because it's what we know. It feels safe. Suddenly having your stuff and your stories about your life messed with makes everything feel out of control, don't you think?"

"Yeah. Your identity gets jacked around. Right now I'm not sure who I am anymore."

"So, when do you think the lightning bolt hit your life?"

"The big bolt? The day I was termed."

"Are you sure?"

Neil released his squashed napkin and turned his attention to the onion straws. He untangled them one by one from the pile, gazing at each before putting it in his mouth and chewing. He was zoning out and letting the answer come to him instead of chasing it. I admired Neil's ability to do that, even under stress. As I watched him, I suddenly realized I was witnessing an eating meditation. I visualized a big yellow legal pad. To the list of sitting, lying, standing, and walking meditations, I added "eating" with an oversized blue crayon that magically slid over the paper to do my bidding. *What else? Hmm...gardening.* The blue crayon made my addition with a flourish and hovered over the page for my next instruction. *Fishing?* The crayon again scribed across the page.

"Hello. Did you hear me?" Neil asked.

My big blue crayon evaporated as my eyes refocused on Neil's face. "Uh, no, I'm sorry. What did you say?"

"The lightning struck my life a long time before I was termed, but I thought I was still in control. The first hit was the lay-offs and the dissolution of my department. That was when I started scrambling to put things back together, although I hadn't accepted that they'd blown apart. The second hit was when you left. Everything unraveled from there."

"Yeah, but I left because your department was dissolved, so that really..."

"What?"

"I left because your department was dissolved."

"Right, I heard you but I didn't know that. You didn't tell me that."

"Yes, because I didn't want you to feel guilty and I didn't want you to try to stop me. I told Steve the night I decided to quit that I couldn't work for a company that would decommission its strongest leader. He told me that I was naïve and didn't understand the politics. I asked him if that was what we'd become — a political machine that wasn't concerned about getting the job done or living up to the ideals so many of us had bought into. He was shocked that I'd speak to him like that, but he's the one who gave me Scotch on an empty stomach and I just kept rolling. Told him I'd signed on to push the envelope, not to be an anonymous component of the corporate machine relegated to pumping out status reports."

"Whoa. Talk about burning bridges with a flamethrower. That is totally not you. How did Steve respond?"

"He offered me a raise and stock in the parent company if I'd keep it quiet, toe the line, and stay through the next merger. But I'd just seen a hawk fly by his office window. It was tempting me to come fly with it through this amazing blood-red sunset. And right before that meeting, I'd started having the dream about the people in the valley. I'd become obsessed with the people going up the paths toward unknown adventure and I saw myself doing that if I could get my confidence up. As hard as that seemed, the prospect was better than staying on and watching in silence as my friends were picked off one by one."

"Okay. Umm, did you tell Steve all that?"

"No, I didn't tell him about the dream or the hawk. He wouldn't have had patience for that. I told him I needed to pursue something. That I needed to live my passion — that I hadn't found it yet and still wanted to try."

Neil's eyebrows shot up as both of his eyes went wide. "What did he say to that?"

"He got irritated and called me a kid. And then he told me to think about his offer and get back to him. I submitted my resignation the next morning."

"I see." Neil cocked his head to the side and stared hard at me through slightly beer-addled eyes. "Well, first off I need to thank you. I'm grateful you had my back and said something. A lot of people had my back and remained silent."

"I'm just glad you're out of there. I've been really worried about you."

Neil blushed and became engrossed in the label on his beer bottle. I zoned out and watched him, not expecting the words that came out of his mouth next. "And, secondly, you are a kid but in the best possible way."

I rose up in my seat and gave Neil my best indignant glare. "You're calling me immature, too? I thought we were friends."

Neil grinned and raised a palm to fend off my flash of anger. "Steady…steady. I said in the best possible way and you went the exact opposite direction on me."

"Well, if that was meant as a compliment, you'd better explain it."

"I think I'd better before you throw your drink at me." Neil smiled and reached out to give my forearm a reassuring squeeze. "You're a kid in that you still have a sense of wonder. Do you realize how special that is? Most of the rest of us…we've lost that. We look at the world and see opportunities to get ahead…to get ours. You look at the same world and see hawks inviting you to come out and play. Your version of the world is full of unexpected treasure. You're a kid in that way…the best possible way."

"And you think that's a good thing."

"For sure. I'm jealous. And I'm also jealous that who you really are still shines through. The dust of life doesn't really stick to you — not the way it sticks to most of us, building up until it changes who we appear to be."

"Well, don't be jealous. I actually wouldn't mind fitting in once in a while."

"Because you think that would make things easier?"

"Yeah."

"Better be careful what you wish for — personalities made of dust are fragile things and take a whole lot of brushing to keep groomed. They apparently also attract their fair share of lightning bolts." Neil caught Jeremy's eye and signaled for refills. I polished off my drink and definitely felt my left ear stumble and slur a few words as the vodka goaded me into finally admitting to Neil how lonely and disconnected from the world I normally felt. I lifted my eyes to his and was about to speak when he suddenly changed the subject. "So, what happens next? In the dream. How does it end?" Neil asked.

"The dream?"

"Yah, we were talking about a dream here, weren't we?"

"Oh, yeah. We were. The end is weird. The dream cuts away to my house. All the windows are open and the curtains are moving in the breeze. The house is almost completely empty — like it's moving day and whatever's still there is being left behind. I'm in the living room and can see the sky out the windows. There's this expectant energy in the air but it's hard to tell what time of day it is. I must have had the dream a dozen times before I finally realized it's dawn, but storm clouds obscure the sun. There's this tension...will the thunderheads move past and allow the dawn to break or will the storm come and drown out its beauty? It's so quiet. Even the birds are holding their breath waiting to find out if they'll be singing or diving for cover. And then I notice something in the dining room — an axe stuck in the table. It's pinning down a note. I walk over to read the note but wake up before the words come into focus. And that's it."

Neil stared blankly at me. "Oh, yeah, I couldn't have heard this eight months ago. I wasn't there. You needed to wait until I was ready. So, what does it mean?"

"I don't know. Any ideas?"

"No, but we should figure it out." Neil grinned. He was ready for adventure, too — was already strapping on his pack and scanning the terrain for the path that was calling his name the loudest. Jeremy came back with our refills and quickly gathered up the empties. He was becoming more rushed as the afternoon wore on and the restaurant started to fill up. The noise level at the bar was increasing with each tick of the clock.

"Do you want to finish these and get out of here?" asked Neil.

"Sure."

"Good. I want to go back to the gallery with you. I want you to show me what you looked at. Everything that caught your eye. Here — eat the last burger. It'll soak up the alcohol. I don't want you falling on your face again. You have a knot on your forehead, you know." Neil pushed the plate holding the last slider and the pile of onion straws toward me. I dutifully ate the burger and drank my final spiked lemonade as Neil worked on the onions and finished his beer.

"What time does the gallery close?"

"Seven."

"Perfect. Plenty of time."

"Aren't you going back to the office today?"

"Clearly, you are intoxicated. I emptied my office out over the weekend and am just biding my time until the final bell rings. Everything has been transitioned and, honestly, most of my programs aren't even being carried forward. I spent all morning in one-on-ones trying to help my former team members cope with my departure. It's been like one long receiving line at a funeral." Neil wrinkled his face into a mask of mock bewilderment.

"Well, your people do love you, Neil. Let them take you out Friday night to say goodbye — that's going to be important to them."

"Yeah, maybe too hard on me, though. Are you ready?"

"Yep."

"Great. I've got this." Neil signaled Jeremy for the check and he came over immediately with it. No doubt he was ready to turn the table. Neil handed over his card without reviewing the bill and Jeremy scurried away to run the charge.

"You feeling better?" Neil asked me.

"Yep."

"Good, because it's time for some detective work. I want to figure out which battle you saw." Neil rubbed his hands together in anticipation and bugged his eyes. He definitely brought energy to whatever journey we were about to embark upon.

Jeremy came back to the table with the check and a pen.

"Stay right there, Jeremy," Neil said as he added a tip to the total, signed his name with a flourish, and handed the slip back to the waiter. "Thanks for your service and for your patience while we used this space. Have a good evening!"

"No problem. You have a good evening, too." Jeremy grabbed the slip and took off but only made it halfway back to the staircase before he turned and held the check up in his right hand and called out to Neil.

"Thank you so much, sir! I really appreciate this."

"You're welcome," said Neil. "Use that to do something you love."

CHAPTER 17

ASSAULT ON THE NATIONAL PORTRAIT GALLERY

"I want to take my shoes off and walk in it."

"Of course, you do," said Neil. "Go for it if you want. I don't mind."

"Nah, that's okay."

We were standing together in the massive rectangular courtyard of the National Portrait Gallery examining the water feature that took up nearly half the space. It consisted of a row of rectangular sections of the dark gray granite floor, the largest at least thirty feet by six feet, that were simply wet. The water appeared at one long edge of each rectangle and disappeared down unobtrusive drains on the opposite sides. The sound of moving water provided soft background music for the muffled conversations coming from small tables clustered in one corner of the space.

"This is brilliant," I said. "I bet they turn it off for big events in here."

"I bet they do."

I looked around and took in the rest of the space, which had to cover over half an acre. An undulating canopy of frosted, rectangular glass panels covered the courtyard. The sunlight coming through the canopy was muted and had an otherworldly quality, making the day appear overcast even though the sun was still blazing in a bright blue sky studded with puffy clouds. Perfectly maintained trees grew under the canopy in massive marble planters that mirrored the water feature in size and orientation. The atmosphere was magical and at the same time strange.

"There's no breeze. Does that bother you, Neil? It bothers me that there's no breeze to move the leaves on the trees."

"Oh, yeah. It sort of does bother me. The trees look artificial. They're too still."

"And there are no bird sounds. It would be cool to have an aviary in here."

"Hmmm. A little messy. How about some piped in bird noise instead?"

"Yeah. That would be cool. Birds and tree frogs, too."

"Do you want to sit down for a minute? To plan our assault?"

"Sure. Yeah."

We moved over to a table and sat down side by side. Neil pulled a tiny notebook out of his shirt pocket and I handed him a pen. We spread my map of the gallery on the table. "Okay, show me your route through the building."

I carefully recreated my earlier visit for Neil, first tracing my route from the F Street entrance through the "Eye Pop" exhibit and the magic portal to the past. Neil took careful notes as I indicated with my finger my path through the first two teal galleries and my tangent into the main hall to follow the apparition that had distracted me from the portrait of Sagoyewatha.

"Are we sure we want to call that an apparition?" asked Neil. "Not a kid who was screwing with you?"

"Wasn't a kid. Was an apparition."

Neil leaned over and drew a tiny ghost near the doorway of the gallery through which I'd followed the cloaked figure.

"And there's actually a partition here in the main hall," I pointed out. "The apparition slipped around it but there was a tour group on the other side talking about Edison."

Neil looked at me like I'd clearly lost my mind, but cooperated and drew a partition where I'd indicated.

"I stopped there for a minute and then started through these galleries." I pointed out the second set of interconnected galleries — the yellow rooms. "This first room is authors and artists. The second room is explorers of the New World. The third room is full of abolitionists and activists." Neil placed careful numbers on the map and made corresponding notes in his book.

"Anything weird happen in any of these rooms?"

"Yeah. In the corner of this first gallery there's a bust of Ralph Waldo Emerson. I was standing in front of it reading a quote about taking responsibility for your own salvation and I heard someone tell me to always follow the little arrow to the North."

"You needed to walk north? Was that a clue?"

"No, it wasn't like that. It was like there was always spiritual guidance available to follow. That Emerson was saying you were responsible for yourself, for your our spirituality and salvation, but you weren't alone."

"Like, 'follow the North Star?' "

"Yes, like that but North was another word for God and you could follow God without a tour guide."

"Oh. No tour guide, huh? Was anyone in the room with you?"

"I don't know — I didn't turn around."

"You didn't turn around...hmmmm." Neil drew another little ghost on the map. "Ghost of Emerson speaks of salvation and the need for a good compass," he said out loud as he made the notation in his book. "Anything else?"

"No. Oh, wait, yes. I talked to a guy in the activists' room. I thought he was a spirit at first but turned around and it was a security guard. He said he'd just gotten there, so wasn't the voices in the other rooms."

"Okay. What's next?"

I pointed out the stairwell and described to Neil the massive portrait of Grant and his generals. "I was hungry and was going to go to the café to get soup but I saw a portrait of John Brown right here and I wanted to look at it. I dubbed the boys hanging in this alcove The Hair on End Posse. The group includes John Brown and a group of Congressmen who argued about slavery and keeping the Union together."

"John Brown from Harpers Ferry?"

"Yes, and something happened here. My hair...well, uh...I think I was initiated into the posse and one of the portraits might have spoken to me."

"Spoke to you, did it? Probably your imagination…don't you think?" Neil indicated the back corner of the main hall. "This is where the Civil War exhibits are?"

More relieved than annoyed that Neil had brushed past my experience in the alcove, which I didn't really feel ready to share anyway, I nodded and pressed on. "Yes, and these two side galleries are Civil War, too." I pointed out the gallery on the right. "I went into this one first. Something really weird happened here when I looked at a portrait of a Union general. There was a lot of anger in this room that didn't belong to me."

Neil raised an eyebrow at me and wrote "WEIRD!!!" in tiny block letters next to the room I'd indicated.

"And then I went into this room straight across the hall. I didn't really look much at the collection in the main hall. Oh, and along this back hall here there's a display of photos of Union generals." I pointed out the back hall that led to the café and G Street lobby. "I heard a voice here that suggested I focus on a few of the photos that piqued my curiosity."

"A voice, huh?"

"Yeah, a different voice than the one I'd been hearing. Decidedly Southern."

"I see. So, uh, where was the vulture?"

I pressed my finger to the map. "In here. Looking at a portrait of Stonewall Jackson."

Neil drew a tiny, hunched bird on the map and then added a little stick figure splayed on the floor. "That's you," he said as he pushed the map toward me so I could admire his handiwork.

"Nice."

"So, I'm thinking we can probably skip the first part of your sojourn and go straight for the Civil War exhibit. Maybe just start with *Grant and His Generals*." Neil marked our current location on the map and drew a line back through the G Street lobby, down the back hall, and then to the right down the main hall to the stairwell, where he placed a star. "From there, let's take a tiny peek at John Brown and his colleagues." He drew another star and continued the line to it. "And then we'll pop around the corner, like you did, and look around in this room." He continued the line into the first side gallery and swirled the tip of the pen around, creating a whirlwind. "And then this room." He continued his line, ending it with a solid, black dot at my prone stick-figure body and the lurking vulture. "But we won't fall down this time." Neil laughed at his own joke and continued. "Anything I missed?"

"Yes, we shouldn't skip the photos of the generals in the back hall. I picked the two that shouted the loudest and took pictures of them and their information. I was planning to study them for clues. You should pick two, also."

"They didn't really shout at you, did they?"

"No, of course not, Neil." I rolled my eyes at him. "But there were two that I gravitated toward. You might pick the same ones or you might pick others that we should check into."

"Sounds fun. Let's make a video of all the photos, too, while we're here."

"That's a great idea. I should have thought of that."

Neil popped to his feet. "Let's roll!" He shot across the courtyard with me in his wake and pulled open the heavy glass door that led back out to the G Street Lobby. I hurried to catch up, knowing that Neil would hold the door for only a heartbeat before moving on. I caught the door right as Neil let it go and walked with him past the café and through the recent acquisitions.

"Slow down. Stop here for a minute, Neil." I stopped his advance under the arch separating *American Origins* from the rest of the museum.

"That's weird," said Neil.

"What's weird?"

"The atmosphere on the other side of the arch is completely different. Can you feel that?"

"What does it feel like to you?"

"It feels like a door is opening and this hidden world is appearing. Do you see the air shimmering?"

"No, but I saw two blue…"

"Who's that?" Neil pointed to the end of the hall.

"That's Daniel Webster of The Hair on End Posse. He was a senator who battled to keep the Union together. He died ten years before…"

"He's glaring at me."

"He has that tendency. We'll get to those guys — ready for the generals?"

"Ready."

"Okay, there are ten on the right and ten on the left. I picked one from each wall. Whoever caught my attention."

"I'll pick first from the right wall." Neil plunged forward through the portal, took two steps, and stopped.

"This one, for sure." Neil pulled out his notebook. "Ambrose Everett Burnside," he said as he added the name to his notes. It was the same general I'd picked first — the one with the outrageous sideburns.

"Are you sure? Why'd you pick him?"

"Absolutely sure. He reminds me of someone, maybe. I feel like I know him."

I pulled out my phone and snapped a picture, so as not to tip Neil off that the same general had shouted the loudest at both of us.

"Ready for the left side?"

"Yes." Neil backtracked to the arch, spun around on his heel, and strode down the hall. He scanned the generals to his left as he walked the length of the short hall, then turned and walked back, still scanning the faces. He made two additional passes up and down the hall before stopping and turning to me with his hands on his hips. "No one here is calling my name."

"Are you sure?"

"Yeah. I want to look at the rest on the right. Is that okay?"

"Sure, we can bend the rules."

"That's what I like to hear." Neil strode down the hall again, scanning the photos on the right. He stopped in his tracks halfway down the lineup. "This guy. This guy pisses me off. He's an uppity little peacock."

I stared at the photo in shocked silence. "Why did you call him that?"

Neil looked at me with steel in his jaw and fire in his eyes. "Because he's full of himself."

"We have to deviate from the plan. Follow me."

This time I took off with Neil in tow, leading him down the back hall and through the Civil War exhibit to the first blood-red side gallery. I stopped at the doorway and stepped aside so Neil could see the portrait of George McClellan. Neil's eyes locked onto the portrait. He strode into the middle of the room and stopped with his arms crossed in front of him, his fists clenched, and his jaw set. I cautiously joined him, being careful not to stand too close.

"It's George McClellan," I said. "He led the Union Army. He organized the troops and molded them into a fighting machine, but was reluctant to let them fight. Lincoln shit-canned him. I heard voices in here, too. I heard someone call him an uppity little peacock."

Neil spun to face me. His features were twisted in rage. I took two steps back, putting my nose out of reach if he happened to swing. "He didn't let us fight! We could have ended it! We were too slow. We were too tentative. Thousands of boys died because of McClellan! We needed to move! We needed the reserves brought up when things got hot!"

"Neil?"

"What game were we playing? Were we trying to lose? Were we trying to prolong the war so Little Mac could play general? The boys wanted to fight and go home!" Neil dropped to his knees and grabbed the back of his head with both hands, squeezing the sides of his face with his forearms. He rocked back and forth from his waist as if he were in great pain.

"Neil?"

"I didn't get to finish it. I didn't get to finish it."

"Finish what, Neil?"

Neil dropped his palms to the floor and supported himself on his hands and knees. He was breathing hard and moaning. I went to him and put my hand on his back, feeling his ragged breaths.

"Neil?" When he didn't answer, I dropped to my hands and knees next to him and turned to look into his tortured face. "Neil, are you okay?"

"Yeah," he finally whispered in a broken croak. "Please help me. Please. I need to get out of this room."

"Okay. Um, close your eyes. Close your eyes and I'll lead you out. There's a bench right outside the door and I'm going to lead you there to sit down for a minute. Does that sound good?"

"Yeah."

Neil closed his eyes. I helped him to his feet and led him away from George McClellan and over to the black, upholstered bench occupied earlier in the day by the couple locked in loud debate. "Turn around. The bench is right behind you. Keep your eyes closed and sit." Neil followed my instructions and sat on the bench with his palms pressed on his knees. "Loosen up your hands. You're pressing all the color out of your fingers. Loosen up your arms and your hands and imagine your fingernails going pink again. Send some love down to them." Neil lifted his hands and shook them vigorously. "Let your shoulders go. Unclench your jaw." He rolled his shoulders back a few times and wiggled his lower jaw. "Soften your face. Let all the anger drop out. Let it drop to the floor." Neil's face softened and I began to recognize him again. I imagined the anger melting from his face and gathering in damp, black pools at his feet. I watched as the pools formed up into little soldiers who scurried for the corners of the alcove and disappeared under the baseboards. "Keep your eyes closed and loosen up your back now. Stretch and let the anger drop away." Neil raised his arms to the ceiling and stretched deeply. I leaned back just in time to avoid getting clobbered as he swung his arms down and out to his sides. He took a wide horizontal stretch out to his fingertips and then pulled his elbows into his ribs, flexed his fingers a few times, and dropped his hands loosely to his lap. "Better?"

"Better."

"Excellent. Take a few minutes to settle completely back into yourself. I'll orient you to what's around us before you open you eyes. Sound good?"

"Yes."

As we sat together on the bench, Neil's shoulders slumped gently and his face relaxed into a serene childlike expression that made me want to tuck a blanket up under his chin and kiss his forehead as he drifted off to happy dreams. Instead of nodding off, however, Neil straightened up and his lips tightened into a smile. He was back. "So, we're sitting in the alcove between the two side galleries. The room we just left is behind you. We're surrounded by Civil War photographs. Groups of men standing together. Some in front of tents. Probably group shots of more generals and officers. It's hard to tell from this bench who anyone is. At the end of the alcove there's, like, a memorial display for someone. And there's a portrait of Lincoln here. Do you think you'll be okay opening your eyes? Maybe focusing on Lincoln, or something?"

"Yep."

"Go for it."

Neil opened his eyes and blinked. He turned to me. "That was weird."

"Yeah. You okay now?"

"Yeah."

"I felt that anger in there myself, Neil, but I knew it didn't belong to me. And I heard a conversation between two men. They were saying some of the same things you just said. Did that anger feel like yours? Or did it feel like you were picking up someone else's emotions?"

"That was mine. It was memories. Memories came flooding back to me."

"What kind of memories?"

A look of intense sadness came over Neil's face, weighing down his features. "Something traumatic happened to me and it was connected to George McClellan. I was angry and frustrated with him when..." Neil paused and looked curiously at me as his face lifted. "I'm so sorry, I can't share the details. But I need to tell you thank you."

"Uhh, okay. For what?"

"Something you did. There was something you did for me that was very kind and immensely courageous. Remembering that made it easy to see how you could have spoken up to Steve on my behalf. You really are a special person."

"Um, okay. That's, okay, confusing, but really sweet, Neil."

Neil wrapped me up in an unexpected one-armed hug and kissed the top of my head. Seeing as he'd clearly just lost his mind, I reassuringly patted his chest. "Uh, how do you feel now, Neil?"

Neil gave my shoulder a squeeze and let me go. "Well, actually pretty good. I feel clear. Like something I was holding onto that was making my mind murky is gone. It's like everything is suddenly in sharper focus."

I peered at Neil, trying not to look too incredulous. "Oh. Well, that sounds good..."

"Yeah, it is good. It feels really good." Neil grinned. He looked relaxed and happy.

"So, what do you want to do now?"

"See the vulture room, of course."

"Of course."

Neil pulled the folded map out of his pants pocket. "Let's get oriented to the topography first, though." I watched silently as Neil put his finger on the star denoting the courtyard. "Okay, we started here. And then we came down the hall..." He traced the line across the courtyard and part way down the back hall. "...to here." He pulled out the pen and carefully drew an arch on the map where the photos of the generals started. "Magic portal dully noted." Neil ran his finger through the lineup of generals and stopped at the corner of the hall. "And then instead of going right to see Grant, we cut diagonally across here and went into this room." He slid his finger to the side gallery. "This room where I'd drawn a whirlwind...a tornado...a dervish." Neil looked up at me.

"I guess we met your dervish," I said.

Neil looked back down at the map. He swirled his finger in the little square representing the George McClellan room and then flicked the map like he was flicking a bug. He looked up at me. "I just sent the dervish out to sea to cool off." I laughed. Neil jumped to his feet. "Let's go!"

Without pausing to realize I was still planted on the bench, Neil strode through the doorway in front of us with gusto and disappeared without looking back. I lingered on the bench, suddenly not sure if I wanted to revisit the vulture room. As I attempted to rationalize letting Neil explore that gallery on his own, his fingers appeared on the door jamb. He was gripping the molding for all he was worth. Horrified, I imagined his body stretched out horizontally, as an unseen force attempted to suck him into a vortex that had opened in the corner of the gallery. He clung on for life as the energy ripped off and swallowed his shoes and then his socks. I jumped to my feet. Neil's face popped into view around the door jamb.

"No birds in here. It's safe for you to enter." He laughed and disappeared again into the room.

"Asshole."

I walked in and found Neil with his back to the door, examining the portrait of William Tecumseh Sherman. I stood next to him as he read the information about Sherman posted next to the portrait.

"I'm mixed on this guy," Neil said. "I kind of like his style but did he swing too harsh? Was it really necessary to open Pandora's Box and allow "total war" to pop out? Maybe it was. Maybe it was necessary to dismantle the Confederates' support system if we weren't finishing it on the battlefield. But why didn't we just finish it on the battlefield?"

With a start, I recognized Neil's mantra — "Finish it on the battlefield and then go home and enjoy the rest of your life." How many times had I heard him use that phrase to implore his team and colleagues, including me, to focus and get a job done so we could leave the office at the office and enjoy our free time?

"Does he seem familiar to you, Neil?"

"No, not really. I'm curious about him but he doesn't trigger anything."

"How about this guy?" I pointed to the photo of A.P. Hill hanging to the left of Sherman's portrait. "Does he look familiar?"

Neil stepped over and leaned in to study the general's tired face. "No. Nothing there. Why?"

"He was a Confederate general — A.P. Hill. The vulture told me I needed to remember him, too."

Neil raised his left eyebrow at me and then turned back to the photo. "Nah, I'm not feeling anything."

"Okay. You want to meet Stonewall Jackson?"

"Sure!"

We moved to the right and stood before General Jackson in his glittering uniform.

"He didn't make it through the war, did he?" Neil asked.

"No, he didn't." I pointed to the placard next to the portrait. "It says here that he died in spring 1863 at Chancellorsville, Virginia. His own men accidentally shot him."

"Okay. I don't want to read that yet." Neil focused on Jackson's profile. His eyes went blank. After several minutes, he spoke again. "Foreboding. Seeing this portrait brings on a sense of foreboding. Makes me tense. I don't feel like I knew Jackson but I knew the force that was him. It was the height of stupidity to delay long enough to allow Jackson to show up. He brought it and didn't back down. Does that make sense?"

"Yes. Makes sense in terms of the dream in the field, too, doesn't it? You knew Jackson was coming but couldn't rally the troops to move fast enough?"

"I couldn't rally them faster because I didn't have the power to do that. I was powerless. I was responsible but had limited authority." Neil paused before continuing. "I think I was an officer, but wasn't calling the shots. I was implementing someone else's plan and had no control over the timing. I had very little control over anything beyond taking care of my men."

"So, do you think you were a line officer? Or maybe a field officer?"

"What are you asking me?"

"One of my ancestors on my mom's side, John Palmer, was an officer in the Civil War. I have pictures of him in his uniform. He was a lieutenant — a line officer. His brother was a major. He was a field officer. A line officer…"

"That's interesting. Oh, wow, look at this portrait of Grant! Look at the frame! Whoa." While Neil examined Grant's portrait, I pulled out my phone and typed myself a note — *Find out what unit Palmer brothers fought for.*

"Check this out," Neil called over to me. "Mississippi is spelled wrong!"

I walked over and saw that he was pointing at the map of Vicksburg painted in the corner of the portrait.

"See? There's an "s" missing."

I leaned in to see the label on the Mississippi River. The fourth "s" or the third, depending on how you wanted to call it, was missing. It was perfectly Neil that he'd immediately noticed and perfectly me that I'd been oblivious. "Oh, yeah, you're right. I hadn't noticed that. What do you think of Grant?"

"He's the guy on the fifty-dollar bill. That's about it. Why's he standing in a hole?"

"I think he's in a ditch. There must have been ditchworks at Vicksburg. You know, like in World War I?"

"Did you see ditches on the battlefield you flew over?"

"No. No ditches."

"Okay, let's go back to the courtyard and put all this together."

"Did you want to see *Grant and His Generals* first?"

"Oh, yeah, I forgot about that. I'd like to see that."

I led Neil from the room and down the main hall to the bottom of the stairwell. We gazed up at the painting of uniformed men on horseback that loomed half a story above us.

"Pretty cool, huh, Neil?"

"Yeah, it is. Look, there's Sherman next to Grant. Ambrose Burnside is there over Grant's shoulder. And there's George Custer along the left edge."

"Do you recognize anyone else?"

"Yeah, see that guy in the back? One, two, three, four, five, six, seven over from the left? In the back with the pointed goatee. Who's that? He looks familiar."

I looked at the key on the pedestal and found the name. "George Crook." Neil took out his notebook and wrote down the name. "See the clean-shaven guy behind Grant?," I said when he'd finished his note. "The one with the big hat? I picked him out of the lineup in the back hall."

"Who's that?" asked Neil.

"Joseph Hooker."

Neil wrote down that name, too, and then looked up from his book with a grin. "Ready to go put this together?"

"Yep."

Neil took off and headed back toward the courtyard. As we walked down the back hall past the café, he suddenly slammed on the brakes and pulled the café door open. "Let's grab some waters." I caught the door and followed Neil into the small rectangular café. There was a serving line in front of us that seemed to be closed down for the day. On the opposite wall was a well-lit open case of expensive sparkling waters, beer, wine, juices, and soda. Neil stepped over to the case and plucked two sparkling waters from a shelf. He held them up for me to inspect. "Will this work for you?"

"Sure."

A young man sat reading behind a cash register at the far end of the room. Neil stepped over, put the waters on the counter in front of the register, pulled out his wallet, and handed the guy a ten without waiting for him to ring up the sale. "Keep the change."

"Uh, okay. Thanks."

Instead of heading back out into the hall, we exited the café through a door at the end of the serving line and were instantly back in the surreal world of perpetual overcast and motionless trees. Neil walked over to a table near the water feature and set down the bottles. I pulled out a chair and sat down, reaching for one of the sparkling waters.

"Not so fast. Didn't you say you wanted to take off your shoes and walk around in this?" Neil pointed at the nearest wet rectangle.

I laughed. "No, that's alright."

Neil pulled a chair away from the table, sat down, and bent over to untie his shiny oxfords. He pulled them off and then peeled off his thin, black dress socks. "Are you coming?"

"Sweet." I pushed out my chair and pulled off my shoes and socks, too.

Neil and I waded in together. The water was cool and I could feel the current move over my feet. I imagined tiny fish and tadpoles wiggling up to check out my bare toes. A water strider skated by on the surface of the water. It was followed by another that stopped in front of me and allowed the current to carry it away. The dark granite became a sandy bottomed creek peppered with rounded stones and small boulders. A mud-colored crayfish shot backwards through the sand to hide behind an algae-covered rock about the size of my fist.

"It feels like a stream," I called out to Neil, who had waded away from me. He had his back partially to me and didn't answer. He appeared to be suddenly quite interested in one of the immobile trees. As he studied it, he lifted his hand, flicked his cheeks with an index finger, and wiped the finger on his shirt. I teared up, turned my back, and waded back to the table. I chose a chair facing away from the water feature, twisted open one of the bottles, and carefully sipped the bubbly water. A few minutes later, I heard gentle splashing behind me and the chair next to me being pulled out. Neil sat down and picked up the remaining bottle. He twisted it open, set the cap on the table, and swirled the bottle for a good minute until much of the carbonation had dissipated. He took a long swallow.

"Thank you for quitting over me," Neil said to his bottle.

"Thank you for being worth quitting over," I said to mine.

We drank in silence. My bottle was sweaty and cool in my hand. I ran my thumb up and down the wet green glass, closed my eyes, and let my mind go completely silent.

"He needs you right now, you know."

"I know, Mick. I'll stick with him."

"He'll stick with you, too. You two have a journey to complete together. A stitching of old wounds so that you might both move forward."

"I know. I've been waiting for him."

"Good. That's good. You're going on a quest, but you needn't direct the proceedings. Your guides are prepared for you and will meet you there. Allow things to unfold and permit your friend to lead the way. You'll see beyond the veil for him and he'll protect you. The door has been opened."

"Okay, Mick."

"Are you ready? Hey, wake up." I felt someone rhythmically poking my right biceps. *Poke...poke...poke...poke...poke.* "How'd you fall asleep that fast?"

"Neil, stop poking me." I opened my eyes. "I wasn't sleeping — I was meditating."

"Oh. I'm sorry. Were you done?" Neil looked at me like a puppy who had peed on the dining room rug even though he knew better.

I laughed. "Yes, are you ready to pull our notes together?"

Neil had his notebook out and pen poised, making the question irrelevant. "Yep. Let's start with our list of players. I'll leave room by the names so we can fill in relevant details later. So, we have you...me...your brother. What was that girl's name again? The one I saw in the dream?"

"Terri. Terri Martin."

Neil looked up from his list. "I hate to go off on a tangent, but did we ever talk about that date?"

"Uh, yessssss. You two did not hit it off, as I recall."

"No, we didn't. She seemed like a nice girl but was way too driven and insecure. I felt like we were in competition the entire evening. Why did you think we'd be a good match?"

"I was hoping she'd drop her guard with you and you'd have a good time together. You really do have a lot in common — high energy, athletic, both driven with a sense of urgency beyond the norm. I imagined you might go on adventure vacations, or something. Remember, it was right after your divorce was final, too, and I wanted to introduce you to someone who wouldn't remind you of Kelly."

"Oh." Neil let that sink in. "She seemed to think that life had shortchanged her — that she wasn't getting everything she deserved."

"I think you brought out the worst in Terri instead of the best for some reason. I doubt it was anything you did, though."

"Why do you say that?"

"What did you say she was doing in the dream?"

"She had a rope over her shoulder and was glaring at me. She wouldn't help me."

"So maybe you have some old history going on."

Neil rubbed his temples and squeezed his eyes shut in mock agony. "You're making my head hurt."

"Such a drama queen."

"Oh, shit!" Neil lifted his head and slid his fingertips down to his cheekbones. His eyes were wide and unfocused with both eyebrows lifted.

"What did you just remember? Did you miss an appointment?"

"Huh? No, I didn't miss anything. I just thought of something. What if Terri Martin has been having the same dream?"

"What?"

"What if she's having the dream, too? You should ask her. She might have additional information that could help us figure this out."

"Oh, wow, Neil. It was hard enough to even mention it to you. Terri's pretty grounded into what she can see and touch."

Neil flipped to a clean page in his notebook and wrote "ASSIGNMENTS" across the top. He made a vertical line to divide the page and put my name in the first column. "Interview Terri Martin and Andy concerning rope dream," he said aloud as he jotted in my first assignment.

"Andy, too?"

"Stop whining. Of course, Andy, too. He's never struck me as someone who would limit himself to the see and touch realm — he's going to be easy to approach. Let's try to get this knocked out by Friday evening, shall we?"

"Okay."

"Alrighty, then. Back to the players." Neil flipped back in his notebook and added Terri to his list. Next to her name, he added "ANTAGONIST" and underlined the word three times. I rolled my eyes but didn't comment. "Now, let's get all the generals accounted for. We had George McClellan...Stonewall Jackson...William Tecumseh Sherman...Ulysses Grant. Who else?" Neil kept his pen poised over the paper waiting for my additions.

I pulled out my phone and quickly flipped through my photos. "Uh, Ambrose Burnside...Joseph Hooker...George Crook...that seems to be it." I watched Neil carefully add the names to his list. "Oh, and add A.P. Hill. The vulture said he was important. Something about snatching victory something-something. I can't remember exactly, seeing as I was busy passing out at the time."

Neil peeked at me out of the corner of his eye. "This is all sounding crazy again, you know?"

"Yeah. You're right."

"My disbelief comes in waves and right now it's high tide."

"I understand. You want to stop and walk away?"

"Nope." Neil added A.P. Hill's name to the list and looked up. "Is that everyone?"

"I think so."

"Alright, let's run the list now and write down what we know. First, you and Andy were on the battlefield as Union soldiers. I'm pretty sure I was a Union officer and given the fact that you and Andy fell in behind me in the dream, I'd say it's likely you were both in my unit. Terri was there, too, and likely in the Union Army, as well, but very doubtful that she reported to me." Neil bent over his book and made quick notes by each name as I watched quietly. When he was finished, he looked up at me, looking slightly uncomfortable.

"Now, uh, how do we reconcile the fact that you and Terri are women?"

"You mean in this lifetime?"

"Uh, yeah. Are you okay with the idea of, you know, switching teams?"

"Um, well, I honestly don't have my head completely around the idea of living inside a guy's body, but I'm not going to fight it. I mean, I'm pretty sure we've all taken our turns as men and women and..."

The color came up in Neil's cheeks. "Okay, then, we'll just say you're fine with it and move on to the generals." Neil turned back to his list, making notations as he spoke. "I think we can say without a doubt that George McClellan was important. We'll keep our assumptions loose, but let's say that he led the Union Army at the time of the battle. And we know Stonewall Jackson is import- ant — his name just keeps on coming up. We were apparently locked in a race with him. Trying to beat him to the punch somehow. Could have involved battling through a mountain pass or that could have just been symbolic of the uphill battle to get where we were going before he did. Would you agree?"

"Yeah, that dream is highly symbolic. The orbs, the rope, the mountain, the storm, the fact that we turned into animals. I wouldn't take any of it too literally."

"Agreed. So, we know McClellan and Jackson were important players and you said A.P. Hill was, too." Neil carefully jotted "victory snatcher" next to Hill's name. "What about the rest of the generals? Any thoughts?"

"In terms of Grant, I was definitely more drawn to his picture frame than his portrait."

Neil nodded. "The names of the battles?"

"Well, that, but more the acorns than anything."

"The acorns." Instead of making a note next to Grant's name, Neil looked up at me with amusement dancing on his lips. "Do you thing that's important or just a symptom of your forest imp nature?"

I rolled my eyes and shook my head. "You're visualizing me with little wings and an outfit made of lettuce leaves right about now, aren't you?"

"And if I were?"

"Suit yourself. I'm confident I can rock that look."

Neil cackled deep in his throat and jotted "acorns" next to Grant's name. "Anything else?"

"Nothing. You?"

"Nope, not at this point. Let's move on to the battle. When did the Civil War start and end?"

"It started in 1861. There was a poster in the exhibit hall that said something about South Carolina and 1861."

"And A.P. Hill was killed in 1865, just a few weeks before Lee surrendered. So, we can probably safely say 1861 to 1865," Neil added.

"Damn, you read for comprehension back there. I'm impressed."

"I did, thank you very much, but I don't listen well. When did you say Stonewall Jackson died?"

"Spring of 1863."

"Excellent. That eliminates half the war and will probably make things easier." Neil turned to a clean page and pushed his book toward me as he handed me the pen. "Okay, now go ahead and sketch the battlefield you saw. Start with the big picture and then we can add the details."

I took the pen and carefully drew what I'd seen — the long, wide valley, the creek, the river, the town. At the north end, I drew the cornfield full of men, the woodlots, and the burning buildings. I drew the small white building and indicated where I'd seen Stonewall Jackson with the other men on horseback. Farther south, I sketched in the country lane where the Confederate soldiers lay in wait. Near the bottom of the map, I carefully drew the stone bridge over the creek with its three arches and interesting parapet of short, weathered boards. Then I sketched in a long ridge to the east of the creek and two small knolls near the bridge. "This is where Andy and I were lying on the ground," I said as I pointed to the southern end of the long ridge. "The ground was plowed and I could see corn stubble mixed in the soil. There were cannons here to our north along this ridge and they were firing across the creek at another line of cannons, which was firing back."

"How do you know which way was north?"

"It was dawn. The sun was coming up here — behind Andy and me." I sketched the sun rising behind the long ridge and added a hawk wheeling around in the sky.

"It was dawn and the battle had already started?"

"Yes, but only at the north end of the valley. There were soldiers everywhere but most were waiting."

Neil took the pen back from me and flipped back in his book to make some more notes. "Soldiers everywhere? How many total, do you think?"

"Thousands…tens of thousands. And more were arriving."

"So this was a big battle! This should be easy to pin down. Do you think it was Gettysburg?"

"I guess it could have been. What time of year was Gettysburg? I woke up cold and wet in the vision and the corn in the fields was tall. It seemed like late summer when the weather starts to turn."

Neil scribbled more notes in his book. "I don't know when the Battle of Gettysburg was, but it seems like a good place to start. There might be a lot to sort through. I know there were numerous big battles within just an hour or two of DC. Kelly and I did a lot of day trips with the kids. I don't really remember too much about the battlefields we visited, though. The kids got bored and started whining pretty early on those trips — we'd take a few photos and then leave for ice cream and shopping."

"Well, that's better than me. I remember going to Gettysburg as a kid and not understanding what I was seeing. I have no recollection of studying the

Civil War in school. I found out recently, though, about my ancestors who fought for the Union. I started doing genealogy research a few years ago when those 'find your roots' shows started running on cable and…"

"If you think there might be some sort of family connection, definitely dig around a bit, but don't get distracted from your assignment, soldier. You need to interview Andy and Terri Martin and see what they can add." Although tempted, I held back from giving Neil a flippant salute and let him finish what he was saying. "I'm going to spend the next few days and the weekend doing some research. Are you free to travel on Monday?"

"Monday? Uh, sure, yeah. Andy sold the landscaping business. Did I tell you that? So, I'm not working for him anymore. Actually, not since July. Did I tell you he went out West?"

"Yeah, I think you did."

"Yeah. So, my time is pretty much my own right now."

"Okay, be ready to travel on Monday, then. Might just be day trips next week or we might have to stay over someplace. Perfect time to check out some battlefields with the weather so nice. Anything we seem to have missed? Anything else we need to see here?"

"No, I think we're good."

"Excellent." Neil glanced down at his watch. "It's ten till seven. We'd better get out of here before we get thrown out." He pushed back his chair and pulled on his socks and shoes while I did the same. "I'm getting rid of these shoes on Saturday morning," Neil said as he tied his laces. "Have most of my dress clothes packed up already for Goodwill along with some other stuff that doesn't make sense in my life any longer."

I raised my head from my shoes to smile at him. "Cool."

"Did you get rid of your clothes?"

"Yeah, but it took me a little longer — they went on their way one bag at a time. I probably still have some more to give away."

"You should get back to that."

I laughed. "Okay, I'll finish that this week, too, and have my own Saturday morning purging ceremony."

Neil patted me on the shoulder. "That's what I like to hear. Ready?"

"Yep. Let's use the F Street exit. It's closer to the Metro."

I grabbed the empty bottles and found the recycling bin while Neil waited for me at the exit to the F Street lobby. He pulled open the door and held it for me. As I walked through, I noticed my security guard friend right ahead of me near the reception desk. He was locked in animated discussion with another guard. I led Neil to the right, hoping to slip behind the guard's back without him noticing us. *Don't look over here. Please, don't look over here…*

"Hey! Well, you're looking better. Glad to see you have a guardian to get you home in one piece. Have a good evening!"

"Have a good evening! I'll try the soup next time."

The guard laughed and went back to his conversation.

"I don't want to know, do I?" Neil whispered near my right ear.

"Naw, just keep walking."

I led Neil through the middle set of exit doors. We descended a short flight of interior steps and then popped out of the museum onto the wide marble staircase in front of the building. Magical evening light swept over us as we both paused at the top of the stairs. My eyes immediately shot to the sky where the sun was moving rapidly toward the horizon, casting an orangey-pink glow on the sides of the clouds. I continued standing at the top of the stairs studying the clouds while Neil ran ahead, taking the steps two at a time with his long legs. We'd stumbled upon an absolutely gorgeous sunset — the colors were changing by the second, becoming more and more saturated until the clouds appeared to be on fire. But only the sides of the clouds were burning. The orange, pink, and gold of the sunset was framed by unobtrusive gray shadow at top and bottom, which presented the masterpiece without vying for attention.

"It's the contrast that makes things beautiful," I whispered.

"Come down! Come down! You have to see this!" Neil called to me.

I descended the stairs to stand with Neil on the sidewalk. He was gazing west down F Street with a look of rapture on his face. "Just look at that." I followed Neil's gaze and saw that F Street jogged north at the end of the block, lining up the sidewalk where we stood with the middle of the street and giving us a clear view straight west all the way down to the colonnaded Treasury building on 15th. The sky immediately above the Treasury was glowing bright gold. A towering bank of pink and orange clouds hemmed in the golden light from above and extended over the low gray buildings lining both sides of the street. To complete the scene, the shiny glazed sidewalk on which Neil and I stood blazed with reflected sunlight.

"A tunnel. We're looking down a glorious tunnel. I'm going to skip the cliché about the light down there, though," Neil said.

"Wow. Yeah, skip the cliché — let's just enjoy it."

We stood silently on the sidewalk together and watched the colors brighten further before fading away to deep purple. As the evening dropped into darkness, we turned and headed toward the Metro station.

"Did you think to snap a picture?" asked Neil.

"No, did you?"

"No, but that's okay. I'm not going to forgot that."

"Me neither."

CHAPTER 18

KARMA REVEALED: GOING DEEP TO REMEMBER WHAT I LOVED

I was up early the next morning watching the sun rise from my back deck with my cellphone in my lap. As the sun lit up the sky in ravishing golds and pinks, the songs of the night chorus began to fade until only a few stubborn crickets remained to eke out a thin tune. Dawn was usually my favorite time of day, but I was impatient with the slow revolution of the Earth this morning and ready for the crickets to give it up and go to bed.

I tapped my phone and checked the time. *7:13 — it's only 7:13 a.m.* I worked the phone like a fidget stone, rubbing my thumb over the impossibly smooth glass of the screen. I needed time to move faster so I could call Andy. The two-hour time difference and the fact that he was often well beyond cell range made reaching him tricky. And I needed to reach him on the first try — the conversation we needed to have felt too important to leave a message. So, I sat waiting impatiently until ten in hopes of catching my brother awake enough not to cuss me, but not yet engrossed in something amazing. I slumped more deeply into my chair and watched the sky evolve from a smear of pastels to a crisp play of white clouds against an azure canvas. I really needed to get up and take a walk to burn off my anxious energy, but instead stayed where I was and played games on my phone, checking the time every few minutes as the morning slipped away.

At precisely 10 a.m., I picked Andy's name from my contacts list and tapped his number while my heart attempted to kick its way out of my chest. My call went immediately to voice mail. I resisted an impulse to immediately hang up and, instead, listened to Andy's instructions to call Carmichael's Landscaping Solutions for my landscaping needs, his assurances that he'd call me back as soon as possible if this were a personal matter, and finally the beep signalling that I was up. I stared at the phone, suddenly unsure of how to string together a message.

"Uh, Andy, hey, hope you're doing well. Uh, well, uh. Just wanted to catch up and, uh, I've been having this recurrent dream with you in it and wanted to talk to you. Could you, uh, give me a call back? It's kind of important. Thanks, talk to you later."

Damn! Maybe he's out shooting photos somewhere and will call me back later in the day when the light gets harsh. Maybe he won't call back for days. Oh, crap, I don't want to talk to Terri first. But I also don't want to let Neil down by missing my deadline. Should I wait for Andy or suck it up and call Terri? And what the hell happened in that gallery yesterday, anyway? Neil's acting like we're on an urgent mission. Maybe it's not so urgent. Maybe he's just latching onto the Civil War thing as something to keep himself occupied as the minutes tick down on his time with the company. Maybe we need to process for a while and see where things go. Maybe that's what the rope dream means — that sense of urgency doesn't mean squat. But then there's everything that vulture spirit guy showed me. If it wasn't urgent, why would he waste time with me? Or was that just a random dream provoked by low blood sugar and a crack to the forehead? I wish Andy would call me back. Maybe I should text him...

"JAY! JAY-JAY-JAY!"

...or maybe I should just suck it up and call Terri. I wonder if she'd answer. I wonder what time she teaches on Thursdays...

"JAY! JAY! JAY!"

I looked up. A bright-eyed blue jay was jumping from branch to branch above me through the big ash tree that shaded the deck.

"JAY!"

That's weird. The bird feeder is full. The birdbath's not empty. What the hell does it want? I set my phone on the table next to my chair and gave the bird my full attention.

"JAY! JAY!"

It came closer...

"JAY!"

...and closer...

"JAY! JAY! JAY!"

…and stopped not two feet away from me on a low-hanging branch. I could have reached out and touched the bird, but kept perfectly still as it cocked its head to the side and regarded me out of one eye. I followed suit, closing my right eye and cocking my own head to regard the jay.

"JAY!"

The blue jay jumped from the tree to the table, knocking my phone to the deck boards. I was too mesmerized to protest. The bird, which was now inches from me, was gorgeous. The indigo blue of its feathers was amazingly rich and deep this close up. Its eye was bright and direct. The bird spread its wings…

"JAY! JAY!!"

…and was gone around the corner of the house.

I retrieved my phone and turned it over in my hands. The glass was intact. I checked the time and fidgeted with the phone again, running my fingers over the case. *What was the jay trying to tell me? Well, cocking his head helps him see more clearly — lets him look directly at what he wants to see. Helps him eliminate distractions and gain clarity. Eliminate distractions!* I put the phone back on the table and pushed it away from me. *Where did I want my focus? Or, more simply, what did I really want this morning? Well, clearly I wanted Andy to call me back. But not really.* I suddenly understood my problem — I didn't know what I wanted and was fighting the flow that might take me to what I needed.

I picked up the phone, pushed myself up out of my chair and went back into the house through the French doors to the office. I stopped first at my desk to plug the phone in to charge. *No distractions.* I put the phone on vibrate and left it behind as I walked down the short hall to the kitchen. *Now what?* I pulled open the refrigerator and looked inside. *Yes, there's still food in here. Why am I staring at it?* I closed the refrigerator and went into the dining room. *I need to vacuum in here. Should I vacuum? Sure, might as well.*

Back in the office I pulled the vacuum out of the closet, but paused before closing the closet door. The closet was packed full, but with the exception of the vacuum and a cardboard box of spare lightbulbs, I never accessed anything stored here. I pulled a small box from the shelf in front of me and lifted off the lid. Inside were hundreds of slides packed in neat rows separated into groups by small tabbed dividers. I selected a slide at random and held it up to catch the sunlight streaming through the office window. Squinting into the bright light, I could make out the title of a research presentation I'd given before the birth of PowerPoint. I did some math in my head — *was that two careers ago or three? Maybe four.* I carefully replaced the slide in the box and plucked out another and another and another, offering them up one by one to the illuminating sunlight. I could make out tiny color-coded maps, tables of statistics, and bullet lists of conclusions. At one time in my life, these little pieces of film mounted in white plastic frames defined me as a professional. Now they just held an old parade of emotions — excitement, pride, confusion, disappointment, frustration, boredom — that I no longer wanted marching endlessly through my life. I plopped down in my office chair with the box on my lap, swiveled around to face the shredder, and began to feed slides through the little slot usually reserved for expired credit cards. When the box was completely empty, I tossed it toward the wastebasket. I immediately felt lighter.

I returned to the closet and scanned the rest of the contents. On a low shelf I noticed a pile of nylon duffel bags. I pulled the pile out and dumped the bags on the floor. A heavy black duffel that looked brand new caught my attention. Turning it over I noticed the name of a regional consulting company embroidered in gold thread across the zippered front pocket. I remembered the name and the fact that my old department hadn't partaken of that particular company's services. I felt a pang of guilt. I dropped the duffel and picked up a small blue tote bag screen-printed with the logo of another consulting firm. Hadn't used them either. My guilt rose up another notch. I stirred the pile of bags around with my toe. Other brands and logos peeked out at me. Insidious damn logo gifts always made me feel horrible — I'd never been able to use, toss, or give away these offerings drenched in hope and anticipation.

I strode back to the kitchen, grabbed a big black trash bag from the cabinet under the sink and brought it to the office. I snapped the bag open, stuffed in the entire collection of synthetic guilt trips, and plopped the bag on the floor. *What else needs to join the going-away party?* My eye fell on a briefcase hanging from a hook on the back wall of the closet. It was empty when I left the office with it for the last time in early January. I lifted the strap off the hook. There was a swipe of mildew across the front flap. I wondered for an instant if it could be cleaned and then wondered why I'd bother — this bag would always remind me of that long, solitary last walk to the Metro through the twilight of a cold, wet winter evening. I opened the pockets to make sure I hadn't left anything behind and then unzipped the main compartment. I flipped the case over and gave it a good shake. A handful of small white business cards fluttered out and settled on the floor. I picked one up. Printed neatly in conservative font below the company logo was my name and former title. A wave of disappointment crashed over me and pushed me down into my chair. I suddenly felt short of breath. My vision blurred. I rubbed my eyes and blinked as the room filled with shimmering blue-green light. The light sparkled and danced as if sunlight were playing upon it. *Water. Water!* I imagined myself reaching up and simultaneously kicking with my legs. *Need to gain control. Need to find the surface.* I swept my arms and kicked, swept my arms and kicked, attempting to propel myself upward. I wasn't moving.

Don't panic, just keep swimming, things are okay, just keep pushing toward the surface, everything is fine as long as you're still moving your arms and legs.

A face appeared from my right and swam across my field of view. *Who was that?* The face came around again as if it were circling my head. Jeff from Finance. *How many mornings had I spent facing Jeff across a conference room table?* He came back around again, joined this time by Kristi from Marketing. Jeff and Kristi shared a knowing glance before disappearing behind me. On the next circuit, Rich from IT, his ubiquitous stained coffee mug still clenched in his hand, had been added. Nico from Ops and Rita from HR joined next. One by one all my old colleagues entered the spinning cavalcade, their faces slipping past through the shimmering light like a school of fish doing laps around me. This felt so familiar — so safe and easy. *Why was it that I'd left them?* With a start, I realized that although I was still moving my arms and legs, I'd lost any desire to find the surface of this ocean. I was placidly treading water — not allowing myself to fall into the depths, which scared me, but no longer concerned about feeling sunlight on my face. *Had we all just been treading water?* An invisible hand grabbed my ankle and jerked me a few feet farther down into the depths. I writhed against the manacle, attempting to twist my foot free so I could rejoin the group. *No! No! They need me! They need me.* I looked up toward my colleagues for help, but the faces continued on their circuit above my head, oblivious to the fact that I was no longer with them. They hadn't even noticed I was missing. I stopped struggling and watched as bodies appeared below the faces. Arms and legs moved in harmony, keeping everyone perfectly suspended like a troupe of synchronized swimmers. I cringed, realizing that I'd never gotten the dance moves down. There was a sharp tug at my ankle. *Okay, sure, I surrender, let's go.*

Relaxing completely, I crossed my arms over my chest and allowed myself to be pulled downward. The shimmery quality of the water dissipated as I moved farther away from the sunlight and the ring of dancers, who had now taken on the jerky movements of crude marionettes. I opened my eyes wide to gather as much light as possible and turned away from the group, peering down my body and into the dim ocean below to see who was dragging me. A shock ripped through my body and settled into the nape of my neck. Where I'd expected to find a swimmer in human form was a massive tail, undulating slowly through the dusky purple water. I wasn't held by an invisible hand — I was tethered to the fluke of an enormous whale that was pulling me down into the dark depths of the ocean. As I struggled to make sense of what was happening, my ears filled with melancholy whale song. The sound came from everywhere at once as haunting pulsed tones that seemed to vibrate every cell of my body. *Coming back. I'm coming back home.*

An object swam into view through the murky still water — a small object that floated tantalizingly close to my right hand. I saw my hand reach out in slow motion and catch the object. Gently pulling it close to my face, I could see it was a small bronze-colored medal strung on a blue and orange ribbon. Embossed on the medal was what looked like a genie's lamp perched on a stack of books — the lamp of knowledge with flames leaping from the spout. It was an academic award. I didn't need to read the word printed below the lamp, but I brought the medal close to my right eye and squinted through the darkness anyway. "English". *There should be two of these. The second one*

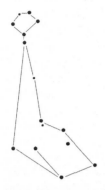

was gold. And there it was, swimming toward me, glinting in the half-light. I turned my left palm upward and the second medal dropped into my hand. Bittersweet emotions flooded through me, carried by the whale's song. I'd won the school-wide junior high writing contest two years in a row, but my father had extinguished my happiness.

"You know that award you got last night? Well, the teachers got it wrong. They don't really know you. They don't really know what an ass you are. You're not smart. You can't write worth a shit. You're just an ass." I opened my hands to let the medals float away, but they stayed, resting gently on my palms. I spread my fingers wide and pushed my palms flat, giving the currents permission to sweep the tainted medals away.

CETUS (THE WHALE)

The plaintive moan of the whale broke into sounds that I could understand. "No…no…no. You keep…keep…keep them. Keep…keep…keep the happy… happy…happiness. Let the pain…pain…pain wash away."

The happiness. Sure. Where had I left the happiness? I reached back through time and found the memory of sitting in a crowded auditorium with my friends. We were packed shoulder to shoulder on metal folding chairs at the front of the darkened room with parents and siblings packed behind us. My seventh-grade English teacher, Mr. Duffy, was at the podium speaking. People began to applaud. I was applauding. A girl from my class was working her way out of the crowd to claim the grammar award. I wondered how I did on the grammar test as I applauded for the girl with curly black hair who was on the stage now collecting a small box and a handshake from Mr. Duffy. The girl melted back into the crowd and there was a pause as Mr. Duffy waited for all of us to settle back down. Then he was speaking again — talking about the essay contest. The winning essay was so well-written and so funny. Mr. Duffy looked down and began to read. I blushed red and a tingle ran up my spine and over my scalp. *My words — he was reading my words!* The crowd erupted in laughter. I smiled. The crowd laughed again. My friend, Max, turned around in his seat to find me.

"That's yours, isn't it?"

I smiled and nodded yes.

"It's really good."

"Thank you."

And then I heard my name and I was working my way through the crowd to the podium, both mortified and ecstatic that all eyes were on me.

"Congratulations. Very well-deserved."

"Thank you."

I carried the small white box back to my seat and sat down. I lifted the lid. The bronze medal was inside, pinned to a piece of black velvet. Max turned around again and put his hand out for the box. "Let me see! Let me see it!" I beamed as I handed the box over. "Nice! Nice! Congratulations!"

"Thank you."

The whale song pulsed again through my body. "Stop there…there…there. Stop there…there…there." I closed my hands over the medals and felt joy course through my palms and up my arms. It spread across my shoulders and down my spine, then down my legs to the tips of my toes. A heaviness that I hadn't even realized was there unraveled from my heart, releasing joy to spread up my neck and into my face. I tipped my head back and laughed, unable to contain my happiness. I opened my hands. The medals were gone but the happiness remained.

I smiled and looked down to find the whale, and noticed out of the corner of my right eye another object swimming toward me. I turned to look at it. This item was larger than the medals. As it came out of the gloom, I could see that it was spinning on a small waterspout that was moving rapidly toward me. The waterspout stopped a few feet away and supported the object at eye level. I reached out. A tan ceramic urn with a footed base was deposited in my outstretched hands. I felt the weight and the rough texture of the glaze. It felt familiar. I turned the urn over and cringed when I saw the Grecian figure playing a lyre painted on the other side. Another writing prize, but this one was from Mr. Manzanelli's high school humanities class. I'd won this urn — thrown and decorated by the ceramics teacher — for my essay on the influence of classical Greek art on contemporary design. I turned the pot and looked inside, expecting it to be full of sea slugs and apocalyptic flesh-eating zombie eels. It was empty. *What am I supposed to do with this?*

A male voice boomed from the depths of the ocean, causing me to cringe again. "Well, I have good news and bad news about the essay contest. First the good news — I've decided to award two prizes, so Miss Snyder has provided not one, but two, Grecian urns for us. These really are lovely and I can't thank her enough for her generosity in providing them. Now, drumroll, please!" The sound of twenty sets of hands thrumming on desks filled my head. "The first winner wrote an outstanding essay! I'm sure you'll be happy to learn that Max has won the first urn! Max, come collect your prize!" Pairs of clapping disembodied hands zipped through the gloom at me. I ducked and danced to avoid them as Max collected his applause. "And the second winner? Well, that's the bad news. I didn't want this to happen and I'm sure you'll be as disappointed as I was, but it was unfortunately a very well-written essay. The second urn regrettably must be given to…"

The second urn. I turned it upside-down and found the crack in the base that I knew would be there. I'd always wondered if Max's urn had been cracked, too. I guessed it had not been. I turned the pot back over and stared at the figure playing the lyre. *If Mr. Manzanelli hadn't wanted to give me this, why hadn't he just given the prize to Max? Why the second urn and the scene in the classroom that had left me humiliated and my classmates confused?*

The little Grecian man turned from his lyre and looked at me. "Mr. Manzanelli was loved by all, yet you were unresponsive," my little Greek friend reminded me.

"He was so much like my father. I wanted so badly for him to like me but whatever I said or did in that class was wrong, so I pulled away."

"Yes, Mr. Manzanelli chose to interpret your aloofness as arrogance and your nervous jokes as disrespect. He felt you needed to come down a few notches. He didn't realize that you needed, instead, a hand up. The only thing you need to remember from that experience is that Mr. Manzanelli's behavior is his burden, not yours. Oh, and the Golden Rule of Thirds — you should remember that, too. It really was a good essay, you know." The little man winked at me and went back to his lyre.

"Um, excuse me," I said.

"Yes?"

"Uh, would you mind terribly much if I smashed this pot?"

"Well, no. Go right ahead." The figure pulled his right arm free from the pot's glaze, grabbed his shaggy mane of hair in a tight fist and peeled himself from the urn. Leaving his lyre behind, he frog-kicked a few times and disappeared into the dark ocean.

I felt a tug at my ankle and realized the whale was diving again. I tucked the urn into the crook of my left arm and relaxed into the ride. We went farther down, down, down until the ocean was devoid of all light. It was so quiet and so dark. So still. I waited. I strained my ears to hear, but there was no sound to vibrate my eardrums. I strained my eyes to see but was met with only inky darkness. There was no movement below me — no current, no twitch of the whale's tail. My frustration welled up.

"Why did you bring me here?"

There was no response.

"Why am I here?"

Silence.

Why am I here? That's it, isn't it? Why am I here? I know what I don't want. I know what I tried that didn't work out. What is it that I want? Why can't I wrap my arms around that? Relax my mind. Don't reach out for understanding. Relax and let the answers flow toward me. My awareness sank to the middle of my chest. I imagined double doors swinging open to reveal my beating heart. Golden light beamed out through the doorway to illuminate the darkness. Figures were moving in and out of the light. Children. Heavy drapes appeared to frame the light on either side. The children were moving around on a stage. Some were dressed as animals. Little leather shoes peeked out from beneath bedsheets painted to look like shaggy creatures. Pairs of children gave life to each creature — one child in the front and one in the back. Little hands held up enormous paper-mache masks that were childishly painted to represent the creatures' shaggy, horned heads. A bridge built of cardboard appeared in the center of the stage. *I knew this place. I was one of these children.* Mrs. Alexander's first grade production of *The Three Billy Goats Gruff* flickered to life in the shimmering, golden light.

The stage melted away and I realized I was peering through the oval eyeholes of a mask. I saw people in rows through the holes. People in a darkened room were watching me. Rows of women with smooth bouffant hairstyles wearing simple flowered dresses and cardigans were looking up at me as they clapped and laughed. *They're clapping for me! But, how will they know it's me behind this mask?* I dropped the mask and beamed out at the audience of mothers. The women laughed louder and clapped again. *They know it's me now. They're clapping for me!* Pure joy filled me up. Mrs. Alexander whispered from the wing for me to put my mask back on and go over the bridge. Grudgingly, I lifted my disguise and became invisible again, but I was still smiling.

I opened my eyes and was back in my office chair, blinking against the bright sunlight that was still streaming through the window. The light danced across my desk and rested upon two academic medals — one bronze and one gold — strung on blue and orange ribbons. I picked up the bronze-colored medal and rubbed a thumb over the embossed lamp. I laughed. "I wonder if a genie will pop out and grant me my three wishes," I said aloud. "Genie, oh, Genie! Come on out and play!"

No genie appeared, of course, but I noticed again the flames spewing from the spout of the lamp. I rubbed them gently with my thumb. *Flames. Action. Passion. Screw the genie — let's get this fire started.* I allowed my eyes to close again as I tossed my golden coins into the cosmic wishing well, visualizing not only the words of my wishes but me acting them out.

I wish to explore.
I wish to go on adventures.

And when I come back from my adventures, I wish to write about them
So that I might fill up the dark Universe
With the light that shines through my words.

And I wish to publish and present my words.
Because I wish to be visible.
I wish to be seen.

Yeah. That.

I opened my eyes again, stood up, and realized I was clutching the Grecian urn to my chest. Without a second thought, I dropped it into my trash bag and went to the kitchen in search of a suitable weapon of mass destruction. I grabbed the big cast iron skillet off the back of the stove and marched back to the office with it.

"Good-bye, Mr. Manzanelli!" I swung the skillet over my head with both hands and brought it down on the trash bag like I was chopping wood. The skillet made solid contact with the urn, which collapsed with a bang. I put down the skillet and opened the bag to find pot shards mixed in with my mildewed briefcase and the nylon duffel bags. *Sweetness.*

My phone suddenly danced to life — vibrating so aggressively that it slid off the corner of the desk. I reached out, caught it in my left hand and looked at the screen. *Andy!* I tapped the screen to accept the call.

"Andy! Hi!"

"Hell, yes! Hell, yes, I'm having a weird dream! We're all pulling on a damn rope. You, me, that guy from your office that I met at the picnic last summer, and freaking Carla! The last person I want to be dreaming about and here she comes popping in every other night. Is that the dream you're talking about? We're all pulling a rope through a freaking war zone?"

"Uh, yeah. Uh…Carla's there?"

"Hell, yes, she's there. Right behind me in some sort of cosmic tug-o-war."

Chapter 19

Karma Revealed: Andy Dreams a Dream and There's Whiskey

"Oh, shit, I have to talk to Carla, too?"

"No, why would you have to talk to Carla again? You performed your final duty admirably. Who else would have covered me while I cleared my stuff out of her place? I still owe you some hazard pay."

"Except that she was at work and there really was no danger involved. You just wanted company."

"Oh, yeah, that's right."

"So, describe the dream. From start to finish, what happens?"

"Well, it always starts out the same. It's night and I'm sitting around a campfire under some trees with maybe a half dozen guys. Nobody I recognize and I always think it's fascinating when I dream about people I don't know. But, anyway, we're sitting on logs and wooden crates around this campfire, passing a jar of whiskey."

"This doesn't sound like the same dream. You didn't walk through a field of floating orbs of light?"

"Oh, yes, I did! Settle down and let me tell my story."

"Okay, I'll settle down."

"I would appreciate that. So, we're sitting around the campfire passing a jar of whiskey and shooting the shit when I notice someone lurking around in the shadows. The fire flares up, illuminating the face, and I realize it's Carla. But the weird thing is I can't tell if Carla's a chick or a guy."

"Seriously? That's really interesting."

"Yeah, I know, right? Carla, the epitome of femininity and I can't tell if she's a chick. But I know it's her! So I make room next to me and call Carla over to the fire. She sits down next to me and I'm just about to hand her the jar of whiskey when I hear you yelling, 'Help! We need help!' Well, I drop the jar, shout to the other guys to come on, and start running toward your voice. I come out of the woods and step into a field that's lit with these beautiful floating orbs — although you've ruined the surprise by jumping forward and I'm not so sure I care to continue."

"Andy! Stop screwing around and keep going — you're killing me here."

"If you insist, I will continue. Where was I?"

"Andy!"

"Walking through the orbs, yes. I slow down when I get to the field and I'm walking through the glowing orbs almost in a trance. And it's beautiful and peaceful but then I see the faces. Thousands of faces are glowing like ghosts in the eerie light. My eyes begin to adjust to the light and I realize it's not disembodied faces but thousands of men standing like statues in the field and blocking my way. I push past them trying to get to you, but they seem to be multiplying. It's one of those dreams where you're in a hurry, you know, to get somewhere but it feels like things are taking forevvvvvver." Andy paused.

"Yeah, I experience that sometimes," I said.

"So you know what I'm talking about. All these guys are in my way and I'm shoving them aside right and left, with Carla right on my heels, but it's taking forever to get to you. And then all of a sudden the crowd parts. Everyone just steps aside and we find you in the middle of the field pulling this massive rope. Your friend...you know the one I mean? The tall guy that we stood around the keg and cracked jokes with at that picnic? What was his name?"

"Jeff?"

"Jeff? No, not Jeff. Stop playing, you know who I mean."

"Neil?"

"Yes, Neil! Neil is totally distraught trying to pull this massive rope and you're right behind him yelling for help. I jump in and help."

"When you jump in, do you say anything to me?"

"Yeah, I do. I tell you that I'm there. And I grab the rope behind you and start pulling. Carla jumps in behind me and then other people get on the rope and we start to move forward. Neil gets excited and starts encouraging all of us. And, I've got to tell you, at that moment I loved that guy and would have followed him anywhere. Anywhere. And we start going uphill. We're moving up a hillside and I can see a pass ahead between low mountains. Rounded eastern mountains — not craggy at all. And I see a huge storm forming over the pass. Thunder starts to boom in the distance. We drop the rope and charge into the storm screaming. Lightning is hitting the ground and throwing up dirt. You're running to my left and Carla's to my right. The air is full of dirt and smoke. I lose sight of you and look to my right to see if Carla is okay. And this is where things get really weird."

"Like they're not already weird?"

"Uh, yeah, that's true, but Carla's not next to me anymore. I look to my right and there's a swan...a freaking big trumpeter swan...flying at my side through the smoke and debris. It was completely surreal. The mountain is being torn to pieces, but here's this beautiful white swan flying calmly through the chaos."

"Oh, wow."

"Yeah. And the really weird thing is I know that swan is Carla — not the squirrelly, nervous new Carla who believes she doesn't deserve happiness, but the beautiful, graceful woman that I loved."

"Wow."

"Yeah. And that's about it. We battle though the storm and the whole time I'm totally getting the metaphor. It was a physical battle, but there was also an emotional or mental battle going on, especially as far as your friend, Neil, was concerned. And this might seem strange, but it really felt to me like it was Neil's dream. It was his nightmare and we were all welcome to it."

"Yes! I thought it was his dream, too! Did you see me or Neil again after you saw Carla as the swan?"

"No, I'm watching the swan and I wake up just as it turns to look at me."

"That's really cool, Andy. That's the same dream. Except I don't start in the woods — I'm walking through a field of Queen Anne's lace. The flowers float up and turn into the orbs."

"Cool! I could totally see that happening."

"And, as we race through the storm, Neil turns into a wolf."

"Ohhhh. Wolf Medicine. Yessss. The Instinctual Guardian. I can feel that on him. That makes sense."

"And you didn't see any other animals?" I asked.

"No, why?"

"Neil's having the same dream, but he sees me turn into a hawk. I see him as a wolf and he sees me as a hawk."

"Really? Did you see me as an animal? Did you see my Animal Guide?"

"Your Animal Guide? Oh. No, but maybe Carla did."

"Oh, wow."

Andy paused. I stayed silent while he collected his thoughts.

"I can't talk to Carla about this," Andy finally said. "That wouldn't be fair to her. She's needs to be able to move on."

"Would you mind if I talked to her? I think this is part of something bigger. It's not just the one dream."

I spent the next several hours telling Andy about my recurrent valley dream, my vision of the battlefield, and Neil's experience in the gallery. He asked a few questions but mostly just listened and soaked it all in.

"So, you think we all fought in the Civil War together. Wow," Andy finally said.

"Yes, and you remember Terri Martin?"

"Hell, yes, I remember Terri. That girl from your class. The shortstop on the boys' baseball team. Is she still around? I haven't seen her in years."

"She's still around — she's a biology professor at George Mason now. I set Terri and Neil up on a date a few years ago. They didn't hit it off but he remembered her. Neil saw Terri in the rope dream but she wasn't helping him. She had her own rope over her shoulder and glared at him when he asked her for help."

Andy laughed. "Well, that sounds like Terri. She always did like to compete with the guys, didn't she?"

"You didn't see her in the dream?"

"No."

"I didn't either. But Neil saw her and he wants me to talk with her and find out if she's also having the dream."

"You're going to have to," Andy said. "And you're going to have to talk to Carla, too. What if this is exactly what Carla needs? What if it helps her dump whatever she's dragging around so she can be happy. You have to figure out how to tell her about the swan, too. I think she'd really like that. Did you know she used to dance?"

"Oh, yeah, I do sort of remember that."

"Yeah, Carla was a beautiful dancer. She belonged to a local troupe when I met her. Carla was good — so good that she was invited to audition for a big regional company. She drove all the way out to a yard I was sodding in Alexandria to tell me. I'd never seen her so excited or happy. I picked her up and spun her around while she laughed into the sunlight. But Carla didn't get to go. She didn't get to audition. She only needed two weeks off from work to do it and she had the vacation time, but her boss wouldn't let her go. He just wouldn't let her go. He told her she needed to think about her career and either make a commitment or move aside for the next person. I told her to quit and move in with me, but she was already two rungs up the corporate ladder. She was afraid to let go and make the leap, so she stopped dancing entirely. Turned out her light like she was hitting a switch." Andy paused. When he continued, his voice was small and tight. "You have to figure out how to tell Carla about the swan. Okay?"

"Sure, okay. Uh, what energy does Swan bring? What should I tell her?"

"Just tell her she was a swan. She'll know what it means. You judge whether or not you want to tell her it was me who saw her."

"Okay."

"And I hate to end this conversation but the light is coming down and I have a twilight shoot planned with a couple other guys — we need to get on the road. Where are you going from here with this?"

"I need to talk with Terri and Carla. I need to find out if they can add anything. Neil has the sketch I made of the battlefield and notes about my vision and he's trying to figure out which battlefield I saw. Neil wants me ready to travel on Monday. He wants to visit battlefields."

"Oh, wow, that's heavy. You be careful with that. Does Neil understand how powerful that might be? What it might bring up?"

"I think in a way, yes. His experience in the gallery was intense, but it didn't rattle him. He knows something is holding him back and he wants the release. He wants to flip the rock and he's not afraid to see the horrors that are crawling around underneath in the darkness."

"Okay, as long as you both realize you can stir up quite a bit of horrific, negative energy kicking over stones on a Civil War battleground. Get thee to the metaphysical shop and grab a handful of hematite before you go."

"What's hematite?"

"It's a crystal that provides protection against negative energy. It'll ground you and make you feel safe."

"I didn't know you were into crystals!"

"I wasn't until I got out here. You really should fly out and visit — you'd fit right in. Are you still thinking about what you want to do next?"

"Uh, yeah. Sort of. Not really chasing it this time but letting it chase me, I guess. I knew I needed to wait for Neil — that we had to do something together. I didn't expect it to be this, but I am kind of excited to see where it leads."

"Even though you're a little scared?"

"Yeah."

"Don't be afraid to leap. It's only a cliff. What's the worst that can happen when you have wings?"

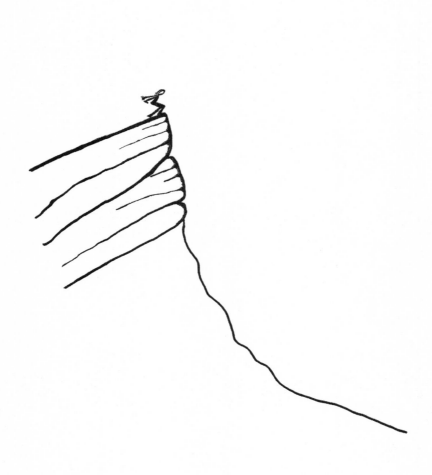

CHAPTER 20

KARMA REVEALED: TERRI DREAMS A DREAM OF ALL WORK AND NO PLAY

By the time I was done talking with Andy, the sun was dropping rapidly. I glanced at the time — 7:30…7:30 on a Thursday night. *If I really want to catch Terri, this might be my opportunity.* I found her name on my contacts list and tapped her mobile number. She answered immediately.

"Hi! Hi! I'm so glad you called! Let me put you on hold for just a minute while I finish up another conversation. I'll be right back." Terri put me on hold without waiting for a response.

I wandered out to the deck while I waited and plopped down in the chaise. I put the phone on speaker and let it fall into my lap. As the sun dropped, the breeze picked up and rustled the leaves of the ash tree. I heard crows cawing somewhere nearby and a cardinal calling for "cheer…cheer…cheer" from the yard below me. The blue of the sky deepened and a few wispy clouds to the west began to glow soft orange.

Terri came back on the line sounding tired and flat. "Sorry about that. It was one of my colleagues. We're publishing together and he needed my thoughts on a peer review of our manuscript that we just received. Let's just say that it wasn't glowing. I never thought I'd say this, but I'm tired of the competition. And, I'm no good at the politics. The school year started a month ago, too, and I'm still not finding my groove. A new batch of seniors always used to energize me, but this year they're just so draining. But, anyway, I've, uh, been thinking about you lately and I'm really glad you called. Something's been happening and I wanted to get your take on it. I haven't really been sure, though, how to broach the subject. It's a little bit uncomfortable."

Oh, shit, Terri had a faculty mentor to guide her and I certainly wasn't qualified to give anyone career advice. Maybe I could lead her around the block to look at her frustrations from a different vantage point. "Not to change the subject completely on you," I started, "but are you doing anything for fun? Anything to just relax and unwind?" I visualized an old-fashioned wooden teeter-totter roughly hewn from a single plank. One end sat firmly in the dirt. It was weighed down by a pile of academic books, an open laptop, and a stack of PowerPoint presentations, all neatly printed and spiral bound. I threw on a rack of test tubes and a centrifuge in deference to Terri's time spent in the lab. The wood creaked and cracked. A few large splinters sprang up from the surface of the board. The other end of the plank was high in the sky. A single wilted daisy had been left behind there. "It feels like you're a little out of balance," I added.

"That's completely fair — I am out of balance. The last thing I did for fun was that hike we took at Rock Creek Park and, if I remember correctly, I bitched the entire time and didn't even bother to ask how you were doing. I'm really sorry about that."

"Not a problem — don't even worry about it. You were there many times to listen when I needed an ear — I can be there for you once in a while. It's okay. I just hate that you're so unhappy."

"I am unhappy and it's affecting my sleep, too. I'm having the strangest dream. I'm hoping you can help me figure it out."

"A dream? Really?" *Ding! Pay dirt!*

"Yes, but I'm so sorry — you called me and I've taken over the conversation."

"No, no, it's okay. We can talk about your dream. How can I help you with it?"

"Well, first, and this is the slightly uncomfortable part — do you remember several years ago setting me up with one of your friends from work? Just a few months before I met Tony. Nice guy, kind of tall and athletic. We met for drinks. Do you know remember who that was?"

"Uh, yeah, that would be Neil."

"Neil! Yes! That was his name. Do you still, uh, keep in touch with him?"

"I do, actually. I just saw him yesterday."

"You did? Oh. Well, he's in this dream I keep having."

"Realllllly? Does Tony know you're having sex dreams about other men?"

"Oh, my god, did you seriously just say that? That is not the least bit funny. It's not a sex dream. It's just a weird dream and your friend, Neil, is in it. He's trying to get me to help him with something and I won't do it. I won't help him."

"Oh. Well, that's not like you."

"Ha! I call bullshit! It's exactly like me!"

I laughed. "I'm so sorry," I said. "I'm not laughing at you. Well, maybe I am. Okay, I'm laughing at you! I admit it!"

Terri started laughing but continued trying to get her story out. "It's...it's...it's why...," she started before giving up to compose herself. "Okay!" she said and blew out a big breath. "The dream's why I'm co-writing this damn paper with Fred Jenkins. He asked me to help him with it and I said yes."

"Oh. How's that going for you?"

"I hate it."

"Of course, you do. Group projects were never your thing."

"I've always hated them."

"I know and it's because you, Terri, are a person who presses the envelope. You naturally set the bar to exceed expectations. Most people don't do that — they're fine with meeting expectations, or even less. As a result, you often end up trying to tackle group projects with people who aren't as willing to bring all their energy to the table. You're not able to lower your bar, so you try to push your teammates to greater heights. Unfortunately, they usually dig in and refuse to follow your lead and you wind up frustrated with your name on a mediocre result. When your teammates do bend to your will, they often don't or can't step up to the challenge. You refuse to fail so end up carrying most of the load, produce something stellar, and then resent the fact that anyone else's name is on it. And, I'll tell you a secret—you're not wrong in keeping your standards high." I sucked in a breath to replace the air I'd just expended getting my thoughts out with no interruption.

"Oh, wow. That's completely…wow. You just nailed it."

"Yeah, I get lucky once in a while. So, why did your dream push you to try a partnership with this Fred Jenkins guy?"

"I…well…okay, first, this dream is making me feel really bad about how I treated your friend. I was really rude to him and I'm not even sure why. I definitely didn't let him be the man that night. I insisted on being in charge the entire evening."

"How so?"

"Well…I picked the restaurant so I could make sure we were on my turf. I insisted we split a bottle of wine when I knew he wanted something else. I ordered the appetizers for both of us and didn't bother to ask what looked good to him…"

"Whoa, whoa, whoa…you made Neil drink wine? Neil doesn't drink wine. It gives him migraines. Please tell me you didn't order crunchy granola-girl food."

"Uh, we had a bottle of Chardonnay and I probably ordered something light."

"No doubt on a bed of arugula. Did Neil go along with all that?"

"He did. And he never once objected. I'm sure he told you all about it."

"Actually, no, he didn't. He mentioned that you were really competitive with him and he wasn't sure what he did to set that off, but he never shared the details."

"Oh. I always assumed he had."

"Nope."

"Well, he really is a nice guy, then. That makes me feel even worse."

"It kind of should, Terri. What else did you do to poor Neil, who was just recently divorced and looking for nothing more than a pleasant evening?"

"Uh, I wouldn't let him pay."

"Hmmm."

"Or walk me to the Metro."

"Ewwww. Who are you?"

"I know, right? And I'd completely forgotten about it until a few months ago when I started having this dream with him in it."

"Well, do you want to describe what happened in the dream or are you too embarrassed to tell me? I mean, we've already established it wasn't a sex dream, so how bad could it be?"

"Yes, I do want to describe it. I'm hoping you can help me figure it out because you're in the dream, too."

"Ahhhh. Okay, shoot."

Terri cleared her throat. "It always starts out the same way—I'm in a field and I'm struggling with a heavy rope that's over my shoulder. It's night-time and very dark. The rope stretches out behind me and is attached to something, but I can't see what. All I know is it's really heavy and I'm struggling to pull it forward."

"Okay, I'm with you."

"I'm struggling to pull and nothing is moving. I'm getting tired and frustrated and am just about to quit when these lights float up and illuminate the field. I can suddenly see that I'm surrounded by men who are just standing and watching me. I stop struggling with the rope and start yelling at all of these guys. 'What the hell is wrong with all of you? Why are you just standing there while I do all the work alone? What is wrong with you?' I'm so pissed at these guys and I'm screaming at them. One by one they turn their backs on me. Just turn their backs. And then the crowd of men to my left starts to part. I think they're moving out of the way to let someone through to help me, but that's not it at all. They part and I see your friend with his own rope. He's also trying to pull but he's asking for help instead of cussing the dumbasses out. He sees me and smiles. He looks relieved to see me there and says, 'Let's pull together. We can do this together.' But I'm not having it. I'm so pissed and I'm not having it."

"What happens next?"

"You come charging out of nowhere to help him! And your brother is there, too. All the men start rushing over to help and I'm left by myself." Terri paused.

This is my opportunity to tell her that we're all having the same dream. Should I tell her about the Civil War connection, too? I'll have to see if I can work that in without freaking her out. "Terri, there's something I have to..."

"And then my rope goes slack and I hear this incredible racket behind me — horses galloping and marching feet. I turn to see men on horses charging right at me. I drop the rope and jump to my left to let them pass. Right behind them are literally thousands of men who swarm past me. They swarm past like they don't even see me. And then they're gone. I'm standing in the field completely alone."

Okay, here's my chance. "Terri..."

"Then I hear thunder in the direction that everyone has gone. I see lightning strikes in the distance. I hear men yelling in unison. There's something going on and I'm missing the action. I start running in the direction that everyone has gone. I'm running through the field, trying to find everyone when I feel a tug at the back of my neck and at the same time my feet lift off the ground."

"You're flying?"

"Yes, but something has me. Something is carrying me. I'm carried high up above the field and away from the thunderstorm. I struggle at first to get away, but then realize that I'm so high up that I'd probably die if I fell. As I'm carried away from the field, everything becomes pitch dark and I start to get worried about where I'm being taken. And then, all of a sudden, I realize I'm falling. I'm free-falling straight down."

"Do you wake up before you hit the ground?"

"No, because I don't hit ground, I hit water."

"Oh, cool."

"Yes, I hit water and I go under, but the water feels very familiar and safe. I open my eyes wide and realize there are animals in the water. Big brown animals are swimming all around me. I dive deeper to get away from them, but they follow me. I swoop up through the water and pop to the surface. The animals come with me. I start dog-paddling through the water and look back. It's beavers! A big colony of beavers is following me and I realize that they're not just following me — they're allowing me to lead them. At that moment, I realize I'm a beaver, too, and I raise my tail and slap it hard on the surface of the water. And that's it. I wake up right there every time."

"Wow."

"I know. And I've had this dream at least a dozen times. It unfolds in exactly the same way every time."

"That's really something."

"Yes, and I suddenly realized how horrible I'd been to Neil. I walked into the restaurant that night and immediately picked him out sitting at the bar waiting for me. I took one look at him and instantly hated him."

"You hated him? Seriously? No one hates Neil."

"Well I did. I felt overwhelming jealousy as soon as I saw him. I should have just left, but instead I walked over to the bar, sat down next to him, and proceeded to make him as miserable as I possibly could."

"And you're sure you'd never met him before?"

"Okay, that's what's weird. I was sure I knew him but we couldn't come up with a single commonality. Nothing. And I felt like I knew him well — well enough that my reaction to seeing him made some sort of logical sense, even though it didn't."

"Terri, have we ever talked about reincarnation?"

"Not really. I mean, you've tried to share your thoughts with me a few times, but that's not been somewhere I've wanted to go."

"Are you ready to go there now?"

"You're going to tell me I knew Neil in a previous life, aren't you?"

"Yeah. How do you feel about that?"

"I think you're right. And I think he was an effective leader in that previous life and I was a wanna-be. I think I missed out because I didn't work with him."

"And that's why you're writing a paper with your colleague?"

"Yes, I want to try to work with people more, but I'm frustrated. It's not going well. I'm trying to, uh, squelch myself and defer to Fred but he's taking things in the wrong direction. I'm trying to be patient, but I don't know how to get things on track. The whole thing is making me feel bad about myself. I want to feel like that beaver. The other beavers trust me and follow wherever I go in the dream. Oh, my god, I can't believe I just said that out loud, but swimming around with the other beavers following my lead felt so great and so right. And since I'm putting it all out there — I might as well tell you that I did some online research about beaver symbolism after I'd the dream a few times. I found out that beavers represent doing the work necessary to make your dreams a reality. You know I'm always willing to do whatever's needed, but beavers also suggest teamwork and how much easier it is to build something when you're part of a team. You know, even when I played sports,

I never felt like a teammate — I felt like a star. I competed against myself and I tried to make my parents proud, but I didn't really care about my teammates. I didn't even care if we lost games as long as I played well. I know that sounds bad, but that's how I felt and it worked for me."

"But you think this dream is telling you that not being a team player is holding you back now?"

"Yes, and it's weird because being a solitary rock star works for so many of my colleagues. It's definitely not productive for me, though. Not at this point in my life."

"That's really interesting. Are you looking for help around this?" I suddenly realized what I was going to suggest and just as quickly realized I had no idea how to pull it off.

"Yes. My faculty mentor is pushing me to be more collegial and I'm trying, but it's really not working out."

"Well, how would you feel if I told you that Neil was a highly effective leader and team-builder in this lifetime, too, and that you're maybe supposed to make a business connection with him?"

"That would make me feel like I completely blew it by acting like such a bitch."

"Well, sometimes timing is everything. Maybe it was just a little too early for you to meet him."

"So, how do you think I'd go about asking him for help?"

The image of Neil carefully writing ADVERSARY next to Terri's name in his little book swam in front of my eyes. "Honestly, I'm not sure. I think it might be something that can't be forced and just has to unfold. You might ask your beaver pals for guidance, though. See if they might bring you some specific advice."

"Are you making fun of me again?"

"No, not at all. Ask them. And then keep your eyes and ears and mind open for messages. And with that I'd better let you go."

"Okay, yeah, I'd better go, too. I have homework to grade and it's getting late. Thanks so much for listening. Good night."

"Good night. Sweet dreams."

"Ha-ha. That's funny. I'm hanging up. Bye."

The call ended and I put the phone on the side table. It was dark now and I could see the bats swooping around the yard below me. The tree frogs were singing for all they were worth and the katydids were getting raucous. I closed my eyes and processed what had just happened. Terri absolutely confirmed that we were all players in a shared dream, and she'd completely exposed her vulnerabilities to me, but I felt held back throughout the conversation. I wasn't able to tell her that we were all experiencing the same dream from different vantage points or that it was apparently tied to our service during the Civil War. I hadn't even told her about the valley dream and the baggage. Maybe that would have helped her. I'd let her down — I could have pulled her in closer and made this easier for her but instead had simply mined her for information to take back to Neil.

I kept my eyes closed and just rested — breathing easily in and out. My awareness dropped to the middle of my chest and I felt instantly lighter. The sounds of the night creatures blended into a comfortable hum and then disappeared from my consciousness.

"Sometimes we scatter seeds, you know, and have to wait to see if they germinate and take root."

"Hey, Mick. I feel like I let her down."

"No, you've never let her down. The things she told you about herself tonight — you knew those truths years ago, didn't you?"

"Decades ago."

"But you've never pointed them out to her. Why?"

"Being the shining star is Terri's identity. Her parents helped her create that image of herself and it's still who she thinks she is. Fighting against the system and competing with other people give her the energy to keep it up...to keep shining."

"And you don't want to rip her mask out of her hands, do you?"

"No, she needs to put it down when she's ready. If it gets snatched away too early, she might be left with nothing. I don't think that would work out for Terri."

"No, it wouldn't. Insight will come to Terri as she's able to process it. How she applies it will be up to her."

"Okay, Mick."

I visualized a sleek beaver with a good-sized aspen clenched in its massive, orange incisors. It was knifing through still water with a "V" of other beavers trailing behind it, each carrying a sapling of its own.

"Mick?"

"Yes?"

"We spend an awful lot of time forcing masks onto some people and snatching them away from others, don't we?"

"Yes. That's interesting, isn't it?"

"Yes...interesting and sad."

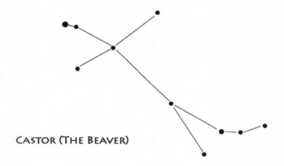

CASTOR (THE BEAVER)

Chapter 21

Karma Revealed:
A Magical Gift for Carla

I rolled over and looked at the clock. *Six twenty-three a.m. It's Friday already. Did Neil mention what time I needed to report back today?* I yawned and rolled back over, tucking the pillow under my cheek and getting comfortable again. *Naw, he didn't...his mistake. I really haven't gained any insight into the location of the battle I saw, anyway, but he'll probably be interested in what Andy and Terri added about the dream.* I curled up and nestled more deeply into the warm bed. *I wonder if Neil will remember Carla from the picnic. Carla!* I sat up and rubbed the sleep out of my eyes. I needed to figure out how to discuss the dream with Carla. Andy clearly was waxing sentimental over her and wanted me to play nice, but I hadn't figured out a specific approach before I'd gone to bed. I was leaning toward stopping by her place unannounced, rather than hoping she'd take a call from me. *But what's my excuse for doing that? And how am I going to just casually mention the swan without giving Andy away? And why the hell am I now caught between Andy and Carla in addition to Neil and Terri? What have I done to deserve this?*

I threw the covers off and swung my legs out of bed. I stretched my arms up toward the ceiling and then pulled them down and back to open up my ribcage and give my lungs some room to function. I wondered if I could channel Swan and do that once more but with more grace. I stretched my arms up again but added some hand-flourishes at the top. I swept my arms down and back again with heightened drama, baring my throat as I stretched my neck and turned my face to the ceiling. The neck stretch felt good but unfortunately didn't shed any light on the best way to start a conversation with Carla. *Maybe an image of a swan will stimulate my brain.*

I slid out of bed, found my slippers, and padded downstairs to the office. I sat down in front of my keyboard and hit the button on my computer monitor. The screen flashed to life. *Six thirty-five a.m. Carla's already on her way to the Metro — probably locked in traffic on I-270.* I opened a browser window and typed *swan image* into my search engine. A collection of swan photos appeared. Curiously, several of the birds pictured were doing almost exactly the stretch I was attempting earlier, but with much more dignity than I'd mustered. As I scrolled through the photos, the pictures progressed through images of live swans to images of objects that had been crafted to look like swans. They ranged from gaudy swan teacups and a hideous swan-shaped kettle, which was oddly enameled a bloody shade of red, to exquisite porcelain renditions of swans tending eggs or rising up with wings raised. *Hmm. I wonder if I can find Carla a porcelain swan to set on the shelf behind her couch. Maybe use it as a conversation starter.* "Hi, Carla! I was out poking around at Nickerson's Antiques and this beautiful Bavarian swan just sang out to me. I knew it had to be yours." *Yeah, that's natural. Not. But, not a half-bad idea if I can work out the dialogue.*

I showered, got dressed, and spent the rest of the morning sipping mint tea and typing up detailed notes for Neil before I forgot any of the interesting tidbits from my conversations with Andy and Terri. By the time I was finished, it was pushing 9:30. *Perfect timing — rush-hour should be dying down right about now.* I carried my tea out to the kitchen and dumped it in a travel mug then grabbed my keys off the kitchen table and was out the door.

Thirty minutes later, I pulled up in front of J. W. Nickerson's Antiques Emporium. Nickerson's Emporium filled the space in a low brick building that was once cordoned off into individual offices for a selection of dentists, Realtors, and insurance salesmen. The network of rooms and short halls had been transformed into a rabbit warren of a place that was packed from floor to ceiling with glassware, collectibles, and small pieces of furniture. I'd arrived several minutes before opening, but Judy Nickerson came to the front door of the shop, unlocked it, and waved to me through the glass before disappearing back into her enchanted lair. I drank the last bit of my mint tea, slid out of my car, and walked the few steps to the door of the shop. As I put my hand on the door handle, I felt a surge of energy course through me and saw a few deep blue flecks of light zip past on the other side of the thick glass. Another mystical portal to traverse, but I always found happy energy whenever I plunged through this particular rabbit hole.

I pulled the door open and heard the familiar sound of a brass sleigh bell announcing my arrival. Deliberately happy piano music with a clipped beat, likely originally scored for the harpsichord, swirled and laughed from somewhere deep within the burrow. Antique lamps and chandeliers added to warm, natural light that filtered in through small square windows near the ceiling. I took a big breath in and let the smoky, herbal scent of the place fill me up while I glanced around. The merchandise in the room where I stood was arranged to look like a nineteenth century parlor — except for the tiny white price tag on each item, you'd think you had just entered your Auntie Mabel's front room. I shook off a wave of sleepy comfort and wondered why I hadn't had a little caffeine this morning.

"Judy?" I called out.

"Back here! Come back to the children's bedroom!"

As many times as I'd visited Nickerson's, I still didn't have the floorplan down but knew if I kept moving toward the back I'd eventually stumble upon the children's bedroom and its expansive collection of antique toys. I wove through the parlor, a formal living room, and a comfortably cluttered dining room full of cut-glass goblets and transferware plates decorated with historical buildings and National Park scenes. I paused in the kitchen to admire a salt-glazed pickle crock that hadn't been there the last time I'd visited and then continued on through the old-time laundry facility, complete with wringer washer, wash boards, and a collection of laundress implements that I couldn't begin to recognize.

"Judy?"

"Where are you?" she called out.

"In the laundry room."

"Head to the right, then the left, and then come straight back."

"Okay."

I continued on through a series of bedrooms, a bathroom with a beautiful claw-foot tub, and two well-appointed closets, before finally finding Judy on a ladder in a room almost bursting at the seams with vintage toys and games.

"I'm just about finished here," she said without looking down. A flurry of indigo blue sparks danced around Judy's head and then whizzed away to hidden corners of the room.

I walked around the ladder and looked up to see what Judy was doing. She seemed to be suspending some sort of large, winged creature from the ceiling. I squinted up at the crackled off-white surface of the object — it appeared to be crafted of painted cloth. "Is that a bird?" I asked.

"Yes, a rather fabulous one, too. Hold on just a sec." Judy finished what she was doing and clambered down the ladder. She stepped back and looked up to admire her work. I stepped back and looked, too. Suspended from the ceiling as if it were coming in for a landing on an invisible pond was a beautiful, white folk art swan with a wing span of at least four feet. I gasped.

"I know, right? It's really unique. All hand-painted kidskin leather. No doubt has its original stuffing — I couldn't find a single opened seam. See the bill and feet? Hand-carved chestnut. My son created this nifty little harness so I could hang it up out of the kids' reach. Isn't it an exquisite piece?"

"Yes. Yes, it is. Um, I'm actually looking for a swan this morning. But smaller. Porcelain?"

"Really? Oh, I love synchronicities! Just a sec." Judy folded the ladder and carried it out a doorway in the back of the room. I backed up to where she'd been standing and got a better view of the swan. The bird gazed past its chestnut bill at me with intelligent black eyes. My morning excursion suddenly felt so incredibly right.

Judy bustled back into the room with a happy smile on her face. "Now, did you notice the swans in the dining room? There are at least a half dozen in the big breakfront."

"No, I didn't stop to look, actually."

"Okay, well, let me be your tour guide!" Judy slipped past me and set off at a quick clip toward the front of the shop. She brought me back to the dining room and led the way to a massive antique cabinet with glass doors. "Oh, no wonder you didn't notice them. Let me get the lights." Judy reached around the back of the cabinet and its interior sprung to life. Delicate porcelain flowers shared space in the cabinet with beautifully decorated birds. The collection included a robin tending a nest of pale blue eggs, a jeweled hummingbird investigating a morning glory blossom, a red-winged blackbird with its head thrown back in song perched on a cattail, and numerous swans in a variety of poses.

"Do you have anything specific in mind?"

"Well, no, but something graceful. Oh, and powerful. It's for a dancer — something that would appeal to a dancer."

"Does it have to be antique?"

"No, not really."

"Follow me." Judy led me back out to the front parlor. She wove her way through the furniture and display cases to a tall glass curio cabinet in the far corner of the room, reached up on tiptoes to the high window ledge above the case, and produced a key.

"This might be it," she said over her shoulder as she unlocked the curio's double doors. Judy leaned forward and reached into the depths of the cabinet. She emerged holding a porcelain swan that was clearly about to take flight. The muscles of the bird's chest were engaged and its wings were sweeping back. I could see each shaft and each tiny vane of the delicately detailed feathers. The swan's long neck was half-extended — a subtle S-curve was still visible but the swan was unmistakably reaching upward. Its black bill was opened slightly and there was a look of determination about its expression. The bird's feet were partially visible emerging from a base of porcelain water spotted with lily pads and blue flowers. It was the same blue that I'd just seen whizzing around the shop.

"Yeah, that's it," I confirmed and nodded. "Can you wrap it?"

CHAPTER 22

KARMA REVEALED:
BREAKING THE ICE AT CARLA'S PLACE

I pulled my car into the short driveway in front of Carla's townhouse and turned off the engine. The wrapped porcelain swan had ridden shotgun up to Germantown with the seatbelt snugged down to keep it from taking unexpected flight. I set it free and then fished in the elegant gift bag that Judy had selected for me, finding tucked in the tissue the miniature folded card that I'd chosen from a rack near the register. I pulled a pen out of the console between the car seats and surveyed the four square inches of space that I had to write a message. Brief and to the point.

> HI CARLA,
> SAW THIS AT NICKERSON'S AND
> IMMEDIATELY THOUGHT OF YOU.
> HOPE YOU ARE WELL,

I signed my name and carefully printed my phone number along the bottom edge. Just enough room. I sealed the tiny card in the tiny envelope, wrote Carla's name with a flourish across the white square, and tucked the card back into the bag.

I'd decided as I pulled out of Nickerson's parking lot that I would leave the gift on Carla's porch for her to find when she got home from work. Just as I'd hoped, her bundled copy of *The Washington Post* was still on the porch by the front door. I imagined Carla coming home after a long commute, opening the door to retrieve the newspaper, and finding the exquisite gift. If things went exactly as planned, she'd immediately call and thank me, but if she didn't call back until the weekend, that would be fine, too. I mean, this was extra credit — the above and beyond portion of my mission. Neil would certainly be amenable to spotting me a few extra days, if needed.

I pushed open my car door and stepped out onto the small patch of grass in front of the townhouse. A bit of crabgrass had muscled its way into the little lawn since I'd been here last and the bright petunias in the bed around the lamp post were now scraggly and faded. Involuntarily, I bent down, plucked a few dead petunia blossoms, and dropped them into the mulch. If Andy were still living here, these would have been replaced with fall mums weeks ago. I straightened up, followed the short sidewalk to the porch and climbed the two steps to the front door.

As soon as I stepped up on the porch, I knew something was wrong. There wasn't just one copy of *The Post* here, there were four — the one by the door and three more hidden behind the overgrown hollies at the back of the front flowerbed. *Shit, she's out of town.* I flipped over the papers and found the dates — Tuesday, Wednesday, Thursday, Friday. The last paper Carla had picked up was Monday's. *Okay, no worries...must be on a business trip...she'll be home tonight.* I carefully piled the papers to the right of the door and tucked the gift in amongst them so no one could see it from the street. I now imagined Carla dragging her little wheeled suitcase through the living room and pausing to retrieve the papers on her way upstairs to shower and get comfortable after a long commuter flight from, say, Dallas. *Yeah, she's flying in from Dallas and this will really brighten her day.* I surveyed the scene one last time.

The tissue paper had slid down into the gift bag a bit and wasn't as nicely fluffed as when Judy had first arranged it. I bent over to adjust the tissue and noticed out of the corner of my left eye that the front door had opened just a crack. *Oh, shit!* My heart leapt to my throat as I jumped back from the door. The cartoon version of Carla's cat that I'd conjured the last time I was at her place flashed to mind as I stood frozen — today, though, the cat's head had been replaced by my own. As I stood gawking, the door continued to swing open, revealing a tall, barefooted woman in a long, white terry bathrobe. The strange woman had a puffy, bloated face and shoulder-length hair that hung lank from her head. In one hand, she held a roll of toilet paper and in the other she clutched a wad of tissue.

"Carla?"

"Yes, it's me. I know I look horrible. What are you doing here? Do you want to come in?" Carla looked over her shoulder and surveyed the living room. "The place is a mess," she continued, "but do you want to come in?"

Before I could accept her invitation, Carla lifted the wad of tissue to wipe her nose and suddenly started weeping. Her face reddened as she attempted to breathe through sobs that racked her slender body. "Please, please, will you come in and talk. I'm sorry. I'm a mess. I'm so sorry. Please will you come in?" Carla held the door open and stepped aside so I could enter.

"Sure." I bent down and gathered the newspapers and the gift, hugging the load to my chest.

Stepping into Carla's living room, I could see what she meant. It was obvious that she'd been camped out on the couch for quite some time. The little trash basket from her powder room was tipped over next to the couch and had spilled a full load of used tissue across the usually spotless white carpet. Several empty tissue boxes shared space on one of the end tables with dirty dishes and a teetering pile of tissue wads. The side chair held Carla's briefcase and one of her beautiful business suits, which apparently had been wadded up and thrown from across the room. A pair of simple black heels, a lacy black bra, and a Coach purse were dumped on the floor beside the chair. Judging from the strong smell coming from the laundry room, cleaning out the cat box had not been a priority for quite some time. I used one of the rolled newspapers to sweep tissue wads off the glass coffee table and deposited my load next to a sheaf of official-looking paperwork and a stack of magazines.

Carla gathered her suit and briefcase from the chair and dropped them next to her shoes. "Would you like to sit down? A cup of tea? Would you like a cup of tea?"

"Tea would be great. I'd love a cup of tea. Thank you." I made myself comfortable in the chair as Carla gathered the dirty dishes and padded into the kitchen. I heard her wash her hands and then commence opening and closing cabinets and setting things on the kitchen counter. The striker on the gas stove clicked several times, followed by the rush of ignition. I leaned forward and picked a copy of *Forbes* off the stack of magazines. Before I could flip it open, however, Carla's cat leapt to the arm of my chair and stared at me through sapphire blue eyes.

"Hi, Bianca. You doing okay?" Bianca took one tentative step onto the magazine, pinning it to my lap. I slid the magazine out from under her paw and tossed it back onto the coffee table. Bianca immediately pulled the rest of her body into my lap and circled a few times, purring audibly as she settled in and made herself comfortable. I stroked the cat's thick white fur as Carla continued to move around in the kitchen. She seemed to be unloading the dishwasher and putting things away. Dishwasher racks slid in and out, glasses clinked as they were put on shelves, pots banged together, and silverware rattled into a drawer that slid shut with a soft thump. The dishwasher rack slid out again. Running water, more glass clinking, the sound of plate scraping and the whir of the garbage disposal signaled that Carla was now loading up the dirties. The tea kettle screamed angrily and then settled down with a few whimpers as Carla filled a teapot. With a few mechanical clicks, the dishwasher hummed to life.

Carla reappeared in the living room with an ornate silver tray holding the teapot, cups, and two small plates of square shortbread cookies. I slid the newspapers over to clear a spot on the coffee table for the tray. "Thank you," said Carla as she set the tray on the table. She'd pulled her unwashed hair back into a short ponytail and had probably held a cool, wet cloth to her eyes, which were now a little less puffy. Even in this disheveled state, she was beautiful.

Carla carefully poured two cups of tea and handed me one on a saucer. She set a plate of cookies in front of me and then sat at the end of the couch near me, putting space between herself and the mountain of tissues at the other end. "Bianca has really missed you. No one else brings her treats. Is that what's in the bag? Were you dropping off a gift for her?"

"Oh, no, that's for you. I found something at Nickerson's this morning that made me think of you for some reason. I think you were meant to have it."

"Really? It's for me?"

"Uh-huh."

Carla smiled a weak but real smile that started in her bloodshot green eyes. "You didn't have to do that. But that's so nice of you. Can I open it now?"

"Sure, please do. I hope you like it."

I sipped my tea as Carla set the gift in her lap, extracted and read the card, and then carefully removed the tissue paper and the box. She slid a manicured nail under the box flap and lifted it to reveal another layer of tissue, which she pushed aside. Carla gasped as the swan's head was revealed. She grasped the box with her right hand and covered her mouth with her left as her eyes welled up again.

"I'm so sorry," I said. "Is it okay?"

Without moving her hand from her mouth, Carla nodded yes. To my relief, she collected herself and continued unwrapping the figurine, allowing the tissue paper to fall to the floor as she set the swan delicately on the coffee table. Both hands now went to her mouth as she stared at the swan and rocked gently back and forth. When she finally dropped her hands from her mouth, Carla was smiling. "This is so amazing. This is…this is perfect," she said.

"I'm so glad you like it. I was hoping…"

"No, no, it's more than liking it. This is…this is…I was asking for reassurance…I was asking for a sign and this is it."

"It is? What do you mean?"

Carla ran a finger lightly over the swan's left wing, following it from the shoulder to the tip. Then she stroked the bird's back, dragging her fingertip down to the tail. "I was laid off Monday afternoon," Carla said without looking up from the swan. She gently touched each of the blue flowers. "Do you realize these flowers are the same color as Bianca's eyes? This is so special." I hadn't realized, but Carla was right. The tiny waterlilies and Bianca's eyes were exactly the same magical shade of blue.

"I was laid off. I wasn't the only one. It was a mass RIF. Jill from HR took me and eight other middle managers into a conference room and handed out our termination packets. She explained the procedure, explained our rights, and then each of us was escorted back to our cubicles where our personal belongings had already been packed up for us." Carla ran her finger along the strong line of the swan's head and neck. "Our key fobs and our company phones were collected and then we were escorted out — dispatched out onto the sidewalk. There were guards at every entrance so we couldn't go back. A hundred or more of us were standing out on the sidewalk with our cardboard boxes, looking at each other. Some of the guys were pissed. They started creating a scene. One flung his box in the direction of a guard. These were armed guards. I just wanted out of there. I took what I wanted out of my box, stuffed it in my briefcase, and left the rest on the sidewalk. No way was I going to carry that damn box on the Metro. Then I started walking. Halfway to the station, I started crying. I haven't stopped crying since."

Carla looked up at me through her swollen eyelids. I couldn't imagine crying for four days straight. She must have felt miserable. "I'm so sorry that happened to you. You didn't deserve that."

Carla picked up her cup and took a small sip of tea. "No, I didn't. I committed to them. I threw everything away for them and they put me out on the sidewalk. I was so humiliated. I wanted to call Andy, but knew I couldn't. Even if he did take my call, what could he possibly say? — 'I told you so?' He did tell me so. He told me to quit years ago before I got too invested." Carla took another sip of tea. "I couldn't call my parents. My mother would have just turned it around to her upset and I don't have the strength to comfort her this time. My friends were all work friends — I'd let everyone else slip away. I didn't have anyone to talk to." Carla picked up a cookie and nibbled a tiny nick out of one corner. "So I lay here and cried and slept and cried and slept. And then yesterday I asked for a sign. I asked for a sign that I could make it through this." Carla turned the cookie and nicked off another corner.

"What happened?" I asked.

"I fell asleep and realized I was dreaming but it wasn't a normal dream because I could remember every detail when I woke up."

"A lucid dream. That's called a lucid dream."

"Really?" Carla looked up and made eye contact. "That's interesting. I knew it was different." Carla returned her cookie to the plate. "Can I tell you about it?" she asked. "I'd like to tell you about it because it has to do with the swan."

"Sure, you can tell me. There are a lot of us having lucid dreams right now."

"Seriously? Okay, now that's really interesting because you and Andy are both in this dream. And that tall guy you brought to the picnic last summer was in it, too."

"Okay. Um, well, all of us have actually been having different variations of the same dream. Andy, me, my friend, Neil, who you met at the picnic, plus another friend, Terri Martin, have all been having pretty much the same dream."

"Terri Martin from high school? The baseball player?"

"You remember her?"

"I certainly do. I went to Walt Whitman. We played against your school in baseball. My oldest brother, Chris, was a pitcher. Terri Martin hit a home run off him and got him pulled from his last home game. Senior Day — she got him pulled on Senior Day."

"Uh, yeah, that would be Terri."

"Well, maybe my dream is different. I didn't see Terri, but I saw the rest of you."

"I didn't see Terri, either, but I saw you and Andy working on something together in the dream."

"Yes, the second part of the dream I was helping Andy do something. At the beginning, though, I was on my own. It was night time and I was running along a dirt road. I was completely alone and very afraid. I'm not sure where I was going — maybe it didn't matter as long as I got away from where I was. I was running and running through the darkness. And then I heard a noise in front of me — a horse whinnied. *A horse.* I stopped and listened. I heard more horses in the distance and what sounded like an enormous group of people walking up the road. I completely freaked. There was forest on both sides of the road and I was afraid to go in there, but I was more afraid to go forward. I turned around and started running the way I'd come. As I ran, I started to hear voices coming from the forest. I slowed down and walked slowly, trying to figure out where the voices were coming from and what was being said. I came closer and closer to the voices until I noticed firelight flickering through the forest just ahead of me on my left. I could see the shadows of figures cast on the trees by the firelight and I could hear men talking and laughing. I felt drawn to the light and I crept forward through the trees to get a better look at the men around the fire. I recognized Andy right away. He was telling a story and the other men were laughing. I was drawn to him. Like a moth to the flame." Carla laughed a tiny, sad laugh and took another sip from her teacup before continuing. "That's the way it was with me and Andy. He drew me right in the moment I met him — I was always the moth to his flame. I felt safe with Andy — he's not afraid of anything, is he?"

"No, not much scares Andy — he's always been one to suck out all the marrow of life." Carla winced. "Sorry, it's Thoreau. Maybe not the best visual for a vegan."

"No, not the best visual. Anyway. I crept through the forest, getting closer and closer to the fire — so close that I could feel the heat from the flames. It felt good…it felt safe. Andy looked up and saw me. He was still telling his story but he waved me into the group. Slid over to make space for me on the log where he was sitting. I stepped forward into the firelight and Andy smiled. I sat down next to him and started to relax, but then there was shouting from somewhere on the other side of the forest. I heard your voice. You were yelling and calling for help. Andy and the other men stood up. Andy looked at me and said, 'Come on!' He ran out of the forest with the other men. I ran as fast as I could and caught up with Andy. We all ran into a field, but it wasn't a normal field — it was lit with magical globes that were floating just over our heads. The globes lit up the field and I could see thousands of faces looking at us — thousands of men were standing in the field just looking at us. I heard you shout again and followed Andy through the field toward you. We pushed through the men and found you with your friend…" Carla looked at me expectantly.

"Neil?"

"Yes, Neil. The two of you were pulling a rope that stretched back through the field and into the darkness beyond. Andy got behind you and started pulling the rope, too. I got behind him and pulled, but that's when I saw my hands." Carla's face wrinkled up in disgust.

"Your hands? Was something wrong with them?"

"Yes. I had man-hands."

"Man-hands? Are you sure?"

"Oh, definitely. *Those* were *not* my normal hands."

I looked at Carla's small, feminine hands with their delicate fingers and perfect manicure. "That must have been shocking,"

"Yes, it was — I was quite upset about it and wanted to drop the rope and run, but all the men in the field were suddenly joining us in pulling the rope. There was a crush of men and I was afraid to leave Andy, so I kept pulling. Then Neil started shouting encouragement — he told us we could do it and to keep pulling. As soon as I heard his voice, I felt safer and I didn't want to lose that feeling by running away — I think I would have followed him any-where and done anything for him at that moment. So, I pulled and pulled and whatever the rope was tied to started moving. We got some momentum going and started moving forward quite rapidly. At one point, I looked over Andy's shoulder and realized we were going up the side of a hill. I put my head back down and kept pulling, but then I heard the thunder — huge claps of thunder. I looked up again and saw a thunderstorm straight ahead of us. We dropped the rope and I was expecting Neil to direct us to safety, but he pointed right into the thunderstorm and told us to charge! Well, I was standing there next to Andy going, 'No way, no freaking way,' but Andy grabbed my arm and we ran into the storm together. Lightning crashed all around us and I was so afraid at first, but then I felt an incredible surge of strength."

Carla leaned forward and picked up the swan. She carefully traced the strong curve of its neck. "I felt like something that was holding me back had sprung loose and I was flying free. I turned to look at Andy and I had wings!" Carla smiled and her eyes lit up. She held the figurine up for me to see. "Wings! Swan wings!"

A prickle of electricity surged through my body. "Ooooh, cool."

Carla laughed and replaced the swan on the coffee table. "Yes, my man-hands had been replaced by swan wings and I was flying."

"That's really powerful, Carla. *Really* powerful."

"Yes, yes it was and I *felt* powerful. It was amazing."

"I bet it was. Where was Andy? Was he still running next to you?"

Carla laughed again. "Well, yes and no."

"Yes and no?"

"There was a coyote running next to me."

"A coyote? Really? How do you know it was a coyote?"

"Well, do you remember the dogs that disappeared in Damascus a few years ago? All those sweet, little Chihuahuas and Yorkies who vanished out of their own yards?"

"Yes, the police suspected a dog-napping ring, but it was coyotes. Coyotes were coming into the suburbs and snatching dogs out of fenced yards."

"Yes. That was very traumatizing to me. I imagined Bianca being carried away by a coyote. I was anxious for weeks."

"But Bianca is an inside cat — how would a coyote get to her?"

"I have no idea and it didn't matter. I was so anxious that she'd be snatched. I read all the articles in *The Post* and studied the pictures of coyotes. I stood on the deck every night and scanned the field behind the development for coyotes. I was so relieved when more townhomes went in back there. I mean, I like the idea of wilderness as much as the next person, but that's certainly not where I want to live." Carla picked her cookie off the plate and bit it in half. She chewed forcefully for several minutes with her eyes focused somewhere behind me. Happy to see her looking stronger, I waited patiently while Carla devoured the rest of the cookie and then plucked the second cookie from her plate. She devoured it, also, and glanced toward my plate, which I lifted from the tray and handed to her. We sat in silence for several more minutes as Carla finished off the rest of the cookies. Eventually, she made eye-contact again. "Where was I?"

"With the dream?"

Carla nodded.

"You'd just looked over toward Andy and saw your wing, but he wasn't there — a coyote had taken his place."

Carla nodded again. "Yes, but Andy was still there. I knew he was the coyote but I wasn't afraid of him. He didn't look blood-thirsty. His tongue hung out of his mouth and he was letting it flop around as he ran. He had a big, goofy grin on his face and he was thoroughly enjoying the run through the thunderstorm. At that moment, I realized we weren't a perfect match. I looked at him — this crazy coyote that sucks marrow bones — and I didn't see a single trace of me. That should have bothered me, but it didn't. And then I remembered the conversation we had about the dragonfly and I wanted to call you, but I couldn't."

Bianca stirred in my lap and began purring again. I stroked her back and she looked up at me through her sparkling blue eyes. I suddenly realized without a hint of doubt that Bianca had somehow, some way, orchestrated my visit that day. *Oh, Bianca, you devious cat. You know the swan, don't you?* Bianca stood up, bumped her head against my cheek, and gently bit my chin. Then she turned and leapt into Carla's lap. *Of course, Bianca knew the swan.*

"Carla, it's just about lunch time. Do you want to get out of here for a little while? Can I take you out for lunch?"

"Really? I would love that. It would take me a while to get ready, though."

"That's okay. You do your thing and get ready. I'll hang out here with Bianca and look at your magazines. Think about where you want to go. I like every-thing — you pick."

"That would be fabulous. Thank you so much." Carla lifted Bianca off her lap and set her on the couch. The cat turned and sat upright on the cushion, keeping her eyes on Carla as she set her teacup and the plates back on the tray, tightened the belt on her robe, and stood up. "Thank you for listening. That helped so much."

"You're very welcome. Take your time — enjoy your shower." Carla smiled and headed upstairs. Bianca curled up and closed her eyes, disappearing into the white upholstery.

I waited until I heard the shower start and then began cleaning up the living room. I found a trash bag under the kitchen sink, gathered all the spent tissues into it, and then flattened the empty tissue boxes. I returned the trash basket to the powder room and then held my breath as I entered the laundry room. Finding Carla's trash and recycling in the far corner, I made my deposits. Bianca had been making deposits of her own into the overflowing cat box by the washer, which I dumped into another bag and refilled from the giant tub of kitty litter that I found stashed between the wall and the dryer. I washed my hands in the powder room and went back to the living room where I gathered the tissue paper and box into the gift bag. I then carefully folded Carla's suit, tucked her bra into the jacket, and put the clothes, Carla's shoes, and her briefcase in the hall closet, closing the door firmly behind them. She didn't need those reminders of her last day at work staring at her from across the living room any longer.

Satisfied that things looked tidy, I went back to my chair, poured myself another cup of tea from the teapot, and settled in. I knew it would be at least ninety minutes before I saw Carla again, but I couldn't begrudge her the time. I reached forward and lifted the swan from the coffee table. My fingers traced the line of its neck and I knew Carla would be okay. Graceful and elegant. And powerful beyond all comprehension.

The Swan and the Coyote

The swan and the coyote
Lived in the 'burbs
In a beautiful new townhouse.

They were madly in love for a time, you might say,
But the swan, well, she always held back.

She'd folded her wings and deferred to the beast,
Ignoring his stark lack of grace,
Cuz he still made her laugh and still soothed her soul
And was still really good in the sack.

But the Swan woke one day
And looked in the eye of the man that she'd loved for so long
And saw not a whit of herself in his gaze,
So, knew it was time to move on.

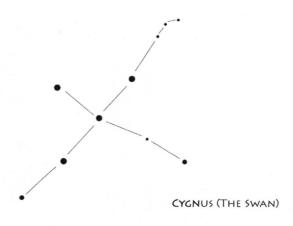

CYGNUS (THE SWAN)

CHAPTER 23

KARMA REVEALED: THE GANG'S ALL HERE, NOW WHERE ARE WE GOING?

I felt unsettled that evening. I badly wanted to report back to Neil, but also wanted to give him as much space as he needed on his last day at the office. But, although I had committed to letting him lead, I hadn't heard a thing from him since we'd parted to find our vehicles in the Park and Ride lot on Wednesday night and my patience was being tested. As the hours ticked by with no contact, I paced around the house, picking things up and putting them down, unable to focus long enough to clean a dish or read a magazine article. Finally, my will broke and I plucked my phone off the kitchen table. "How was the last day?" I typed. I hit "send" and before I could set the phone back down, it rang.

"Hey, Neil."

"Really kind of anticlimactic," Neil said without preamble. "I realized by 10 a.m. that I'd already made the transition and was fine. People came by to wish me well through the morning and then the folks still around from my old team took me to lunch and surprised me with a big farewell party. People who had moved on years ago made it. Everyone I'd lost in the last RIF and the reorganization was there. Every single one of them."

"That probably felt great, Neil. That wasn't anticlimactic at all."

"Oh, true. That part of the day…yeah, you're right. Walking into that restaurant and seeing the crowd was an important moment for me. Made me realize I'd made a difference in a few lives."

"More than a few, my friend. How'd the afternoon go?"

"Oh, I left after lunch. Got back to the office around two feeling good and saw that Steve had left several messages on my landline. Wanted me to come upstairs and debrief. Have a drink. I wasn't interested. Maybe not the best career move, but I went over to HR instead of calling him back and found someone to take my fob and company phone. Got out of there and spent the rest of the day on the computer doing Civil War research. Was hoping you'd call. Don't want to press you, but did you make any headway on those conversations?"

"I did and you were right — both Andy and Terri have been having the same dream."

"You talked to both of them? Good job, recruit. How was it? What did they have to say?"

"Well, Andy, of course, was completely cool with it all. I was also able to tell him about my valley dream and the Civil War connection. He thought my battlefield vision was epic, especially his role in it. Andy did add to the shared dream. He was in the woods with other men sitting around a campfire passing a jar of whiskey when he heard me calling for help. And, get this — his ex appeared at the campfire and joined him in helping pull the rope."

"Carla? He and Carla aren't together anymore?"

"You remember Carla?"

"Of course, I do. Every man at that picnic last summer remembers Carla."

"Of course. No, they're not together anymore. They broke up before Andy went out West this summer. They hadn't been getting along for a while. It was a messy ending with a lot of shenanigans on Andy's part. You don't want the details."

"No, probably not."

"The really interesting thing was that Andy saw Carla as a swan at the end of the dream."

"A swan? What does that mean?"

"Well, Andy told me that Carla had been a talented dancer but had given up a big performance opportunity to commit to her corporate job."

"You're going to tell me that was a mistake, aren't you?"

"Of course, I am. She went all in with her company years ago. Completely abandoned her passion for dancing. She was laid off on Monday."

"She was? How do you know? Did you talk to her, too?"

"I did. After I talked with Andy, I stopped by to see her — brought her a swan figurine and it completely resonated with her. Carla had the dream, too, and had seen her own wing at the end. She knew she was a swan and really seemed to have a good feel for what it meant. The dream gave her some closure because she saw Andy as Coyote and realized they weren't compatible."

"Coyote? Andy turned into a coyote? What does that mean?"

"From what I understand, Coyote is the trickster and the clown. He's intelligent but has a happy irreverence for life. Sound familiar?"

Neil laughed. "Yeah, and all of this is feeling freaky again."

"Well, the option to stop and walk away is always open."

"Oh, no, I definitely want to keep going. I'm invested now. Did you tell Carla about the valley and the Civil War connection, too?"

"No, no, no. Carla was in no place emotionally to handle all that. I spent most of today with her, but I was focused on listening and giving her support. Carla felt very afraid at the beginning of the dream. She was running away, but didn't know which way to go. She stumbled upon Andy with his friends around the campfire and he seemed to take her under his wing. She needs to be in a better place if I'm going to share more — I don't want to trigger memories before she's ready."

"Okay, good thinking."

"Oh, and before I forget, Carla mentioned you, too."

"She did?"

"Yeah, and don't ask — she didn't want your number."

"Damn!"

"I know. But, she did recognize you in the dream and mentioned that she felt safe with you there — that she was willing to follow your lead. Andy said the same thing. If this really is a reincarnation dream, Neil, you've carried your personality forward."

"Wow. Just *wow*. I really like that. It sounds like Andy did, too, from what you said. What about Terri? Her, too?"

"Definitely. Her version of the dream was fascinating and did suggest bad blood between you two."

"Oh, great."

"I knew you'd be excited. In her dream, Terri was in the same field as you but with her own rope. She also couldn't get the men standing around in the field to help her, but she tried to motivate them by screaming at them. They turned their backs on her."

Neil laughed. "Is it okay if that makes me feel vindicated?"

"Yes, carry on and let me know when you're ready for me to continue."

"Keep going! Keep going!"

"Okay, but I have a question for you — in your version of the dream, do you and Terri have a conversation?"

Neil went silent for a few beats. "Yes, well, I don't know if you'd call it a conversation, but we exchanged words."

"Hmm, it seems you forgot to tell me that part."

Neil cleared his throat. "I asked her to help me. I suggested that we could work together. She shut me down."

"Okay, that matches her version. Right after you spoke, she saw me running to your aid with Andy in tow. From what Andy said, Carla was right behind him, but Terri didn't recognize her and I didn't either. But I think Carla looked like a guy in the dream."

"A guy? How could that be?"

"Well, Andy said he knew it was her but it didn't look like her. I think he was recognizing her essence or her soul for who it was even though her appearance was different. And Carla said she had man-hands."

Neil snorted. "Man-hands?"

"Yes, she saw her hands and I think she knew that she was in a different body. All of us would have been in different bodies if that dream is representing a past-life experience, but she's the only one who noticed it. I think it's maybe because her appearance is so important to her."

"So, you think there was a message there for her?"

"Maybe, but it's not for us to decide what it might be. You know, Andy is the only one who knows I'm talking with you about any of this. He and Carla know that we're all having this dream together, but I'm a little bit uncomfortable that neither Carla nor Terri know about the other dream or..."

"You didn't tell Terri about the valley dream or the Civil War either?"

"No, but I was having trouble getting a word in edgewise with her. She doesn't even know that the rest of us are sharing the dream."

"How did you bring it up, then?"

"She just started talking. It was on her mind. Do you want to hear how the dream ends for Terri?"

"What you told me wasn't it from her?"

"Oh, no, no, no. Terri might be having the most complex version of all. She was left behind when we moved forward with the rope. She was left standing in the field. Men on horses came up from behind her followed by an army of men. They moved past her and left her there. She could see the thunderstorm in the distance and knew something big was going on but she was left out."

"Wow. Okay, that makes it sound like we're really on the right track — that I was trying to get the army to move and was frustrated by the lack of urgency."

"Yes, you and Terri both, but there was a clear clash in leadership styles."

Neil paused to mull that over. "So, maybe I should be looking for a situation where there was a personality clash between officers as well as a strong difference of opinion in terms of strategy."

"That seems reasonable. It might also be reasonable to look for a situation where an officer or a unit was left out of the action, although I'd imagine that might have happened a lot."

"Okay, hold on just a minute. I'm writing all of this down."

As I waited for Neil to make his notes, I deliberated on how much of Terri's Spirit Animal story to tell him. I seemed to be the only one in the group who knew and cared about all the others and, as difficult as Terri could be, I still felt protective of her. Something was pulling me, though, to put it all out there.

"Alright, I'm caught up now. You have anything else?"

"Yes. Terri had an animal encounter, too, and it was pretty intense. I'm not sure now to say this…"

"Then just say it — don't edit yourself."

"Okay, the unedited version is I think Terri was forced to meet a better version of herself through her animal."

"Really? What did she turn into?"

"A beaver. She was picked up out of the field by the scruff of the neck and carried to a pond. She was dropped into the water and realized that she was the leader of a colony of beavers. Terri and the other beavers were building a dam together or something, but Terri was apparently leading the effort as all the beavers were following her. She researched beaver symbolism and came upon the idea that beavers accomplish their goals by working with others. The dream seems to have really impacted her — she's even trying to write a paper with a colleague for the first time ever. I think she's trying to recreate the feelings she had in the pond, but she's struggling so far."

"Oh. She's going to have to put the work in to build the team before she can lead it. Does she understand that? That it's more work at first? And that it takes patience to build trust and respect? And a large measure of self-sacrifice to keep that trust and respect?"

"Umm, I think she's figuring out that it's not easy, but there's more. Terri realizes she might have known you in a previous life. When she met you at that bar, she felt this overwhelming hate crash over her. She wanted to purposely make you miserable."

"Well, she did a good job."

"Yeah, she shared some of the details and I was pretty appalled. I'm really sorry I put you in that situation, but I think there might have been a reason for it. What Terri told me about the emotions rushing over her the night you met made me think of what happened to you in the gallery when you saw that portrait of George McClellan."

I heard Neil inhale hard through his nose and blow it back out. "I don't know how to respond to that," he said.

"Maybe you don't need to. Maybe just let it sit."

"Okay, we're going to let that just sit. Let me make a few more notes."

I stayed silent as Neil added to his notes. *Why had I found it necessary to make him tense on what sounded like a great day for him?* A little black cloud condensed from the atmosphere and hung about a foot from my nose. I clapped my hands together and crushed it between my palms.

"What are you doing?" Neil asked.

"Vanquishing the guilt I feel for making you tense. Hold on a second, I need to wash my hands." I walked over to the kitchen sink and plucked a molded soap out of the ceramic dish I kept on the counter. The little soap was shaped like a sunflower and was scented with lemongrass oil. As I rubbed it into suds under running water, I resolved to let go of any guilt by the time I was done washing my hands. The lemongrass aromatics released into the air and filled my lungs, making me feel calm and focused. I rinsed my hands and turned off the water. The guilt was gone.

"All clean now?" Neil asked from the kitchen table.

"Yep," I called out to him as I dried my hands. "What's next?"

"Well, first, the additional information you gathered from everyone is invaluable. I don't know if it'll help us identify the battle, but it does confirm in my mind the connection between the dream and the Civil War. The details Terri provided, in particular, are pretty compelling. Second, the vision you had with the vulture didn't occur at Gettysburg."

"It didn't? How do you know?"

"The dates are wrong. I did some preliminary checking. Stonewall Jackson died on May 10, 1863. The Battle of Gettysburg happened two months later in early July. So it's out of the mix."

"July would have been too early anyway. The corn I saw was too high and some had already been harvested. Some of the fields were plowed."

"That's right. I forgot about that. We're probably talking summer or fall of 1861 or 1862. And I've already limited the geographical area. Stonewall Jackson fought mostly under Robert E. Lee and exclusively in Virginia with a few forays into Maryland and present-day West Virginia. McClellan fought a battle or two in West Virginia, too, but he was stationed primarily in DC and also did most of his fighting in Virginia and Maryland."

"Sweet! We're probably talking about somewhere nearby."

"Probably so, but I've been a little distracted from tracking down the battle. Once I started researching the generals, I became intrigued with the wide variety of leadership styles represented in our group. And from there I branched out to other generals who drew my attention. What a study in strengths and weaknesses and every historian has an opinion on these guys. There's a gold mine of information online and I've picked up a stack of books already — the start of a Civil War library. Do you want to hear what I've found so far?"

I suddenly felt exhausted and put my head down on the table next to the phone. "It's really nice of you to offer, but I don't want to interrupt your flow. Do you want to just continue at it and loop me back in as you need to bounce things off me?" I said without lifting my head.

"You're good with that?"

"Sure. I want to do some research on the war, too, to get an overall understanding and to figure out where my ancestors were, but not tonight. I'm pretty tired."

"Yeah, you do sound tired. I'll say goodnight, then, and dig back in. Really great job with the conversations. I'm impressed that you pulled those off so quickly."

"Thanks. It was actually pretty easy. Everyone wanted to talk."

"I'm still impressed. Now, I'll get back to what I was doing and will let you know if anything looks promising. Maybe check in tomorrow afternoon? I'd still like to travel on Monday if we get things narrowed down."

"Okay, that sounds great. Have a good night."

"You, too. Talk to you tomorrow."

The call ended. I carried my phone upstairs and plugged it in to charge on the bedside table. The remainder of my Friday night consisted of crawling into bed and falling almost instantly into a deep sleep.

CHAPTER 24

THE PART WHERE NEIL INTERRUPTS MY BEAUTY REST

I'm flying again over the valley full of people with their boxes and bags. This time I know for sure that I'm soaring — riding the thermals that rise up from the hot valley floor. I feel peaceful and detached from what I see happening below me, but I'm drawn to the southern end of the valley. I shift my body slightly and find myself floating in that direction. There's a woman below me whom I realize I'm supposed to see. I float down. Perched on a cardboard box in a white robe is Carla. Her head is bowed and her hands cover her face. Her feet are bare. She looks sad and defeated down there on the valley floor. My shadow crosses over her. It is the shadow of the hawk. Carla lifts her head and shades her eyes so she can see me against the bright midday sky. She raises her right hand and waves — a small, tentative wave as if she's unsure. I tip my wings and circle back around so my shadow slips over her again. She smiles up at me. My shadow slips over Carla again and again as I wheel over her. She stands now and watches me with both hands shading her eyes. I fly over Carla once more and notice the play of sunshine and shadow across her face. She smiles through the sunlight and smiles through the darkness.

Carla turns and looks down at the box where she sat. She gives the box a hard kick and it spins across the valley floor, coughing up its contents. A framed motivational print extolling the virtue of sacrifice flies out. As it hits the ground, the frame bends and the glass shatters. A coffee cup sporting a red and black company logo takes flight and shatters against a rock. A leather-bound notebook spins across the valley floor, skittering like a flat stone skipped across a pond. Papers fly from the notebook and flutter back down as the ground is pelted with a rain of colored paper clips and teabags. Carla surveys the mess. Another smile crosses her face. She tugs at the knotted terrycloth belt at her waist. Her robe falls open and slides down her smooth shoulders. The sleeves slip down and cover her hands. She lifts her elbows to free herself. As the robe slides down to Carla's waist, white wings emerge from the sleeves and stretch toward the sky. The robe drops to the ground and a powerful feathered breast rises to meet the sunlight as a graceful neck unfolds. The puddle of terry cloth runs over the valley floor and transforms into a crystal lake.

The swan now reaches up, reaches up, reaches up. Its feet emerge from the surface of the lake as it begins running smoothly over the water in sync with the beat of its wings. Delicate white mists rise up from the lake and transform one by one into an entire flock of swans, all racing across the water's surface to the graceful beat of their wings. Carla's body rises slightly and her feet lift from the lake. She drags a toe across the water in farewell and then raises her foot, breaking her final connection with the terranean world as she rises powerfully with her neck fully extended and her feet stretched out under her tail. The other swans rise with her. I scream my encouragement as the swans fly strongly toward the valley's rim. Carla opens her bill and an insistent snatch of music emerges. It's a tune I know. It plays again. The swans and the valley melt away as I fumble for my phone.

"Wha? What? Neil? It's three in the morning. What's wrong?"

"I found it."

"What? What?"

"Wake up! Wake up!"

I flipped on the lamp and sat up, squinting at the room.

"What do you need at three in the morning, Neil? I was flying with the swans. You interrupted."

"I'm sorry. Are you awake now?"

"Yes, I'm awake and, no, I don't want to be. What's wrong with you?"

"I found the battlefield."

"What?"

"I found the battlefield and it's nearby. It's in Maryland."

"You found it? Which one is it?"

"Antietam. I'm sure it's Antietam. It matches your sketch almost perfectly and Jackson was there."

"Where's Antietam?"

"West on I-70. South of Hagerstown. At a town called Sharpsburg."

"Is it on a river? The town I saw was on a river."

"Yes, it's on the Potomac and Antietam Creek runs north to south just east of town. I think that's the creek you saw. Part of the battle was fought back and forth across Antietam Creek and there was a bridge across the creek at the southern end of the battlefield. A stone bridge. With three arches. And get this — it's still there."

"Seriously?"

"Yeah, seriously. And guess whose corps on the Union side was active in the fight for that bridge."

"What's a corps?"

"A corps is an organizational unit of an army — around twenty-six thousand men commanded by a major general and on the Union side designated with a numeral. Did you realize there were numerous Union armies fighting in different geographical areas during the Civil War?"

"No."

"Well, there were. The Union Army wasn't just one big army — it was a group of several distinct armies that weren't all run the exact same way, but all of them were organized into corps. Each corps included two to three divisions of infantry, or foot soldiers, also commanded by major generals. The divisions were made up of two to four brigades commanded by brigadier generals. And each brigade was made up of two to five regiments, ideally commanded by a colonel with a lieutenant colonel and a major under him. There were ten companies in each regiment, each commanded by a captain with lieutenants, sergeants, and corporals under him. Each company was a hundred volunteers recruited from a local area, but all of this was best-case scenario. As the war dragged on..."

"Uh, Neil? This isn't going to be on the test is it?"

"No, but guess whose corps fought for the stone bridge."

"McClellan's?"

"No, but he was there. He was leading the entire Army of the Potomac that day against Robert E. Lee's Army of Northern Virginia. Do you remember who we both identified from the lineup of generals?"

"Oh! The guy with the muttonchops."

"Yep, Ambrose Burnside. He led the fight for the bridge and it was later named for him — Burnside Bridge. If you were up on that hillside above the bridge, you and Andy would have been in the 9th Corps, the unit Burnside commanded."

"Oh, wow. What about the other generals? Did any of those make sense?"

"They certainly did — Joseph Hooker commanded the 1st Corps. His troops were at the north end of the battlefield where you saw the small white building. I think that was Dunker Church. I found photos of it online that were taken right after the battle. There's a cannon and dead soldiers in front of the church in one of the photos. You'll need to look at those and tell me if the building looks familiar."

A wave of trepidation coursed through me and I shivered. "Okay," I said.

"And get this — Hooker's Corps did the initial fighting against Stonewall Jackson's men."

"Near the church? Jackson was near the church?"

"Yes, and just as you suggested, Confederate troops came up past Sharpsburg to join the battle after it began. They crossed the Potomac early in the morning, passed through town, and then massed behind the church. Those guys had marched all night from Harpers Ferry, which is seventeen miles south of Sharpsburg. Actually, in the days leading up to Antietam, all of Stonewall Jackson's divisions were in Harpers Ferry taking the federal garrison there. They came north piecemeal — only about a third of them were in place when the battle opened. Jackson himself only reached Sharpsburg the day before the battle."

The rope dream. Jackson has arrived. I was suddenly nauseated and dizzy. I lay back down on the bed.

"And remember George Crook, who I thought looked familiar from that big portrait of Grant in the stairwell?"

"Yeah."

"He was there, too. He was a colonel at Antietam and commanded a brigade in 9th Corps, so he was also at the southern end of the battlefield."

"Whoa. What about Sherman and Grant?"

"No, neither one of them were there. They were engaged at the same time in the Deep South. Fall of 1862 was leading up to the siege on Vicksburg, which began that December. Remember the earthworks in the portrait of Grant? Vicksburg, Mississippi, was heavily fortified and…"

"Neil, I don't mean to interrupt, but did you say it was fall? When exactly was the battle fought at Antietam? The leaves were still green in my vision. It wasn't autumn."

"Mid-September of 1862. September 17, 1862. Leaves were still on the trees and the corn in the fields was tall enough to conceal a man."

"Oh."

"Perfect, right? And the Confederates burned a farm during the battle to keep the Union sharpshooters from using it as a sniper nest. The house and barn burned early in the morning as a tremendous battle was fought at the north end of the field. As the day wore on, the bulk of the fighting shifted to the middle of the battleground. Union troops launched a major assault from the northeast on a high-banked, sunken lane where Confederate soldiers lay in wait. A small force of Confederates there did massive damage to the approaching Union ranks but their position was eventually overwhelmed and the Confederate line was decimated. That lane is still known as Bloody Lane."

Neil was becoming more and more excited as he recounted the details of the battle. I was becoming more and more apprehensive, but I squeezed my eyes shut and tried to focus. "What about the south end of the battlefield near the town and the bridge? Were things bad there, too?" I hoped they hadn't been. Maybe Andy and I had stayed safely tucked up on that ridge while the battle played out. Maybe…

"Yep, another blood bath down there. A thin line of Confederate defenders, five hundred men at most, was positioned high up on a bluff above the western bank of the creek. The 9th Corps, over ten thousand men, was on the other side of the creek and was ordered by McClellan to take the bridge. Burnside launched assault after assault that subjected his men to Confederate fire from the bluff. The Union guys were completely exposed, but regiment after regiment was sent forward on the same approach — sent forward and stopped in their tracks by Confederate fire. Five hundred men were killed or wounded taking that bridge — five hundred! And the reconnaissance was pathetic. One division got lost — couldn't even find the bridge. Another division that was supposed to cross the creek a mile or so south of the bridge wandered around all morning looking for a usable ford…"

I let Neil's voice fade away as I visualized noise and confusion around the pretty arched bridge that I'd seen in my vision. I wondered if Andy and I ended up tramping around lost in the woods or dodging bullets as we stormed the enemy.

"…complete chaos and keep in mind the artillery fire pinning the guys down. Did you realize they had exploding ordnance and rifled guns during the Civil War?"

"No. I didn't know that. Neil, did the Union army ever get across the bridge?"

"Huh?"

"Did they ever make it across?"

"Yeah, but it took all day. Two regiments were finally sent flying downhill straight at the bridge instead of marching in from the side. At the same time, part of a regiment from Ohio waded the creek upstream of the bridge and the division lost to the south finally found the ford and came charging at the Confederate line from the side. If the lost division hadn't been misdirected by McClellan's engineers, they would have been able to clear the Confederates off the creek bank ahead of the bridge assault. So many lives could have been saved. But they were too late. Much too late."

Too late. I imagined Neil with his rope trying to pull the entire 9th Corps across the stone bridge. "What happened next?" I asked.

"The Confederates retreated across the fields toward Sharpsburg while the rest of the Union troops were brought across the bridge. Things looked good for the Union at that point — Lee had moved men north from the south end of the battlefield all day and had just a few thousand men left around Sharpsburg to prevent the 9th Corps from cutting his entire army off from its only escape route back across the Potomac. The Civil War might have ended that day."

"Really? Why didn't it? What went wrong?"

"I know this is going to come as a shock, but lack of urgency is what went wrong. Once the 9th Corps was over the bridge, it took hours for Burnside to get the men organized and ready to attack. Some of the regiments were exhausted and needed to rest, others were out of ammunition, and everyone was hungry and thirsty. Since the men had crossed the bridge before being fed or resupplied with ammo, the ordnance and supply wagons had to be brought across the bridge to them. The wagons could only come one by one. Time was wasted. Hours were wasted." A thread of anger had woven itself back through Neil's voice. I imagined his jaw tightening. "By the time we charged up the hill it was too late. Too damned late," Neil barked into his phone.

"You were there, Neil? You were there at the bridge?"

"What?"

"Um, well, it sounded for a minute like you might have been there charging up the hill."

"Maybe. I don't know. One minute I feel like I have a personal stake in all this and the next minute I don't know what the hell I'm thinking. All of it's crazy."

I couldn't have this conversation from the fetal position — I sat back up on the bed and shoved my pillows behind my back. "Oh, yeah, that's still hitting me, too, but I'm working hard to keep my mind open to anything that might come with no expectations. You know what I mean?"

"No, not really."

I paused so I could fully feel the combination of apprehension and curiosity in my body before trying to describe it to Neil. "Well, it's like there's some fear and disbelief settled in my gut about the dreams and the visions — the vulture man honestly freaked me out — but I'm also curious. And, I'm willing to see where things go without needing to force things to a specific conclusion.

So, we might get to the battlefield and just spend a nice day outdoors or we might experience something that helps one of us in some way. In my mind, any outcome is fine."

"Okay, I get that, but I don't know if I'm curious or just looking for something to do right now. You know, other than sitting around thinking or drinking too much."

"Well, then maybe this crazy puzzle has come precisely to get you through this rough patch so you stay awake in the moment instead of stewing or numbing yourself out. Keep yourself completely open to more than that but also just be grateful for the distraction that's being provided — although distraction isn't really the right word for it."

"Focus is the word. It's giving me an objective to focus on."

"Yeah, focus, is better but don't let that your focus get too tight now. I think you've been doing a great job remaining open to where the process might lead. Don't cut anything off that attracts your attention. It's possible that you're being led out of the valley, you know, but that the route isn't obvious."

"What's that supposed mean?"

"Uh…" I was suddenly self-conscious and unsure of myself — afraid that I'd over-stepped my bounds and was about to alienate Neil. How could I back away?

"No, no, keep going. You're doing fine. You're putting things together quite nicely, actually."

"Are you sure, Mick? I feel like I'm fumbling and making him mad."

"Making him mad? Yes, perhaps. Fumbling? I believe not. Keep going. Take a risk and stand your ground. What's the worst that could happen?"

"The worst that could happen? He might stop speaking to me and I might lose my best friend, Mick!"

I was answered with silence.

"Mick?"

"Mick?"

"Okay, then."

"Well, before you called, I was flying over the baggage valley again, but this time I saw Carla down in the valley kicking her old job to the curb and taking off with the swans. A lake appeared for her and dozens of swans rose up out of the mists like they were waiting for her. She held herself out of the game for a while, but the swans needed her back, so her job and her relationship with Andy both ended. See? She was released so she could follow her heart and do what she came to do." I held my breath for Neil's response.

"Uh, you believe that?"

"Yeah, I guess I do. Remember the donkey in the hole? How she's your life purpose? You willingly remove some things that cover her up, but only those that you're not afraid to let go. What happens, though, if she's really, really supposed to come up out of the hole but she's blocked by something you cling to?"

"It gets ripped out of my hands? Is that what you're saying?"

I flashed to an image of a three-year-old Neil locked in an epic struggle to retain possession of a grubby security blanket. "Yeah, but it's not your mom who's trying to take your blankie away to wash it — it's the Universe trying to wrestle away something that your soul is yearning to let go."

"Really? My soul wanted me to be treated like a pariah in an organization that I helped build from the ground up? My soul wanted Kelly to cheat on me not once, but three times? My soul wanted me to see my kids every other weekend and on national holidays? Is that what you're saying?"

"Keep going."

"Damn you, Mick."

"You're welcome."

"Yeah, I think that's what I'm saying."

"Why? Why does that make sense?"

"I'm not sure. Are you open to allowing the answer to come to you?"

"What?"

"Can you let your anger and pain drain away enough to silence your mind? Can you push your fear aside so it doesn't drown out the answer from your heart?" I gulped hard, not sure if the question was for Neil or for me.

"Doubtful."

"Well, at least you're honest."

"Honesty is one of my best qualities, you know."

"Yeah, I do know that, and you shouldn't drip your sarcasm all over it. The company changed, Neil, and you didn't change to stay in step."

"I couldn't."

"Exactly. But other people could. They moved right in sync with the new dance. But you stayed true to yourself."

"And now I'm out of work."

"Yes, thank God you're out of there. And thank God you're free of Kelly. And thank God you're now in a position to start a new life that will include more time with your kids."

"Okay, that's the problem. That right there is the problem. I know all of that intellectually, but something's still wrong. I can't even completely wrap my head around it, but I feel like I've let everyone down. I can't see an upside here."

"Even after what happened yesterday?"

"Yes, and I don't understand what the hell's wrong with me."

"Neil, do you feel like you didn't deserve that party? Like if people really knew you, they'd realize you failed them somehow?"

"Yes!"

"But at the same time you know that's not rational."

"Exactly."

"Have you always felt that way, even as a kid?"

"Yes, and it didn't come from my parents. There were supportive and thought I was too hard on myself."

"Damn. There's something there to throw off your back. You might want to ask to be released from it."

"Uh, who would I be asking?"

"Well, since you don't have a religious preference, why don't you try the Universe?"

"Seriously?"

"Yeah. It'll work. Just ask to be released from that feeling of letting people down. It's not rational and it's jamming you up. Keep asking and be open to what happens in response."

"You mean pray? I have no idea how to do that."

"Uh…"

"Do you recall what Mr. Emerson recommended?"

"Uh, yeah, he said the little needle always knows the North, and you should let it be your guide."

"So, perhaps you might like to remind your friend of that guidance. I don't believe he embraced it the other day. And, there are no rules, you know. The approach he undertakes in good faith is inconsequential to the result."

"All paths lead to God. Andy told me that."

"Ah, very good. Yes. All paths lead to God and your friend is waiting for your instruction."

"Okay, thanks, Mick."

"You can follow your own compass, Neil. Do what feels right to you. Use your own words and ask for what you think you need. And don't forget to say thanks for things you appreciate. I, um, started by talking to the clouds, if that helps."

"The clouds? And they answered?"

"Well, yeah. And the answers they sent came in all kinds of amazing packages."

"Interesting. And you do this often?"

"Sure, all the time. I have a few things holding me back, too, in case you hadn't noticed."

"Well, maybe we'll both figure a few things out at Antietam."

"Uh-huh. But remember — be open for anything, even just a nice day spent outdoors."

"Okay, I'll try."

"Neil, I'm really tired. Are you going to sleep tonight? If you planning on it, I hate to break it to you but you're running out of night."

"I'm crashing fast. I guess we do need to hang up."

"Okay, but before you fall asleep, make yourself ask. It doesn't have to be anything elaborate — just put it out there."

"Okay."

"And, Neil?"

"Yeah."

"You might as well accept the fact that you deserve to be outrageously happy."

CHAPTER 25

LONGING FOR HOME: OF DEER, GRIEF, AND RESEARCH AT THE WITCHING HOUR

Once Neil hung up, I turned out the light, snuggled down into the covers, and imagined I could go back to sleep. After tossing around for twenty minutes getting no closer to unconsciousness, I flipped the light back on, threw off the blankets, and sat up at the edge of the bed. I was thirsty. Maybe hungry, too, but definitely thirsty. I slid into my slippers and quietly padded downstairs to the kitchen for a glass of water. As I filled my glass at the sink, I noticed soft moonlight through the window in front of me. The moon wasn't bright enough to cast shadows on the lawn, but the light it threw was sufficient to create an ethereal glow across the entire backyard. I felt strangely drawn by the moonlight. Maybe it was time to follow my own advice.

I carried my water through the office and gently pulled open the French door to the deck. The slightest whisper of a breeze slipped through the screen and moved my hair. A jet hummed from somewhere far off in the distance. I searched the sky and made out a dim contrail chasing a pair of blinking lights. *A red-eye flight — how many of those had I endured over the years with a migraine building behind my eyes?* The jet noise faded away, allowing my attention to shift to the background music of the night insects — a light chorus so ubiquitous at this time of year that I sometimes forgot to hear it. I slid open the screen and stepped out onto the deck. The three-quarter moon was low on the horizon and seemed to be particularly large this morning. *Is it rising or setting?* I wasn't sure, as I hadn't been paying attention to its comings and goings lately. I settled into a side chair, holding my water glass in both hands. With my eyes closed, I imagined the moonlight soaking into my skin and infusing the water I held. For ten minutes or more, I sat inviting the moon's soft energy to fill me up and then opened my eyes. I drank my water while visualizing the moon pulling on the water in the cells of my body exactly as it pulled on the waters of the oceans. High tide and low tide, high tide and low tide, emotions up, emotions down, emotions up, emotions down. Always making life interesting.

I put the empty glass down, dropped my hands to my lap, and gazed at the moon, letting my eyes go softly out of focus. The spectral moonlight took on a bluish tint and became an indigo haze that filled the yard and my consciousness. I closed my eyes again and imagined myself becoming the blue light. The tides of my emotions gently relaxed into a tranquil still pond — a luminous indigo point of stillness. I saw myself standing by the pond, gazing out across its surface.

"Please release me from the grief I carry that I cannot understand. Please release me." The indigo pond softly swirled and rose, gathering into a blue mist. "Please release me. I open my heart to your guidance."

The gentle face of a doe appeared through the mist. She stepped forward, revealing a strong body on impossibly slender legs. The doe looked into my eyes and dipped her head. The mist lifted a few feet from the ground, revealing a narrow path that swept away from the deer to disappear into the darkness. Without breaking her gaze, the deer dipped her head toward the path. The mist parted and the doe turned away from me. She looked back to meet my eyes one last time and then stepped onto the path. The mist gently swirled into a three-quarter moon that glowed brightly, silhouetting the deer, who stepped silently and confidently away from me down the path. The moon dipped below the horizon and the deer disappeared into the darkness.

"Trust your intuition. You'll recognize the path."

"Thank you, Mick."

"Always. I'm always here."

I opened my eyes again. The moon had set below the horizon and the night was now enjoying its darkest moment. I was back in my body — back on my deck. A mosquito buzzed my left ear, singing soprano, as the katydids crooned back up. I waved the diva away and went back into the office to search the desk for a flashlight. I intended to scour the yard for signs of the deer, but as soon as I sat down to open the desk drawer, I felt compelled to turn on my computer monitor and open a search engine. I typed in the name of my great-great-granduncle from Ohio, who I knew from family lore had fought in the Civil War with his older brother. I let my right little finger linger in anticipation for just a moment and then stretched it over to hit "Enter". The very first result to pop up included a link to an Antietam battlefield database. *Whoa.* I clicked the link. Without any fanfare, the portrait of a young bearded man in a Union officer's uniform popped onto my screen. The brief biography under my uncle's portrait indicated that he and his brother helped raise a company of the 36th Ohio Volunteer Infantry Regiment, which fought at Antietam. A chill rushed through me. My uncles were at Antietam and I had identified their unit. With a little more research, I might even be able to walk in their footsteps. *How cool is that?*

Not ready to go back to bed when I was on a roll, I searched the database for George Crook, who Neil had said was also at Antietam. The face of another bearded man appeared on my monitor. I studied this new face and felt a slight hit of recognition, so scrolled down to read his service record. Just as Neil had said, George Crook had commanded a brigade that was temporarily attached to the 9th Corps at Antietam, but there was additional detail here. Crook's Brigade consisted of a company of cavalry from Chicago, an artillery battery from Kentucky, and three Ohio infantry regiments — the 11th, the 28th, and the 36th. If I had been standing, I probably would have passed out and put a lump above my other eye. George Crook hadn't commanded just any old brigade in 9th Corps, he'd led the one that included my uncles' regiment. As the significance of my discovery sank in, I felt my hair move as if someone had lightly stroked my head. I suddenly sensed someone behind me and spun to look over my shoulder, but the room, of course, was empty. "This is why it's always good to be asleep during the witching hour," I commented to the room. "But, I'm going to accept that as confirmation that I'm on the right track."

I turned back to George Crook's picture and realized how young he looked. His birth year was given, so I did the math in my head — thirty-four years old and he was a colonel leading thousands of men in battle. *Had Crook's men loved him as much as Neil's team loved him? Was there a young family waiting for him back home? An impatient wife complaining bitterly about his career?* I was just about to imagine a harping letter from home for poor George when I noticed beneath his portrait a little link to his battle report. I pulled my nose out of Colonel Crook's personal life and clicked the link. On the page that opened were two reports, the first for a battle that occurred on September 14, 1862, at someplace called South Mountain and the second for the battle of Antietam three days later. Neil hadn't mentioned a place called South Mountain and from the brief, disjointed descriptions in Crook's reports, I couldn't see how the two battles fit together.

I left the Antietam database, did an Internet search on the Battle of South Mountain, and clicked on the first link to appear. The page that popped into view started with a short summary of a day-long battle for four mountain passes just east of Sharpsburg.

 I felt the heavy rope drop onto my shoulder and heard the crash of thunder in the distance.

The Union Army pushed hard through the passes defended by Confederate troops in an attempt to attack and overwhelm Lee's Army, which McClellan knew was spread out over the countryside west of South Mountain.

 I leaned against the weight on my shoulder and drove forward into the storm.

McClellan's Army of the Potomac eventually prevailed, but the Battle of South Mountain had become prolonged, keeping the roads west of the mountain open long enough to allow the Rebel troops to fall back toward Sharpsburg. In spite of the victory, McClellan became uncertain and wary. Progress west slowed to a crawl.

 I pushed the rope off my shoulder.

By the time the Union army was ready to fight again on September 17, Stonewall Jackson had successfully taken the garrison at Harpers Ferry and had arrived in Sharpsburg, where Lee was massing his army in a strong defensive position.

I turned off the monitor and rubbed my eyes. Knowing Neil, if he'd been present for the approach on South Mountain, he would have been desperately frustrated with the pace. And, if he'd been aware that Lee's Army was scattered and vulnerable, his sense of urgency would have been through the roof. My friend would have seen the opportunity to get the job done and get home — and he would have felt that opportunity slipping away. The rope dream had fallen neatly into place.

I rubbed my eyes again, straightened from my chair, and walked back to the French doors. The faint light of approaching dawn was softening the darkness now, painting the sky an impossibly deep blue. I glanced at the clock — 5:37 a.m. The sun would rise in about an hour. Hopefully, Neil was asleep now and would miss the pinking of the clouds in the east. I'd have to wait to tell him what I suspected — that a few lifetimes back he'd been George Crook, who led my uncles into battle at South Mountain and Antietam. I pulled open the door and stepped out onto the deck. From far off in the distance came the clatter of crows.

CHAPTER 26

ROAD TRIP: A ZOO OF GENERALS

Bright and early on Monday morning, Neil pulled up my driveway. I was sitting on the front porch in the pre-dawn darkness waiting for him with my travel mug of coffee and a cheese sandwich wrapped in a paper towel. As instructed on Sunday night, I had my overnight bag packed and at my feet just in case our day trip stretched into a longer adventure. Before Neil could turn off his headlights, I'd grabbed my bag and was down the porch steps, headed toward his idling SUV. I'd been on enough business trips with Neil to have the protocol down — if you dawdled long enough for him to turn off the lights, you'd be buying coffee for everyone. If Neil had to come to the door and fetch you, you'd be buying lunch. As much as I didn't mind buying lunch, I hated to lose and was always ready on the porch regardless of the weather.

Halfway down the sidewalk, I heard the cargo latch on the SUV release. I went to the rear of the vehicle, set my bag in the cargo area next to Neil's and slammed the hatch closed. Neil was grinning as I slid into the passenger seat. "I always did like traveling with you. Do you have your sandwich?".

"Yep, right here."

"Excellent," Neil said over his shoulder as he backed out of my driveway. "Unless we hit early traffic around Frederick, it should be smooth sailing all the way to Antietam. We'll probably see the sun rise over the battlefield."

"Cool."

I put my mug in the cup holder and unwrapped my breakfast, spreading the paper towel across my lap to avoid scattering crumbs over Neil's interior. I bit off the corner and chewed. I'd learned early on to bring a sandwich if I wanted to eat before lunch.

"I always feel like there are eyes watching me out here," Neil said as he navigated the narrow lane out to the main road.

"That's because there are. Slow down. See the deer?"

Neil braked as his headlights reflected off three pairs of eyes staring from the side of the lane not fifty yards ahead of us. As he approached them at a creep, the deer decided to saunter across the lane and stop in front of the SUV.

"Try parking lights," I suggested. "I think you have them blinded."

Neil dimmed his lights and the deer moved on, disappearing into the scrubby woods on the other side of the lane. "Have you ever considered moving someplace a little more civilized?" Neil asked as he eased on the gas and started up again.

"No, never. Especially since I don't do the commute anymore." I considered for a split-second sharing my recent vision of the deer with Neil but decided to keep it quiet. Although we'd been friends for years and shared almost everything, the experience felt too deeply personal to speak out loud.

"Speaking of the commute, are you still aimlessly riding the Metro?"

"Not as much. Maybe once or twice a week. I'm able to meditate other places now, although a Metro train will probably always be my favorite spot."

"You know, some people would consider that a little weird."

"Yeah, but not everyone. Right?"

Neil laughed. "No, not everyone. Especially not those of us who benefit from it."

"What do you mean?"

"I mean you give damn good advice. You see life from a unique perspective that probably comes from riding around on the Metro with your head cracked open to the cosmos. You're an enigma to people like Steve who know your value but struggle to classify you or figure out what motivates you. It would blow his mind if he realized you were guided by visions and voices and vultures who visit you in art galleries."

"Well, that's only been recently, but you followed my advice, didn't you? You asked."

Neil looked over at me with smiling eyes. "Damn straight I asked. I asked to be released from feeling like I let people down as soon as we hung up Saturday morning and then I fell asleep — precisely as instructed. And it felt great. Not that I got an answer, but it was a weight off my chest just to say it out loud. I asked again on Sunday and again this morning. I listened but I didn't hear anything. And then I realized this morning that I didn't hear anything! Nothing at all, as in my brain wasn't jabbering on about the issue."

"Neil, that's great — that's really great. Is this what you wanted to tell me last night? I realized after we'd hung up that I'd kind of hogged the conversation and you probably had more on your mind than what time I needed to be ready this morning."

"Yeah, but that's okay. We got the logistics for the trip mapped out and you were so excited about South Mountain and that dream finally making sense that I didn't want to change the subject. Actually, the news about South Mountain really blew me away, too."

"But you're still not sure about the 36th Ohio Infantry and George Crook?"

"No, I'm not. I mean, it's one thing to suspend disbelief and entertain the idea that I fought in the Civil War, but identifying as someone specific who had a name and lived a whole separate life is something else. I guess I'm just not there. I know something happened in the portrait gallery that I can't explain, but it's like, well…it's like…"

"Like you can't sit in your living room in broad daylight and rationalize an explanation?"

"Yes! I need the experience. I need to experience Antietam — I feel like I'm being drawn there with you but that all of this is a package that's being unwrapped bit by bit so I don't get overwhelmed. You know what I mean?"

"Yes. You feel like things will come to you according to your ability to handle them."

"Exactly."

"Okay."

"But the seed is planted, and I think that's good."

I went back to my sandwich, taking bites of thick wheat bread and slightly tangy mozzarella. I'd been frustrated yesterday when Neil hadn't shown more interest in my ancestors' infantry regiment, and now he'd made it clear that he wasn't going to entertain a past-life connection with George Crook. While I was excited that the connection seemed to make everything feel more specific and purposeful, Neil was hesitant and seemed more comfortable keeping things abstract. Hesitant and abstract weren't exactly what I'd envisioned for the day. I chewed and swallowed.

We were on I-270 now, headed north to I-70. Even this early, there was traffic on this six-lane super-highway out of the Maryland burbs, but we were cruising right along in the center lane. Our headlights picked up the dashed white lane line and I settled my focus there. Dash, dash, dash, dash, dash, dash, dash...I imagined the white dashes peeling off the road one by one and rolling up into pure white birds that were illuminated by the headlights for just an instant as they left the roadway and disappeared into the dark sky. I tried to get all of them to look like doves, but each was different — a dove, a heron, an egret, a snowy owl, a swan, an osprey, an ibis, a pelican, a kite, a snow goose, a stork, a seagull, a cockatiel, a gyrfalcon. One by one they peeled from the highway and took flight. And each one, I noticed, approached flight in a different manner. Dash, dash, dash...a barnyard chicken rolled off the highway and ran alongside the SUV for a few hundred feet. It stared in the side window at me with indignant eyes and its beak open in a squawk, keeping pace at seventy miles per hour before spinning off toward the shoulder.

"Each approaching flight a little differently and not all getting off the ground."

"That's true, Mick. I don't always appreciate that."

"But you're experiencing it now as your friends find their truths, aren't you?"

"Yes."

"Remember the ancestors you recently visited — all those who found their wings and flew high enough to have their portrait in a national gallery. Each flight unique and none perfectly successful, but all fueled by individual passion."

"I've been thinking about them, Mick. It seems they were so sure of who they were. They expressed their passions and they were remembered for it. How does that happen?"

"Ah, I think the better question is how does that not happen? How do things so often go off track?"

"We get in our own way a lot, don't we?" I blushed, remembering Neil pointing out my own tendency to block myself from flight. Mick continued on as if he hadn't noticed my embarrassment.

"Yes. People craft boxes of fear and limitation and stuff themselves inside. Worse, they pull others in with them."

"Ahh, Nathaniel Hawthorne?"

"Yes, he did have a tendency to use fear and shame to champion a code of conduct not appropriate for everyone. He likely meant well, but others don't. Rules are so often made in attempts to control others and shift power, you know. Those rules have a way of squelching expressions of passion."

"What is passion, then, that we've created codes of conduct to snuff it out?"

"It's nothing more than a way of being that allows you to be in the moment without editing yourself. A way of living that leads to happiness. Some get confused and judgmental, though, about what that should mean for others. Just because the bird is white, doesn't mean it has to be a dove, you know."

Dash, dash, dash, dash, dash, dash.

"Doesn't that make you carsick?" asked Neil.

"What?"

"Staring at the lane marker. I'd be puking in my lap if I did that."

"Oh, I'd never puke in my lap. If I couldn't get the window open in time, I'd sacrifice your floor mat."

"Umm, good to know."

"Where are we?"

"Almost to Frederick. We're actually driving through the middle of Monocacy National Battlefield right now."

"Really?"

"Yeah. Outnumbered Union troops made a stand here in 1864 against fifteen thousand Confederate troops who were attempting to push east to take DC."

"How did that turn out?"

"It was a Confederate victory in that the federal troops eventually fled to Baltimore, but the Rebels were delayed long enough for the Union to get reinforcements to DC. Monocacy was the battle that saved Washington."

"Interesting. You're really getting into the Civil War stuff, aren't you?"

"Oh, yes, I've done my homework, but..." Neil paused and chewed his lower lip, apparently trying to decide if he wanted to share something with me. "But, I'm, uh, not learning all this for the first time. It's strange. It's like I already knew and I'm, uh, just waking up to the memory." I opened my mouth to comment but Neil cut me off. "Are you ready to hear what I found out about the generals?"

"Sure."

"Excellent, because I think they might be more than just breadcrumbs leading us to Antietam. They also seem to have a story to tell about passion and measures of success."

I immediately sat up straight, ready to soak up everything Neil had to share. Neil laughed. "Yeah, I thought you might be interested. I can't guarantee this will be as engaging as your donkey story, but here goes. First off, three of our Union general friends — and I use "friends" loosely — McClellan, Burnside, and Hooker, held the position of commander of the Army of the Potomac. One after the other, they each struggled in the position and ultimately failed."

A light went on as I remembered from the gallery that McClellan had been removed from his command after Antietam. "If all three failed, it must have been a difficult position to nail," I suggested.

"You could say that. In my mind, it required opposing skill sets. The commander of that army needed to be a skilled administrator with masterful strategic and communications skills plus had to have the heart of a warrior."

"Earth, Air, and Fire."

"Huh?"

"Those are Earth, Air, and Fire energies. Earth energies make for a good, grounded administrator, who can organize and use resources well, but who also might be risk-adverse or tend toward getting stuck in a groove. Air is all intellect and communication with little use for intuition and feelings. Fire is action and passion — it drives the warrior, but can make him planning-adverse and ungrounded."

Neil glanced at me with his eyebrows raised.

"I'm sorry, I didn't mean to interrupt your story," I said.

"Oh, no, you're fine. Where did that come from? Did you come up with it?"

"No, it's not mine. I learned about the importance of the four elements from a spiritual perspective at the American Indian museum downtown this summer. The elements are used in cosmology — how the tribes describe the Universe and their place in it. But, I put a little astrological spin on things for you."

Neil's eyebrows went back up. "Astrology, huh?"

"Yeah, I've just started poking around a little bit with it. The four elements are used in astrology to describe different cosmic energies that impact us and also help define our personalities."

"Fascinating. It's kind of a sweet classification system. I like it. But where's the water?"

"Uh, Water is the emotions, deep, dark emotions and flowy light emotions. And, Spirit can be considered a separate element or you can think of it as being woven through the other four. I like to think of it as being woven through everything."

"Spirit, huh? Interesting. All the tribes believe that?"

"Well, not exactly. I kind of borrowed and put my own slant on things, but the elements and the four cardinal directions are used by a lot of tribes to describe the Universe, especially the unseen energies. I really like that way of thinking because it breaks the Universe down so our small minds can understand it. Animals are really important, too — both the behaviors of the animals we know on Earth and the energies that the Spirit Animals bring to us. That really speaks to me, too."

"Oh. So, you think the animals in the rope dream are what? Spirit Animals?"

"Yes."

"Like mascots?"

"No, like guides. They seem to be bringing powerful energies to us — giving us guidance to stay on track or pushing us onto new tracks."

"Huh. Interesting. I have Wolf energy around me? Huh. I like that. Anything else you want to insert?"

"No, that's about it."

"Okay, then. Interesting. Back to the generals?" Neil shot me a curious glance.

I grinned back, probably looking like the lunatic he now suspected I was. "Yeah, back to the generals."

"So, McClellan, Burnside, and Hooker each held the job of commander of the Army of the Potomac, a job that required strong Earth, Fire, and Air energies." Neil shot me a thumbs-up without looking over. "The first of our heroes to come up to the plate for a shot at the position was George B. McClellan, a skilled engineer with, uh, masterful Earth energy, I'm gonna say suspect Air energy, and, alas, not as much Fire as his boss, Abe Lincoln, desired in a commander. Our hero, George, had mad organizational skills and knew how to train his troops, but lacked the warrior's fiery heart. His Earthy propensity caused him to be most comfortable dealing in certainties and to be rather adverse to risk." Neil glanced over and gave me a wink. "That might have extended to his personal safety, too. I stumbled upon a collection of critical comments concerning how far he stayed from the battlefield at Antietam, even though he couldn't see the action well. He also kept thirty thousand reserves between himself and the fighting at Bloody Lane. Very Earthy, wouldn't you say?"

"Yes, very Earthy. How was his Air energy suspect?"

"You said Air was intellect and communication, right?"

"That's right."

"Well, intellectually our man, George, was brilliant — a boy genius — and strategically not bad, but his communication skills just were not honed. He shared his plans with few and was a bit of a sneak. George also struggled at times with his independent streak — being unable to submit to Lincoln's oversight and, perhaps, not approaching his job with pure intent."

"A hidden agenda, you say?"

"Hidden? Ha! General McClellan might have hidden his strategic plans but he kept his personal agenda on the table for all to see — he supported a limited war and a negotiated peace that would have allowed the Confederate states to leave the Union. And he had his eye on a political prize — the Presidency. After McClellan left the army, but while the war was still raging, he ran against Lincoln on a negotiated peace platform. Lincoln was re-elected, obviously."

"Uh, that's a pretty serious conflict of interest. Sounds like some deep, dark, murky Water running through McClellan's veins. Why did Lincoln have him commanding the army if he knew all that?"

"He needed McClellan's mad organizational skills, of course. The huge volunteer army that had been raised was suffering from lack of organization and training. I mean, you're talking thousands of farmers, clerks, shoemakers, carpenters, laborers, farmers — did I mention farmers? — all thrown together and given muskets. There weren't nearly enough experienced officers to train and lead them and the regimental officers up to the rank of colonel were elected by the men from the ranks. Lincoln had a big issue there and he needed to tap the talent he had available. Everyone was learning on the job and I'm sure

Lincoln hoped that he could take advantage of McClellan's strengths and then compel him forward to engage and pursue the enemy. But, he couldn't. So, McClellan ended up failing in Lincoln's eyes due to insufficient Fire, compounded by what you've identified as a serious case of deep, murky Water."

"Do you think McClellan lived his passion as commander?"

"I think he might have."

"You do?"

"Yes, because I think above all else he wanted to be his own man — to be in charge of something on a grand scale on his own terms. And that he was, if only for a short time."

"But McClellan had his eye on something much grander."

"Absolutely. And if he'd won the war for Lincoln, he might have been elected President at some point, but, again, McClellan's success needed to be on his own terms, so he was probably destined to drive Lincoln to remove him from command. Little Mac did end up a successful politician, though — he was the governor of New Jersey after the war."

"Interesting."

"Yes. And you know what's weird? In spite of my ingrained and irrational hate for George McClellan, I find something insanely appealing about his attitude. Why the hell mute yourself so you fit into someone else's system? Why bend yourself to someone else's will so they can exploit the skills they have a use for while attempting to manage the rest of your personality away. I know that's simplified and I'm pretty sure the man was an asshole, but there's something there I connect with. Ready to move on to Burnside?"

My head was spinning but I wasn't going to object. "Um, sure. Burnside was next up?"

"Yes, he certainly was. Ambrose Burnside, the man with the whiskers, was forced to take command after his dear friend, George, was removed for not pursuing Lee's army out of Sharpsburg."

"Forced?"

"Yep, Ambrose Burnside was ten degrees beyond reluctant to take command from McClellan. He tried to refuse, and being a consistent man, had turned the promotion down twice previously. He knew he wasn't qualified. In the end, he was ordered to take the command and was motivated to do so by the threat of it otherwise going to Joseph Hooker, whom he despised."

"Ouch."

"Yeah, a lot of these generals were close friends from way back, but just as many seemed not to be able to get along. Lots of strong personalities stewed up into an HR nightmare, I take it, but back to Ambrose Burnside — he was an interesting character. A likable sort who struggled to find a place for himself in the world. Flowed from one thing to another like a meandering stream." Neil winked at me. "George McClellan was a good friend to Ambrose, though, and helped him move up the ranks. Although I'm not positive that was helpful in the long run."

"Ahh. So, what did our friend, Ambrose, bring to the plate?"

"Well, he was emotional and exceedingly modest — not at all confident, so must have brought Water with little Fire to offset his flow. I'd say Burnside was also an Earthy chap, but maybe not in a good way. He wasn't a good administrator and quickly undid all the organizational good McClellan had done. And, once he got something in his head, everyone needed to hold on for the ride because he wasn't going to let it go even if conditions changed and it became a really, really bad idea. If we hold Burnside up to the job requirements, we'd have to admit that he knew best and wasn't qualified."

"Why did Lincoln promote him then? Especially since the man clearly didn't want the job?"

"Well, Burnside had enjoyed some success. Early in the war, he'd led a very successful coastal campaign in North Carolina — he was one of very few Union generals in the East who could claim a victory. And, Burnside was in a good position to step into McClellan's shoes. He commanded two corps under McClellan, the 1st and the 9th, and it was probably reasonable to think he could step up and oversee the rest, too. Interestingly, though, McClellan had demoted Burnside right before Antietam and took leadership of the 1st Corps away from him. Burnside ended up at the south end of the battlefield with command of just the 9th, while Joseph Hooker was at the north end with the 1st."

"That sounds like a bit of corporate maneuvering."

"Well, it might have been some sort of maneuvering, but General Jesse Reno, who had been the commander of the 9th Corps, was killed at South Mountain and the change of roles might have had more to do with that. I don't know a lot about Reno, except that he was a warrior with a lot of experience. He intrigues me, though, and I want to understand what made him tick. I suspect he was the perfect subordinate for Burnside, too — brought qualities to the table that his commander didn't possess. We'll…uh…do you have any more questions about Burnside?"

"Yeah, what happened to him? How did things go with him in command?"

"Badly. Things went badly. Burnside got one chance in command at the Battle of Fredericksburg in December — three months after Antietam. His Earth energy hurt him when the frontal assault he ordered against a strong Rebel line behind a stone wall failed. Instead of listening to his generals and trying something else, Burnside stuck with his plan, stubbornly throwing regiment after regiment against the wall. After the battle, his Water kicked in. His subordinate officers, including Hooker, complained bitterly about Burnside's leadership. He did not take the personal attack well and asked Lincoln to remove all the complainers. Instead, Lincoln removed Burnside and the command went to Hooker, while Burnside was sent to Ohio in a non-combat role."

The image of a spotted salmon swimming doggedly upstream in spite of the odds slipped through my consciousness so clearly that I could almost hear the rush of water and feel the dampness in the air. I blinked and the image was gone. "Well, I feel kind of bad for Ambrose Burnside. It seems like he was self-aware and Lincoln should have respected his refusal."

Neil pursed his lips and shook his head. "No, you shouldn't feel bad for Burnside. He cost thousands of men their lives at Fredericksburg. And he was involved in another debacle later in the war that cost thousands more. The same single-minded determination and inability to change direction as things fell apart were at play there, too. Some historians suggest that his assault on the bridge at Antietam showed the same inflexible tendencies and was micromanaged by McClellan, maybe for good reason. There seems to be a big lesson there. Something along the lines of not every big challenge we come upon is for us to embrace — opportunities are sometimes tests to see if we can be true to ourselves and walk away. Something like that."

"Interesting. And not something you hear too often. Quitters get a pretty bad rap."

"True, and especially during the Civil War. Deserters were shot or hanged on both sides of the conflict."

"Really?"

"Yep."

I immediately flashed to Carla running along that dark, dirt road. "Oh."

"Alright, on that happy note, we have next up at the plate Joseph Hooker — the fiery enigma of this group. In complete contrast to Burnside, he had huge confidence in his abilities and was uniformly described as an exceedingly brave, if somewhat flamboyant, field commander."

"Flamboyant, huh? You know that makes me imagine him riding a zebra into battle wearing a neon jumpsuit and a crown of peacock feathers, don't you?"

Neil rolled his eyes, but didn't miss a beat. "He rode a white horse and maybe flamboyant isn't the right word, but Hooker didn't mind an audience. He seems to have been quite aware of himself, shall we say, but he was also good to his troops, really took care of them, and it seems they had confidence in him. He did have a bit of baggage, though, of which Pamela might not have approved — his headquarters were described as a combo barroom and brothel. And he freely ran his mouth about his superiors, including Lincoln."

"Never a good idea."

"Nope, not if you have career aspirations, which Hooker certainly did. He was vocal about his desire to command the Army of the Potomac and even suggested that he might make a good dictator for the country. And, when he finally got his chance to lead the Army of the Potomac, he was so openly brash and overconfident that he had himself set up for a limited run if he didn't deliver immediately."

"Nothing like putting undue pressure on yourself."

"No, nothing like it. Now, in terms of organization, Hooker apparently did an amazing job but came at things from a more emotional perspective. He wasn't an engineer like McClellan, so didn't see the army as a machine to fix. He was, instead, very invested in getting morale up and getting his men emotionally ready to fight."

"Fire and Water? In the same package?"

"Uh, sure, I think that might describe him."

"Without much Earth or Air?"

"Hmm, yeah, I'll go along with that. You could say Hooker lived his Fire on the battlefield as a corps commander. He was right out there on the front lines moving troops around in the heat of battle at Antietam. Descriptions of Hooker in battle convey absolute confidence and an ability to live in the moment." Neil shot me a quick glance. "That's, uh, something I crave, you know…that, uh, experience." I opened my mouth to respond, but Neil had moved on. "In the one battle Joseph Hooker led as commander of the Army of the Potomac, though, he was indecisive and confused."

"His Water?"

Neil laughed. "Maybe, but more likely his Fire. He had his bell rung by a shell that hit a pillar he was leaning on but refused to relinquish command even though he was flat out. That was the Battle of Chancellorsville. Lee and Jackson tore Hooker's army to pieces there — it was their greatest victory of the entire war."

"And that was it for Hooker?"

"It was. He wasn't immediately removed but a short time later got into a big row with Army Headquarters in DC about something unrelated. In the heat of the moment, he offered to resign. Lincoln took him up on the offer and sent him down to Tennessee where he had some success but was passed over for promotion, so quit. He ended up behind a desk."

"That's a sad ending."

"Well, I wouldn't cry for Hooker. He got hot-headed and offered to resign and then didn't get the promotion he wanted and quit. Strong passion and strong emotion in the same package seem to be difficult to manage."

"Ahhhhh, he made steam. And it disappeared into the atmosphere." I waved my hand in front of me to scatter Hooker's residue to the winds.

Neil smiled and shook his head at my antics. "Well, that's one way of looking at it."

"Are you going to count him as a success?"

"Um, I'll give him a partial success in that he took care of his troops. He and McClellan were similar in that regard. They both prepared an army, but didn't use it to quickly end the war, which is what Lincoln wanted. Of course, they were up against Lee, Jackson, and a group of other talented Confederate generals, so the task wasn't easy."

"Jackson! Did you find out anything about him? The vulture, uh, pointed Stonewall Jackson out specifically."

"Oh, yeah, Jackson. Definitely. He was an interesting guy. A strange bird with a somewhat magical ability on a field of battle. Jackson could move men and artillery around on the fly as conditions changed during battle, and he wasn't afraid to try the unexpected or untested tactic, even if it flew in the face of convention. He had an elevated sense of duty, too, so his agenda was Lee's agenda and Lee was able to trust Jackson with vague orders. That sense of duty combined with Jackson's intelligence made him highly valuable as a commander because he could be trusted to work without micromanagement."

"You think Jackson rocked his Air energy, then?"

Neil shook his head at me. "Um, sure, he definitely used his intellect, but he wasn't the best communicator in some ways. I found a treasure trove of eloquent quotes attributed to Jackson that suggested a man who could express heady, almost mystical, concepts in plain English, but he was also painfully shy. Struggled with public speaking. And, wouldn't take his subordinates into his confidence even when it came to battle plans. Created a lot of confusion and frustration in his generals."

"I'm guessing he probably wasn't too well liked."

"I'm guessing you're right. I don't believe Jackson let his Water flow too freely." Neil laughed. "Or his Fire. He was buttoned-up and rigid — didn't drink, didn't gamble, was staunchly religious. Liked to follow all the rules and have those who reported to him follow all the rules, too."

"Well, now he's just waving his Earth flag."

"Waving it like a fiend, I'd say, and now that you mention it, a heavy dose of earthiness was probably what helped Jackson stay contained and controlled in battle. He gave outcomes over to God and tried to do his job. And stayed acutely focused on that job. Didn't get confused trying to work a second agenda."

"Oh! Do you think Jackson was able to live in the moment without editing himself?"

"Yeah, sure, that's a good way to say it. And I think he was able to grow into his role — he got better and better at tactical leadership as the war went on."

"Jackson lived with passion and rode his donkey!"

"Hmm." Neil glanced over at me. "Sure. Yes. From what I know, if you look at just that little snapshot of his life, I'd say he might have. He seemed to have been true to himself. Not perfect, not without limitations, and not without controversy, but true to himself."

I couldn't be completely sure, but thought I heard a hideous hiss of approval from somewhere across the dark landscape. "What about A. P. Hill? Did you find out anything about him?"

"Oh, hell, yes. Ambrose Powell Hill — pure Fire in a red battle shirt. Well, maybe not pure Fire. Probably had some of McClellan's deep Water going on, too." Neil grinned. "Independent and frequently at odds with people, especially people who outranked him, but inspirational to his men even when he drove them hard."

"Describe him in one word."

"Passionate."

I bobbed my head in understanding. Just as the vulture had suggested, A. P. Hill wasn't merely an exhausted face hanging in a portrait gallery. "Was Hill important at Antietam?"

A shine rose in Neil's eyes. "Important? Hill was the Confederate savior at Antietam! His division was left behind to secure the garrison at Harpers Ferry, but at the last minute Lee called for him. Hill brought his men north on a forced march to Sharpsburg while the battle was raging. Those guys did seventeen miles in eight hours on foot under dusty, hot, miserable conditions with little food or water. Hill drove his men north like cattle, even breaking his sword over the back of a lieutenant who tried to leave the march and hide behind a tree. Guys collapsed along the sides of the road and didn't get back up."

"Whoa."

"And Hill made it just in time. His division arrived in a cloud of dust at the south end of the battlefield just as the taste of victory had begun to tickle the buds of thousands of Union troops battling towards Sharpsburg and Lee's only route of retreat across the Potomac River. The Union boys crept tantalizingly close against a determined but collapsing defense and then…" Neil glanced over to make sure I was paying attention. "And then Hill's men rolled in and hit the Union troops from the side, sweeping them off the battlefield and back to the creek. And that was it."

"What do you mean that was it?"

"That was how the battle ended. There was no counterattack by the Union and there was no reengagement the next day. By the third day, Lee had moved his army back over the Potomac to safety in Virginia."

"Oh."

Neil looked back over at me. The shine had gone out of his eyes. "Yeah. There were over twenty-three thousand casualties at Antietam and it essentially ended in a draw. There might have been an opportunity there to end the war, but it didn't happen that way and we can't go back to refight the battle, can we?"

"No, I guess not."

"But, I think there's something here. Something that I'm supposed to learn from this group of men. From their strengths and weaknesses. Their successes and failures. I feel drawn to putting all of this together and getting it out there so it's of service to people. You know what I mean?"

"Sort of. But, not exactly. What's the "it" you're talking about?"

"Well, I might as well say it out loud. Leadership training with my own unique spin on it. Feels like it's time to stop espousing and implementing other peoples' systems. I'm bored with that. And, a future of continuing to stuff my best ideas so I can work within someone else's box looks downright bleak."

I reeled back my immediate urge to whip out my pompoms and cheer Neil on, choosing instead a bit of massive understatement. "Cool. That sounds like good insight." Neil nodded almost imperceptibly as he gazed at the highway, deep in his own thoughts. I picked pieces off the cheese sandwich still on my lap and chewed them thoughtfully as I imagined the battlefield at Antietam. I saw again the rolling farm fields, the white church and burning buildings to the north, the men in the farm lane in the middle, the creek and bridge to the south. Soldiers were on the field engaged in horrifying combat and smoke filled the air again, but this time the action was frozen.

 I soar around on my hawk's wings and make a few additions to the scene. First, I place Stonewall Jackson as a huge golden eagle in the sky over the small, white church. He wheels around in the air, surveying the woods and fields of the northern battlefield with intense focus and resolve. Next, I place a beautiful white horse on the battlefield below the eagle. I set Joseph Hooker as a striped tiger in the saddle. Then I fly high up on a ridge to the southeast where I scrape rock and earth together with my talons to form a safe cave. I conjure George McClellan as a hungry bear. I put field glasses in his paws and tuck him in the cave. Before I leave, I place thirty thousand soldiers and a line of cannons in front of the cave to protect the bear. Finally, I soar to the south end of the valley and summon Ambrose Burnside as a sleek, spotted salmon with outrageous sideburns. I place him on a knoll overlooking the bridge. He flops and gasps in the sun as a knot of perplexed officers look down upon him.

I scream as the Hawk and the battlefield becomes animated. I fly to the north and find the Eagle, who circles the scene below for just a moment before swooping down to pick up a cluster of Confederate soldiers in his talons. The Eagle rises up in the air clutching the soldiers, soars to the edge of the woods near the church, and sets the men down. As the troops run into the woods with a Rebel yell, the Eagle flies up into the air again. The giant bird makes one circuit over the scene and then dives once more. This time he plucks cannons from behind the church and places them closer to the cornfield. The Eagle rises up again and screams. A tiny kestrel rushes to his side and he softly whispers a message in its ear. The kestrel dips its head in understanding and swoops south to Sharpsburg. I turn to follow the kestrel but am blown backwards in a tumble of feathers as an even larger golden eagle emerges from behind the town, dives down to the farm lane in the middle of the battlefield and sweeps up several thousand Confederate soldiers in its talons. It swings to its left, deposits the men behind the church, and then flies south to disappear again behind the town. The repositioned troops swarm around the church, through the woods, and into the cornfield. I see the Tiger on his white horse weaving amongst the opposing Union soldiers. He has raised his sword in a massive paw and is roaring orders and encouragement. The men around him are infected by the Tiger's brave passion and fire. They yell as one and surge forward against the Confederates swarming toward them. The Tiger wheels on his horse and roars again — revealing the tail of the Scorpion draped behind his saddle.

I soar to the southeast to check on the Bear and find him still in his cave. He's squinting through his field glasses with tiny eyes as he struggles to see the battlefield action from the safety of his lair. The Bear feels protective of the army he has created through hard work and his ability to organize men and resources, but he's not satisfied — he's still hungry. The Bear strains to see through the thick smoke and at the same time imagines himself riding on the back of his army to the White House where he shrugs the Bear's pelt. He squints through his glasses and they reflect back to him the image of a Griffin. The Bear spreads his illusory eagle's wings and shakes his tawny mane. He will master the Earth *and* the sky.

I fly to the south to find the Salmon. I see thousands of Union soldiers massing at the creek bank. They have already run across the bridge and have waded the creek. The Rebel soldiers are massed high on the hill above them, along the outskirts of Sharpsburg. It's late afternoon and the sun is dropping to a hard angle. The Union soldiers line up elbow to elbow and start running up the slope — into the sun and into the Confederate cannon fire that had been bombarding them all day. I see George Crook and the men of the 36th Ohio running up the hill with the thousands of others, but where is the Salmon? I swoop down and find him still on the knoll, still on the east side of the creek, flipping and flopping as the day drains away. The other officers are gone. They are across the creek now, leading the soldiers up the hillside. A cloud of dust rises at the south end of the slope. Thunder rumbles and the ground shakes. The men look to the south as A. P. Hill, reimagined as a glorious red Dragon, emerges from the dust and strafes the battlefield with his flaming breath.

I look up into the sky and the clouds roll aside to reveal the gargantuan face of Abraham Lincoln peering down on the battlefield, which is quiet now as the Confederate troops slip across the Potomac. Lincoln's eyes fill with both sadness and resolve. A huge ghostly hand reaches down through the clouds and into the cave of the Bear. The hand pulls the Bear out by the scruff and gives him a shake. The Bear's pelt falls away to reveal not a Griffin, but an Adder. The Adder twists and turns in Lincoln's hand, attempting to bite him, but its attempts are futile and it bites only the air. Lincoln tosses the Adder away. The hand of Lincoln then grabs the Salmon from the knoll, and tosses him upstream into the creek. The Salmon swims determinedly against the current until he gets to a dam. He throws himself forward over and over until he's dashed senseless against the face of the dam. Lincoln's hand comes down again, plucks the Salmon from the water, and tosses it into a small pond in Ohio.

Lincoln's attention next falls to the Tiger. He had watched the Tiger in battle and was well-pleased; however, Lincoln also had noticed the tail of the Scorpion draped lazily across the horse's haunches. Lincoln's giant hand parts the smoke and lifts the Tiger from his horse. He gives the cat a little shake and its barbed tail goes limp. With his other hand, Lincoln sweeps away the cave and fashions a coliseum from the ruins. He installs the Tiger in the coliseum and tells him to get ready to fight. The wings of a mama bird emerge from the Tiger's thick pelt. He builds his gladiators a nice nest and feeds them well, but at night he retires to the Scorpion's den and parties like it's 1999. In spite of the extracurriculars, the Tiger with the wings of the Robin and the tail of the Scorpion crafts an elegant battle plan. He marches from the coliseum to fight but is set upon by the Eagles. They tear him to pieces and he retreats into the night. The stars part and Lincoln's face appears in the midnight sky. The Tiger trembles and offers to quit. Lincoln's giant hand reaches down through the night sky, picks the Tiger up by the scruff, puts him back on his horse, and sends him to Tennessee.

"Hey, Neil, who commanded the Army of the Potomac after Hooker?"

"George Meade took over after Hooker. It was a few days before Gettysburg. He was credited with a win for the Union at Gettysburg, but let Lee retreat back to Virginia. Lincoln had something to say about that, of course. Why? Why are your eyes glassy? What are you up to? Oh, Lord, what kind of crazy scenario are you playing out in your head?"

"Well, since you asked — Lee and Jackson are magnificent golden eagles who command the sky and the winds. McClellan is a bear in a cave with the heart of an adder — he tries to bite Lincoln when Lincoln fishes him out of his cave but Lincoln's a little too quick for all that. Burnside is a salmon. He flops around on a knoll at Antietam and then dashes himself half to death against the dam that was Fredericksburg. Lincoln plucks him out of the stream and tosses him into a little pond in Ohio. Hooker is a tiger with the wings of a mama robin and the tail of the scorpion. He marches out of his coliseum and the eagles pounce on him. Oh, and A. P. Hill is a dragon who strafes the hillside below Sharpsburg."

Neil looked at me in wide-eyed amazement and then started laughing hysterically. The SUV swung back and forth between the lane markers as Neil fought to stifle his laughter. "Oh, my god, that's so freaking perfect. Oh, my god!" Neil choked out as he wiped his eyes.

"Dude, you need to watch the road or pull over and compose yourself. Get over in the right lane here — there's the sign for Alt-40. Are we past Frederick already? How long have we been on 70?"

"Long enough for you to fill a zoo with Civil War generals, that's how long," Neil said as he signaled and changed lanes. Neil exited the interstate and followed the long gradual ramp to the traffic signal. He turned left with the light onto Route 40 headed west.

"You mapped out the route?" Neil asked.

"Yeah, last night and you're gonna have to stay calm now. This road has a few curves. And it's dark."

Neil laughed and glanced over at me. "You're going to have to write that story down," he said. "There's something interesting there. And you need to write more, anyway."

"Okay."

"And just to round things out, George Meade's men called him a goggle-eyed snapping turtle. Apparently, he had buggy eyes and a bad temper. You might want to fix him a bed in your zoo."

We drove the next few miles in silence as the dark, rural landscape slowly filled with ranch houses and gas stations. Large housing developments and shopping centers slipped past next. A sign announcing Middletown appeared and disappeared as we rolled into the outskirts of a small town. The steady stream of headlights now coming at us suggested this was a bedroom community for people who commuted to Frederick and points east. I couldn't remember ever having been through here, but as we rolled into the downtown area a shock of familiarity hit me. "Some of these buildings — they were here at the time of the Civil War," I said and pointed out a massive white rectangular church with four solid columns in front to support a beautiful steeple, clearly not crafted of fiberglass. "That church there. That was a hospital."

Neil glanced across me to look at the imposing church. "You getting déjà vu here?"

"Yeah."

"I am, too."

"A lot of these houses. They were here," I said as I leaned forward and pointed out historical clapboard and brick houses, including some beautiful Victorian homes, that streamed by on both sides of the road.

"I think you're right."

We came out on the other side of town and I relaxed my shoulders, which I realized were hunched almost to my ears. I sank into my seat and imagined the tension in my body draining out my right big toe. Hopefully, Neil's floor mat wouldn't show the stain. I closed my eyes, suddenly aware of how early I'd gotten up. I could trust Neil to find Antietam from here — all he needed to do was head straight to Boonesboro and then take Route 34 to Sharpsburg. We probably would see the sun rise over the battlefield. *Sweet*. I settled in for a nice little doze and was just about to nod off when I heard Neil's turn signal and felt the SUV slow down. My eyes popped open just in time to catch Neil turning left onto a rural road lined on both sides with a disparate collection of houses.

"Neil, where are you going?"

"Hold on just a minute, you'll see."

As the houses gave way to barns and farm fields, I could just make out a low mountain to our right front. My eyes went wide as another wave of familiarity washed over me. Neil rolled up to a stop sign at a T-intersection. Our headlights picked up a road sign and I leaned forward to read it. "RENO MONUMENT RD," the sign shouted in all caps to make sure we'd noticed. Neil swung right and started up the narrow country road. "We're following in the footsteps of your ancestors," he said. "They walked this route on the way to South Mountain."

I was suddenly completely awake and could not possibly get my eyes open wide enough to take everything in. We seemed to be riding along a bottom with a steep slope to our right and flat land to the left. Alternating patches of field and woods were just visible covering the dim, colorless landscape. Not more than a quarter-mile up the road, Neil stopped where a side road angled to the right. "That's Fox's Gap Road, but look here to the left," he instructed as he pointed to the ridge just visible behind a freshly mown field. "That's South Mountain." I was too mesmerized to respond.

Neil pulled up to a narrow gravel lane at the end of the mowed field and put the SUV in park. He reached into the backseat and grabbed a thick, hard-cover book that bristled with bookmarks. "Look what I found this weekend," Neil said as he showed me the cover. "It's filled with maps that show regimental movements during the battles of South Mountain and Antietam." Neil turned on the SUV's map light, flipped the book open at one of the bookmarks, and showed me a map of the area where we now sat. "See, this is where we are now. This paved road we're on was called Old Sharpsburg Road at the time of the war — obviously, it wasn't paved back then. Now, see right here? See this lane on the map called Loop Road?"

"Yes."

"See the gravel access road right over there on our left?" Neil leaned back so I could see past him.

"Yeah."

"That's the remnant of Loop Road. It swung away in a big loop and then came back to meet Old Sharpsburg Road ahead of us at Fox's Gap. There were two brigades of three regiments each from Ohio involved in a morning battle for this gap. They took Loop Road from where we are now and headed for the Confederate flank. The early battle for the gap ended up taking place almost entirely within the area circumscribed by Loop Road. See the symbols here on the map? They indicate what type of vegetation covered the various portions of the battlefield. The area within the loop was mostly pasture with a few cornfields and it was all surrounded by woods."

"Oh, my god, Neil, that's the field in the rope dream."

"Wait, there's more." Neil flipped forward in the book a few pages and showed me an enlarged map of the area. "See here? This blue bar is the 36th Ohio. They marched along Loop Road for a half mile or so and then went through the field along this stone wall toward troops from North Carolina, who waited just below the gap. See this Confederate artillery battery? It was sitting right in the gap firing on the 36th and the other Union regiments."

"The thunder and lightning."

"Yes. We'll drive to the gap now where the most intense fighting occurred. Ready?" I nodded yes even though my heart was suddenly in my throat. Neil closed the book and handed it to me. He turned out the interior light, smiled over at me, and set off slowly up Old Sharpsburg Road. My eyes and mind bounced all over the place, attempting to find the familiar in the scenery, as we rolled past fields, a few houses, and then thick woods. We'd gone steadily uphill about a mile when a concrete enclosure with an iron gate appeared on our left in the half-light. The soil was built up inside the enclosure so that a lone obelisk could be seen over the concrete wall. Neil passed the monument and pulled into a small gravel parking lot on the same side of the road. He turned off the engine and looked over at me.

"And this is it. Your ancestors were here," Neil said.

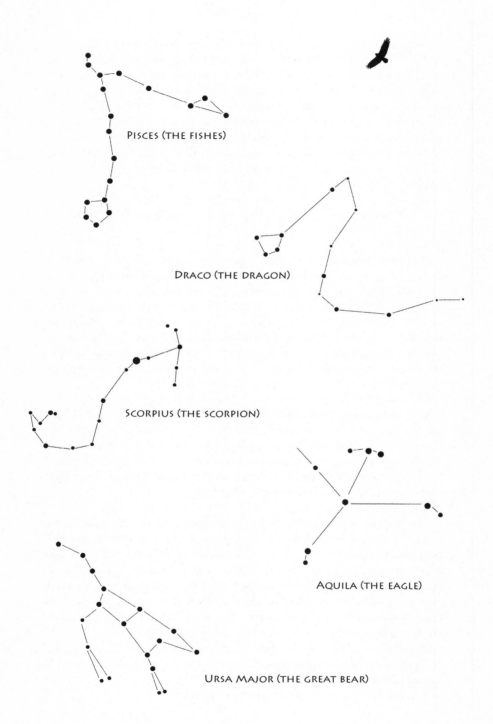

PISCES (THE FISHES)

DRACO (THE DRAGON)

SCORPIUS (THE SCORPION)

AQUILA (THE EAGLE)

URSA MAJOR (THE GREAT BEAR)

CHAPTER 27

ROAD TRIP:
SOUTH MOUNTAIN MEMORIES

Neil put the SUV in park and left the engine running. He flipped the map light back on, took the book of maps from my lap, and laid it open again where we'd left off. He then spent the next ten minutes or so explaining the lay of the land and the sequencing of the all-day battle for Fox's Gap. I learned that the 36th Ohio had made a bayonet charge here and had engaged in hand-to-hand combat with North Carolinians led by a General Samuel Garland, who had been killed not far from where we sat. We flipped through a dozen maps detailing an intense battle within a confined space under constant artillery fire. Neil got more and more animated as he pointed out blue bars and red bars on the maps that represented the reinforcements that were added to fill the gap with twelve thousand Union soldiers and seventy-five hundred Confederate troops. He then explained how General Jesse Reno was shot from his horse near the Old Sharpsburg Road while repositioning troops as night fell. "That was General Reno's monument we passed coming in — it was erected where he was hit. I'm sure the fight at Antietam would have been different if General Reno hadn't been killed here — he was a soldier's soldier. You know what that means, right?"

I shook my head. "No."

"He was a fighter and wasn't averse to fighting shoulder to shoulder with his men. I suspect things might have moved along much faster and with better effect on the south end of the battlefield, if General Reno had been at Antietam."

"Just saying?"

"Just saying."

"Umm. Can we look at his monument?"

"Sure, let's start there."

Neil reached in front of me and pulled a flashlight out of the glove compartment. "There's one in there for you, too," he said. I took the other flashlight and got out of the vehicle. Except for an orchestra of crickets, the woods and fields were silent but also pregnant with something that I couldn't quite identify. The sun would rise in about twenty minutes and the few thin clouds visible in the sky were just beginning to color up. The pre-dawn air was cool and damp. I zipped up my fleece jacket and snuggled my shoulder blades down into its warmth.

Neil had set off briskly from the vehicle and I scrambled to catch up, following the bob of his flashlight and the crunch of gravel to General Reno's monument. As we walked to the front of the protective wall, a light breeze stirred my hair. I strained my ears for the sound of an owl — the only thing the creepy scene was missing. I followed Neil through the open iron gate and up a few steps to stand in front of the marble obelisk erected in memory of Jesse Reno. As Neil circled around reading the inscriptions on all four sides, I looked up the road toward the mountain gap and strained to imagine the area filled with soldiers. I heard ever so faintly, drifting back over the intervening decades, the clop, clop, clop of a horse moving in the dim light, a short volley of gunfire, and a choked intake of breath as General Reno felt a musket ball enter his chest. A cold breeze shot through my jacket and I suddenly felt someone standing behind me in the dark. I froze and held my breath, straining for the reassuring rustle of leaves that would tell me it was only a squirrel foraging for breakfast. When no sound came, I slowly turned my head to the right as I peered out the corner of my eye. A dark object whistled past my ear and bounced hard off the front of the monument. I swung my flashlight to the base of the monument and stared in wide-eyed horror. Whatever had just missed my head was buzzing and whirling in the grass. Neil's head popped around the side of the monument and I nearly jumped out of my skin.

"What was that?" he asked. As I watched mutely, Neil trained his flashlight on the ground and studied the projectile that had nearly plunged through my skull. "Oh, wow, look at this. It's a big, green dragonfly. I wonder why it flew into the monument."

I took a tentative step forward and looked down at the badly damaged insect whirling its broken wings in a futile attempt to become airborne. Looking down at it, I suddenly became overwhelmed with grief. "How many died here, Neil?" I asked, still staring at the struggling dragonfly.

"No one knows for sure. Several thousand maybe? So many boys died in the woods and were hidden in the dense undergrowth. They weren't all found."

"Oh. Could you step on it so it won't have to lie out here all day dying?" Neil stepped forward. The crunch of the dragonfly's death magnified in my ears and seemed to ricochet off the surrounding trees and mountains.

"Thanks."

"Uh, are you scaring yourself?"

"Maybe."

"Good to know. Do you want to take a little walk in the woods? There's a monument to the North Carolina regiments just a short way back in the woods."

With the creepy lighting and heavy energy settling at the nape of my neck, the last thing I wanted to do was beat around in the woods.

"Sure, I'm game," I said.

"Cool. Let's go." Neil led the way back through the iron gate and onto the grassy lawn behind the monument. He swung his flashlight back and forth across the woodline in front of us until the beam of light revealed a small sign marking a narrow opening in the woods. "There's the trail," Neil said as he took off across the grass. Unwilling to admit I was scared out of my mind, I followed Neil across the lawn. As we stepped into the woods, I felt forcefully drawn forward by an energy that couldn't be identified as friendly. I took a few quick steps to put Neil within arm's reach just in case I needed to grab onto to him to avoid being pulled into the underbrush by my ankles.

"There was a small woodlot here at the time of the battle," Neil said, "but not all these woods. It's grown over quite a bit."

"Okay." I kept my light trained on Neil's back as we walked. There was no sense losing sight of him for even a split second. He, however, swung his light around looking at everything. Weird shadows appeared in the heavy underbrush and then disappeared. Thick vines that hung in curtains from the trees loomed over me and then receded. Trees creaked and rubbed together in a light morning breeze. I took another quick step to keep myself right on Neil's heels.

"The 36th Ohio was in this area right around noon. They and three other Ohio regiments had the 13th North Carolina surrounded on three sides. The Southern boys were fighting for their lives."

Desperation welled up out of the underbrush, threatening to engulf me. My heart raced and I felt suddenly winded. I was getting lightheaded. I swayed on my feet. A cardinal chipped somewhere behind me and I jumped mostly out of my skin. I was now trembling, but was unwilling to admit I was afraid and wanted to run back to the vehicle. Keeping my light trained on Neil, I stumbled along the path and visualized myself kicked back in a rope hammock in a…uh…well-lit forest. No. Between two palm trees on a white sand beach. I leaned back and got comfortable, even slipping a fluffy tropical-print pillow beneath my head and clutching an umbrella drink in both hands while I sucked rum through a straw. I paused on the trail and closed my eyes. *I am completely relaxed and happy to be here. I am completely relaxed and happy to be here. I am completely relaxed and happy to be here.*

I opened my eyes and screamed in terror as the shadowy face of a dying soldier with open mouth and vacant eyes loomed up right in front of me. Suddenly, I was blinded by a piercing white light. "What? What's wrong with you?" Neil asked from behind the light. "The monument? Did the monument scare you?" Blobs of blue replaced the glaring white light as Neil swung his flashlight from my face to the monument for the North Carolina regiments that had fought in these woods. The specter I'd met revealed itself as a bronze sculpture of a Confederate flag-bearer lying prone on a tall, black marble base. The man's upper body was still off the ground, propped up by his left elbow. But, he was falling back in death while clutching his flag with one hand and his chest with the other. I imagined the soldier continuing his collapse to the ground as the bullet-riddled flag softly settled to shroud his face.

"Uh, yeah. I had my eyes closed and when I opened them, there he was."

Neil reached out and grasped my shoulder. "Keep your eyes open from now on. What are you trying to do? Scare the shit out of yourself?"

Neil and I read the inscription on the front of the monument that included a few sentences about the battle and the mention of the desecration of Confederate dead whose bodies were dumped down a nearby well. We then moved to the back of the monument and read an account of the death of a Confederate color-bearer who stood up on a stone garden wall with his flag, refusing to surrender it to Union soldiers who eventually shot him and took it. The passage ended with the suggestion of a squabble over who should have received credit for capturing the flag. I imagined Union soldiers grabbing the flag from the dying color-bearer's grip and parading it around with glee as the man took his last few breaths in the dirt without aid or comfort. I heard an officer's voice demanding the treasure so that he could claim its capture and make note of his accomplishment in his battle report.

"Neil, do you think people ever recover their sensitivity to suffering after an experience like this?"

"Like what? Like the battle here?"

"This battle or just the Civil War, in general."

"Oh. Well. I think some must have. Others, well. Some were probably mean to begin with…I don't know. Why are you making me think about this?"

"I don't know. It seemed important to ask. Do you know how many men died in the war?"

"Of all causes — estimated at well over half a million."

"That's a lot of misery."

"Yes, a lot of misery."

I swept a few handfuls of fallen leaves from the Confederate soldier's clothes before Neil and I headed back up the trail. I turned as we left and found the soldier's face with my flashlight. I looked into eyes that I now realized were not vacant, but gently closed.

"Do you see that?" asked Neil. He'd stopped in his tracks ten feet up the trail and was peering into the woods on our right. "Were you shining your light over there?" he asked.

"No, I have it pointed at the monument."

"Come stand by me and turn it off for a minute. I think I saw a light in the woods." I walked over and stood next to Neil. We shut off our flashlights.

"There. See that to the right?" said Neil as he pointed into the woods. I looked to where Neil indicated and saw a strange, round light bobbing a few hundred feet back in the woods. It was faint and appeared to burn brightly and then ebb, like the memory of a flame that was being teased by a light breeze.

"There's another one," said Neil. "And another one over there."

Very slowly the woods filled with dozens of the faint baubles of light, which flared and ebbed, flared and ebbed. "The orbs. The orbs of light in the field," I whispered.

"Yes."

As we stood transfixed, the orbs began to move through the woods. Starting and stopping every few yards, they moved carefully and deliberately among the trees while bobbing about head high. "Neil, it looks like they're being carried."

"It does."

As we continued to watch, the orbs moved silently through the woods, dipping on occasion to knee-level. My hands suddenly became cold and I clasped them to my mouth, ready to warm my fingers with my breath, when a pure white mist swirled up from the ground not fifteen feet in front of us. An orb flickered to life through the mist and moved gently forward. It was followed by the upraised arm, shoulder, head, and then chest of a slight, young man who stepped out of the mist and stopped in front of me. The man, who was really only a boy of eighteen or nineteen years, was dressed in heavy light blue pants and a long-sleeved white button-up undershirt stained with sweat, dirt, and splatters of blood. The boy's face and his right hand, which held a candle lantern aloft, also were spotted and streaked with blood. The boy looked at me with desperate worry in his eyes. "Have you seen my brother, Eli? I can't find him," the soldier said in a clear voice.

I dropped my hands from my mouth. "No, I haven't. I haven't seen him."

"I have to keep looking. I have to find him." The boy turned to his left and went the way we'd just come, stooping for a moment with his lantern to peer under a tangle of mountain laurel before moving away from us. As the soldier's light became smaller and fainter, the breeze picked up and stirred the fallen leaves along both sides of the trail. Carried on the breeze was a light moan, almost imperceptible at first, that softly broke open to release a momentary cacophony of cries, shrieks, and pleading voices. I reached up to plug my ears, but just as quickly as they'd risen, the voices fell away as the breeze stilled and the pinkish glow of the dawn sky brightened the gaps in the tree canopy. Neil and I stood watching in silence as the glowing orbs winked out one by one in the rising daylight. And then we were alone again.

"Okay, so, if I were fifteen again, I'd be running like hell right now," Neil said.

"But, that would be disrespectful."

"Yes, so let's walk quickly, but respectfully, back to the vehicle."

"I'm game for that."

In spite of our show of respect, it felt like we literally flew down the trail and were suddenly out on the grass behind General Reno's monument again. Neil didn't pause as he strode to the SUV, which beeped to declare it was open and ready to receive us. We dove into its welcoming arms and Neil immediately started the engine. I expected him to throw the vehicle in reverse and spin gravel getting us out of there but he didn't. Instead, he reached forward and cranked up the heater. "I'm freezing. Are you freezing?" Neil said as he held his fingers up to one of the vents, which was not yet blowing warm air. I realized that my teeth were chattering. I clenched my jaw and nodded yes, knowing Neil would rib me endlessly if I answered sounding anything at all like Elmer Fudd.

We sat in silence for a good five minutes as the SUV started to warm up and Neil continued to rub his fingers together in front of the vent.

"I can't freaking believe you just had a conversation with a ghost," Neil finally said.

"You heard him, too?"

"Damn straight, I heard him. He was looking for his brother, who was probably lying dead or wounded on that field. The orbs are lanterns. Oh, my god, the orbs are lanterns. That battle didn't end until after dark and the Union soldiers spent all night on the field with the dead and dying from both sides.

They probably searched by lantern light for their friends and relatives as soon as the Confederate troops had melted away. Oh, my god, do you realize what this land remembers? What's still here and will probably always be here?"

I looked at Neil as I contemplated his question. If the land remembered the horror, didn't it also remember the beauty that regularly passed through? The baby birds born, the spring wildflowers in bloom, the snowflakes filtering down through the naked trees, the gentle rains that tickled the ferns until they gave up their clean fragrance? How many summer showers would it take to wash the horror from the land?

"I'm starving. Could you eat? Do you want to take a break before Antietam and find a diner? Eat some eggs or something?" Neil asked.

"Yeah, that sounds good. A break would be good. I could eat some eggs. I had a few bites of my sandwich but that seems like three days ago."

"Does time feel messed up to you, too? Like it folded in on itself back there in the woods?"

"Yes. Yes, that's a good way to put it. Time folded in on itself back there in the woods."

CHAPTER 28

ROAD TRIP: WHERE WE EAT OMELETTES WITH AN OLD FRIEND

Neil and I rode in silence for several miles. I watched the scenery change as we drove through Fox's Gap and dropped steadily off the western slope of South Mountain, following in the footsteps of the 36th Ohio and the rest of the 9th Corps to Antietam. Heavy, tangled forest gave way to rolling hayfields followed by perfectly flat farmland and then more rolling hayfields as we crossed Pleasant Valley, a beautiful wide expanse that showed just a few discreet marks of suburban sprawl. The sun had not yet lifted clear of the mountain behind us, but the thinly stretched clouds in the west were glowing pink and salmon against a soft blue sky. I lowered my window a few inches so I could hear the morning birds — a chickadee, a jay, a field sparrow, a titmouse, a goldfinch, another jay, a cardinal. Their voices, mixing together to score the beautiful landscape, promised a day of easy magic and I reached out with my fingertips to touch that bit of joy, rather than worrying about what lay ahead. I raised the window against the chilly breeze as Neil stopped and yielded to an oncoming pickup crossing the one-lane, humped stone bridge in front of us.

"This has to be an historic bridge," Neil said as we took our turn to cross. "Bet it's arched just like Burnside Bridge. This is the Little Antietam Creek. We're getting close to Keedysville. I'm pretty sure the 9th Corps made camp somewhere to our left the day after South Mountain, which would have been September 15th. Instead of continuing on through Keedysville the next day, though, they likely swung southwest from here and dropped into position east of Antietam Creek via a more direct route."

I looked at the peaceful scene to our left and, as much as I tried, couldn't imagine the valley filled with thousands of men, tents, campfires, horses, mules, and covered supply wagons.

"The diner is on the other side of town — out on Route 34. We can take the shortest route to 34 or ride through downtown Keedysville. Do you have a preference?" Neil asked.

"Downtown, please."

"Downtown, it is."

Past the bridge, the farms quickly gave way to neighborhoods of all sizes and configurations. Neil pulled over in front of one of them so we could get a close look at a section of old stone wall that guarded its entrance. The wall was three or more feet high and built of at least a dozen courses of dry-stacked flat, gray stones. An additional course of flat stones was set perpendicular along the top of the wall, creating a somewhat foreboding sharp-toothed barricade.

"This is probably what the stone walls back at Fox's Gap looked like in 1862. Can you imagine a long wall like this bristling with enemy muskets? And being told to charge it?" Neil said.

"I kind of can." I didn't mention to Neil that the version I imagined included the thick smoke of gunpowder, flashing gun barrels, and the bloodied bodies of young men piled up on either side, but saw in his eyes that I didn't need to.

"Ready?" Neil asked.

"Yep, I'm starving."

"Less than five minutes."

We skirted around a few more large housing developments and rolled into town. Neil turned right on Main Street and drove it slowly. Although smaller than Middletown, Keedysville looked similar, but with a main street mostly devoid of businesses and lined instead with big historical houses and churches. Lights were on in most of the houses we passed and people were stirring but the impatient energy of the DC suburbs was missing here. And that felt good.

"I wouldn't mind living here," I said.

Neil laughed. "I was thinking exactly the same thing. I bet this is the type of place where kids can still play outside all day as long as they come in when the porch light goes on."

"Yeah, I like that. I'm thinking I might move away to a place like this. Some-place just off the edge of the frenzied energy of the metro area. Well, and then a little bit farther to stay out of range of the sprawl. I'm kind of waiting to see what Andy does, though. I don't want to follow him around like a puppy, but I can't imagine not living close enough to see him all the time."

"Well, you'd better not move too far away — I'd miss you. Do you realize we've had a least a text conversation almost every day for the past five years?"

"Oh, you'd have to come, too, of course. I don't think it would be possible for us to part company."

Neil grinned. "No, probably not possible. I doubt we've been able to shake each other off over more than one lifetime."

"You think?"

"Yeah, pretty sure."

We'd gotten to the end of Main Street and Neil made two quick lefts to get on Route 34. A few hundred feet down the highway, he pulled in front of a relatively modern low building with aluminum siding and tidy awnings sitting just off the road behind a large gravel parking lot. There were five or six other cars in the lot. "Cool, not too busy," said Neil, "but busy enough to confirm that the breakfast is pretty good."

I was just glad the diner was in a modern building free of Civil War mem-ories. But, as I stepped out of the SUV, I realized I was feeling strangely out of it, like a thick fog had rolled in, muddling both my mind and my vision. I followed Neil through the front door of the restaurant and to a long counter across the back wall.

"Counter okay?" asked Neil.

"Sure."

I slid onto the stool that Neil indicated and put the palms of my hands on the counter in front of me. The white Formica was smooth and cool. I watched as my hands sank into it and disappeared from view. *Interesting. Where have my hands gone?* Neil nudged my leg with his foot.

"Coffee? Do you want coffee?" he asked.

A waitress in a blue polo shirt stepped forward through the fog. She had a white ceramic mug in one hand and a glass pot of coffee in the other.

"Uh, sure. Thank you."

The waitress set the cup in front of me and filled it with hot, black coffee. Steam curled up from the slightly oily surface of the coffee and sat like a vapor above the cup. As I gazed at the steam, it reorganized itself ever so slightly. A chill gripped my thighs and ran up my back as I found myself staring into the face of a vulture. I scattered the steam with a wave of my hand and the vulture disappeared. It was replaced by a laminated menu, slipped in front of me by the waitress, who also brought an offering of silverware wrapped in a white paper napkin. I looked over at Neil who was studying the menu.

"Did you notice the meat-lover's omelette?" I asked.

"I'm all over it. Not sure how you're going to fare, though — don't see any salad omelettes."

While Neil was laughing at his own joke, the waitress came back over. "Have you two decided?"

"I'll have a meat-lover's omelette with home fries and rye toast," Neil said and then looked over at me.

"A western omelette, please, but with no ham."

"No ham?"

"Yes, please. And I'll have home fries and wheat toast."

"Would you like tomato and mushrooms in place of the ham?"

"Sure, that would be great." I glanced at Neil as the waitress gathered the menus and slipped away to put our order in. I was about to gloat over scoring an off-menu veggie omelette when an older man in jeans, a dark fleece jacket, and a ball cap approached Neil.

"Mind if I sit here?" the man asked as he indicated the empty stool on the other side of Neil.

Neil turned and smiled up at the man. "No, not at all. Have a seat," he said.

"Don't mean to bother you, but not really in the mood to eat alone this morning."

The waitress came over with coffee for the new arrival as he settled in and unzipped his jacket. "Good morning! The usual today?"

"Nope, let's mix it up a little, Amy — the ham platter seems to be calling my name."

"Wheat toast with that?"

"Yep. Thank you much."

Amy left with the man's order and he turned to Neil. "You two headed to the battlefield today?" he asked.

"Yes, we are. Is it obvious for some reason?" Neil said.

The man gave a quick laugh. "No, you're blending pretty well. It's just the anniversary of the battle always attracts a crowd, although you're a day early for most of the happenings."

"Ah, that would be intentional. We're hoping to explore a bit without too much company."

"I understand. It's a good time to do that. The veil is always just a little thinner around the anniversary."

"The veil?"

"Uh-huh. The curtain between this world and that. The separation gets amorphous this time of year. Things become a lot more, uh, fluid. And the land is more willing to give up her memories, if you will. It's a good time to seek answers to your questions."

Neil raised his eyebrows. "It's interesting you should say that. We experienced something up on South Mountain this morning. Someone stepped through the curtain to speak with us — a soldier looking for his brother."

The man nodded. "Yes. I knew you belonged to this place. It scratched its talon across you a long time ago — took a part of you that it holds yet. You can tug yourself loose or leave that bit of yourself here. It doesn't really matter which." The man lifted his mug and took a long sip of coffee. He set the mug back on the counter and I watched transfixed as the steam rising from the cup swirled into the shape of a circling vulture with outstretched wings. The man noticed me watching and swept his hand through the steam, scattering the vapor into dozens of vultures that rose up and melted into the foggy mist that now seemed to fill the entire diner.

Neil was studying the man and appeared not to have noticed what had just happened. "Do I know you from some place?" Neil asked. "I feel like we've met before."

"Could be. I run into a lot of folks who get drawn back here for one or another reason. Some remember me and some don't." The man leaned forward slightly to make eye contact with me and smiled. His face softened and then sharpened, allowing me to recognize a man thirty years younger in a slouched Union cap and jacket with red collar, epaulettes, and braid on the sleeves. I cocked my head slightly to the right as I studied his face. I knew this man as an artillery officer. But there was something more. As I squinted through the fog at the man's smiling brown eyes, a rush of memory swept over me as a series of rapid-fire images that included this man as a boy. Drinking lemonade together on the porch of a white farmhouse with a yard full of chickens. Walking a snowy track through the woods to a one-room schoolhouse with smoke curling from its fieldstone chimney. Slaughtering a hog together on a cool autumn morning. Running barefoot in his wake through a pasture. Playing hide and seek in tall corn as grasshoppers jumped from all directions. Riding horses side by side along a dusty road. Swimming together in the cold, clear water of a wide creek. Climbing with him high into the crown of a tall oak thick with acorns. Throwing green apples at each other as we wove and dodged through an orchard. I knew this man well as a child. He was family.

Older than me — always several steps ahead. I'd worshipped him as a boy. *Isaiah. Cousin Isaiah.*

I involuntarily reached in front of Neil for the hand that the man offered. He squeezed my hand firmly and I squeezed back. Pure joy coursed through me and I teared up with the intensity of the emotion. "I remember you," I said.

"I remember you, too, and I don't really want to let go again," he said as he held onto my hand. His smile had turned wistful and I could see that he was tearing up, too. As I looked into his soft misty eyes, I knew that I'd held his hand before. On a battlefield a century and a half ago, as he took his last breath.

Neil glanced at me out of the corner of his eye. His eyes then shot to the opposite corners so he could get a look at Isaiah without moving his head. Neil's eyes shifted over and over between my face and Isaiah's, my face and Isaiah's as he tried to read the situation without interrupting our reunion with questions. Neil's rapidly darting eyes were too funny to ignore. Isaiah and I laughed together and released our grip at the same time.

"Okay, I have a special veggie omelette for you, a meat-lover's for your old pal here, and a country ham platter for your new best friend," Amy announced as she winked at me and set white china plates loaded down with breakfast food in front of each of us. "I'll be right back with more coffee."

As Amy refilled our coffee cups, we all dug into our meals. We ate in silence for the next ten minutes — the only sound was the metallic pings and scrapes of silverware on the heavy plates. When I finally looked up from my breakfast, the air filling the diner was light and clear. I glanced over at Neil and noticed on the stool next to him an older man in jeans, a dark fleece jacket, and a ball cap, who was eating a breakfast of ham and eggs. It was odd that he was sitting right next to us when the entire length of the counter was otherwise empty, but I wasn't at all surprised when Neil struck up a conversation with him — Neil was insatiably curious about most people.

"You live around here?" Neil asked the man.

"I do. Actually right outside of Sharpsburg. Have a blacksmith and metal working shop. Craft all kinds of implements for the Civil War reenactors and sell decorative pieces at the summer craft festivals."

"Oh, interesting. What kind of decorative work do you do?"

"Just about anything you could imagine. Lots of fireplace sets, all kinds of hanging brackets, miniature farm implements, coat hooks, fancy hinges — all kinds of things. I have a whole series of little animals." The man put down his fork and reached into an interior pocket of his jacket. "Here, these are for you." The man set two intricately crafted coiled snakes in front of Neil's plate. He smiled at me and pushed one of them my way. I reached for it as Neil picked up the other one.

Holding the black iron snake on the flat of my palm, I lifted it close to my nose as I studied it. The snake was coiled in a tight clockwise spiral. I counted one, two, three, four, five, six revolutions of the intricately patterned body that ended with a wide diamond-shaped head. I lifted the snake up higher so I could see its eyes more clearly. They were perfectly round and tranquil.

"It looks friendly," I said.

The man laughed. "It is. See the blunt nose? It's modeled after a hog-nosed snake that hangs out around my shop. More than once he's shed his skin on the back step of the place. I like the symbolism of that. You know, casting off the old container so we can expand into a new one. Constantly reinventing ourselves." Neil nodded vigorously in agreement.

"I really like it, thank you," I said.

"Yes, thank you. It's beautiful," Neil added as he held his snake in his left palm and ran his right index finger along the coils.

"You're both very welcome."

"Do you have a business card?" I asked as I slid my snake into my jacket pocket.

"I do." The man dug through his jacket and produced a loose handful of embossed black business cards. He handed one to me and another to Neil. The heavy card looked exactly like a smooth piece of black iron tooled with the image of an anvil and the man's contact information in metallic gray — "Battlefield Metalworks, Isaiah W. Knapp, Blacksmith" with a Sharpsburg address, phone number, and email.

"Are you Isaiah?" Neil asked.

"I am," the man said. "And you're both welcome anytime to visit the shop if you're interested. See? I have my hours on the back of the card."

"I'd enjoy that," Neil said as he shook Isaiah's hand and introduced himself. Neil then leaned back so I could do the same. As I took Isaiah's hand, he looked at me quizzically and for a fleeting moment I felt that I knew him from somewhere.

"Have we met before?" he asked.

"I was thinking the same thing, but I don't think so. Isaiah is such an unusual name that I'm sure I would have remembered you and I definitely would have remembered your work."

Isaiah nodded thoughtfully as we retrieved our hands and let Neil get back to his breakfast. "Isaiah is pretty rarely used these days — used to be more popular. I'm actually named after my great-great-grandfather, Isaiah William Knapp, who was a first lieutenant in the 1st Ohio Light Artillery during the Civil War. He was killed by a Minie ball to the chest at Fox's Gap during the Battle of South Mountain. Left a young wife and three little boys, one of whom was my great-grandfather."

"Oh, wow, what a coincidence," Neil said. "We just came from Fox's Gap. We're sort of following in the footsteps of the 36th Ohio Infantry."

Isaiah's face lit up. "Part of the Kanawha Division! The 1st Ohio was attached to the Kanawha Division. Small world."

"Yes, it is. My great-great-granduncles were officers in the 36th. They were there at Fox's Gap, too," I said.

"Really? Our ancestors would have known each other, then — the units fought together through most of the war. I'm sure there must have been some association between the men. Maybe that's why we seem familiar to each other — maybe there's a long-standing association that we know nothing about."

"Well, that's an interesting thought," I said as I smiled at Isaiah. I did feel a strange connection to him that I couldn't explain and I knew that I'd be following up on the invitation to visit his shop. I glanced over at Neil, who had polished off his omelette and toast while Isaiah and I had been talking. We both went back to our breakfasts, finishing up as Amy came back with our checks.

"I'd like to buy," Neil said as he swept up all three checks, stacked them with two twenties, and handed the pile to Amy in a single fluid motion. Amy accepted the cash without comment and immediately took off for the register at the far end of the counter. The crowd in the restaurant was picking up and she, no doubt, didn't want to linger long enough for Isaiah or me to launch a time-consuming protest.

"Very nice of you. Thank you," Isaiah said.

"You're very welcome. It was a pleasure meeting you."

"It was," I added, "and I'm going to take you up on the offer to visit. I'd love to see more of your work."

Isaiah smiled at me and a new current of familiarity swept through my body. *It makes me happy just to be around this guy. Strange. Maybe I do know him from somewhere.*

"Anytime. Come anytime."

Neil and I left Isaiah at the counter finishing his coffee as we headed back out to the SUV. The sun was up now but the light of the day was still soft and expectant.

"Ready for whatever's next?" Neil asked as I buckled my seatbelt.

"Ready."

CHAPTER 29

ROAD TRIP: HAPPENINGS AT A LITTLE WHITE CHURCH

Less than ten minutes later, we pulled into the parking lot at the Antietam Visitors Center, and I was suddenly unsure if I really was ready. The trip from the diner had been much quicker than I'd anticipated. We'd driven southwest from Keedysville on 34 for just a few minutes before Neil had pulled over at the end of a gravel lane and had flipped open the map book. "Okay, we won't drive back right now since it's not open yet," he'd explained, "but the Pry House, which McClellan used as his headquarters, is back at the end of this lane. Look here on this map. McClellan and his staff stood on this ridge behind the house with his field glasses and could, in theory, see the middle and northern portions of the battlefield. Not a bad position for a wide view of the battle, but the fog and smoke from the burning farm buildings and all the gunpowder limited visibility. And, he couldn't see the southern end of the battle at all. McClellan came onto the battlefield only once all day. Almost all of his communications with his commanders were by courier. In contrast, Lee was all over the battlefield throughout the day." Remembering the white birds peeling off the interstate, I'd felt an unexpected pang of understanding for a man not naturally invigorated by the idea of bullets zipping around his head, and a simultaneous rush of respect for the man who put aside personal safety in favor of a more intimate view and direct contact with his commanders. I hadn't been sure, though, which approach I would have taken.

We'd continued on, but a mile past McClellan's headquarters, Neil had pulled over again as we approached a wide, modern highway bridge. "We're about to cross the Antietam Creek and enter the battlefield," Neil had told me. "There was a stone bridge here at the time of the battle that looked a lot like the Burnside Bridge. A majority of the Confederate troops retreating from South Mountain on the fourteenth crossed here. They were followed a few days later by about a third of McClellan's army. Once we cross the creek, we'll be driving straight across the battlefield south of Bloody Lane to Sharpsburg. Then we'll turn north and go up the western edge of the park so we can start things off at the visitor center. There's a driving tour that starts near there that will give us an overview of the battlefield."

It had taken us just a few seconds to roll over the Antietam, allowing only a quick glimpse of a tranquil tree-lined creek still clinging to its morning mists. The easy crossing had felt strangely wrong and I'd turned in my seat to prolong things by watching the bridge disappear behind us. A half-mile farther up the road and Neil had stopped again, this time at the intersection of a road that crossed the highway almost perpendicularly. "To our left is the southern portion of the battlefield and Burnside Bridge. We'll be back this way on the driving tour," Neil had said as he pushed back in his seat to allow me to see past him. A narrow paved road lined on both sides with zig-zags of split rail fence followed a rolling path between two golden cornfields and then disappeared over a slight rise that blocked any view beyond a few hundred yards. The soft light of morning had played magically across the corn, filling the landscape with a burnished, beckoning glow. I'd felt pulled in that direction, but knew that I needed to wait.

We'd continued on, past the cornfields on our left and mowed fields peppered with red cedar on our right. Both had given way to patchy woods, which had opened to reveal extensive cemeteries on both sides of the road. "We're coming into Sharpsburg now," Neil had said. "Confederate brigades and batteries were up here on the high ground firing down on the Union troops as they advanced late in the day up the hill that falls away to our left. That was the final attack — the last assault that was swept off the field by A. P. Hill's division. We'll have a much better view later."

The road had dropped steadily between stone retaining walls as we left the cemeteries and entered the small town of Sharpsburg. I'd watched a few big white houses loom up and then recede and had been settling in to study the buildings when Neil had slowed in front of a brick church and turned right. We were suddenly out of town and driving along a long stone wall on our right that delineated the western edge of the battlefield. The landscape offered an interesting limited palette of green grass, golden corn stalks, and the deep cerulean sky but had seemed strangely empty, like a canvas on which only the background had been painted or a stage that held only scenery.

"The Park Service tries to keep the land use in line with historical patterns," Neil had said as I gazed out my window at the rows of corn that stretched for a half mile or more. "I guess there was a lot of corn in the fields at the time of the battle."

The rolling cornfield had given way to rocky pastureland interrupted by a few big rangy trees. The pastureland had then become manicured lawn. A copse of trees appeared and we'd turned right into the visitor center parking lot where we now sat with the engine running. Before I was truly ready, Neil reached into the backseat and grabbed a folder stuffed with papers. He opened the folder and pulled out a single sheet. "Okay, before you accuse me of being over-prepared, I'm going to just own the fact that I'm over-prepared. I put a lot of work into understanding this battle as well as I possibly could in a limited amount of time."

"Um, so you're saying in a nice way that you got totally obsessed and just rolled with it."

"Precisely and now I'm ready to share." Neil leaned toward me and held out the paper so we could study it together. "This is a map of the driving tour. See the dark blue line? That's the tour route. Here we are at the bottom of the northern battlefield — the Dunker Church is right across the road from us." Neil pointed out a little black rectangle that represented the church and swung his fingertip around the top of the map and back to the church. "We'll trace a big P that starts at the Dunker Church, goes straight north past the West Woods along the Hagerstown Pike, cuts east between a large farm and what's known as the North Woods, drops south through the remains of the East Woods, and cuts west across the cornfield and pasture where a lot of intense fighting took place in the morning. From there we'll drive south down the Hagerstown Pike and end up back at the church."

I must have looked boggled because Neil traced the route with his finger again. "See? This end of the battlefield isn't confusing if you think of it as a big field surrounded on three sides by woodlots. The fighting here, though, definitely was confusing, but don't worry, I prepared a little something that'll help you visualize at least part of the battle."

I smiled at Neil's twinkling eyes and then turned back to the map, imagining soaring over the area with the vultures circling above me. A little stick-figure horse and rider galloped in from the edge of the paper and stopped behind the rectangle indicating the church. The horse reared slightly. "This is the spot where I saw Stonewall Jackson on his horse," I said as I pointed to the horse and rider that Neil apparently couldn't see.

Neil reached into his jacket pocket and produced the little notebook that he'd used at the gallery to organize our battle plan. He flipped the book open to the map I'd drawn and held it next to the tour map. "Look — look how similar," Neil said. "You have the church, the cornfield, and even some of the woodlots in the right places. And see where you drew a burning farmhouse? That was the Mumma Farm — right here — that the Confederates burned on the morning of the battle. The house and barn were rebuilt, though, and we'll see them on the second leg of the driving tour. See how the tour route continues? From the Dunker Church we'll loop behind the visitor center and then drop straight south to Bloody Lane. See where you drew the farm lane with the Confederate troops massed? Bloody Lane. You got it in almost the exact right spot."

I looked at the blue line that zigzagged down through the middle of the battlefield and felt tension bubble up in my gut. I suddenly felt impatient and ready to get on with things, but Neil continued the orientation session. "The route continues to drop south from there and crosses Route 34 right here at the intersection where we just stopped on our way into Sharpsburg." I leaned in and carefully studied the map. The blue line of the tour route continued for about a mile southwest through the rolling cornfields I'd seen from Route 34, tracing an almost straight path equidistant between Sharpsburg and Antietam Creek. About halfway down, a spur road wiggled its way east toward the creek and then ended in a loop. Indicated near the loop as a black bar over the sweeping blue line of the creek was the bridge I'd seen from the air. Everything seemed very right and I was ready to roll.

"I downloaded trail maps for all the interpretive walks and figured we could take the hikes that we felt drawn toward," Neil said as he glanced at the clock in the dash. "It's almost 8:15. We'd better get started. The visitor center opens at nine and I'd like to finish our first circuit of the tour route before things start to get crowded." Neil put the SUV in drive and was finally about to hit the gas when Mick's voice swam into my awareness.

"Perhaps an invocation might be nice before we begin."

"A what?"

"An invocation. A prayer as you begin this leg of your journey to clarify your intent and to ask for assistance."

I touched Neil's arm. "Hold on a second."

Neil stepped on the brake and peered over at me with one raised brow. "What's wrong? You were wiggling around like you wanted to get on with it and now you want to stop?"

"Um, yeah, I feel like we need an invocation or something."

"A what?"

"An invocation — you know, a prayer as we begin this leg of our journey to clarify our intent and to ask for assistance."

"Oh, okay. Uh, you wanna go for it?"

"Uh, sure. Let's get our intents straight first and then I'll word them as an invocation. You want me to go first?"

"Yes, please."

"Okay, Mick, you need to help me out here."

"Ah. Just tell him. Tell him where you'd like more clarity in your life. And name that from which you would like release."

"Out loud?"

"Yes, certainly out loud. Trust your fellow traveler."

"Okay. My intent is to gain clarity about what holds me back from enjoying life and finding my place in the world. I'd like to understand the numbness and sadness that hangs over me and would like to be released from those feelings…"

"And are you open to surprises? Even surprises that might not assist you personally?"

"…but I'm also open to whatever I might learn here to help myself or others."

Both of Neil's eyebrows rose. "That sounds like depression. Do you think you're depressed?"

"No, I don' think so. Just kind of emotionally flat in a way and, uh, not sure who I am, I guess."

"But not depressed…"

"I don't think so. I mean, I'm nowhere near the peaks of joy that I deserve, but I'm not that bad off."

"Ahhh, but you don't really think you deserve joy, do you?"

I felt my cheeks flare up but responded anyway. "No, I don't. Something's wrong. There's some sort of weight I carry that says happiness is for everyone but me."

Neil snorted a laugh through his nose. I pursed my lips and shot him a mild stink-eye. "I'm sorry," he said, "I just imagined you schlepping around a fifty pound iron bar with 'no happiness for me' inscribed across it."

"That's about right but it weighs at least a few hundred pounds. And I'll have you know it's stainless steel — I polish it every morning. What's really weird is that until recently I've always just kind of accepted that message without question and focused instead on what I could do to help other people be happy without…without getting too overly attached to them." My cheeks got hot again. "Which I know sounds nuts because it is."

A small smile played around Neil's eyes. "Well, that explains a few things. Can I ask you something that might seem unrelated?"

"Sure," I agreed, happy to have the subject changed.

"Do you think you'd have ever left the company if I hadn't been forced out?"

"No, I would have stayed as long as Steve wanted me there if things had stayed the way they were. I wasn't happy but I felt, uh, safe and unchallenged — there were worse positions to be in. But that changed with the reorganization. Seeing you marginalized pissed me off and woke me up. I could ignore everything else that was going on, but the stupidity and inequity of how you were treated was a slap to the side of my head. And I, uh, also didn't want to be there without you."

Neil nodded enthusiastically. "It's interesting what we do in the pursuit of safety, isn't it? I was willing to ignore everything and go along, too. I stayed with the company years longer than I should have because I was so afraid of letting people down, especially the people who reported to me. I'm completely secure in my definition of myself as a leader of people, but I take on too much and stay too long in situations that I know are stagnant and draining. I carry a huge load on my shoulders that I put there and apparently only I can see. Carrying that weight of duty feels safe to me — it's my status quo. Without it, I'd feel, well, I guess exposed is the best word for it."

"Pursue that, please."

"Pursue what, Mick?"

"Your friend has revealed his intent. Restate it for his review, incorporate it into your invocation, and send your request out into the Universe, please."

I quickly charged ahead. "Are you ready to put the weight of duty to others down, though, and risk being exposed, Neil? Is that your intent today?"

"You mean beyond spending time with you, going on a grand adventure, meeting ghosts, and distracting myself from losing my job?"

"Yeah."

"I'd say yes."

"Relax now and let the prayer flow through you."

"Okay, so here's our invocation." I closed my eyes, let my awareness drop into my chest, and allowed the words to come tumbling out. "Great Spirit, we have come here today seeking insight into that which holds us back from becoming who we are destined to become. We ask for release from the burdens that we carry and your guidance as we discover our true purposes in life. We ask that you show us how we can best serve you, ourselves, and others. We surrender to your wisdom, opening ourselves to the messages you wish to share with us."

"Was that okay, Mick?"

"Could not have done better myself. Carry on."

I opened my eyes to find Neil with his eyes closed and his head bowed. "Amen," I added.

"Amen," Neil repeated as he lifted his head and opened his eyes. "That was a little deeper than I was expecting," he said, "but I concur and honestly do surrender to anything that might happen. Thank you. Are we ready now?"

"Yes, I think we're ready now."

Neil put the SUV in drive again and swung north through the parking lot in front of the visitor center. As we wheeled around, the Dunker Church appeared on a small rise in front of us. The morning sun illuminated the front of the neat, one-story white building, making it glow like a beacon. The woods enclosing the back and north side of the church were shorter than I'd expected but they still formed a protective enclave around the structure. A tingle of familiarity prickled over me and then drained away as I noticed the monument across the road from the church. The tall obelisk was jarring and out of place. As we neared the church, I saw another monument back behind the obelisk. This one, even larger and in the shape of a large green cupola supported by a ring of stout columns, sat along a road running at a forty-five degree angle east across the battlefield. As Neil maneuvered the SUV into a pullout in front of the obelisk, I realized that the roads were wrong. The modern asphalt surfaces lined with power poles and neatly sheared lawn irritated me, as did a tree in front of the church that didn't belong there. I felt strangely disoriented and annoyed by the easily recognizable building that appeared in a setting different in detail than what I'd been expecting. I looked over at Neil, who was watching me expectantly.

"The church is right, Neil, but it feels like it's been transported to a strangely different location."

"Really? The original church did collapse and was rebuilt in the sixties, but it's supposed to be on the same spot."

"No, it's not that. It feels like the building is right but that everything changed around it. Like I've gone back to the old neighborhood and I recognize my childhood home, but nothing else is quite right. It's not completely wrong, but all the little details have changed and I'm missing the emotional connection."

"That does make sense. The battlefield wasn't preserved immediately. The land was farmed for decades after the war. Woodlots were cleared, the roads were modernized, buildings came and went — there were probably a lot of changes over time that haven't been completely rectified. But, do you feel like you knew this area well? You know, beyond what you saw in your, uh, vision?"

"No, not really. Can we go in the church?"

"I think so. Let's go check it out."

Neil and I got out of the vehicle and walked across the road to a short, curved set of brick steps. We climbed the steps up a small rise to an arched concrete walk that swung right across the narrow lawn in front of the church and led to a pair of interpretive signs at the edge of the hill. I glanced over my shoulder at the battlefield. *Not a bad view — I can understand why Stonewall Jackson sat his horse on this hill.* Turning back to the church, I found a modern apron of red bricks beckoning us off the sidewalk and toward two stone slabs that formed a rustic stoop in front of the tiny church. Neil led the way, climbing the stone steps and sticking his head through the open doorway. "Not much in here, but no sign saying we aren't welcome to explore," Neil said as he disappeared into the dark interior of the building. I watched him go and lingered at the bottom of the stoop for just a moment, trying to dispel my irritation that nothing felt right. I'd expected some sort of magic as soon as I stepped foot on this land, but just wasn't feeling it. I breathed deeply to settle myself and climbed the steps.

As I stepped into a single open room, my foot creaked on heavy, vanished floorboards and I immediately recognized the familiar cologne of old wood, coal dust, and wood smoke worn by so many historical buildings. I scanned the room and found a small black wood stove in the middle of a space packed with simple plank pews all facing a plain wooden table at the north end of the building. A narrow door, likely the entrance used for Sunday services, sat closed in the middle of the south wall. The lighting was natural and uneven. Panes of morning sunlight from pairs of long windows on the south and east walls played across half of the pews, while reflected light from identical pairs of windows in the west and north walls cast a soft gloom within the shaded half of the church.

Neil was sitting on a pew along the sunny south wall of the church. He was half in and half out of the light, sitting staunchly upright with his shoulders squared and his palms resting on his thighs. He appeared to be watching a shifting show of blue sky, green tree leaves, and golden morning light through one of the windows opposite him. So as not to disturb Neil by tromping over the squeaky floorboards, I slid into a pew to my right and sat quietly contemplating the west wall of the building. The wall was painted white, as were all the walls, but was cast in uneven gray shadow. In contrast, a bright scene of green trees shone through the windows, making me feel as if I were in a dark theatre watching a movie screen. The movie that should have been playing would have included General Jackson on his small red horse — I was, after all, gazing at the small patch of real estate behind the church where I'd seen him. *But, where is he today?* Staring hard at the view outside the window, I attempted to smear away the trees and will the appearance of smoke, soldiers, and horses. *Is the wood smoke I smell actually the Mumma Farm burning?* I leaned across the pew and peered through the open doorway. The asphalt roads and monuments were still right outside. The visitor center was still sitting on a rise to my right and the parking lot was beginning to fill up with vehicles, none of which were tethered to horses, mules, or oxen. There was no smoke on the horizon. Feeling frustrated, I closed my eyes and let my mind empty out. Almost immediately, I felt Mick settle in next to me on the pew.

"Expectation has a rank tendency to dampen wonderment, you know."

"What do you mean by that?"

"Your expectations are too high. You're chasing the experience away."

"I thought I'd feel a connection to this land, but it seems to be repelling me. I also

was expecting to feel Stonewall Jackson's presence, but he doesn't seem to be here."

"Remember to look at things through wide open eyes — the expectation of specific results makes the gap too narrow for the mystery to slip through."

I visualized a tiny pinhole in the mottled white wall of the church through which I was expecting a man on horseback to come flying into my arms. Light flickered through the pinhole, suggesting that the messenger was repeatedly passing by, not able to find the portal.

"Oh. I see what you mean, Mick."

"What were you expecting at South Mountain?"

"Nothing. I mean, I didn't even know we were stopping there."

"And what did you receive?"

"A full-on visitation."

"Yes, and do you think that was a random soldier? A random visit?"

I suddenly realized that I'd been so rattled by the soldier's appearance that I might not have fully appreciated his message.

"No, he wasn't random. He explained the floating orbs in our shared dream and he tied that dream to a real place."

"Yes, but what else?"

"He was searching. Searching for someone who was missing."

"Yes. And why does that sit so heavily with you?"

"Who says that sits heavily with me?"

"Ah, yes, touched a nerve. Consider that the soldier might have been probing a wound that you'd prefer remain unmolested. Closing yourself off to any further prodding might feel safer, but will cause you to squander the opportunity you have been given today."

With that, Mick stood, folded his arms across his chest, and began spinning. I watched in amazement as his energy spun down into a little dervish that lifted a swirl of fine dust from the plank floor and bounced away from me into the sunlight streaming through the open doorway. The miniature whirlwind spun in the light, allowing the morning rays to sparkle from the suspended particles of dust, transforming them into golden glitter.

"Life can be a spiral path, you know, that leads you back, time and again, to that familiar pain guarding the heart of a matter. For those with the courage to stay the course, however, each revolution brings new awareness and the promise of release. You are on just such a path. Don't jump from the lovely swirl just as you approach your answer."

The dervish continued to spin in the sunlight, picking up speed as it shrunk to a fist-sized ball of light rapidly rotating around a dark object that had formed up in its center. As I strained forward to see what was held within the light, the small object popped out of the glittering glow and bounced against the side of my foot. A hot pain immediately shot through my foot and up my leg. I squeezed my eyes shut, doubled over in the pew and clutched my chest as the pain shot up my body to my heart, where it lingered for just a moment before draining away. When I opened my eyes, the golden dervish was gone and there beside my foot a large blackened acorn spun on its pointed tip like a top. I nudged the acorn cautiously with the toe of my shoe. It rolled harmlessly to its side and lay still. Doubling over again, I brought my face within a few feet of the odd, black acorn. Suddenly resolved to have a little bit of courage, I reached down and touched the acorn quickly with my right index finger — fully expecting a new pain to course through my arm and knock me off the bench. When the pain didn't come, I extended my fingers to pick up the acorn, but stopped with a sharp gasp when the toe of a muddy boot materialized not six inches from my fingertips. Without moving a muscle, I took a few shallow breaths. The boot was still there. I allowed my eyes to scan slowly upwards, taking in the strap of a spur and a tall leather boot top that ended at a blue worsted wool knee. I slowly lifted my head, following a double-row of gold buttons up a gray coat to the face of the man who stood before me. His mouth was obscured by his heavy beard, but his light blue eyes were dancing.

"I believe this belongs to you," said General Jackson as he tapped the acorn with the toe of his boot. It skittered forward and landed between my feet. I looked down at the blackened nut and then back up into the general's face. "No need to fear it. Pick it up."

I leaned down and picked up the acorn. It looked quite ordinary in my hand. The shell was smooth and supple, as if it had been freshly plucked from the tree. The cap was firmly attached and, in spite of a heavy layer of soot, I could plainly see the rows of tiny overlapping scales that covered the flat cap. I bent my index finger around the nut and held it firmly against my curled middle finger, rubbing the shell vigorously with the pad of my thumb.

Stonewall Jackson chuckled. "No use trying to clean it up. The char is part of that nut's character. Accept it as it is." I blushed and closed my palm over the acorn, resting my fist on my thigh. I looked back up into General Jackson's eyes. "So you know, I did enjoy the zoo of generals, regardless of what your friend over there had to say." Jackson almost imperceptibly gestured in Neil's direction with his left thumb. "I would have loved to have flown over this battlefield and seen what was ahead and on all sides of me. I had to rely on trust instead. Trust that I was divinely directed, and conviction that I was ready for death no matter when it might arrive, allowed me to think clearly in battle, unsullied by fear."

All of the decisions I'd made under the influence of fear swept around me in a swirl of shame. The acorn burned in my grip. Jackson nodded. "Fear is a funny fellow. An unpleasant visitor but so few are willing to bar him at the door. I have told more than one soul to never take counsel of his fears. Trusting that the how and when are taken care of gives you the freedom to take things as they come without projecting fear out into the darkness." An expression of rapture came over Jackson. I looked into eyes that glowed like bright blue headlights and suddenly felt a sense of complete release.

"Remember that feeling. You have felt it before. And remember, too, that you may be whatever you resolve to be." A sly smile played around Jackson's eyes as he winked at me and turned toward the open door. "Watch this."

Thomas Jackson raised his arms into the sunlight and leapt through the doorway as his boots fell away revealing strongly clenched talons and heavily feathered golden-brown legs. I jumped to my feet and stood at the door as Jackson's uniform dropped to the sidewalk, releasing the magnificent golden eagle I'd seen in my mind's eye. The first powerful sweep of the eagle's wings lifted it up almost vertically. Two more sweeps of its wings and the bird was above the roof line of the church and headed for the battlefield. Three more sweeps and it was above the obelisk across the road. As the eagle continued to gain altitude with powerful strokes of its wings, I suddenly realized that I wasn't the only one who could see it. A winding sidewalk through the field between the visitor center and the Dunker Church was dotted with people looking up and pointing as the eagle swung wide right over the roof of the visitor center. People craned their necks and scrambled for cameras and smartphones as the eagle banked to its left and flew straight at the side of a majestic columnar monument that dominated the hill beside the building. With the bird now in profile, I could see that its body and head were in absolute alignment — it was locked on its target with unwavering intent. Time slowed to a crawl as the eagle's wings lifted slightly, gathered the morning beneath them, and then pushed the golden sunlight down and away. Lift, gather, push. Lift, gather, push. The eagle charged unwaveringly and just as it was about to collide with the monument, screamed and rose, dragging its talons across the head of the stone eagle that topped the column. A gasp emerged from the assembled witnesses as a voice rang in my head.

"The eagle never questions the ability of his wings to carry him — he just picks his target and flies."

"Whoa," Neil said from over my right shoulder. "Is that an eagle?"

"It is," I confirmed. "Being what it resolved to be."

CHAPTER 30

ROAD TRIP: WHERE THE PENNSYLVANIA RESERVES TEACH US THE ROPES

Neil and I watched together at the door of the church as the eagle rose up high against the brilliant blue sky and headed north over the battlefield. Across the road, a white Honda pulled in behind Neil's SUV and disgorged a trio of tourists with camera straps around their necks. I looked up at Neil and saw that his eyes were glassy. "Are you okay?" I asked.

"Yes, let's get out of here and drive the northern battlefield. Something happened, but I'm not prepared to talk about it yet."

"Okay." I let Neil slip past me as I pushed the acorn deep into the front pocket of my jeans. Ignoring the niceties of sidewalk and steps, which he left to the approaching tourists, Neil strode down the rise and across the road to the SUV. I rushed to catch up and slid into the passenger seat just as Neil threw the vehicle into drive. I hurried to shut the door as the SUV rolled out from under the shade of a stocky maple tree and passed by the road leading east across the battlefield. Neil drove straight north on Hagerstown Pike, past five-rail fence on our right and tangled woods on our left, not slowing for sightseeing as we passed a series of black interpretive signs and what looked like a park on our left. He suddenly swerved to the right and pulled over, though, when we came to an intersection guarded by a bronze soldier on a tall stone column. Neil put the SUV in park, opened his door, and stepped out to look at the figure high up on the monument. I quickly followed suit, squinting into the strong morning sun at a soldier brandishing a sword above his head with his right hand while balancing himself with his outstretched left arm.

"He was an infantry field officer," said Neil. "He marched into battle in front of his men and signaled their movements with his sword. I can't see from down here if he has a sash. He should have a sash around his waist—a red sash. Men like this were unbelievably brave. They led lines of soldiers forward under artillery fire to within a hundred yards of the enemy. So many of these officers were shot down as they led their troops forward." Without looking at me, Neil slid back into the SUV and slammed his door. I immediately jumped back into my seat to avoid being left on the side of the road. We were again moving forward before I had the door shut.

Neil gestured over the dash toward the fields on our right. "Does this seem about right for the cornfield you saw? I mean, about the right location where you saw all that fighting?"

I nodded, just barely moving my head. "Yes, it does seem right."

"We're going to make the loop around it. The loop of the P that I showed you on the map. There was more of a woodlot back there on our left at the time of the battle and, oh, on the right now is the Miller House." Neil pulled over at the bottom of a gravel driveway leading to a white two-story farmhouse. The front door and small front porch of the house were strangely offset to the right corner.

"Yes, that house was right there! Everything's been cleared out around it, though. There should be a stone wall with a gate out front. And the trees are missing. There were trees all around this house, including a big one right in front. But the porch is right and the windows are right, too. There were soldiers all over the place here."

"Now, there's the enthusiasm I was hoping for. Would you say without a doubt we're at the correct battlefield?"

"Oh, yeah. Without a doubt."

Neil took off again. We passed farm fields on both sides and a modern house on our left. Rounding a slight curve to the right, I could see a wide two-lane road in front of us. If not for the guardrail separating the two roads, we could have driven straight north off the battlefield by continuing on the larger road. "See how the Hagerstown Pike was rerouted? The road we're on used to be the main route between Sharpsburg and Hagerstown. Now it's just a short spur that runs between the church and the Poffenberger Farm, which is right…." Neil turned right before we had a chance to crash through the guardrail. A beautiful farm property complete with outbuildings and a low white farmyard fence appeared on the left. A strong sense of déjà vu swept over me. I'd seen this land from the air but alive with Union soldiers. "…here. This is where your tiger on horseback spent the night before the battle. The 1st Corps camped up here on the 16th."

A rush of conflicting emotions hit me as we wheeled by the Poffenberger Farm — overwhelming anticipation, excitement, anxiety, fear, and downright dread all stirred together in a confusing emotional stew that was just an inch from boiling over and burning all over the stove. I wanted to throw myself out of the vehicle, run screaming back to the guardrail, and flag down a ride to Hagerstown. "Cool," I said.

"First thing in the morning, Jackson's troops were waiting for the Union attack along the Hagerstown Pike, in an open field south of Miller's cornfield, and in the East Woods, which we haven't gotten to yet. Let's stop here for a few minutes." Neil pulled into a small parking lot on our left and reached over the seat for the book of maps. He chose a bookmark and flipped to a map that included a large mass of blue bars at the top and an equally large mass of red bars at the bottom. "Over the weekend, I read whatever I could get my hands on about Antietam and Civil War battle tactics. Then I organized what I learned so I could share it with you."

A smile spread over my face. "Still prepping me for the big meeting."

Neil winked at me. "Someone has to do the attention to detail thing. Now, the battle started at this end of the battlefield right as dawn broke. What happened between where we're sitting and where the visitor center is now located was gory, horrific, chaotic, and confusing. Individual participants on either side had only basic knowledge of what they were to do, which usually consisted of either taking a defensive position or marching into position in columns four men wide and then spreading out to form two lines, which could be a mile or more wide depending on the topography. The men would march shoulder to shoulder into firing range and then the line in front would fire en masse at an enemy line, which might be advancing, charging head-on, or waiting protected behind a fence or rock ledge. Once the soldiers in the front line had fired their rifles, they would reload as the line behind them fired. This would continue until one side or the other broke."

"What do you mean by broke?"

"The lines would become full of holes as men were killed and wounded. Artillery, in particular, could be used to create big holes in infantry lines. Both sides used exploding cannon balls and canisters that exploded and sent small shot, the size of musket balls, into opposing infantry. It was critical to plug any holes by moving men around and bringing up reinforcements because if enough men fell, the survivors wouldn't be able to fire fast enough to slow the enemy line, which would come closer and closer until being ordered to charge. In most cases, a collapsing line would be called into retreat because once the enemy punched through a hole, they were able to shoot down the line and decimate it. And that's it for basic tactics."

"That's it?"

"Pretty much so. Any questions?"

"Well, yeah. Why was lining up a mile wide and plowing head-on into the enemy a good idea?"

"The intent of the frontal assault was, at least early in the war, to rattle the enemy and intimidate them into retreating. A frontal assault could also be effective if you had numbers or surprise on your side. A bigger force, in theory, should be able to overwhelm a smaller force by charging right at it, but that wasn't always true, especially if the smaller force had taken a defensive position and had time to really dig in."

"But, if hitting the enemy line from the side was so effective, why wasn't that always the plan?"

"It often was. Getting around the end of the enemy line and charging was called flanking, and it was a devastating tactic. It's what A.P. Hill's division did on the south end of the battlefield. Both sides tried to guard against being flanked by using impenetrable topography to anchor their flanks. If that wasn't possible, cavalry might guard the flanks and, if we're talking about a long line, it was usually the practice to position veteran regiments at the flanks because they were better able to turn their line to face a flank attack. You know, your eagle friend, Jackson, was legendary for his flanking moves. He..." A quizzical look spread over Neil's face and then bled away. "Uh, you ready to learn about the general strategy on this end of the battlefield?"

I nodded silently, glad that Neil wasn't going to probe the connection he'd obviously just made between Stonewall Jackson and an eagle that was inexplicably flying around strafing monuments. "Okay, um, so as I mentioned, Lee and his army arrived here first and took up defensive positions in anticipation of an attack from the north and the east. They placed their artillery on high ground to the west of where we're sitting right now and to the south in front of Dunker Church and along the ridge where the visitor center is now located. The Union objective was to simply drive the Confederates back and take the church and high ground. The Confederate plan was to hold their ground and then drive the Union forces from the battlefield."

"Did the Confederates have any hope of doing that?"

"Yep. Lee's army had been mostly victorious early in the war and was just coming off a huge victory at Manassas, so Lee had emotion on his side. His plan was to ride that emotion forward to his first big win on northern soil. The biggest challenge the Confederates faced was the toll of scrambling to get assembled here. The men had been marched hard and fast with little food or water, so were in rough shape on the day of battle. Thousands didn't make it here with their regiments — they fell out on the side of the road or called bullshit on the entire ordeal and just melted away. By the time everyone arrived who was going to arrive, the Confederates were outnumbered about forty thousand to eighty-five thousand, and those forty thousand were exhausted, filthy, starving."

"And they were still confident?"

"Apparently so. Lee knew McClellan well and counted on him to overestimate the Confederate strength and to take a cautious approach. He was right on both counts. McClellan was convinced Lee had over a hundred thousand men here. He was expecting all day to be overwhelmed by Lee's reserves just as soon as he overcommitted his own. So, McClellan didn't overcommit."

"Little Mac's accounting weren't far off. Ev'body knowed one Johnny Reb was worth ever' bit of three Billy Yanks 'specially with Marse Robert on the field."

I spun around in the direction of the voice and found myself gazing into the empty back seat. "Neil, did you…?"

"What?"

"Uh, never mind."

"You sure."

"Yeah, keep going."

"Okay, then, let's shift focus to what actually happened out here." Neil's attention went back to the book and the map of blue and red bars. He first pointed to the red bars spread near the bottom of the map. "On the Confederate side, Jackson had most of his divisions here. He was supported by General John Bell Hood's two divisions. Hood and his men were crazy aggressive. He had this brigade from Texas that just never stopped. They…no, wait, I'm jumping ahead. I wanted to show you the Union corps now. There were three infantry corps involved in the fight up here. They entered battle one after another. General Hooker went first with the 1st Corps…" Neil swept his hand top to bottom across the map.

"…then came General Mansfield with the 12th Corps…" Neil now dragged his fingertips from the right top corner of the map and spread them as he moved down the page.

"…and finally came General Sumter with part of the 2nd Corps." Neil swept his hand right to left across the map.

"In terms of how the battle was fought, you can think of Miller's cornfield as the center of a good deal of the action early in the day. The cornfield changed hands several times as both sides repeatedly attacked, retreated, and counterattacked. But it wasn't as simple as a fight for the cornfield. There was also intense fighting in the West Woods, which we just passed coming up here, along the Hagerstown Pike, and in the East Woods on the other side of the cornfield."

I let out a heavy sigh.

"Overwhelmed already?"

"No, not really that. Don't get me wrong, what you just explained was helpful, but it was also really impersonal and…"

A grin spread over Neil's face and his eyes lit up again. "I was hoping you'd say that. Let's get out of the vehicle for a few minutes. I have a story I want to tell you that starts right here." Neil grabbed his book and we both got out of the SUV. He led me to the hood of the vehicle and set his book down carefully, so as not to scratch the paint. "First off, let's take a look around. Notice anything interesting about the four tall monuments arranged along this road?"

I peered up and down the road. Four monuments, each topped with a stone soldier, were stretched out along the northern edge. "Definitely, they're a matched set — though each soldier has struck a different pose."

"Yep, meet the boys of the Pennsylvania Reserves. These monuments were placed in honor of four of the thirteen regiments that made up General George Meade's Division of the 1st Corps."

I nodded. "Ah, Meade. The snapping turtle."

"Goggle-eyed snapping turtle to you, soldier. He did Pennsylvania proud here and I'd like to tell you about seven of his regiments, including the four with statues along this road."

"I do believe I'll allow you to do that, but how'd you know these monuments were here?"

"I found a cool app online. Had maps and pictures of all the monuments. I'm hoping that seeing the men depicted on the monuments will make it easier to connect with the soldiers as I tell you what their regiments did out here. Now, let's go meet our new friends."

Neil and I walked over to the stone soldier to the left of the parking pullout and looked up at him. His right foot was forward and he was holding the muzzle of his musket with his right hand. The sunlight illuminated the face of a clean-shaven boy probably not yet out of his teens with thick hair that swept back along the edges of his cap as if blown by an invisible wind.

"He looks really young," I said.

"The average age of the Union soldiers was just under twenty-six and there were a huge number of teenagers out here. Eighteen was the minimum without parental permission, but thousands of younger boys lied about their age and enlisted."

"You looked that up?"

"It seemed important."

"What's he doing?"

"I think he's about to pull out the gun's ramrod."

"He's on the battle line? He looks so calm."

"He does."

"No way would I be that calm."

We walked back across the parking pullout and slightly downhill to the next Pennsylvania Reserves monument. The stone soldier here was loading his musket, his right hand working a phantom ramrod. This man was a little older — maybe early twenties — and also clean-shaven.

"I can't imagine using a muzzleloader in battle," Neil said.

"Well, you're ahead of me, then, because I can't imagine being in battle, period. If I was here, I hope Andy really was next to me, taking the edge off. Otherwise, I suspect I might have left a hole in the line as I ran like hell in the opposite direction."

Neil clucked his disapproval like an old mother hen and led me a little farther down the hill to the third monument. It was topped by a mustachioed stone soldier with his hat raised in his left hand. A bandage was wrapped around his head and he seemed to be looking for someone on the horizon.

"He looks like he's waving farewell," I said.

"I don't know. Look at his right foot. He's standing on a cannon. I think he's celebrating the victory."

"He looks sad. Like his comrades are walking away and leaving him. His buddies were killed here."

"No, he's celebrating. You know, low-key. He's pleased but tired."

"Hmm, I don't know if I'm buying what you're selling."

I followed Neil down the road into a swale occupied by the last of the boys from the Pennsylvania Reserves. The final stone soldier was standing at attention with his musket at his side. Forever ready to march back into battle, if called.

"This is the monument to the 8th Regiment," Neil explained. "These guys started out from about this point and marched south and then east to the corner of the East Woods. They fought until their ammunition was exhausted."

The sight of the young soldier standing at the edge of the road, never to return home, filled me with a hollow sadness. "Okay. I've connected with the guys now," I said softly.

Completely missing my melancholy, Neil grinned and gave me a quick one-armed hug that almost knocked me off my feet. "Great, I was hoping you would. Let's walk back up to the pullout. It makes more sense to tell their story from there."

I silently followed Neil back past the stone soldiers to the hood of the SUV. He opened the book to a new map and leaned forward to begin his explanation, but then changed his mind. "This would be better on the other side of the road. Let's go stand over there."

We walked around the SUV and crossed the asphalt to a split rail fence where Neil picked up the thread of his presentation. "Okay, so the monuments mark the positions of the four regiments that made up the left half of a line that stretched the full length of this road. The remaining three regiments were lined up in front of us and to our right — all the way to the Hagerstown Pike."

I looked back up the road the way we'd come in case I'd missed the monuments for the last three regiments, but couldn't spot them.

"Where are their monuments?"

"At Gettysburg. The state of Pennsylvania gave the regiments enough money for one monument each and theirs are at Gettysburg. Just imagine that there are three more statues spread out kind of evenly in front of the Poffenberger Farm."

"Okay."

Neil opened the book and balanced it on the top rail of the fence. He pointed out a strip of little green blobs near the top of the map with his left hand while waving his right hand in an expansive sweeping gesture to introduce the landscape in front of us. "Now, if this were 1862, we'd be facing into the North Woods. Imagine this as a mature woodlot…"

I gazed out at the tall grass and sparse trees covering the land in front of us and easily conjured up sixty-foot tall oak and walnut trees in thick, green summer foliage. I made the trunks straight and clear and grew them out to diameters of eighteen, twenty-four, thirty-six inches. Beautiful timber. I hoped it had been used for lumber, not firewood or fence rails. I placed a sparse understory of short, skinny gray-barked beech and maple saplings beneath the canopy and then imagined myself standing in the woods with the morning sun filtering softly down to dance across the forest floor. *What's missing? Ah, low-growing greenery.* A carpet of ferns, small woodland plants, and red-capped mushrooms emerged from my magician's brush. *But, maybe that's wrong — cattle and hogs probably grazed these woods.* As I contemplated whether or not to erase the bloodroot and low-bush blueberries in deference to a gang of marauding livestock, Neil's voice faded away and I found myself standing alone in the woodlot I'd imagined.

The light immediately dimmed to predawn gray and the details of the woodlot became indistinct. The sound of a single chirping cricket intruded from somewhere in front of me. I drew in a stuttering, shallow breath and slid my eyes in the direction of the cricket as a fine mist rose up from the earth, which was now springy and saturated beneath my feet. Faint breeze tickled the tree canopy, knocking moisture loose from the leaves high above my head. The resulting shower of heavy drops pummeled me and then abruptly stopped as the breeze settled. I strained my eyes to see in the misty gray light, realizing that the presence or lack of bloodroot and blueberries didn't much matter in the dark. The crack of a twig breaking ricocheted through the dark woods and I spun around to see what was behind me. I stretched my eyelids as wide as they'd go but couldn't see through the darkness pressed tight against my eyes. And then I heard the breath. The hollow cacophony of thousands of men breathing the thick moist air rushed forward through the dark, drowning out the cricket, and slamming me to my knees. The cool damp of the morning fled, replaced by the heat emanating from two thousand simmering soldiers. I clamped my palms over my ears and sunk down in the wet soil beneath the trees.

"…and as the Pennsylvania Reserves waited in the woods around dawn, Doubleday's Division and then Ricketts' slid over from the east and advanced south through their ranks to meet the Confederate troops who were waiting below the cornfield. Why are you looking at me like that?"

I blinked and pulled my eyeballs back into my skull where they belonged. "I was imagining the woodlot."

"Apparently it looked a little freaky?"

"Yeah, dark, wet, and full of dangerous men. A lot of heavy breathing going on."

"Ah."

Neil paused.

"Do you want to hear what happened next?"

"Yes."

"The divisions that went ahead of the Reserves stepped from the edge of the woods into a plowed field. The hill to the west of the Hagerstown Pike belched Confederate fire like a volcano, as did the high ground to the south. 'Welcome to artillery hell, boys,' the big guns shouted. 'Welcome to artillery hell.' The Union lines struggled south as Confederate shells slammed into them, throwing men and body parts into the air. Eventually, the survivors reached the relative cover of the tall corn…"

 The grass and trees in front of me shuddered and fell away in a ruddy cloud of dust as lush, bright green cornstalks emerged from the earth and surged ten feet into the air. I could hear the artillery roar, but the crash of explosions seemed strangely muted. As I stepped forward into the corn, the bright morning dimmed again to misty predawn and my nostrils filled with the musty, sweet smell of corn silk. The hollow tromping of feet and continuous swish of leaves indicated that I was not alone in the corn. In fact, ragged breathing to my immediate right and left suggested that my nearest comrades were just feet away. I lifted my arms to fend off the cornstalks that I could barely see through the damp morning mist and cursed as a sharp-edged leaf sliced my ear. The soft curses of others engaged in hand-to-hand combat with the corn drifted through the darkness. I pulled a strappy leaf away from my eyes just in time to see a long line of flashes ahead of me in the dark. Pop-pop-pop-pop-pop! The leaf was ripped out of my hand as a whispered hum filled the air. I

threw myself to the damp ground between the cornstalks as shredded
leaves and bits of corn tassel rained down upon me.

"...and as the Union troops advanced through the cornfield, lines of Rebel
troops rose up and fired into them from open pasture to the south. Men dove
for cover and fell by the dozens. Before the morning ended, thousands more
will have joined them as casualties of war."

"So, you got me all attached to these boys from Pennsylvania and they're
about to be sent into a killing field?"

"Yeah, but not yet. They have about ninety more minutes to wait."

"Ninety minutes seems like a long time for the guys already in the cornfield."

"It was. In the course of that ninety minutes, they battled their way to the
southern edge of the corn and held a line that stretched nearly eight hundred
yards east to west from the Hagerstown Pike to the East Woods..."

The sound of continuous artillery fire filled my ears again, but this time
the mute button was off. From in front of me, from behind me, and
from both sides came the roar of cannons and the crash of exploding
ordnance. It was dawn now and I could see more clearly, although the
air had become filled with sulfuric smoke. I was still on the ground
in the corn, but now was behind a pile of wooden rails with a musket
clenched in my hands. A stirring "hu-RRAH", carried by thousands of
voices, rose from somewhere in front of me and to my right. Raising up
on my elbows, I peered over the fence rails to see lines of Union soldiers
racing at an angle across a green field littered with bodies. I watched
fascinated as the lines changed direction with the precision of a starling
flock to sweep a ragged line of Confederate soldiers south before being
swallowed from sight by the rolling landscape.

"...swept the Confederate line all the way back to the Dunker Church, giving
the Union temporary command of the battlefield. But, the Union troops
holding the line along the south edge of the cornfield were running low on
ammunition..."

I reached down for my leather cartridge box and pulled open the flap.
Only one cartridge left. One bullet in my musket and one in my box.
*Where are the damned reinforcements? We need to pull back. We need to
pull back now!* A new commotion of men arose from the other side of
the fence rails. I lifted myself up again to see what was going on. To my
horror, the Union lines were thundering out of the field, headed in my
direction. "Companee! Retreat! Reg-i-ment! Retreat!" Not waiting for
the lieutenant to ask twice, I scrambled to my feet and raced back into
the corn.

"...and then, finally, the Pennsylvania Reserves were called in. They marched south in columns through the woods and into the plowed field, where they, too, were pummeled by the Confederate artillery. As they headed to a stout rail fence that lined the northern edge of the cornfield, they encountered the first of the dead and wounded from the divisions that had moved past them at dawn. By the time the heads of their columns reached the fence, bloodied and exhausted Union troops were streaming north through their ranks in a mass retreat."

"Wait, what happened? Why did the other guys retreat?"

"Oh, sorry. Jackson's men had been forced off the field, but General Hood answered with an aggressive Confederate counterattack. Ten regiments, including his Texas Brigade, came charging north. They broke the entire Union line and chased the guys back through the cornfield and out of the East Woods."

"So, the Pennsylvania Reserves marched straight into a tempest."

"Yeah, and while still in their columns they began taking fire from Hood's men. The regiments to our right spread out into a defensive line behind the fence and propped their muskets on the bottom rails. Unfortunately, even though they were already within Confederate musket range, the four regiments to the left had been ordered to march east to shore things up in the East Woods…"

The pulses in front of my ears began to throb and I realized my heart was racing. My peripheral vision contracted until I seemed to be looking through binoculars. *No, no, no. I can't pass out!*

I strained to see through billows of thick acrid smoke that burned my throat and lungs. Something solid was pressed against my right cheek. My shoulders were tense and my hands were cramped. A sharp pain in my left shin told me my legs were folded tight in front of me and wedged up against something hard and unforgiving. The smoke thinned just enough to reveal that I was sitting on the ground — doubled up behind a pile of rocks sighting a rifle between the rails of a stout fence. My ears were ringing, muffling my hearing. I wiggled my jaw to pop my eardrums and a sharp pain shot through my head. I reached up and touched my forehead. My hand came back bright red with blood. I wiped my fingers on the sleeve of my dark blue coat just as the ground shook with an explosion that I couldn't hear. I turned back to my rifle and waited, sighting down its length toward an enemy I couldn't see or hear. A small window cleared in the smoke and a trampled cornfield filled with prone human forms appeared in front of me. Wavering figures began to move through the smoke. The enemy racing toward me. *Wait for the shot. Wait for the shot. Wait. Wait. Wait.* I involuntarily coughed to clear my lungs.

"You alright there? Sounds like you have the croup."

I snapped my head up toward the voice and found myself staring into a haggard face that seemed strangely familiar. It was that of a man, probably in his early thirties, but was a little hard to age due to a liberal coating of black soot and a tawny goatee that covered most of the mouth.

Playful gray eyes danced in the soot, inviting me to recognize them. I cleared my throat but found there was nothing there to clear. "Who are you?" I asked.

"You don't recognize me? I told them you wouldn't recognize me. Maybe this will help." The man dug into a pants pocket and pulled out a dirty rag. He extracted the cork from the flat metal canteen slung around his neck and carefully shook a few drops of water onto the rag. "Damn, out of water again." He replaced the cork in his canteen and rubbed the damp rag over his face, revealing strikingly handsome features that I immediately recognized in spite of the fact that they now apparently belonged to a Confederate officer.

"You're the guy at the Shady Grove Metro Station! The homeless guy on the sidewalk who I save my change for!"

The officer grinned and swept the high-crowned brown felt hat off his head in an expansive bow. "That I am. Lieutenant William Dupree at your service. You can call me Bill. Would you care to stand up and commiserate a spell?"

I snapped my head back around, suddenly remembering the horde approaching through the smoke.

"Don't worry 'bout my boys. They'll still be here when you get back."

"They're your boys?"

"Yep, 1st Texas. Howling, raucous lot have outrun our ability to corral them and are about to meet you here in a moment of destiny. Let me help you up. See you got yourself in a right knot there." Bill dangled a hand down for me to grasp but my attention was drawn past it by his right foot, the heel of which was pointed toward me while the toe was pointed away. Bill followed my horrified gaze. "Oh, forgot about that." He reached down with both hands, grabbed his ankle, and gave his leg a sharp twist to the left, bringing his toes to the front. "That'll fix 'er." Bill extended his hand again and pulled me to my feet. "Up we go. Your head is bleeding. Looks like you got a little nick there. Don't worry none about it, though. You just popped into this feller's memory for a little look around. You ready to take that little look around?"

"Uh, sure." Even before I'd finished agreeing, Bill snapped his fingers by his right ear. In the next instant, we were both flung bodily onto a damp patch of ground. Bill sat up next to me and wiped at a new swipe of dirt on the sleeve of his gray coat.

"Always a mess out here. Sorry 'bout the rough landing. This is my first go at tour guide."

I stretched my arms out, looking in wonder at the muddy tan coat I was now wearing. "How did I change clothes?"

"Oh, that. You're one of us now. I put you with the 2nd Mississippi. Welcome aboard! Now pick up your musket and get in line. There's Yanks up there in front of us making a run for the woods. See 'em? See 'em run?" I squinted through the smoke and could make out a continuous stream of dark figures half running for a stand of tall timber looming out of the smoke and mist to our right. "Reminds one of a carnival game, don't it? All we need is the calliope. Get up there with your pals if you want a piece of the action." Bill gestured forward toward a line of shadows not twenty feet in front of us. The pops of musket fire and periodic celebratory shouts coming from that direction indicated the Mississippians were hitting their marks.

"No, I…" Bill snapped his fingers again and I found myself back in blue but this time jogging along a fence line with pops of musketry coming from my right. Bill ran along beside me with a wicked grin on his face.

"Better?" The head of the man in front of me snapped to the side as his cap flew off in a spray of blood and gray matter.

"No!"

Bill snapped his fingers again and I was suddenly standing behind a cannon with the end of a long cord in my hand. "Turn away and pull the cord! Them Mississippi boys have broke through the line! Pull it!"

"No, I can't!"

Bill snapped his fingers and I was a Confederate again, but was now 20 feet off the ground tumbling through the air. "Ah, guess somebody else pulled that cord," Bill commented from below me. "We'd better move on to the Pike before you hit the ground."

Before I could catch my breath, I found myself attempting to squeeze my body between the rough rails of a fence. "Look at you, a Texas boy! Who whudda thunk it? Don't get stuck now. Them Yanks over on the other side of the Pike are waving around a Rebel battle flag. We can't have that, now, can we? Go get it, son!"

I clumsily extracted myself from the fence and tumbled to the ground at Bill's feet. "Oh, son, not the way we do things in Texas."

Bill snapped his fingers again and I was carrying a heavy can in both hands toward a smoking line of cannons. A bare-headed, dark-haired Union officer with a heavy mustache and at least a week's worth of beard galloped up on a horse and swung down to the ground beside me. "General John Gibbon. North Carolina boy. Shoulda been one of us. Left his infantry division just now to come fire that there abandoned gun. Look at him calling for the teamsters to come up and help him. Enough sightseeing. Hurry up! Hurry up! Give him that canister and go get another. My boys are charging you from the other side of the Pike!"

I stared in shock at the howling mob charging the tall split rail fence right in front of me. "No!"

"Just no satisfying you." Bill snapped his fingers and my world exploded in a pink, misty hell of exploding bodies and flying shards of fence rail. "Dang, slid us in here a little too late for comfort. Mick's gonna have my hide. But I see General Gibbon got that load of double canister off."

I was suddenly sitting alone with Bill by a small campfire in a quiet, open woodlot. My back was against a tree and my legs, again, were folded up in front of me. As I trembled and struggled to catch my breath, Bill fussed with a blackened can, carefully handling it with his dirty rag as he poured a thin brown liquid into two tin cups. He handed me one of the cups and sat down next to me with the other. "Rebel coffee. Boiled corncobs and tree bark but it helps us keep up appearances."

"Thanks."

"Oh, don't thank me till you've tasted it." I took the cup and blew on the steam, unsure if I wanted a hot drink given the river of sweat cascading down my back.

"So, how many boys did your friend say was out here? You remember?" Bill asked.

"Uh, a hundred and twenty-five thousand all together."

"Yep, a hundred and twenty-five thousand, more or less. Never could pin down exactly how many Rebs stumbled in, but one twenty-five will do. Every one of them had a unique view of what happened out here. Quarter of a million unique views. Whaddya think of that?"

I opened my mouth immediately to answer but Bill held up his hand. "Think about your answer, now. This is important. Don't give me something pat just to shut me up."

I stretched out my legs and lowered my eyes to my right foot, which I found wrapped in a rough leather shoe caked with thick red mud. My big toe was pushing through the worn leather. The top of a coarse gray sock was visible between the top of the shoe and my frayed pant leg, which had been torn off a foot or so above my ankle. A hard ache in my belly suggested that I hadn't eaten in days. I folded my thighs back against the ache. "Everyone out here knew the battle intimately, but didn't know it at all."

"Yep, you got that right. How'd it make you feel to share a single moment of just a few of them hundred and twenty-five thousand battles?"

"Confused. You were flipping my brain on and off. Before I could get invested in one guy's battle, you'd moved me on to the next one."

"Invested? Invested, you say? You didn't really try to invest, did you?"

I was embarrassed to be called out and wanted to be released from this conversation. "No, I didn't really try," I mumbled to the ground.

"Why was that?"

I looked up at Bill, pulling on my lower lip with a grubby thumb and forefinger as I answered. "I didn't want to step into their realities."

"Why?"

"Umm...I...uh...I don't know."

"Well, now you're just makin' things too hard." Bill handed me his coffee cup and pushed himself to his feet. He dusted off his jacket and suddenly let out a string of curses. "Damnation! I lost a button!" I noticed then the line of gold buttons marching up Bill's chest. He wiggled his finger through an empty button hole and ranted for a bit before resigning himself to the fact that the button was gone forever. "Well, guess it don't matter none considering how this day is gonna turn out, but damn it."

In spite of my hopes that Bill had forgotten me in his angst over the lost button, he put his palms on his thighs and glared hard into my upturned face. His face flared angry red as he bent down and screamed inches from my nose, "Why wouldn't you try?"

I immediately shot back in the face of the attack. "Those aren't my stories!" I yelled. "I don't have to live someone else's story if I don't want to and...I don't want to!"

"What else?" Bill yelled in my face.

"I'm sick of seeing through a pinhole! I want to see the big picture!"

Bill sunk to his heels in mock exhaustion and put his hands on my shoulders. "I want you to remember that now. Even if you don't end up accepting Vulture's invitation today to uncover your own story, I want you to remember that there. You don't have to live someone else's story and you don't have to accept a limited view of reality. That gets you halfway to where you need to be. And halfway home is better than fullway gone any day of the week."

"Oh, hell, not the vulture again."

"That's Vulture with a capital V for you. Them little vultures...they're out here for your friend. Speaking of which, he's almost to the end of that speech I had him pre-pare and will be expectin' you back."

My mouth fell open. "You put Neil up to that?"

"I did! Been followin' him around for weeks, whispering sweet nothins in his ear. He needed somethin' to ground to...give himself a little control of his situation and what better than to write a speech? He reckons it's all his idea, of course, but I just sat with him a spell back at the church while you was entertaining Old Jack. He's comin' to the realization that he's still got a team and I'm on it." Bill tipped back his head and shared the cackling laugh I'd last heard outside the Metro station. I suddenly panicked, realizing he was getting ready to leave me.

"Will I remember you?"

"Well, sure you will. And I could prob'ly stick close today, if you'd like."

"I would! I'd like that a lot."

"Mick? Whaddya think?" Bill cocked his head and listened for an answer before meeting my eyes again. "Mick says certainly and before I go back to the field to get my fool leg shot off again he wants me to share a little secret, but let's drink up first." Bill tapped his cup against mine and lifted it toward his lips. I tipped my head back and sloshed a bitter gulp of liquid down my throat and immediately gagged. Bill howled with laughter and slapped his knee as I spit the remnants of the brew on the ground. "Now you know why I appreciate your loose change." He dashed his coffee into the fire, smiled at me with his magical gray eyes, and tipped his own head back. "Caw! Caw-caw! Caw-caw! Caw! Caw-caw!"

"...1st Texas emerged from the smoke when they were less than thirty feet from the fence. The Pennsylvanians popped up and poured musket fire into their ranks. At the same time, the Union artillery battery that had been brought into position on the other side of the Pike started blasting the Texans from only forty-five feet away. They were driven to the ground with fifty percent of their men lost. But, the survivors didn't retreat. They stayed prone in the dirt and kept fighting. No quit in those boys. By the time they were done, they'd lost their flag on the field of battle and eighty-two percent of the regiment was dead or wounded, including most of the officers. You look a little nauseated. Do you want me to stop?" Neil asked.

I stared at him in stunned silence for just a beat as I imagined Bill clutching what was left of his right leg. "No, you don't have to stop. Um, how did guys who were wounded usually make out?"

"A lot of them died out here on the field before they could be reached. Both sides used a big, conical lead bullet that spread out when it hit flesh and caused horrendous wounds, even pulverizing bone. It was called a Minie ball. Even if they did make it to a field hospital, there was little hope for guys with gut or chest wounds and there were also huge numbers of amputations. Limbs were piled up outside the field hospitals, which were in houses, barns, tents. And there were no antibiotics. Bacterial infection wasn't even understood back then so…"

"Okay, you can move on now."

"Understand. I have more story I can tell you about the battle along the Pike. You want to hear it?"

"Sure."

Neil patted me on the shoulder and tried to smile sweetly through his excitement to share more gory battle descriptions with me. "Try to just listen without imagining all the details, okay?"

"Okay."

"So, those three regiments of the Texas Brigade that I told you about were still battling the five Union regiments across the Pike with both sides suffering tremendous casualties, which I won't describe, and neither side willing to give in. In the Confederates' favor, they'd picked off a lot of the guys manning the artillery pieces and had two of the cannons knocked out of commission. They were very close to overwhelming the battery — were within fifteen feet. In complete desperation, the artillery officers brought up their teamsters and anyone else who was available. Even a young bugler helped carry ordnance. Seeing that the rag-tag crew was aiming over the Rebels' heads, one of the infantry generals rushed over to give instruction. Still okay?"

I gulped hard at the familiar story and nodded, suddenly not sure if a big breakfast had been a good idea.

"You look green so I'll wrap it up here. The entire Union line then advanced toward the Pike en masse and the Rebel line began to fold. At the same time, the three Pennsylvania Reserve regiments still behind the fence north of the cornfield were ordered to charge. The simultaneous Union charge cleared the field of Hood's men, including the survivors of the 1st Texas, who ran like hell back to that road that cuts across the battlefield in front of Dunker Church."

I glanced down the road to the statue of the soldier waving his hat in triumph. "So, the Pennsylvania boys did get to enjoy the taste of victory."

"Yeah, but it was only a little taste. They emerged victorious from the south edge of the cornfield and were charging through a clover field to claim the high ground when they were met by five fresh Confederate regiments. The Pennsylvanians were forced to turn around and race back north. As they fled, General Mansfield's entire 12th Corps helped out by appearing in a gap between the North and East Woods. That drew the Confederates' attention and allowed the Pennsylvanians to escape the cornfield and work their way back to the North Woods. By 8:15 or so, their role in the battle was finished."

"And that was it?"

"It was for the Pennsylvania Reserves and the rest of 1st Corps, but the battle continued up here for two more hours. The 12th Corps took the field next. Remember those Confederate soldiers you saw in your vision marching north to Sharpsburg?"

"Yeah, a steady stream of them."

"That would have been one of the Confederate divisions arriving late from Harpers Ferry. Those guys joined the battle in time to help push the 12th Corps back. Later, part of the 2nd Corps came in from the east like I showed you on the map. Jackson and Hood reorganized their men and ambushed the 2nd Corps in the West Woods. The fighting continued on until about 10:30, but by then the battle had already started to shift south."

"Oh. So did anyone really win up here?"

"I guess you'd have to say the Union did. They did gain the high ground, which was their objective, and positioned artillery there as the battle moved to Bloody Lane. That high ground was captured at a brutal cost, though. The Texas Regiment alone…"

I let Neil continue rattling off facts and statistics as I looked out over the landscape in front of us, imagining shattered men, their dismembered limbs, and their possessions littering the field. *Baggage. Baggage. Baggage in the valley.* A crow cawed loudly from across the road and I spun around to find the flapping bird fighting to find its balance on the slouched hat of the stone soldier loading his musket. A shadow passed through the peripheral vision of my left eye — a second crow flying from the battlefield to land on the soldier's hat. A tingle started in the middle of my forehead and swept down my body.

"Caw!" Something fell from the second crow's beak and rattled to the pavement.

"…that adds up to almost thirteen thousand causalities just on this end of the battlefield and all before 10:30 in the morning. By the end of the day, that number almost doubled and…"

I walked across the road to the monument occupied by the crows. Oddly, the birds watched me intently and stayed put as I approached and looked up at them. "What did you drop?"

"Caw! Caw-caw! Caw-caw!"

I scanned the asphalt at the base of the monument but didn't see anything, so squatted at the edge of the road and ran my hands through the grass. Neil's shadow fell over me. "What are you looking for?" he asked.

"I'm not sure. One of the crows dropped something. It seemed deliberate."

Neil stacked the book and his phone on the ground and squatted next to me. He swept the grass in front of him with both hands and immediately came up with something. "Could this be it?" he asked, holding out a flat greenish pebble.

I took the stone from Neil's hand and turned it over. To my surprise, a sharp five-pointed star was embossed on the object, which was clearly not an ordinary stone. "Yes! What is this, Neil? Look, it has a star on it."

Neil took the item from my hand and examined it. "It looks like a metal button. See? There's a bump here where the shank must have broken off. And there are letters around the star. This looks like a "T". This might be an "E". This is an "S". I wonder..."

"Texas? Does that say Texas?"

"It might. Yeah, this could be an "X". Where the "A" would be just looks like a blob, but maybe you could clean..."

The sound of flapping wings drew my attention back to the monument. The crow that had dropped the button was hopping up and down on his left leg with his right held comically out to the side. *Bill!*

"Caw! Caw-caw! Caw-caw!" The crows lifted off together and flapped across the road toward the battlefield. "Caw! Caw!"

"This is the valley, Neil."

Neil looked up from the button and furrowed his brow at me. "What?"

"The valley of people from my dream. This is that valley and this isn't just a personal treasure hunt that we've been offered. We're going to have to figure out how to share what happens, so others who picked up a burden here might also be able to move on."

"How did you come to that conclusion?"

"I'm not sure. I just know. I can't make it logical for you except that..." I took the button from Neil and held it up between my thumb and forefinger. "...right as I realized the implication of the valley dream, this confirmation that we're not randomly standing here on the side of the road talking about the battle and the Texans is brought to us."

Neil took the button from me and examined it again. "This *is* a little much to be a random coincidence, I'll give you that," he said and glanced around furtively. "And it's a little creepy," he continued. "I don't know if I like being watched this closely."

"We're always being watched and nudged, though. And we did ask to be led. You know what I mean?"

Neil cocked his head and squinted off into the distance over my left shoulder. He bobbed his head gently for a few beats and then made eye contact again. "I do know what you mean. I've been getting some incredible hits of clarity lately that make me feel like I'm not really alone. It's almost as if I'm being guided by some sort of invisible force. It seems like you just had one of those hits of clarity and I respect that, but I don't understand what we're supposed to do with that connection you've just made. Do you?"

I imagined Neil sharing a pew with Bill and almost wanted to ask what had happened in the church, but stopped myself. "No, I don't either. I think I'm only halfway there and we need to keep going."

"I agree. And, I know I shared a lot of information with you all at once, but were you able to process it? Do you think you'll be able to understand things that might have happened later during the battle if, say, I wasn't here to help you interpret them?"

I glared at Neil through my left eye. "What are you saying?"

"Well, just that you might find yourself alone or something and might need to understand what's going on."

"Uh, you did great, but…"

"Okay, then. Let's go see the rest of the battlefield," Neil said as he put the button in his jeans pocket and started for the SUV.

"I don't think you can keep that, you know. We need to turn it in or something," I called out to Neil's back. I bent to retrieve the book and phone that Neil had left at the side of the road and hurried to the vehicle as the engine started.

CHAPTER 31

ROAD TRIP: THE CORNFIELD AND NEIL'S DOPPELGANGER

"Thanks," Neil said as I handed him his book and phone. He stowed the phone in the console and opened the book to a map showing a mass of blue bars charging south through the cornfield in hot pursuit of the 1st Texas. "We're going to finish the loop around the northern end of the battlefield now. We'll continue west on this road along the historical edge of the North Woods...here...and then take the right to go south...here... through the remnants of the East Woods. From there, it's another right... here...and we'll drive along the southern edge of the cornfield and back to the Hagerstown Pike. One big loop around and back. Ready?"

"Sure." I buckled my seatbelt.

"I'll point a few things out as we go, but let me know if you want to stop anywhere."

"Okay."

We eased out of the parking area and rolled past the regenerating North Woods on the right and our stone friends from Pennsylvania on the left. I purposely tried to keep my mind empty and open to anything that might want to pop in. As we approached the first right, Neil slowed in front of the stone soldier standing forever ready to march and then rounded the corner. We were immediately penned in on both sides by post and rail fence. Strong sunlight caused the rails on the right side of the road to glow golden, while casting those on the left in dark shadow.

"The 12th Corps would have been massed over our left shoulders right about now. The Pennsylvania Reserves marched through the field on our right on their way to the cornfield. It was plowed at that time. See the East Woods up ahead on the right?"

"Yes."

"That's where the 8th Pennsylvania Reserves fought."

"Okay."

I looked through the wide gap on our right between the North and East Woods, expecting to see the cornfield in the distance, but it wasn't visible. "That swale hides the cornfield," I said.

Neil stopped the vehicle. "Yeah, I guess it does."

"The smoke would have hung in that swale."

"Yes, it would have. It was foggy that morning, too. Visibility was poor and it was hard to breathe."

"Do you hear that?"

"Hear what?"

"A bugle. I hear a bugle."

"I don't hear anything. Maybe it was a bird."

"Can we keep going? I'm feeling anxious."

"Sure." Neil put the vehicle back in drive and we rolled forward through the East Woods toward a low, modern barn in a grassy opening.

"Are we off the battlefield now?" I asked.

"No, but that must be private property inside the boundaries."

We jogged to the left and a stone solider appeared ahead of us on a small rise. Neil rolled slowly past a young man with a strong jawline, riding boots, and a wide-brimmed hat. "Pennsylvania Cavalry," Neil said. "Keep going?"

"Keep going."

We rolled up to a stop sign. Neil paused and then turned right. "We just made a little detour around that private property. We're still going south through what would have been the East Woods and we're about in line with the north edge of the cornfield now."

"I can't see it through the trees."

"No, not yet but see that tall monument at the intersection in front of us? That should be General Mansfield's monument. The 12th Corps marched down the road angling in from our left and engaged a line of Confederates in the woods…"

My breath caught sharply as a severe pain cut through my chest. Intense nausea welled up and enveloped my mind. I closed my eyes and realized I was looking down at a grassy field from at least five feet up in the air. I vaguely felt myself slumping forward as unseen hands gripped my shoulders. Another wave of pain rushed through my chest and up around the back of my head, threatening to drive me into unconsciousness. And then I felt the ground against my back and was looking up at a crystal blue sky dotted with fluffy white clouds.

"Damned old man. He shouldn't have been out here in the first place."

"Shush, he'll hear you."

"Don't care. Stupid old man tried to get us all killed marching us out here in columns like that. Go find General Williams. Tell him what happened."

I felt cold. So cold. I shivered and gasped. Hurts to breathe. Small breaths. Small breaths. The sky is so pretty and the breeze is so fair. If I must die, what a beautiful day to do so.

"…General Mansfield rode his horse in front of his own line and tried to convince his men that they were firing on another Union regiment. He was wrong and was shot off his horse. Died later that day, I think. Had only been on the job for two days." Neil had stopped in front of the monument — a tall column topped with a sphere.

"Was he old, Neil?"

Neil pulled his little notebook out of the console, flipped through it, and found what he was looking for. "Joseph Mansfield...yes, he was almost sixty but this was his first field command during the Civil War. He'd commanded garrisons up until Antietam, which was more like a desk job, and he'd badly wanted a field command. McClellan had just given him the 12th Corps."

"And he was shot right here?"

"Near here."

"Can we keep going?"

"Sure. Are you doing okay?"

"Yeah. I just want away from this spot now. I think I just experienced what Joseph Mansfield experienced when he was shot."

"Really?"

"Yeah. He was shot in the chest, right?"

Neil's eyes went wide. "Uh, yeah, he was. Let's move away from here."

Neil put the SUV back in drive and we rolled forward. A heaviness that I didn't realize was there lifted as we went through a short shady allée of trees. Neil gestured toward the trees out his side window, trying to distract me with benign landscape details. "There would have been thick woods here on both sides in 1862, but look—here's more private property." A two-story white farmhouse with a cinderblock garage appeared ahead of us. Neil slowed and turned right at an ornate black street sign that announced our arrival on Cornfield Avenue. On our right was a scrubby patch of overgrown field peppered with tall plastic tubes used to protect tree seedlings from deer browsing.

"They're replanting the East...," I started and then stopped as rows of tall green corn stalks became visible on a swell behind the tree tubes. As we rolled forward up a small rise, a split rail fence appeared about ten yards off the road, separating us from the cornfield that stretched to the north behind it.

"I'd like to stop here and get out," Neil said. "You okay?"

"Yeah," I lied.

Neil pulled in to the last available space in a small parking lot, put the SUV in park, and stopped the engine.

"Would you mind if I waited for you?" I asked.

"Not at all. You sit tight. You look a little pale. Rest for a few minutes. I'll be right back."

Neil lowered my window, got out of the vehicle, and shut the door. I watched as he walked along a low stone wall and joined a group around a pair of interpretive signs. He immediately started up a conversation with a white-haired man wearing a black t-shirt tucked into jeans. I squinted to see what was printed on the man's shirt but couldn't quite make it out. Then I noticed several more men in similar shirts. *Must be a group.* I realized how tired I was from the early morning and closed my eyes. The sun warmed my right cheek, making me comfortably drowsy. "Keep chatting, Neil, I'm catching me a nap," I said out loud.

I quickly dropped into the zone between awake and blissfully asleep and just as quickly was shocked wide awake by an explosion that rattled the SUV. My eyes flew open and I looked out the windshield for Neil but everything had changed — the stone wall and signs were gone, the tourists and vehicles were gone, and a thick white fog obscured the landscape in front of me. *What the hell just happened?* I opened the door of the SUV and stepped out. *And where's Neil?* I took a few tentative steps forward toward the rail fence and heard the sound of the bugle again. *It's calling me. I need to answer the call.* I craned my neck forward and strained my eyes, willing the mist to part so I could see what it was hiding. *Is something moving in there?* I suddenly thought better of walking into the shrouded field and turned back toward the SUV. It was gone. In fact, all the vehicles were gone. The parking lot and the road were also missing. I was standing in a pasture by myself.

Another explosion rocked the ground and then another and another and another and another until the air was filled with continuous thunder. The soil not a dozen feet to my right flew into the air. I dropped to the ground and covered my head against the dirt clods and stones that rained down on me. And then I heard something else. An eerie yipping howl just barely carried above the roar of the explosions. I lifted my head and looked out over the pasture. The sky was still bright blue and dotted with innocuous white clouds. Soft green clover blanketed the roll of land in front of me. A whispered breeze playfully tossed the heads of the little shamrocks. *How ridiculously tranquil.* The howl came again. I strained to make out the raucous mixture of a pack of yapping hounds, a band of screech owls in the night, and the strange twisted yelps of a thousand distressed turkeys. It was closer this time. The hair rose on the back of my neck. I scrambled to my feet and squinted at the horizon. A few hundred yards in front of me, a faint shimmer stretched across the full width of the pasture. It was moving rapidly toward me. I stood frozen, not sure what to do, as the wall of electrified air closed to within a few hundred feet of me and then exploded into a line of ghastly men. My eyes went wide, taking in the sight of their enraged faces and the rifles held at their hips. A tortured howl rose up from the charging mob and shot through me.

I spun around and raced toward the concealing safety of the fog. Scrambling over the fence, I knocked down the top rail as I tumbled into the corn. I popped back up and ran blindly forward, pushing my way through broken cornstalks. My eyes burned and teared horribly as the distinctive smell of burnt gunpowder filled my nostrils and scorched my throat. Feet pounded the earth behind me as the howl grew closer and closer. I angled to the right. The smoke was thinner in front of me now, allowing me to just make out a clearing in the corn. I stumbled toward it over the uneven ground and felt my toe catch. My knees sunk into a soft, warm mound as I pitched face first into damp soil. I pushed myself up to my knees and felt below me. Damp wiry hair met my fingertips.

"This is someone else's memory. Push it away. Push it away."

"Bill? Mick?" I jerked my hand back and scrambled backwards as another loud explosion rocked the earth.

"Damn. I'm sorry. I shouldn't have slammed the door. I didn't mean to startle you."

Neil's face swam in front of me. "Oh, my god, Neil."

"I'm sorry. I…"

"No, not that. I was dreaming I was running through the cornfield. I was being chased by Confederates and I ran through the corn and tripped over a dead guy. The cornfield was all full of smoke and I couldn't see where I was going and I'm so glad you woke me up!"

"Well, that sucks. I was hoping you'd be able to relax a few minutes. Why are your eyes so red? You look like the star of an eye drop commercial."

I blinked my sore eyes and rubbed them carefully. They were wet with tears. "Probably allergies."

"Tissues in the glove box." Neil popped the release on the glove compartment. I found a pack of tissues under the flashlights and pulled one out to wipe my flaming eyes.

"You see the guys in the black t-shirts?" Neil asked.

"Yeah."

"They're from a living history group — they do Civil War lectures and reenactments in character. I just met Robert E. Lee, Joseph Hooker, and John Brown Gordon."

"Who's John Brown Gordon?"

"He was a Confederate general who was wounded five times while leading his men in the defense of Bloody Lane. His final wound was a shot to the face that almost killed him — face-planted into his hat and about drowned in his own blood, is how he told it. He was also the officer who surrendered Lee's army to the Union at the end of the war. Hear tell he accomplished that with great dignity."

"Oh. Okay."

"And Joe Hooker told me that I look a lot like General John Gibbon, the Union general I told you helped fire the artillery piece on the Hagerstown Pike. That was his name — John Gibbon. He actually broke the Rebel line by loading a gun with double canister and…"

"Did you say double canister?"

"Yeah, do you know what that is?"

I shook my head no.

"A canister was an exploding can filled with metal balls. Converted a cannon into a giant shotgun capable of mowing down dozens of men at a time. "Double" means Gibbon loaded a cannon with two exploding cans filled with metal balls. He aimed the gun himself and fired point-blank into the Confederates across the Pike. Blew the fence and the Rebels twelve feet into the air."

My eyes went wide as I understood what Bill had been showing me from both sides of the fence.

"That's what caused the Rebel line at the pike to fold and retreat," Neil continued. "Gibbon was also the one who went over and ordered the Pennsylvania Reserves up and over the fence to charge the remnants of the 1st Texas. He was a real hero at Antietam. The living history guys told me they've never had anyone play John Gibbon before. Look, they gave me this brochure. It's a trail map. There's a walking trail that winds around the cornfield, but look here — it has pictures. Here he is. This is John Gibbon." Neil handed me a pamphlet folded back to a page titled, "The Bugler and The General". At the bottom of the page were two photographs — one of a baby-faced teenager with a sword and a bugle and the other of Neil's doppelganger in a Union officer's uniform.

"Damn, Neil, you look rugged with facial hair. He's eyes are even light. Do you think they're blue?"

Neil took the pamphlet back and brought the black and white photo to within a few inches of his nose. "Hard to tell. They're definitely light." Neil looked back up at me. His own blue eyes were dancing.

"Are you going to do it?" I asked.

"Do what?"

"The living history thing…play John Gibbon."

"Oh. Well. No."

"No? Why not?"

"It's not my story, I guess. I mean…you know. He was apparently a great leader of men and I feel that connection, but John Gibbon killed a lot of people. To bring him back to life, I'd have to drop into the mindset that that's alright with me. And it's not."

Neil lifted his right hip off his seat and dug into his jeans pocket. He pulled out the weathered Texas button. "Chances are this button came from a dead man's coat — someone who traveled all the way from Texas to fight for a horrible cause that, in his mind, was just. When those guys asked if I was possibly interested in playing John Gibbon, I immediately opened my mouth to say yes. And then I felt this button in my pocket and I knew the answer was no. How could I channel one man without the other? And how could I kill the Texan over and over again in my imagination? I couldn't."

The two of us fell into a heavy silence.

"Did you notice the Texas monument across the road? The pinkish one?" Neil finally asked.

"No, I was looking at the cornfield when we drove up."

"It's right across the road. Let's walk over to it."

"Okay."

We both stepped out of the SUV. The morning was now slipping away and the sun was heating up the battlefield. We stripped off our jackets and stowed them in the back seat. Neil locked the SUV with his fob and we walked to the rear bumper, pausing while a line of vehicles rolled slowly past.

"Things are getting busy," Neil said.

With one last glance to either side for vehicles, he led me across the road to a pink granite monument. Unlike the Pennsylvania tributes, this monument was simple — a six-foot tall, rectangular slab on a short base. A straightforward homage detailing the Texas Brigade's actions in battle was engraved on the stone beneath a bronze lone star encircled by a wreath of branches.

"Is anybody watching us?" Neil asked without looking away from the inscription.

I glanced around and pretended to point out landscape features as I scanned the terrain for witnesses. "No, nobody's watching."

Neil knelt in front of the monument and gently pulled the sod back from the base with his left hand. He looked up, showed me the button in his right hand, and quickly pushed it deep into the soil at the base of the monument. He pressed the sod back into place and pretended to tie his shoe before standing up.

"So…uh…whoever brought that to me…uh…thank you. Rest in peace. You guys fought hard." We stood reverently gazing at the pink stone and then…

"Caw! Caw-caw-caw! Caw!" We both ducked and spun as two crows dove right at us and then swept past on both sides to light on the top of a monument directly across the road. They flapped their wings crazily as they tried to find their balance on the round disk that topped the monument. I grinned over at Neil, who was watching the birds in slack-jawed amazement. After fumbling around for a moment like a slap-stick comedy duo, the crows took off, swept just a few feet over our heads, and flapped erratically south.

Neil tracked the birds with his eyes until they disappeared below a rise. Then he opened his hands in front of him as if he were holding an invisible beach ball and glared straight up into the heavens. "Are you freaking kidding me?"

CHAPTER 32

NEIL'S A-HA: THE TWO CROWS AND A BUTTON TRUTH ABOUT MY LIFE

I laughed all the way back to the vehicle. Neil was not amused. As I slipped into my seat, I snorted and choked, trying to get control of myself.

"Why are you laughing at me?" Neil demanded.

"I'm…so…sorry…that…that…that…was priceless…welcome…to…my…world."

The anger melted from Neil's face and was replaced with a smile that lit up his entire being. "Are you telling me I've earned the right to fly the freak flag?"

"For sure — let that baby snap in the breeze."

"Sweet."

I pulled the reins back hard on my laughter and tried to get serious. "One thing, though. You can, uh, ask the Universe for clarification of what that meant if you need to. That seems to always be an option. You know? It's seems to be fine not to pick things up on the first go."

"Good to know, but I think I have it. I was really flattered talking to those living history guys. Way too flattered, especially once they started describing John Gibbon's heroics. Mix in how much fun I've had with the Civil War research and the hook was in my mouth waiting to be set. I was a whisper away from throwing all my chips in with those guys, growing out a moustache and a five-day beard, and joining the reenactors' circuit. I would have allowed it to take over my life and then be my life. Eventually, I would have figured out the marriage was tainted, but I would have been in deep by then and would have felt honor-bound to keep my commitment even if I wasn't being true to myself. I need to break that MO and have more experiences just for the experience. You know, without obligating myself and letting things spin into a huge responsibility that I have to keep carrying so as not to let anyone down. That's exactly what I was thinking right as those crows appeared."

"That's huge, Neil."

"Yeah. I'm gonna call it 'the two crows and a button truth about my life'. And I'm going to do my best to remember it and live it."

"Nice!"

"Thanks. Now, let's get out of here and let someone else have this parking space. Do you want to stop anywhere along the pike or in the West Woods on our way back toward the visitor center?"

"No, I wouldn't mind doing that another time, but I'd really like to maybe stop at the visitor center to use the restroom before we head south to see the rest of the battlefield."

"Perfect."

CHAPTER 33

NEIL'S A-HA: THEY'RE STARING AT YOU, FRIEND

Less than twenty minutes later we were back outside the visitor center with our backs against a maple tree eating tuna sandwiches, carrot sticks, and sweet green grapes from a cooler that Neil had produced from the back of the SUV.

"I'm glad we stopped in there," Neil said. "I didn't realize there was a user fee."

"I don't think they would have hunted us down for not having paid it."

"True, but we might need to stick the ticket in an exit gate to get out. Can you imagine being trapped out on the battlefield over night?"

I must have looked mortified, because Neil burst out laughing and slapped my knee. "Just kidding."

"Yeah, I knew that."

"Okay, for the afternoon portion of our tour, I have not prepared a thing except for what we ran through on the tour map when we got here. You're sure you're good with that?"

"Yes, that's perfect. I'd like to just see where things take us. I'm positive the southern end of the battlefield is important. Something happened there — I'm just not sure where."

"Well, we do have the map book..."

"Would it be okay to put it away from here? Just for this circuit of the battlefield?"

"Absolutely. Are you about done?"

"Yep." I took a final sip of apple juice from my drink box and wadded up my trash.

"Moist towelette?" Neil asked as he handed me a little foil pack.

"Certainly. So civilized."

"It's a dad thing. No sticky fingers in the vehicle. No sticky fingers." Neil gathered up the trash and put it in the cooler. "Let's go. Time's a wasting."

I followed Neil back to the vehicle and got strapped in while he raised the hatch and put the cooler away. He slammed the hatch and then pulled open the back door. "Hand me the map book and I'll put it away." I grabbed the book off the dash and handed it over the seat to Neil. I heard a heavy bag being dragged over the back seat and then a zipper opening and closing. Neil looked up at me. "Do you want the tour map that I picked up at the counter? It's like the one from the web we looked at this morning but includes basic information that goes along with the remainder of the auto tour."

"Yeah, that would be helpful without being too distracting."

Neil handed a glossy folded map over the seat to me, closed the back door, and settled into the driver's seat. "Ready?"

I felt a rush of nervousness well up and suddenly wasn't sure. "Ready."

Neil pulled his door shut, put on his seatbelt, and started the engine. "Okay. We're headed back toward the Dunker Church, but this time instead of continuing north on the Hagerstown Pike, we're going to turn right on Smoketown Road across from the church." I unfolded the auto tour map. Neil leaned toward me and pointed out the road that I'd noticed cutting east across the battlefield past the big monument with the green cupola.

"Cool. I wouldn't mind getting a better look at that big monument on the knoll."

"I'll drive by slowly and we can always come back and walk around later."

We backed out of the parking space but could roll only thirty feet toward the exit onto Dunker Church Road before being stopped behind a line of other vehicles also trying to exit. "I'd say this is the drawback to coming around the anniversary date," Neil said.

"Yeah."

We crept up to the stop sign and turned right. Up ahead, the pullout in front of the church was overflowing with cars. People milled around the monuments and interpretive signs. "I'm glad we stopped there early," I said.

"Absolutely."

We turned right just past the church. I was relieved to see that most of the backlog at the visitor center had gone elsewhere, leaving the road ahead of us empty. Neil pointed out the monument with the cupola as we approached it on our right. "It's the State of Maryland monument. Guys from Maryland fought on both sides."

As we passed, I craned my neck and twisted in my seat to study the substantial monument sitting in a small grove of shade trees on a small knoll above the road. Several people moved around under the shade of the cupola, which could have sheltered twenty or more in a storm. "Maryland did it up right and...," I started as I turned back to Neil. My comment was cut short, however, by a flash of dark brown feathers sweeping over the hood of the SUV.

"Holy shit, what was that?" Neil said as he hit the brakes.

"Vultures! Two of them. Look, they're landing right there in the field." A pair of turkey vultures dropped to a cropped green field not thirty feet from the left edge of the road. They hopped around a bit with their wings extended before settling in. Our presence was clearly not lost on them.

"They're staring at us," I said.

"They're staring at you, friend. You're the one they want."

"Ha! Maybe not. Roll your window down. Are they hissing? Vultures hiss, you know. I learned that recently."

Neil's eyes shot to my face. He scowled at my grin and lowered his window, pressing his left ear toward the birds. "No, no hissing. They're not saying anything. Are they?" Neil peered at me out of the corner of his eye.

"I'm not sure. Were they sitting on that fence?" I pointed to the post and rail fence along the right side of the road.

"Probably. I didn't really notice them until I was on top of them and then they took off."

"They were waiting for us. 'Welcome to your own personal hell.' That's what they're saying. And there are two, not just one. One for you and one for me — to remind us that there's gold to be found in the stinking cesspools of our lives, if only we have the courage to peer into our own foul darkness. Did you know they crap on their feet to keep cool?"

"Seriously?"

"Seriously."

"You're endlessly fascinating. I suppose this means we're on the right track?"

"I guess."

"Well, I was going to point out that this road follows the historic road trace. Hood's men retreated south across the field to our left and regrouped in this road. Most of the men followed it back to the church and the safety of the woods, but not the 1st Texas. They stayed in the road and were reorganizing to go back in. Eighty-two percent of the regiment was down and they were organizing themselves to go back in."

"Maybe they realized their flag was still on the field?"

"Maybe." Neil went silent as he gazed out at the vultures, who returned the favor and gazed back.

"Well, what happened?" I asked. "Did they go back in?"

Neil kept his eyes locked on the vultures as he answered in an almost wistful tone. "The Texans? No. Hood came and got them. They probably got into it in the West Woods later, though."

"You're really taken by those Texans, aren't you?"

"Uh-huh. I'd love to feel that level of comradery and purpose. Band of brothers. The warrior lifestyle. Strap on your sword, set out on an epic adventure, go all in for the cause. Maybe you come home, maybe you don't, but at least you tested yourself…"

I listened to Neil muse, realizing that he was continuing to talk himself out of his life of self-imposed responsibility and into a new role as a swash-buckling pirate. I allowed my eyes to wander past him to the vultures in the field. They were still just sitting, but coalescing behind them on the horizon was some sort of figure. I squinted at the wavering shape that slowly organized into a lone man on horseback. The horse walked deliberately toward the vultures and stopped twenty feet behind them. I smiled, recognizing the white horse and Zachary Taylor in his blue uniform. General Taylor sat expressionless in his saddle with his sword held across his lap and stared at me. Just stared at me. I stared back. If he had a message, I wasn't getting it, but held his gaze.

Just as I was about to detach from the vision, though, and tell Neil what I was seeing, Taylor's horse stepped forward and stopped just a few paces behind the vultures. Taylor cocked his head slightly to the left and then, in one smooth movement, the horse reared up and wheeled to its left. The startled vultures leapt into the air as Taylor whipped his sword off his lap and swung it hard through the flushed birds. The vultures dissolved into a twitching pile of bloody meat and broken feathers. I jerked back and blinked. When I opened my eyes, Taylor and his horse were gone. The vultures were whole and alive, still intently watching me. I understood. Killing was just another day at the office.

"Uh, Neil? I don't mean to cut you off, but before you canonize Hood's Texans, do you really think they were testing themselves? Texas culture was really violent in the nineteenth century. You know, there was the Texas Revolution and the War with Mexico leading up to the Civil War..."

Bill's voice suddenly rang through my head. "That's right, kid. They called us 'bandits vomited from hell' down in Mexico. 'Bandits vomited from hell' "

"...and all the Indian Wars and the genocide. Those Texas guys were weaned on death and violence. It might have been more of a test for them to throw down their guns and refuse to fight."

Neil twisted back toward me and his chin snapped down as if he were peering over a pair of reading glasses. His eyes came into sharp focus and locked on my face. "That's an excellent point. So, what the hell am I picking up about them that I like so much?"

I was about to offer that I had no clue when I noticed movement in the back seat. I slid my eyes carefully to the left and there was Bill, sitting behind Neil and frantically directing my attention back out the window at the vultures. I looked past Neil at the birds. They were still just sitting in the field.

"Uh, maybe the vultures can help with that question, Neil," I stalled. Neil turned back toward the window. The bird on the right suddenly snapped its wings up, creating a heart-shaped shadow on the ground. "They invite us to peer into the shadows and...uh..."

Out of the corner of my eye, I could see Bill shaking his head. He formed a heart with his fingers and held it up for me to see.

"And...oh!...what's in your heart?"

Bill nodded emphatically.

"What's in your heart that you feel is dark, Neil? That you might not even want to admit is there?"

To my relief, Bill grinned and flashed me a thumbs up.

Neil turned back to me and laughed. "You want to know what evil lurks in the blackened depths of my heart?"

"Appears so."

"Well, since you asked, my black heart is sick of being nice all the time. I have an asshole wedged smack in the middle of my right ventricle who wants to take care of himself first instead of worrying about being fair to everyone else."

I peeked back at Bill, who was waving me toward him with both hands — the universal sign for keep it coming. *Keep what coming? Oh!*

"What else, Neil? Don't stop."

Bill shared a melodramatic roll of the eyes as he pursed his lips and blew out a silent whew of relief. I stifled a laugh as his rangy mustache flew away from his lips and resettled.

Neil had continued on. "Why the hell should I come last in my own life?

I'm sick of giving to all the takers without complaint. Sick of trying to make everything work out to everyone's benefit. My black heart wants me to say 'hell no!' when I want to. It wants me to have great sex with no conversation afterwards. And, it would be ecstatic if I pissed a few people off without apology and walked away clean instead of obsessing over how everything was going to settle."

"Is that what the Texans trigger in you?"

"Well, yeah. I love the fearlessness, too. The boldness. I lived that way when I was a kid, but something changed. I got civilized along the way and now I rarely take risks. I gamble only as much as I'm willing to lose. I've become... George McClellan!"

I imagined the bear hunkered well back in his rocky fortress, keeping his tawny hide safe in his lair. I became a dragonfly and buzzed the cave like a drone, looking for a way in. To my surprise, a massive paw adorned with Neil's silver Rolex popped through a fissure in the wall and took a few swipes at the air. I suppressed a snort and tuned back in to what Neil was saying.

"...I've spent my entire life taking the edge off my passion. I've diluted it with scotch and pounded it out of myself on a treadmill. Now my world has blown apart and I need to decide if I pick up my sword or...if I..."

"Sit in your cave?"

"Exactly." Neil leaned out his window and called to the vultures sitting in the field. "Hey! You two need us to move on? You need to get reset to welcome the next carload, you say? That's fine because I think I've got it now."

Neil grinned as the birds stared dispassionately at him. He put the SUV in drive and inched forward. "Watch them as I pull away."

I kept my eyes on the vultures as we started up the road. As Neil accelerated, I shifted my attention from the field to my side mirror, waiting for the vultures to reappear on the fence as we drove a quarter mile up the road.

"Did they reset?" Neil asked as he slowed and turned right. I looked up to see a sign announcing our arrival at Mumma Farm Lane.

"Nope. Maybe you were the only one on the list today."

Out of the corner of my eye, I saw Bill blow me a kiss. I put my hand to my cheek to catch it and smiled like a demure schoolgirl as he waved to me with his fingertips and disappeared.

"Hmmm. Okay, does this look familiar?" Neil asked.

We were pulling up to a big white farmhouse and barn on our left. "Yes, the farm that was burned."

"Feeling any pull to stop here? There's a family cemetery and we can also walk around outside the buildings."

"No, no strong need to stop here right now."

As we passed the house, a cannon appeared amongst the outbuildings. "Look at that artillery piece," Neil said as we kept rolling. "It's pointed toward the Sunken Road. Oh, and look up there. See? The stone tower? That's an observation tower that the War Department constructed so the battle could be studied."

A columnar stone tower with a red tile roof appeared on the horizon and then disappeared as we took a slight left and began to climb a small rise. I felt suddenly hemmed in by the tall post and rail fences on either side of the road. A moody cedar pressed against the fence just below the top of the rise added a heavy sense of foreboding. As we passed the tree and popped up on the higher ground, the sense of entrapment between the two high fences intensified. "Neil, what happened here? I'm getting a sense of being trapped between these fences with nowhere to go."

"Um, I don't think that happened on this road, specifically, but we're coming up to Bloody Lane. The Confederates defending it got trapped when their position was flanked. Union troops were able to fire down the length of the lane and the Rebels couldn't fire back without hitting their own men. The lane filled up with two, three layers of dead and wounded."

An interpretative sign appeared on our left near a tree line running perpendicular to the road, but Neil didn't pause until we were past the tree line and had a clear view to the left. "See the tower now?" Neil asked as he pointed out his window at the observation town, which was now visible again on the near horizon.

"Yes."

"That's where we're headed. The tower sits at the far end of Bloody Lane. You feeling okay to swing past?"

"Sure."

We took off again and quickly rolled up to a stop sign where Neil took a left. "Oh, wow. Look at those two tracks directly in front of us — the road we're on must follow the route of the original wagon road. We just get jogged to the right here to avoid the sunken portion." We swung right and climbed another small rise. As we topped the hill and started to drop down, I could see to our left the entire length of Bloody Lane running parallel to the paved road. The high banks on either side of the deep grassy lane were topped with stacked rail fence that invited the strong sun of early afternoon to mark the boundaries of the lane with deep zigzagged hems of dense, black shadow.

Neil paused to let a gold SUV back out of the small parking area on our left and then pulled into the vacant space overlooking Bloody Lane and the wide, plowed farm field beyond. "Look at this," Neil said as he put the SUV in park. "This is the view the defending Confederates would have had of the battlefield. I bet there were generals up here behind a line of artillery." Neil took a breath and continued. "Can you imagine being a private waiting in that trench of a road all morning listening to the battle rage just north of you?"

"Yes, I think I can — at least a little bit. I think that's what I've been feeling riding between the split rail — hemmed in and anxious. Ready to get on with it, but not wanting it to come to me, both at the same time and equally strong. Just wanting the waiting to end." A wash of concern swept over Neil's features and he opened his mouth to comment. I quickly cut him off before he could suggest leaving me behind in the vehicle as he poked around Bloody Lane. "Did the Union troops come across the field in front of us?"

"Uh, yeah. Uh-huh. They advanced in waves. The Confederates were pretty effective at mowing them down. Eventually, though, the Confederate line broke when one of the regiments misunderstood an order and triggered a mass retreat out of the lane. Uh, I'm kind of feeling drawn to get out and look around and I don't really want to leave you alone in the vehicle again. Would you mind walking out to that overlook with me?" Neil pointed out the windshield at a short stone wall perched along the edge of the lane. An interpretive sign sat at each end of the wall.

"Oh, no, I wouldn't mind."

Neil turned off the engine and popped out of the vehicle. He strolled over to a narrow, pebble-topped concrete sidewalk leading to the overlook and turned around to wait for me. As I walked over to join him, a puff of breeze drifted past.

"Neil, do you smell that?"

"Smell what?"

"I'm not sure." I made a series of rapid-fire sniffs that came up empty. "Never mind. It's gone."

Neil's right eyebrow shot up. "Okay…make sure you let me know if it comes back."

Neil and I followed the sidewalk together under the boughs of a leafy middle-aged black walnut tree and across a short stretch of lawn to the concrete pad and stone wall of the overlook. The small area was clogged with people. Clusters gathered around each interpretive sign and jammed the full width of the wall. I paused, not wanting to intrude, while Neil strolled over and joined the group reading the sign directly in front of us. He quickly engaged a man at the back of the pack in conversation. As I waited for the crowd to shift, I noticed someone disappear down a set of steps at the right end of the wall. I glanced back at Neil who was now engrossed in animated conversation with his newest friend. *Should I wait for him or set out on my own?*

"Excuse me, are you in line to read the sign?"

I looked over my left shoulder to find the owner of the voice — a young woman with long red hair pulled back into a pony-tail. The breeze, which had risen again, played with the loose hairs around her face. The faint salty smell was back.

"No, I'm sorry. You go ahead."

I stepped aside to let her and the young man whose hand she was holding join the fray in front of me. Realizing now that I needed to join in or get out of the way, I opted for the later and skirted behind the mob to the far end of the wall. I reached the top of the steep stairs and for some reason was surprised that they led straight down between two stone walls to the grassy surface of Bloody Lane. I put my right foot on the top step. Everything around me with the exception of the ten stone steps and their protective walls went smeary and out of focus. I rubbed my eyes in an attempt to dislodge the layer of petroleum jelly that had apparently settled on my corneas. Rubbing didn't help. I put my left foot on the next step and glanced back to where

Neil should have been standing. Everyone was gone, replaced by a smear of blue sky. I was moving down a stone tunnel to the unknown and it seemed I was meant to go alone. *Keep going or turn back? Keep going or turn back?* Indecision locked me wavering on the steps.

And, then the breeze carried the scent of the ocean again into my nostrils and curiosity got the best of me. I took a deep breath, let it go through my mouth, and descended the staircase at a run. When I reached the stone land-ing at the bottom, I paused and looked around. The lane was now in sharp focus, but the grassy surface I'd noticed as we'd approached in the SUV had been replaced by deeply rutted bare soil. The banks on either side were badly eroded and the fence rails were in disarray. I leaned forward to see up and down the lane. I seemed to be standing in a bottom from which the grade ascended in both directions — to my left rising gradually and disappearing behind a sweeping curve and to my right climbing straight up a low hill before leveling off. A sharp pop disturbed the heavy silence. My eyes darted to a thin cascade of loose soil tumbling down the eroded bank in front of me. *Something knocked that loose. I wonder what it was.*

I tentatively lifted my left foot and set it down in the dusty lane. A sticky puddle of congealed blood formed around my shoe. I gasped, drawing in a brimming mouthful of salty air. The roar of the ocean rose in my ear, snapping my head to the left. Squinting up the lane, I could just make out a wave of frothy red rushing around the curve. I froze, one foot on the ground and the other on the landing, unable to tear my eyes away from what I was seeing. As the wave surged closer, the roar of its approach shattered into a hundred thousand distinct sounds. Explosions, gunshots, terrified voices, enraged voices, calm voices, the agonized screams of men and horses, creaks and clanks and groans and prayers and curses filled the lane and ricocheted around inside my skull. The wave of blood and noise rose up impossibly high, crested not a hundred feet from where I stood, and crashed down onto the rutted dirt surface of the lane. The hideous cargo carried along behind the foam was now visible. Whole bodies and the severed limbs of thousands of men and animals bobbed in a tumultuous red sea that lapped and splashed against the banks of the lane. It was the flotsam and jetsam not of the ocean, but of war.

I stared spellbound as the frothy red remains of the wave raced toward me before abruptly losing energy and dissipating just inches from my foot. The ground shuddered and then, with a great sucking groan, the bloody sea soaked into the soil and disappeared, leaving a deep, jumbled deposit of overwhelming carnage on the surface. I jerked my foot out of the puddle and back to the landing. A firm hand immediately settled on my left shoulder blade.

"There you are," Neil said, leaving his hand on my back. "I'm glad you waited for me. Would you like to walk the lane together?"

"Uh, sure."

"You're pale again. What's wrong?"

"I just saw a tidal wave of blood come through here. It was carrying dead people and body parts."

"Really?"

"Yeah."

Neil stepped down onto the landing with me and comically craned his head to the left and the right. "I just see grass and sunshine now."

"There were dead horses, too."

"I'm sorry."

"For what?"

"For stopping here. I shouldn't have made you stop here."

I stepped down onto the grassy lane and was struck again by the silence of the place. Neil stepped down next to me. "No, it's okay. I was supposed to see that for some reason." I paused to sort things out, aware that Neil was watching me out of the corner of his eye.

"Let's move out of the way while you contemplate," he said. Neil used his hand on my back to guide me out of the path of a stream of people slipping quietly down the steps. They all veered to the right, beckoned by the statue of a solider with a battle flag that stood on the edge of the lane near the top of the steep rise. Neil led the way to the left. I followed him for a few dozen feet expecting that we were going to explore the opposite end of Bloody Lane, but without hesitation, he hung a right at a sign that pointed down an intersecting gravel road. Apparently, we were visiting the Roulette House.

"Bet most people don't ever walk up this way," Neil said over his shoulder as I took a few quick steps to catch up. We walked side by side for forty or so feet, our shoes crunching lightly on the shaded gravel surface, before Neil abruptly stopped at a stacked stone wall lining the right side of the lane. He leaned into the sturdy wall and gazed up at a line of trees marching across the high ground above us.

My attention was drawn to the wall, rather than the view, and I stood for several minutes studying the wide variety of stones used to build it. All sizes and shapes stacked together in harmony to create a structure capable of holding up the hillside. *Why can't humans stand long in harmony like this wall?* I glanced over at Neil, who was lost in silent contemplation. "Hey, do you remember The Hair on End Posse from the gallery?" I asked.

Neil turned toward me with a flicker of sadness in his eyes that he tried to erase before I could notice. "Daniel Webster? The guy who glared at me from down the hall?"

"Yeah, Daniel Webster was one of them. I guess you didn't get to meet the rest. Do you remember what I told you about those guys, though?"

"Sure, I wrote it down. They were intensely passionate."

"Yeah, they were." I paused to conjure up the posse sitting together on the stone wall — John Brown leaning forward with his legs spread and his palms planted on his thighs, Daniel Webster next to him, eyes dark and smoldering, with his arms crossed against his chest, Henry Clay next with his legs elegantly crossed and his hands clasped loosely in his lap, calmly separating Webster from John Calhoun, who sat bolt-upright with his hands on his hips and his blue eyes flaring. To my surprise, Bill appeared, loping loose-jointed and casual down the road toward me with his hat in his hand. He made himself comfortable next to Daniel Webster and nodded a greeting in my direction. "Yeah...intensely passionate. Their passion helped build the wave that crashed through this place. Their words and actions were rolled into the big tsunami of destructive energy that played out as the Civil War."

Neil looked at me a little blankly but nodded politely before staring quizzically in Bill's direction.

"Since I saw their portraits in the gallery, I've been thinking about the ability of fiery people to provoke amazingly strong emotion in others and..." I paused as I struggled to articulate what the bloody wave represented to me.

"Provoke or expose what's already there?" Neil asked. "Your posse might have provoked emotions in some, but even more importantly exposed the angst that already existed. The country was sitting on the powder keg of slavery and the opposing wills of a collection of strong states only loosely bound together by a traditionally weak federal government that was rapidly becoming stronger. Things were well past the point where the country needed to either come together or blow apart. Efforts at conciliation just held everyone hostage in anticipation of the inevitable. You have to respect the men who helped detonate the powder and break the stalemate. Even recognizing that the ensuing destruction was extreme, their passion helped move the country from stuck to unstuck." Neil turned back to the hillside without waiting for me to respond.

I glanced over at the posse. The Johns and Daniel were now scowling aggressively and throbbing with an intense red glow. Henry Clay had melted into a glowing, aqua puddle. There was a look of mock alarm on Bill's face as he moved a little ways up the wall away from the group. I dismissed the posse from the wall with a disappointed flick of my wrist. Their vestiges popped and sparked as they were caught up by the breeze and scattered. With the rest now out of the way, Bill picked up his hat and moved down the wall to sit directly in front of me.

"What's wrong, kid?" Bill asked as he looked down and played with the braided leather string looped around the crown of his hat.

"I wanted to say something else about the bloody wave I saw, but I can't put words together on the fly like Neil can. My brain hangs up when I have to translate from the pictures in my head and I'm getting frustrated with that."

Bill looked up at me. "Practice on me if you want. I'm all ears."

I watched in horror as dozens of ears of all shapes, sizes, and colors emerged from Bill's head and face. "Bill, that's just disturbing and you're reminding me of the night I decided to quit my job. That's what the CEO of the company said to me — 'I'm all ears.' "

"I know. I was there with you."

"What?"

Bill's extra ears regressed until he was left with just the two he normally sported. "I was there with you. I sat with you on the couch and lent my support. I also put that Steve feller in mind of a drink and I'll be damned if he didn't listen."

"You did?"

"Yes, sir-ee, nothin' like a little whiskey to get your words flowing. Not stuck that night, was you?"

I shook my head. "No, words just flew out of my mouth that night."

"Felt good, didn't it?"

"Yeah, but I can't walk around with a flask in my sock just in case I need to speak up. Can I?"

"Naw, probably not, but why'd you come out here today?"

"Uh..."

"No need to be evasive or to pick out fancy words. I already know the answer. Just need you to say it."

"I want to feel alive."

"Keep a-goin' with that."

Tears welled up in my eyes. "I want to feel alive or I want to die. I can't stay numb lingering at the edge of other people's stories of who I am or what I should want."

Bill brought his brow down in indignation. "Damn them folks making up stories for you."

I pinched my lip between my thumb and forefinger as I realized the truth. "Um, no, it's not their fault. I force them into it by not being honest about what I want. And then I go along. I don't speak up when they get it wrong."

"Ohhhh, fancy that. But you'll speak up going forward, won't you?"

I flashed back to the pink mist of exploded bodies and fence rails that Bill had forced me to experience. "Yeah, I'll speak up going forward."

Bill cocked his head to the side and smiled. "So, what's right for you, kid?"

"I'm not sure. I know what used to make me happy, but I pushed those things away a long time ago and now don't seem to have the energy to reach back and retrieve them."

"You talking about exploring the world and writing?"

I nodded mutely.

"Oh, you didn't necessarily push them things away. They was just put in storage for a spell till you was ready."

"What?"

"Yep, just in storage till you was ready to unstick. But you ain't unstuck yet. You still got a big ol' branch on top of your donkey hole. That's the thing keeping you a little outta sorts."

"Oh."

"But, don't mean you cain't practice your storytelling. What you wanna say about that wave you seen come through here? How'd you want to end that conversation if your friend hadn't taken your stage?"

"Uh, well, uh." Bill set his hat on the wall and leaned forward, giving me his complete attention. I cleared my throat, took a deep breath, and started. "What I wanted to get at was the angst is *always* there to be provoked. We seem to have a huge reservoir of negative energy to tap just below the surface. That's what the bloody wave revealed to me. After it played out, all the blood soaked into the Earth. None of the negative energy carried by that wave went away, it just went underground and it continually bubbles up to the surface so there's always a sticky puddle to put our foot in.

"It will always be easy for passionate orators who prefer a fight to build up a big wave of that negative energy, because there's an element of negative in all of us that can be used to sop up more negative like a sponge. That's what the dragonfly teaches with its cannibal nature presented in a beautiful package. The best of us is a beautiful cannibal — Andy's not the only gold dragonfly in boxers. I mean, even the nicest guy I know has an asshole in his right ventricle.

"I think we need that kernel of negative to exist as humans — it keeps us moving and keeps us alive. I don't think we need to be afraid of that but we need to be careful about dipping our sponge in the reservoir and loading up on too much bloody water.

"We should also be suspicious of forceful people — wannabe dictators, passionate orators, and even people in our everyday lives — who stir up and groom what's negative in us. Because when we aren't careful, we become weapons in someone else's hands."

"Oh, wow. I like that," Neil said. "You only lost me a little bit with the gold boxers." I spun from Bill to face Neil, who was looking at me as if we'd just met for the first time.

I turned back to Bill who now was beating his hat against his thigh and howling in silent laughter. *Rat bastard.* Bill stood up, swept his hat back to his head, touched the brim in a small salute, and disappeared in a cloud of indigo blue sparks that ricocheted against each other in a wild panic and then shot out over the battlefield in all directions.

"Did you see that?" Neil asked. "Did you see those blue sparks?"

"Yeah, I did."

"Thank god. I've been seeing those sparks all day. There was a huge cloud of them back at the church. I thought my retina was detaching or something."

"I'm happy you can see them. That's energy. Purposeful energy. I've seen it before."

"Ahh. Good purposeful energy?"

"Yeah, good purposeful energy. But kind of devious."

"Ahhhh." Neil looked me over as he rubbed his chin and jaw. "You look a lot more relaxed now. You ready to move on?"

I nodded. "Ready to move on."

CHAPTER 34

ROAD TRIP: A BRIDGE, AN OFFICER, AND OUR BOYS IN BLUE

The sun had taken on the hot intensity of mid-afternoon by the time we'd left Bloody Lane and zigzagged across rolling farm fields and through a young forest of red cedar to the stop sign at Route 34. As Neil waited for a steady stream of cars to roll by, I gazed again at the single-lane paved road that I'd seen disappearing into a cornfield under the morning sky. We were finally here. Finally ready to cross the highway and enter the southern portion of the battlefield, where I knew something was waiting for me.

"Wow, look at this traffic," Neil said as his head snapped right and left. "They're piling up behind us, too." I glanced in the side view mirror. There were six or seven cars pressed up behind us. We'd have plenty of company on the southern end of the battlefield.

At a small break in the cross traffic, Neil hit the gas and my head snapped back to the headrest. We zipped across the highway and almost too soon were rolling along through the cornfield. "Are you feeling a little claustrophobic right about now?" Neil asked as we dropped below grade and drove beside a stone retaining wall that elevated the corn on our left.

"Yeah, the line of sight is really cut off here on both sides of the road. Strange topography."

We climbed out of the low spot and the view to the right opened up to reveal a plowed field and patches of woods. I was about to comment on the expanded view when we reached the top of the rise. "Damn! Where'd he come from?" I said as Neil slowed quickly so we could get a look at the monument that had popped into view right along the left side of the road. The stone column was topped by a distinguished looking bronze officer who gazed off at the horizon while clutching a pair of binoculars. Neil rolled forward so he could read the monument's inscription.

"Oh, 50th Pennsylvania. Apparently, that's Colonel Benjamin Christ up there. Here's all the orientation you need right now. Late in the day, the 9th Corps of the Union Army was on the left side of the road and the Confederates were on the right side. The 50th Pennsylvania was on the right flank of a line that stretched north-south for over a mile and was backed up in some places by reserves. The Confederate infantry that faced them was thin, but there was plenty of Confederate artillery at this end of the battlefield. Plenty of it."

My head was swimming just a little bit, so I nodded understanding and left it at that. Neil pulled away from the monument and we continued along the top of the rise. A bright green hillside appeared directly in front of us. The roll of land was bisected diagonally by an asphalt road and edged by a split rail fence along which several monuments were positioned. Just as I was going to ask if we were headed for the road running across the hill, we dipped down slightly and the view opened up on either side of us. A two-story red brick farmhouse with outbuildings and a white board fence was tucked into the hillside right below us on the left. A gentle mosaic of brown, green, and tan fields and woodlots decorated the rise beyond it. The dark green of the South Mountain Range served as the perfect backdrop.

"Neil! Stop here a minute!"

Neil hit the brakes and snapped me forward against my shoulder belt. "Damn, I'm glad no one was right behind us," I said.

"Well, you said you wanted to stop."

"Yes, I did. Isn't this view spectacular?" I leaned toward Neil and peered out his side window, soaking in the scenery.

"The sign says this is the Sherrick Farm. You recognize this area?" Neil asked.

"No, it's just pretty," I said as I rubbernecked to my right and appreciated a green field that fell away steeply, allowing a clear view of a leafy mature forest on the opposite hillside. "Okay, I'm done," I said. "Thanks for stopping."

"Sure, anytime. By the way, I'm pretty sure the 36th Ohio crossed that hillside right in front of us."

"Really?"

"Yep. There should be another farmhouse near the base of that hill. The 36th was deployed in a ravine near that house before they charged up the hill."

"Let's go see the house!"

"Alrighty."

We continued not more than five hundred feet to a short modern bridge. As we crossed, I peered over the parapet at a paved road that traced the bottom of a deep ravine. "That's the bypass road," Neil said. "Keeps cars off the historic bridge. Wasn't there at the time of the battle. So, don't worry too overly much if this doesn't look familiar." Neil eased on the brakes and we rolled to a stop at a T-intersection. A brown metal sign in front of us indicated Burnside Bridge to the left and the battlefield exit to the right. "I'm assuming you'd defer exiting in favor of seeing the bridge," Neil said as he turned left and I craned my head to the right. We were now driving along the toe of the grassy hillside that the 36th Ohio might have crossed. I relaxed my mind, welcoming any hint of familiarity that might come my way, but the grass quickly gave way to a tangled wood that clung to both sides of the road and shut off any sense of recognition. Just as a new niggle of anxious claustrophobia was about to creep back under my skin, the trees and twisted vines on our right parted to reveal a large, old, and exceedingly creepy two-story gray farmhouse. Neil stopped in front of a short flight of concrete stairs that led up a steep bank to the wide front porch.

"And here we have the Otto House," Neil announced as he leaned forward to get a better look out the windshield.

"How exceptionally creepy. We need to stop here and walk around."

"Oh, darn, there's no place to park."

"Chicken."

"Maybe so. Maybe so."

Neil let a line of vehicles pass us and then pulled slowly away from the Otto House. I turned in my seat so I could take in all the details of the building — the eight small-paned windows across the second story, the white spindles lining the porch, the weathered cedar shingles on the roof, the blue glowing woman standing by the front door with her hands on her hips. I shot Neil a catbird look and opened my mouth to comment on the specter I'd just witnessed, but he was focused on the topography. "Okay, we're going almost due east now, skirting along the eastern edge of the Otto Farm, which is where most of the action took place once the Union troops got across the bridge," Neil explained as we wound through the dappled shade cast by the woods on either side of the road. The road curved to the right around a steep bank of yellowed weeds just as a sturdy wooden guardrail appeared on the left. "Antietam Creek is just below us now on the left," Neil said. I lifted myself half out of my seat and leaned across the dash in an attempt to see the water, but thick woods up to the very edge of the road blocked the view of anything below us.

The SUV rolled up a rise and around a curve. A dusty dirt road beckoned us forward along the bank of the creek but that route was blocked by a cable. We were routed instead to our right up a steep, closely manicured green slope. As we mounted the hill, the top of a gray stone bridge popped into view on the left and then disappeared as we swung up the bank and away from the creek. A peaceful landscape of tended lawn and scattered mature trees slipped quietly down the hill to meet us. I lowered my window to hear the chatter of the small birds that flitted back and forth across the road on some mission known only to them. Contentment flowed over me. "This place is so peace... oh, crap, never mind," I said. We'd rounded the curve and crested the hill to join a stalled parade of bumper to bumper vehicles, all apparently vying for the dozen or so parking places that lined the loop of asphalt covering the top of the flat hill. "This looks like the weekend before Christmas at Tyson's Corner."

"It's not that bad. Look, they're just waiting for that tour bus to park. There's plenty of room in the field in front of us." Neil pointed out a sign directing us forward to overflow parking in a mown field behind a majestic columnar monument topped by an eagle. "See? We're moving already." The line of vehicles rolled forward past the tour bus, now tucked in its bay, and onto a narrow gravel road that dropped slightly down the hill and into the field. Neil steered the SUV patiently along the route and waited his turn to pull in next to a white van that was disgorging teenagers at an alarming rate.

Neil put the vehicle in park, shut off the engine, and looked at me with bugged eyes and his mouth pulled back in a grimace — his look of mock appall. I laughed. "Things look grim in terms of a little peace and quiet out there on the field of battle, but we do have the afternoon heat and a selection of trail maps on our side."

"We're going hiking?"

"We're going hiking."

We climbed out of the SUV and into the sticky heat of mid-afternoon. I walked to the back of the vehicle and scanned the landscape as Neil dug around in the back seat. The sun was high in an almost cloudless sky that capped gently rolling farmland rimmed by an irregular line of mature trees that promised shade for any soul willing to stumble toward them. In defiance, the visitors around us were streaming back toward the asphalt parking loop. A drop of sweat broke loose from the nape of my neck and raced south between my shoulder blades. "Wish I'd brought shorts," I said.

"You'll be fine," Neil said from the bowels of the SUV. "I have water and snacks for us." Neil pulled his head back out into the sun and lifted a gray daypack off the backseat. He pushed the door of the SUV closed and shouldered the pack. "I wasn't expecting things to be quite this crowded today, but since they are, I'm thinking we forgo the typical points of interest here and instead explore the areas where the 36th Ohio saw action. That will get us away from the bridge and most of this mob. You like that idea?"

"Yeah, thank you! I love that idea. Do we still get to see the bridge?"

"Yep, follow me." Without any further explanation, Neil took off, striding down the row of vehicles and back to the gravel road. I followed a step behind him as our feet crunched with purpose back up the slope the way we'd come in. When we reached the tall monument with the eagle topper, Neil skirted around a family group posing for pictures and turned right onto a paved walking trail. Neil led the way down a gentle decline and we were quickly well below the level of the flat asphalted hilltop, which rose steeply on our left, and the patchy farm field, which rolled up and away to the right. We slowed as we merged with a steady stream of people flowing down a switchback trail to join us from the paved parking circle. The tour bus we'd earlier seen parking was, no doubt, currently empty. The now crowded trail curved smoothly left under the welcome shade of tall trees that lined the creek and conspired with underbrush to keep the bridge hidden from view.

I was doing pretty well containing my excitement — moving along with the flow and patiently waiting for a glimpse of the bridge — when progress inexplicably slowed. I peered around Neil to see a knot of elderly men carefully picking their way down a small set of stone steps. As we crept forward, the bridge peeked out at me through a gap in the trees. Three graceful arches meticulously crafted of limestone blocks into a gently humped span stretched the hundred or so feet across Antietam Creek. I winced and teared up. Although I'd fully expected this to be the stone bridge I'd seen as the hawk, I hadn't expected the intense sadness that was now washing over me.

Neil and I took our turn descending the three steps that had instigated the traffic jam and then crossed a narrow ravine spanned by a concrete slab. Three final stone steps and we stood on a paved apron at the western end of Burnside Bridge. I looked up at Neil, who seemed frozen in place at the bottom of the last step. His eyes were dreamy and unfocused. "Neil, let's step out of the way. We're holding up progress." I pointed out a low stone wall to our right that jutted out at an angle from the end of the bridge and formed a small refuge from the flow of people. "Want to stand over there for a minute?"

"The regiment started out on the other side of the bridge with the rest of the 9th Corps. We crossed to this side late in the day," Neil said without looking at me. I took his left elbow and guided him over to the wall, releasing the humanity that had been dammed up behind us.

"I saw Andy way up on a ridge over there on the morning of the battle." I pointed diagonally across the bridge to the northeast.

"Yes, that's right. I was there, too. We'd all watched the artillery battle the night before. Hundreds of guns on both sides of the valley. But we moved down to the orchard before the fight started here."

"Where was the orchard?"

"Oh, you remember. Behind General Burnside's headquarters. Behind the brick barn."

"Caw!"

My eyes snapped up to find a crow peering at me from a majestic, double-trunked sycamore growing beside the bridge on the far bank of the creek.

"Caw!"

The crow jumped to a small branch hanging low over the bridge and flapped its wings. The branch jiggled and emitted a faint musical tinkle.

"Caw! Caw! Caw!"

The crow hopped from branch to branch through the old tree, setting off a melody that sounded like a thousand tiny bells moving gently in a soft breeze. I tilted my head to the side and squinted at the tree, which glowed softly green and gold in the afternoon light.

"If only that tree could talk, eh?" I turned toward the voice and found the tanned, well-lined face of a man who had spent many decades outdoors.

"What do you mean?"

"It was here. Photographed in 1862 in that very spot. Lived through the battle and still stands. A true witness to history."

"Oh, wow. I didn't know."

"Well, you do now." The man winked and walked away. I turned back to Neil.

"Hey, we need to go across the bridge now. You need to lead. Are you ready?"

"Huh?"

"Are you ready? There's a story to be told on the other side of the bridge. We're being beckoned across and you need to lead."

"Beckoned? Who's beckoning?"

"That big sycamore, but I have a feeling he was put up to it by a friend of mine."

Neil dropped his chin slightly and cocked an ear toward the tree. "I don't hear anyone beckoning. Just a crow cawing way off in the distance."

I looked back to the crow in the tree and imagined the shrug of Bill's shoulders. "Then you're going to have to trust me, but we need to go now."

"Okay, then, follow me." Neil strode off across the pebbled surface of the bridge deck, weaving around groups of people strolling along a bit more reverently. I took off after him and closed to within a stride three-quarters of the way across the bridge. As we neared the eastern end, Neil veered left to avoid a young couple snapping a selfie in the middle of traffic and I found myself just feet away from the trunk of the old sycamore. I reached over the wooden parapet of the bridge and barely brushed the flaky gray bark with my fingertips. Invisible fingers caught mine, squeezed gently, and then released my hand in a shower of green and gold sparks. I closed my eyes for just a beat to allow the love to envelope me and plowed head-long into Neil.

"You should keep your eyes open. You nearly knocked me over."

"We're over the creek."

"That we are." I looked around and found we were standing on a paved patio that was lined with monuments of all shapes and sizes. The patio seemed to be the final destination for most everyone crossing the bridge. Neil wasted no time in getting me oriented. "There's a loop trail on this side of the bridge that follows the creek upstream for a while before turning and climbing the hillside in front of us. We'll walk back through that strip of woods." Neil pointed across a sweltering field of tall grass and weeds at a shady strip of woods that stood about two hundred feet above us on the hill. I was all for heading directly for the shade, but was willing to play along.

"Okay, sounds good."

Neil headed left, walking behind the patio and taking cursory looks at the monuments along the way. "These must have been the units that fought for the bridge," Neil said. "A lot of guys died down here. A lot of officers. Look at how high that opposite bank is. The Confederates hid up there and shot down at the boys trying to take that bridge. A lot of guys died down here. A lot of guys never made it home." Neil stopped when we reached the last monument. "Look at this! It's a giant granite Minie ball." I looked over the replica ammunition that topped a monument to the 21st Massachusetts and acted suitably impressed as Neil explained again how much damage the soft ammunition did to the human body.

We were then off and away from the crowd, strolling easily beside a stacked limestone wall that followed the course of the creek. We passed a few knots of people who were walking back along the wall to the bridge and then had the trail to ourselves. I swept my hair off my forehead and was grateful that we were tucked just close enough to the creek to enjoy the shade of the tall trees lining the bank. Neil was quiet now and I followed suit, listening to the single calls of small birds moving around in the trees and scrub as we walked a quarter mile or so and then turned hard right to follow the tree line uphill and away from the creek bank.

The sun was now hard on our backs. I shooed a horde of black gnats away from my eyes and leaned into the steep climb. We'd ascended no more than a hundred feet when Neil stopped at a wooden stake into which the numeral "1" had been carved. "This is an interpretive trail," he said. "I have the map that goes with it. Do you want me to pull it out and read the info that goes with this stop?"

I clapped my hands in front of my nose in a futile effort to crush the plague of gnats and shook my head no. "I say skip it for now. I'd rather just experience the place this time through."

"Agreed."

Neil turned and resumed leading our ascent. As we climbed, a rolling hill of tall grass dotted with goldenrod and daisy fleabane became visible above us. The call of a single chipping sparrow, a monotone "chip-chip-chip", carried down the slope. The landscape shimmered and I felt suddenly nauseated. My head was strangely heavy and hot. I reached up, rubbed my forehead, and ran my hands though my hair, surprised that it was dry and not plastered to my head. I rubbed my forehead again but was unable to release the tight band that now squeezed my temples. I was about to call out and tell Neil that I wasn't feeling well when we turned right to follow the trail across the slope. We were now just above the strip of woods that Neil had pointed out from the patio. I plodded along quietly, hopeful that we would be in the shade soon where I might feel better.

"Lord Almighty, how much longer are we gonna wait up here? I'd give my two eye teeth and my first-born child to get off this hill and have it over with."

The booming voice from somewhere upslope caused me to flinch and stop mid-stride. I slowly shifted my eyes left and scanned the field. A soft breeze tossed the green seed heads of rye and fescue and then died away. I glanced back to Neil, who hadn't noticed I'd stopped and was marching forward along the edge of the woods. I watched him disappear into the woodlot and then looked once more upslope. I saw nothing but the grass and heard only the incessant chip of the sparrow marking the passing seconds.

"Chip-chip-chip-chip-chip-chip-chip-chip-chip-chip-chip-chip…"

I turned back to the trail and rushed forward to catch up with Neil. My head swam and bobbed, feeling like a heavy marble swinging around on the thin wire that had replaced my neck. Massive trees surged forward and loomed threateningly, only to fade away as I stumbled toward them. Dappled patches of sunlight swirled up from the forest floor, reforming as a green and gold mist that obliterated the woods and the trail. Realizing that I was dehydrated and about to pass out, I sank to my heels, pulled the sodden wool cap from my head, and dropped it in the dirt beside me. My head felt immediately lighter. I used both hands to push my wet hair off my forehead and straight back over the crown of my head.

"Wondered how long you'd keep that thing on. It must be three hundred degrees out here today. Almost makes a man long for the damp shivers of dawn." I turned toward the familiar voice on my right and was relieved to find my brother reclining on the ground next to me.

"Lay back down before that fine Rebel artillery finds its mark square between your eyes."

I sat down in the dirt of the open woodlot, stretched my legs out in front of me, and leaned back on my elbows, mimicking Andy's pose. I felt something hard pressing into my right kidney and reached around to extract from beneath me a bright green apple with just the faintest glow of red gracing its unblemished skin.

"I wouldn't eat too many of them apples, son. Half the company has the shits from too many little green apples." I looked up at the compact Union soldier who had offered the stern warning. The stripes on his sleeves told me he was a sergeant. He looked to be several inches shy of six-foot tall with a boxy build that would have naturally carried at least thirty pounds more than those currently tucked into his dusty uniform. His black hair was trimmed close and his slouched cap was installed firmly on his head above a pair of glittering dark eyes, a wide nose, and a thick black beard that concealed his mouth and curled down to cover his throat. I looked beyond the sergeant standing at my feet to see fruit trees arrayed in neat rows and columns upon a flat. Plowed land rose beyond the orchard to a little knob that concealed from view the combat in progress below us. I tossed the apple away.

The sergeant leaned down and offered Andy a dusty envelope. "This seems to have your name on it. Just because I think it'll keep you out of trouble a little while longer, I'm giving it to you." Andy accepted the letter with a big sloppy grin on his face.

"Sergeant! Any word on when we might move out?" a voice to my right inquired. I craned my head to see who had shouted and saw that Andy and I were in a long line of men again. This line appeared to start near a big brick barn and farmhouse less than a hundred feet to our right. I noted with wonder that the farmer had monogrammed his barn by leaving individual bricks out of the end wall in the shape of an H and an R. I raised up just a little so I could see to the left. Man after man, a thousand or more men in federal blue, lay in the broken shade of the apple orchard straining to hear the words that would relieve the tension of waiting. All eyes within shouting distance were locked on the sergeant.

"Not yet, boys. No word yet from Colonel Crook."

A voice to the left rang out. "He took the 28th down hours ago! All the fighting's gonna be over before we get our chance at that bridge."

"Plenty of glory for everyone, son. Plenty of fight left. We'll get our chance."

A high-pitched whistle from our front caused the sergeant to collapse to the ground at my feet. An iron ball the size of a nice head of cabbage hurtled over a man in line not ten feet to my left and hit the ground a dozen feet behind him, sending up a tremendous spray of dirt and small stones. The cannon ball kept on going, plowing horizontally through the hard ground of the orchard like a fast-moving mole, before finally losing velocity and stopping with a thump at the base of a tree. The tree shuddered slightly and then stilled.

"Well, boys, it's a right good thing that one was a dud," the sergeant said as he got up and dusted himself off. "And with that, I'll be ambling back to where I come from." The sergeant stepped calmly between Andy and me and headed toward the barn, around which I could see knots of officers on horseback and ambulance wagons lined up waiting to be dispatched. As the sergeant moved down the line, I heard others call out to him. His reassurances became fainter and fainter until they were finally drowned out by the boom of artillery fire.

Now that the excitement was over, Andy's attention went back to his letter. "It's from Maggie!" he announced. He dug in his pants pocket and produced a pocketknife, which he used to carefully slit open the envelope. Once he had the folded letter extracted, he tucked the envelope in his blouse and rolled to his belly to read out loud.

My dearest husband, I pray this letter finds you in good health and spirits. I am happy to report that I am well, as is our little Annie. She is growing fast now and missing her Papa. There is nowhere she goes of late that she is not running as fast as her little feet will carry her. She has your smile still and often shares it. I took her up to see your parents after services Sunday last and she lit up for your father to such an extent that I was sure that she saw you in his face. He was quite pleased and toted her around on his hip all afternoon, even bringing her out to the barn to visit with the horses and milk cows. It was a fine visit and your mother sent me home with a fresh peach pie and a sack of the most beautiful tomatoes. I will be drying the tomatoes in the sun and will send them off to you in a package soon. I have been quite occupied otherwise with keeping the farm and the house. With the help of your sisters, I have picked almost all of the early crop of apples and am making the most crystal clear apple jelly and putting up the most delicious sauce you ever could imagine. The cabbages that I set out six weeks past have now formed nice heads and I look forward to salting them this autumn. I know you said not to fret on it, but I am still aggrieved that I was not able to plant but the one small field of corn this year. I have been working with much industry to replace the funds not coming to us from the extra corn meal this season and am happy to report that sales of my milk and honey soap are quite brisk of late. Mrs. Flannery is selling small bars as complexion soap to many of the finest ladies in town. She has asked for more varieties, lavender for the ladies and bergamot for the gentlemen are among them. I am sorry to not write more often and will do better to send you just a few lines when I am light of spirit. I love you so dearly and miss you so deeply of late that I have been overcome with longing for your return whenever I pick up the pen. It is not my intent to burden you while you are doing your moral and patriotic duty but I pray many times each day for the end of this terrible war so you might come home and hold me tight again. Until that day, I remain your loving wife, Maggie.

P.S. Please give my love to our brother.

Andy's eyes filled with tears. He folded the letter carefully and dug the envelope out of his blouse. As he fumbled with suddenly thick fingers to put the letter away, a rectangular bit of heavy paper fell from the envelope and fluttered to the ground. Andy rubbed each eye with the heel of his hand and wiped his fingers on his blouse before carefully retrieving the paper from the dirt. His face lit up with joy when he saw what it was.

"My baby! It's Maggie and my baby! Looks how big she's grown!" Andy handed me a sepia-toned studio portrait of a young woman in her Sunday best holding a girl of about two years with tight curls and a handkerchief pinned to her little dress. An electric shock of recognition coursed through me. *Ashley. That's Ashley and little Zoe.* My mouth fell open. I looked back at Andy who was waiting expectantly for my response. I shut my gaping pie-hole and smiled broadly at him. He plucked the photo from my hand, rolled to his back, and held his family up to catch a beam of sunlight dancing through the apple trees.

"Maggie still looks so beautiful. She's tired, though. She wears herself down with worry. You can see it in her eyes. Worry about me, worry about you, worry about the farm, worry about that damned cornmeal. Damn the damned cornmeal. I wish she would let it go. She can't do everything on her own. It's just a temporary hardship. Just a temporary hardship while I'm gone." Andy rubbed his thumb lightly over the photo, gently stroking the image of his wife and baby. "I'll be home soon, darling. Don't you worry, sweetie. Don't you worry. I'll be home soon and we'll have all the babies you can handle. We'll fill that house with little feet." Andy kissed the photograph tenderly and sat up to tuck it and his letter into the interior pocket of his blouse. "I'm keeping this close to my heart," he said as he buttoned his top button and patted his chest.

There was a sudden commotion down the line of men to our left. I peered over my shoulder and caught sight of a skinny young soldier scurrying along the line toward us under the fire of good-natured jeers and jests. He was nearly doubled over, clutching his belly and raising dust as he scrambled by the other men. I recognized him immediately as the young soldier who Andy had welcomed at the campfire — the soul I knew as Carla.

"Whoo-whee, Davey, we'd thought the gray backs had got you!"

"Was you out and about fertill-izing them bushes, Davey?"

"A-dancin' the Tennessee quick step, are you, son?"

Davey clambered past me and Andy, kicking a choking cloud of dust into our faces, and threw himself exhausted on the ground next to my brother. He curled in a tight ball and moaned.

"Davey, now, I warned you off them green apples, didn't I?" Andy said as he patted the boy's shoulder and grinned. "From now on, you're gonna listen, right?"

"Oooooo, leave me be," Davey moaned. "Leave me to die."

I noticed a new commotion coming from the right and saw the sergeant walking back along the line. He was in a hurry this time and was shouting out orders that I couldn't hear at first above the roar of the artillery and the din of the battle going on below us. Men gathered their things and scrambled to their feet as he passed. As the sergeant came closer, his words penetrated my skull and set my heart to racing.

"Okay, boys! Up and at 'em! The music is playing and we've been asked to dance. We're marching light. Pile your knapsacks by company. Fix bayonets and form up in columns. We're marching down this here lane with bayonets fixed! Up and at 'em, boys! The bridge is taken and we're going in!"

"Did he say the bridge is taken?" the man next to me asked as I offered him a hand and pulled him to his feet. I nodded yes.

"Well, damnation! We was supposed to take the bridge!"

"Plenty of glory to go around, boys!" the sergeant called out as he passed us. "Plenty of glory for all!"

I squatted on my heels to collect my cartridge box and nearly jumped out of my skin when Andy grabbed my arm and tugged hard. "Hurry! Get up! Hurry!" Panic raced through me. I looked up but couldn't see Andy in the glare of a sunbeam that had pierced the crown of the tree above us. I shaded my eyes with my free hand and Neil's face swam toward me. "Get up! Hurry! You have to see this!"

Neil dragged me to my feet and pulled me along the trail deeper into the woods. I stumbled along behind him, willing my much shorter legs to keep pace with his long strides. The muscles in my upper arm ached under Neil's grip and I gasped for breath as we ran up the uneven trail toward a gap in the woods. Neil stopped in front of the gap and pulled me in next to him. "Look!" he said as he pointed through the opening at Burnside Bridge below us. I gazed through the gap in the trees and oriented myself. We were just a little upstream of the point where the eastern end of the bridge tied into the bank. From where we stood, we could see the side of the bridge from an angle, but only the nearest arch of the three was visible — the remainder of the bridge and the far bank of the creek were concealed by a heavy screen of foliage hanging down from the trees immediately in front of us.

I looked at the bridge and looked at Neil, who was staring awestruck through the gap in the foliage. I directed my gaze back toward the bridge. It sat solidly over the slow-moving creek, anchored at the visible end by the trunk of the witness tree. Two innocuous looking kids stood above the one visible arch and leaned over the parapet to get a look at the water below. Knots of adults strolled over the span and milled about on the near bank, snapping photos and examining the monuments. I looked at Neil again. His mouth was still hanging open in disbelief. Clearly, I was missing something. I softened my gaze and relaxed my mind, allowing my awareness to sink deeply into my chest. I felt a door spring open, releasing my heart. My awareness rushed up to my forehead and another door sprung open, releasing me to perceive beyond the limitations of my eyes. And then I saw them — a steady stream of Union soldiers racing, four abreast, across the bridge.

"Holy shit."

"You see them?"

"Yeah."

The witness tree shimmied ever so slightly causing its branches to bob and dance. I heard the bells again.

"Neil, the tree would like to show us more. Do you accept its invitation?"

I whispered.

"The tree?"

"The sycamore at the end of the bridge. It witnessed the battle. It's inviting us to see more. Do you accept?"

"Yes," Neil said so softly that his reply could have been a puff of breeze.

The big sycamore trembled and began to shrink before our eyes as over a hundred and fifty years of growth retracted. Branches moved about wildly as they shortened and thinned. Bark became smooth and tight as more than a century of girth melted from the tree's trunk. In the span of moments, the witness tree stood before us in the shine of its youth with its supple trunk hidden below the creek bank and its narrow leafy crown pressed tight against the flank of the bridge. The sycamore's leaves rustled into place and the tree fell still and watchful. The soldiers rushing past were indifferent to the change in the sycamore's appearance. We watched them continue to pour across the bridge through the small gap in the woods as if we were watching an old silent film on a frustratingly small movie screen.

"I wish we could see more of..." Before I could get my lament fully out, the hickory bough framing the view from above snapped up and away with such unexpected force that I jumped back and sat down hard on the trail. The entire woodlot came alive with the rustling of leaves and creaking of wood as the woodlot reconfigured itself and slid further up the hill behind us. I scrambled to my feet. Neil and I were now completely exposed, standing together in a stubble field at the edge of the woods with an unimpeded view of the scene below. The landscape was at once familiar and disturbingly foreign. The bridge had not moved but many of the short parallel boards that made up its parapet were broken or missing. Light smoke rolled in from the left and right and settled over the creek. Above the smoke, an irregular line of tall open-grown trees with narrow crowns and branches almost to the ground loomed high above us on the far hillside. Along the water's edge, the witness tree had been joined by a gang of other young sycamores, one of which appeared to be missing a good portion of its crown. Directly in front of us, the patio and all of the monuments were gone, replaced by patchy corn stubble and a dusty dirt road that followed the heavily wooded creek bank from the left and then angled over the bridge.

The Union troops were pouring down from the heights to our left onto the road and across the bridge. On the opposite bank, a few men stopped to fire up the steep bank and were answered with scattered puffs of smoke from the top of the bluff. The majority, though, once across the bridge were moving in a steady stream to the right. The heavy dust rising from their feet indicated that they were continuing to follow the road, which skirted the base of the bluff and then climbed the rise along the same route that the paved road now took. Officers with red sashes tied around their waists were pointing the way with their swords. Federal and regimental flags, most sporting some representation of an angry eagle, identified the units. Regiments from New York, Michigan, Pennsylvania, and Massachusetts ran past with their flags marking their passage.

"Do you see any regiments from Ohio?" I whispered.

"No. I don't see them."

A loud boom from somewhere to our rear made both of us jump and signaled the end of the silent-picture portion of the show. The air filled with explosions, human voices, and popping musketry. A single voice broke free from the chaotic noise and boomed down the hill behind us.

"The whole damned war will be finished before we get there. Why in damnation are we standing here?"

"Dunno. Sergeant Carson! Taylor here wants to know what the holdup might be. Seems he's 'specially eager to shoot some Rebs today."

"Let's maintain discipline, men! No talking in ranks! Maintain discipline!" I spun around and peered through the woods behind us. That was a voice I recognized.

"They're behind us," I whispered. "The 36th Ohio is on the other side of the woods behind us."

"Alright, men! Fix bayonets! We're moving out on the double quick!" A thousand metallic clicks rang through the woodlot.

"Com-pan-eeee!"

"Re-gi-mint!"

"For-ward!"

A whirlwind of dust filtered through the trees, dancing in the shafts of sunlight angling down through gaps in the canopy. The 36th Ohio was finally on the move. I peered around Neil, willing myself to stand still as I waited for the regimental flag to appear from the edge of the woods. "Neil, they're coming!" I looked up at Neil. He was staring at the creek. "Did you hear me? The 36th Ohio is coming. They're moving out behind us."

"Yes, I heard them back there. Yes. There's an officer in the creek. Do you see him?" I turned my attention to the creek, scanning above and below the bridge for a Union officer splashing across. I couldn't spot him in the shadows. I was about to ask Neil to point him out when I noticed that one of the shadows was floating down the middle of the stream. Almost to the bridge, it veered in the direction of the witness tree and disappeared from view behind the stone wall on the near bank. I looked back at Neil and noticed the pained expression on his face.

"What was tha…" My question was interrupted by a loud cheer that echoed through the woods. I looked to our left and finally saw the flag of the 36th Ohio coming down the hill. The navy blue banner, adorned with the most vicious eagle of the lot, flowed out from a standard carried by a confident, clean-shaven color-bearer. Near the front of the column, I saw Sergeant Carson, running forward behind a tall dark-haired officer who led the way with his sword held aloft. The rest of the regiment followed with their polished bayonets glittering in the sun.

"There's Andy!"

"Where?"

"There! Right there! And the young guy next to him is Carla!"

"Carla?"

"Yes. Poor kid, he looks so scared."

"I don't see Andy."

"He's right there, Neil! I must be on the other side of him. Can you see the guy on the other side of him?"

"No, which one is Andy?"

"The one who's grinning at us. Kick ass, Andy! Give 'em hell!"

"He should watch where he's going with that bayonet. That little kid is Carla? He's only a kid."

"Can you see the guy on the other side? Can you see him?"

Another loud "hu-RRAH" sounded as the colors arrived on the bridge and then Andy was gone — across the bridge and lost to the shadows on the far bank. The remainder of the regiment pounded across the dusty bridge and joined the mass of soldiers clogging the road on the other side.

"We need to go now," Neil said quietly. "Before the wagons come down off the hill. We only have a few minutes. You'll need to follow me." To my amazement, the scene didn't dissolve as Neil strode down the hill and across the stubble field toward the bridge. I ran after him, stumbling forward and kicking up a huge cloud of dust. We skirted around the remains of a post and rail fence that had lined the road and stepped onto the bridge. I stopped and looked down at my feet. I was standing in blood again. The packed dirt surface of the bridge was splotched with bloody puddles and littered with debris. I squatted down and picked up a curved shard of black metal. Congealed blood clung to the sharp edge. I dropped the shard and looked up to find Neil leaning over the parapet by the witness tree.

"Join him."

"Mick! I don't want to join him. I don't want to see."

"Exactly why you need to join him. Go now. You don't have much time."

I dusted off my hands and stood up.

"Now."

"Okay, okay."

I walked slowly over to Neil and stood next to him by the tree. I forced my eyes down to the dead soldier bobbing gently in the shade of the sycamore. I was relieved to see that he lay on his back with his head and shoulders hidden beneath the boughs of the tree. He looked intact and anonymous. "His shoes and buttons are so beautifully polished," I said.

"Yes, they are. He was proud to be an officer."

I noticed then the carefully tied red sash around his waist and his empty scabbard. "He's lost his sword."

"He has. It's probably in the water where he dropped it. He was trying to encourage his men across the creek when he was shot down."

"How do you know that?"

"I was watching. Watching from the hill. Five companies of his regiment were sent to ford the creek several hundred yards upstream. They were pinned down behind the stone wall by the Confederates on the bluff. Rebs in the trees. Rebs dug in on the hillside. Shooting down on his men from above. Picking them off one by one. This officer stood up, raised his sword, and attempted to lead the way across the creek. His men didn't follow. They couldn't follow. Was suicide just to stand. Don't think the Rebs initially knew what to make of such a gallant officer. They held their fire. Held their fire until he was almost across the creek. Was almost across when his head snapped back and he dropped his sword. Almost across."

"Why did he do that, Neil? Why did he sacrifice himself?"

"Oh, I don't think he meant to sacrifice himself. I don't think he realized what he was asking of his men. He thought they could take the bluff. Maybe they could have. But the fire was so heavy. So very heavy. He was extraordinarily brave, this officer, and had a good heart. The men knew that." The creek tugged at the officer's legs, trying to work him loose from the eddy beneath the sycamore.

"How did it end? What happened to his men?"

"The colonel was up on the hill repositioning artillery to provide support. He got the battery in place and put it to pounding the Confederate position right as two regiments out of Ferrero's brigade stormed the bridge. Rebels had to run for their lives. When they broke, our boys finally were able to wade the creek. I watched them splash across and capture a group of stragglers. Boys were mad as hornets. Lined those Rebels up for execution. But I stopped them. I raced down off the hill and stopped them. Supervised the march of the prisoners toward the rear, where my regiment was still waiting in reserve."

"What? You were just a witness to someone else's memory, right? You weren't really here watching."

"Oh, no, I was here and I didn't feel I'd done enough for this young officer. He was so young. I could have done more for him if I'd figured out how to reach him. I couldn't have changed anything for him in the moment, but maybe I could have done more to prepare him. Maybe…"

"Oh, shit. Is this what came back to you at the Dunker Church? What you didn't want to talk about?"

"Yes."

The current ever so gently claimed its prize and pulled the officer's head and shoulders into view below us. One vacant golden-brown eye stared up past us at the impossibly blue sky. The officer's other eye and the right side of his head were missing, but I didn't need the face to recognize Terri. *I'm so sorry, my friend. I'm so sorry this happened to you.* Terri quietly slipped beneath the bridge. Neil and I walked to the other side and silently watched her body emerge downstream. Splashing at the near shore caused both of our heads to snap up. Two young soldiers were wading into the creek.

"It's Lieutenant Colonel Andrews!"

"Catch hold of him before he slips under."

Neil grabbed my hand. "We have to go. Don't let go of my hand."

We ran together across the bridge, kicking up dust. Halfway across, I slipped on something soft and slick and went flying backwards. Neil pulled me back to my feet before I could hit the ground and dragged me forward. As I stumbled behind him, for the second time that day trying to match his long strides, the dirt below my feet blew aside to reveal pebbled concrete. The sounds of artillery fire and shouting men faded away.

"Hey, watch where you're going."

"I'm sorry," Neil said as he let go of my hand. "Wasn't watching. Sorry." We were back among the tourists and historians, guides and grandpas, bored teenagers and curious kids that we'd left behind.

"Let's cross and follow the old road trace on the other side," Neil whispered near my ear. "I need some space." We walked more casually now toward the end of the bridge, stepping respectfully around a photographer who was leaning over the parapet to frame the witness tree. *The tree.*

I stopped and turned to face the sycamore, wizened again and still witnessing the doings on the bridge.

"Thank you," I breathed. "Thank you."

I imagined I saw a bough stir in response, but could not be sure.

CHAPTER 35

COMING HOME: SURRENDER

Neil rubbed his forehead and read the tablet again. "I still don't understand what it's saying. There's no way they would have kept marching up this road toward Sharpsburg. They would have gotten mown down in their column. This indicates all the other regiments swept up the hill in their battle lines. Why wouldn't Crook's Brigade have swept up the hill behind them?"

At the end of the bridge, Neil and I had turned away from the crowd and had walked in silence along the trace of the old farm lane to its end at the asphalt road. Both of us felt drawn to keep following in the footsteps of the 36th Ohio and so had continued a quarter mile along the paved road to a black War Department tablet that we'd hoped would provide guidance as to their movements. Its mention of Crook's Brigade had only added confusion.

"What did your book of maps show?" I asked.

"Just that they were down here by the creek and a few hours later were up above. My gut says they would have climbed that hill, just like this tablet says the rest of their division did." Neil pointed up the slope across the road, which seemed impossibly steep from where we stood.

"Uh, I don't think I could climb that without landing on my ass."

"Same. But there's a trail that wanders around up there on the top. Let me find the map." Neil slid out of his backpack, opened the front pocket, and pulled out the stash of maps he'd found online. "Here it is — The Final Attack Trail. Once all the regiments got across the bridge, they reorganized, were resupplied, and eventually charged up the hill below Sharpsburg. That was the final attack of the battle, although I don't think either side realized it at the time."

"I remember."

"You do?"

"Sure. You told me this morning. The Red Dragon swept in at the last possible moment and saved the day for the South."

"That was this morning? Seems like months ago. But, yeah, that's right. The trail starts on the far side of the parking circle. Feeling energetic? We'll need to climb back up the hill on the paved road — same way we drove in."

"Yeah, looks more doable than straight up the side. I'm in." I pulled out my phone and glanced at the time. A little after three. Exhaustion had settled over me as we stood puzzling out the tablet, but I wanted to keep going. Neil seemed to have gotten some sort of resolution, and I was happy for him, but I felt I'd been left hanging.

"Ready?" Neil asked as he pulled on his pack.

"Yep, ready."

The climb up to the trailhead, except for the traffic brushing past us, was quiet and peaceful. I was glad for the time to contemplate and appreciate the view of the creek and bridge as we ascended the bluff. I could see now from the vantage of the Confederate defenders hidden up here why it had been so difficult to take the bridge. And I felt intense sadness for Terri, who had tried to take those defenders on.

"I did it my waaaay..."

"Frank Sinatra, you are not, Mick."

"But, you see the truth in that, I'm sure."

"Yeah, I do. And Terri is still headstrong. She does things her own way. Always."

"Well, raw passion is a bit headstrong by definition, you know — fiery and not easily bent by the will of others. There's much to admire in that. But, the Red Dragons among us find it hard to comprehend those who don't have the same fire in their hearts. They wear blinders, you might say."

"Interesting. I hadn't thought of Terri as a Red Dragon, but I could, for sure, see her getting pissed and breaking her sword across someone's back. It seems important, though, for her to crack the leadership thing."

"Oh, yes, Terri's soul has work to do that will require others. She needs both their support and their audience. She seems aware of that now, don't you think?"

"Yes, but apparently she was aware of it in a previous life, too, and wasn't successful."

"If you can't do it the first time, try and try again. If you can't do it the second time, don't give up, my friend..."

"That's not Sinatra."

"No, Barney the Purple Dinosaur. Oh, and don't neglect to tell Neil everything you know about the other members of your band. He deserves to hear all the lyrics. Ta-ta."

The lyrics? What?

"Okay, here we are. The trail heads kind of west toward Sharpsburg for a ways and then makes a big loop on the high ground that was above us as we stood on the road." I snapped back to the present moment. We'd arrived on the parking circle, but stood opposite and well away from the parked cars and all the action above the bridge. The trail that Neil pointed out was nothing more than a strip mown straight back through a soybean field. The path disappeared at a rich green woodlot that stood a hundred yards or so behind the field and blocked any view of what lay ahead.

"Are you getting a portal feel here?" I asked.

"Yes, but I was trying to ignore that. Do you want to see the map?"

"Sure." Neil leaned in and outlined the route of the trail for me. It looked like we'd be making a big loop to the north and then an even bigger loop to the south before ending up back at the grassy field where the SUV was parked.

"There were a lot of moving parts at this end of the battlefield, too, but, like I said, I didn't study all the movements down here in detail."

"That's alright. It feels right not to know."

"I agree. Are you hungry?"

"Yeah, actually I am."

"Me, too. Let's head up the trail a bit and find some shade. Rest a little and have a snack? I've got apple chips, oranges, peanuts, raisins, granola bars…"

"That's an excellent idea. I have something I need to tell you, anyway."

"You do? What?"

"The details can wait until we sit down, but I had a vision back there on the hill. It was sort of a continuation of the vision I had in the museum."

"Well, let's go find a place to sit." Neil took off down the trail and for the third time I was rushing forward to keep in step. Sweat poured off my forehead and down my back. I conjured up the image of a sleek black rat paddling frantically through a swamp.

"Maintain your spacing, men. No bunching up."

Neil's head pivoted to the right and he stopped in his tracks. I halted a few paces behind him and waited while he listened for more. When no further instruction arose, Neil glanced over his shoulder at me and winked. "Hey, back there, no bunching up," he said and then took off again.

We reached the woodlot, which turned out to be a somewhat spotty collection of young cedars and locust trees undergrown by tall, rough grass. "Best not to wander around out here in the tall grass," Neil said. "Don't want to tempt the ticks." He knelt in the trail under the shade of a big locust, unzipped his pack, and held it open for me. "What's your pleasure?"

I knelt to pick out an orange and plopped to the ground next to Neil. I dug my thumbnail into the end of the fruit and pulled back the thick rind. A mist of aromatic oils from the peel tickled my nose and reminded me of the little handmade soaps that I'd installed by each sink in my house. *Soaps. Ashley. Of course! I need to suggest a home-based business to Ashley. She already has a track record as a mom and a successful entrepreneur!* I pulled off a segment of the orange and popped it whole into my mouth. *I wonder how many kids Andy and Ashley, I mean Maggie, ended up having? I bet I can figure it out if I…*

"Soooooo…," Neil started, trying to appear nonchalant as he focused on opening a bag of apple chips.

I pushed the orange segment to the side of my check. "The vision?" I mumbled.

"Yes. Spill."

"Andy was married." I bit down on the orange segment and felt the sweet rush of juice across my tongue.

"What?"

I chewed and swallowed. "Andy was married in 1862. To a family friend we both know in this lifetime. He read me a letter from her and showed me her picture. I recognized her."

Neil dropped his chin and looked at me as if he were peering over a pair of reading glasses. "Well, that was completely out of left field."

"Yeah, it was. Her name in this life is Ashley Campbell. Her grandparents lived next door to us growing up. They helped take care of Ashley and her sisters and brother during summers while their parents worked. Andy and I both babysat the kids when we were still living at home."

"Oh, that's interesting." Neil fished a chip out of his bag and chewed it slowly. "Were she and Andy ever a couple?"

I laughed. "No, Ashley's fifteen years younger than Andy. He's never thought of her as a love interest." And then I remembered a six-year old Ashley standing on the front stoop in her little pink shorts and Rugrats tank top asking if Andy could come out and play. "She did have a huge crush on him as a little girl, though. Used to follow him all over the place…"

"Oh, wow. Do you think maybe they're supposed to be together?"

"No, I don't think so. Ash is twenty-six now and very happily married to a great guy named Paul Sanchez. He's a rocket scientist at NASA. They have a little girl, Zoe…"

"Why'd you stop?"

"Andy was Zoe's dad, too. He was married to Ashley and Zoe was his little girl. She was in the picture with Ashley. They were Maggie and Annie back then."

"That's weird."

"Uh, yeah, like the rest of it wasn't?"

While I finished my orange, Neil plucked apple chips one by one out of his bag and ate each slowly and deliberately. When the bag was empty, he tapped the loose bits of desiccated apple hiding in the bottom onto the ground and then folded the bag carefully in half again and again until it was reduced to a tiny silver square. Neil worked the shiny square between his right thumb and forefinger like a worry stone, intently watching it glitter in his hand.

"I was hoping you might have seen me up on the hill," he said without looking up.

"Oh. No, I didn't. I mean, not that I recognized you. I was in line with Andy again. We were still on the ground trying to avoid the artillery barrage. It was much later in the day — felt like afternoon — but the shells were still whistling in. One almost hit a sergeant who was standing at my feet talking to me. He wasn't you — just a guy."

"Anyone, uh, hurt when the shell exploded?"

"No, the shell was a dud. It didn't explode. It hit the ground and burrowed through the dirt and had just about run out of steam when it stopped at the base of an apple tree. The sergeant…"

Neil's head shot up. "An apple tree? Did you say an apple tree? Where were you? What did you see around you?"

"Uh, we'd moved since early morning. I think we were farther down the ridge. In an orchard. Closer to the bridge but still a distance away."

"Is that it?"

"No. The orchard was near a big brick farmhouse and a barn…" A jolt of realization shot up through the base of my skull and exited between my eyes. I was mildly surprised that Neil hadn't needed to duck to avoid it hitting him. "Neil, do you remember what you were saying on the bridge before we crossed over to start the hike?"

"Yeah. I agreed to let that tree take us on a tour even though, at the time, I thought you were just a tiny bit nuts."

"No, not that. You were mumbling something about a barn and an orchard."

"I was mumbling? I don't remember that. But you said the house was brick — was the barn brick, too?"

"Yeah, at least part of it was. It was really unusual in that some of the bricks were left out of the end wall to form letters — an "H" and an "R." And there were a lot of officers milling around the barn and the house."

"Yes, there were. There were officers all over the place. What you're describing was General Burnside's headquarters. I was there. I saw McClellan there." Neil's voice had tightened and a dark red flush moved up from his throat to take over his face. "He and his staff briefed us the day before the battle. McClellan had his engineers personally position all the regiments. Took everyone else's head out of the game. I knew trouble was coming — knew the engineers would be gone when things got hot and I wasn't comfortable with the terrain. I was able to pull Colonel Crook aside for a moment to express my concerns but..."

"Whoa, whoa, whoa. You pulled George Crook aside? I thought you were Crook."

"No, I wasn't George Crook — and that never did feel right. But, apparently, I reported to him and he respected my opinion because he heard me out."

A chill came over me. "So we did know each other. You were the commander of my regiment."

"Maybe or maybe not. There were three regiments in Crook's Brigade and an artillery battery. I could have been an officer in any of them. Do you want to hear the rest?"

"Definitely."

Neil unzipped a side pocket of his pack and pulled out our water bottles. He handed me mine and took a long swallow from his. I clutched my bottle and tapped its metal shell with a fingernail, feeling suddenly anxious. We needed to hurry up. Neil capped his bottle and stowed it back in his pack. "You need to drink something before I put that away," he said. I uncapped the bottle, gulped down a few mouthfuls of water, capped the bottle, and handed it back. "That's better." Neil put my bottle away and slowly zipped the pocket of his pack. I was sure I could hear each pair of plastic teeth engaging as the pull traveled along the zipper track. It was time to go.

"Well, George heard me out but told me we needed to sit tight and wait for further orders. We had to trust McClellan's plan." Neil's voice had become dreamy and thick. He was still looking my way but I sensed he could no longer see me sitting next to him. "He wasn't going to carry concerns up the chain of command — no one was in the mood for that. I had to back down but I was still uneasy. I felt that my men were being placed in danger and I needed to do more to protect them. But there was nothing I could do. I had no options." Neil stopped and didn't pick the story back up.

"Did it end there?"

"I'm sorry. What did you say?" Neil's eyes refocused and he was back.

"Did it end there with you feeling uneasy?"

"Yes. And then I slowly realized that I was back in the woods at the bridge overlook and you'd disappeared. I turned down the trail to call your name when I saw movement out of the corner of my eye. It was the soldiers marching over the bridge. I knew it was the next day and the battle was going on, but I was me again and I wanted to find you so you could see what was happening. I was so relieved to find you. I was afraid I was alone in some sort of weird twilight zone."

"Wow."

"Oh, no, look at the clouds!" Neil suddenly scrambled to his feet and stepped out of the shade of the tree to see the sky more clearly. "Thunderheads are building to the south — we need to get moving if we've going to finish this hike today." I got to my feet, grabbed Neil's pack, and handed it to him. No wonder I was feeling anxious — I was picking up the energy of the approaching storm.

"We've got to hustle," Neil said as he swung his pack on. "Try to keep up. And let me know if you see anything interesting." Any fantasies of a leisurely exploration of this side of the battlefield evaporated as I was once again pushing to keep up with a pace that was just short of an all-out run. We tore along the trail, periodically stumbling on clumps of grass and loose rocks, and quickly emerged from the woods. The view opened up spectacularly to the south. It was now clear that we were on what might be considered a rolling plateau, beyond which the next rise of land lay. Although the sky was still clear and bright to the north, a tremendous bank of towering cumulus clouds was pressing in from the south. Neil showed no interest in the scenery and swung hard right through an old fencerow of trees. We popped out on the other side at the edge of a big soybean field — a bright green sea interrupted by spiky clumps of tall grasses scorched golden by the summer sun. The sense of being exposed on the top of a plateau was even stronger here as the land fell away on three sides only to rise again in the distance. Neil led straight ahead toward the near edge of the plateau. At a trail post marked with a "2", we made a sharp left and kept going. Without breaking stride, Neil gestured to the wooded ravine now on our immediate right. "The creek and the spot on the road where we looked at the sign are right down there. Crook's Brigade…"

"Up, up, up! Come on, boys, stay together! Try to maintain your line!"

The sound of crashing on the slope below us froze Neil in his tracks. I stopped next to him and stared mortified at the edge of the ravine.

"That's it, boys! That's it!"

The sound of men crashing through the underbrush and struggling up the hill came closer. My head began to pound.

"Halt and form up! Form up below the crest!"

I held my breath waiting for the tops of the soldiers' heads to appear.

"Follow meeeeee! For-WARD!"

"Hu-RRAH!"

With a rush, a dozen does and fawns, still wrapped in red coats of summer, bounded out of the ravine and charged in front of us at a diagonal across the field. The blood rushed out of my head, leaving me dizzy. I bent over and grabbed my knees. Neil sank to a squat next to me and crossed his palms over the center of his chest.

"Holy shit," he said. "Holy shit."

I straightened up and watched the line of white tails disappear across the field. "We need to pull it together and follow the deer. They're showing us the way." Neil stayed where he was, crouched on the trail. A cool breeze came up from the south and ruffled his hair. "Neil, did you hear me? The deer are showing us the path. We need to follow them."

Neil unfolded to a standing position, planted a palm on his forehead and pressed his hand firmly up and over his head to the base of his skull. He massaged the tension out of his neck and twisted his head side to side a few times.

"Alrighty, then. Let's carry on. Which way did they go?"

"Ahead of us and to the left on a soft diagonal. They disappeared below the horizon where the land falls away over there."

"That's in the direction of the Otto house — the creepy one where you wanted to stop. Let's stay on the trail and see if there's an easy way to cut over there." Neil took off again and led the way to the next trail post. He stopped this time and pointed out the red brick house we'd passed earlier on the opposite slope. A tingle of recognition ran across my shoulders and down my arms. I shook my hands to release the prickle of remembrance from my body. I didn't want to be overwhelmed right now.

"I'm sorry, Neil, what did you say?"

"That's the Sherrick Farm again on the hill facing us. The Otto house is almost right across from it."

"We need to get over there."

"Look at the sky. That storm looks bad. We might be better off spending the night and coming back tomorrow morning."

An overwhelming sensation of being watched was now crushing me. A flash of anger coursed through me and exploded outward. "Are you kidding me? No! What are you afraid of? We need to keep going! We need to finish!"

Neil stared at me with his mouth slack. He was plainly taken aback at having been shouted at. "Uh, okay, let's finish. Follow me." Neil put his back to the ravine and strode off through the soybeans. His pace was again too fast for me but I'd be damned if I wasn't going to keep up. I locked my gaze on Neil's back and willed myself forward.

When we reached the middle of the field, I saw that the land to our right rolled down into an overgrown pasture before disappearing into a deep ravine. That's where the deer had gone. We needed to move downhill, but the trail had doubled back and was returning us to the strip of woods along the old fencerow. The ravine represented safety and we weren't getting there fast enough. Anxiety clutched at my belly, but I said nothing and kept following Neil.

We arrived at the fencerow and, to my relief, the trail turned right and followed the ragged line of trees downhill. We skirted by the last few rows of soybeans and hurried past the pasture of high grass and weeds on our right.

On the slope below us, a picturesque section of split rail fence framed the left edge of the trail and swept to the right around a simple monument that sat near the bottom of the hill. The white granite pillar gleamed against the green and gold of living and dead vegetation like a beacon lighting the way.

Neil headed straight downhill toward the monument, but something made me stop just above the crest of the hill. I pulled in a big lungful of air and blew it out, trying to catch my breath. My heart was beating in my ears. I bent over and put my hands on my knees. The breeze from the south had picked up and was blowing cool on the side of my face. Without straightening, I rotated my head to peer at the approaching storm, which now blotted out a full third of the afternoon sky. A crack of thunder sounded in the distance. We were running out of time. *Why had I stopped here?* The breeze played through the high grass, bringing to mind ripples across a flat pond, but I saw no answers there. *Why did I stop here, dammit? A little help? Anyone?* A hawk screamed from across the field. I immediately straightened up and spun to my right to find it in the sky but my gaze landed and locked, instead, on a trail post marked with a "4." I stared at the post in disbelief. *We've ignored these damned posts all day. Why would this one matter?* I took one tentative step toward the post. And then another. It didn't twinkle, glow, or speak to me in muted tones — it was just a wooden post and it stood resolute in front of me. I took another irritated step forward. Something white in the tall grass at the base of the post caught my eye. I reached down, parted the vegetation, and lifted a beautiful brown and white feather from a tangle of weeds. The tension melted from my body. It was a flight feather. The flight feather of a broad-winged hawk. Another crack of thunder sounded across the hillside. I looked up from the feather to check the sky again and noticed something odd — the trail post in front of me was in perfect alignment with a large gray monument that stood way off in the distance on the other side of the ravine. With a jolt that ripped through me like a lightning bolt, everything became clear — it was the monument we were supposed to see, not the Otto House. I had to find Neil.

I clutched the feather and took off running down the trail. The tall grass to my right and the rail fence to my left formed a chute, which I raced down past the white monument. I banked right along a high stone retaining wall that created a shelf of flat land in the side of the hill for the monument and continued to charge downhill along the length of the ravine. I expected to see Neil ahead of me, but he wasn't in the ravine. Sweat was pouring down my back now and my arms were getting heavy. I shook my hands and kept running, but my arms still felt leaden and my upper back had tensed. The side of the ravine, spotted with dead trees stuck in a snarl of dense vegetation, loomed high and steep on my left. On my right, I was just clearing the bottom of the old pasture and was coming up to a patch of deep green trees.

"Neil!"

Instead of Neil's voice, a hideous hiss answered my call. I froze and closed my eyes, refusing to look up into the trees to see the vulture I knew was waiting for me.

"Come here."

With my eyes still closed, I took a step back and willed my mind to focus. *Protection! I need protection from the hideous creature trying to lure me to it.* My mind raced back to the sturdy stone wall near Bloody Lane. I felt again its unyielding bulk beneath my hands. *I need a wall to protect me. No, a tower!* I visualized massive stones flying up from the pasture in bursts of dirt and sod. The stones spun and rotated around me and dropped with jarring thumps, locking into place to form an impenetrable fortress on all sides of me. I looked up at the circle of sky above me and called one more rock from the field, a huge flat slab of limestone that burst out of the ground in an explosion of debris, knifed through the sky to me, and settled with a tremble on top of my cell, bringing me darkness and security.

"Come here now."

I dropped to my knees in my dark tower, grabbed the back of my head with both hands, and pressed my forearms against my ears. "I'm not listening, I'm not listening, I'm not listen…" I nearly jumped out of my skin when I felt the light tap on my shoulder.

"It's time to surrender now. You know…for real this time."

"No, Mick, I don't want to. I don't want to see it."

"Well, that's entirely beside the point, you know."

"This is a mistake! This is all supposed to be for Neil and Terri and Carla. This doesn't have anything to do with me."

"It's time to surrender."

The thunder cracked again and the ground trembled. A rain of dirt sifted down on me. My tower was swaying and shifting. A small rock popped loose and hit my back. I scrambled to my feet and opened my eyes. Where the stone had been, a needle of light penetrated my shaft of darkness.

"No!"

I put my hand over the tiny gap in the wall. Another stone popped loose and landed at my feet. I pressed my other palm against the new hole. *I can stand like this forever, blocking out the light. I can.* I relaxed into the wall of my tower, allowing it to support my forearms. *I feel safe here. Screw the vulture.*

"The wall is an illusion, Seeker. It does not protect you, but keeps you blind to what would set you free. Push it down and come to me. I offer you the opportunity to put down your burden."

I stood in the dark and listened to my own shallow breathing.

"Do you see what you have dropped? What you must deny to remain in that cage of your own design?"

"What I've dropped? I'm not playing at riddles, Vulture. I'm not…" *The feather!* The hawk feather was no longer in my hand.

"That's right, Seeker. It's there at your feet, but you'll have to lower your hands to retrieve it."

And then I understood. I was at a crossroads and was being offered the higher road — the road out of this valley. The wings of the hawk were waiting for me, but I was still too heavy with baggage to take flight. I needed to surrender to the guidance of the vulture. I dropped my hands. The white feather glowed in the half-light. As I bent to retrieve it, I imagined the walls of the tower exploding outward into space, the stones tumbling away into nothingness. When I straightened up, I was standing in the ravine looking into the eye of a sleek black vulture perched high up in a stately red oak tree.

"Come here."

I walked to the base of the oak and looked up. The vulture cocked its head to consider me and then with a tremendous flapping of wings, rose from the tree and took off across the ravine. I tracked its flight as far as I could with my eyes and then turned to my left to watch it flap with much deliberation up and over the gray monument on the opposite bank. All sound ceased, save the trilling song of a field sparrow, and the vulture disappeared as if plucked from the sky by an invisible hand. As the bird sang, the outline of the monument became fuzzy and indistinct. The gray of the granite slowly faded allowing blue sky to shine through. By the time the sparrow had finished its song, the monument had disappeared from the landscape. There was a moment of silence when I thought nothing more would happen and then the world exploded into a roar of continuous cannon and musket fire. Thick acrid smoke rolled down the hillside in an unbroken billowing wave that crashed into the ravine and across the landscape behind me. I stood in the blinding smoke, deafened by the cannonade and realized that my heart was racing as fast as if I'd just run a hard mile. I badly needed oxygen but every breath I took in seared my lungs, causing me to cough and choke. I gasped and whimpered, desperate for a stream of clean air to miraculously push through the poisonous vapor that had, no doubt, been belched directly from the bowels of hell just for me. With no miracle in sight, I took one last shuttering breath and resigned myself to suffocating in the accursed fog. The smoke immediately rose up fifteen or twenty feet and thinned. I could see the sun now, high in the sky above the slope, and I could see the musket in my hands.

I instinctively looked to my right and there was Andy, his face black with soot and streaked with the tears flowing out of his watering eyes. He caught me looking, gave me a sweet half-smile, and leaned toward me to yell in my ear. "It's gonna be okay, little brother. Try to steady your hands. We're gonna be okay. Rebs is waiting for us up there and we're gonna bring it to 'em."

I tried to give a smile back and looked past Andy down the line of men. I could see little Davey at his elbow and the twenty men beyond him who weren't hidden in the smoke. Everyone was tensed with bayoneted rifles ready at their hips. I glanced to the left. The smoke swirled upward, exposing a long line of crouched men that snaked its way along the base of the ravine before disappearing on the other side of a small rise. A cannon boomed somewhere to the left high above us. A black mass came screaming over the bank and hit the ground hard behind me. I turned and watched it bounce several times before disappearing into a little copse of oak trees at the edge of an orchard behind us.

I looked wide-eyed at Andy, who smiled back at me. "It'll be okay. We'll be okay. We'll be back up in there picking peaches before the day is done."

I smiled and nodded. *A peach would taste good right about now.*

"Here, take a swig of this. It'll settle you. Just a little swig." Andy handed me his uncorked canteen. The sweet, oaky smell of good whiskey wafted up to meet my nose. I tipped my head, gathered a mouthful of the smooth brew, and allowed it to slide down my throat. I felt calmer as I corked the canteen and handed it back.

The cannon boomed again and this time the shell flew high over our heads and tore a branch, big enough to kill a man, off one of the oak trees. With a whoosh and a thud, the branch dropped to the ground behind me. The man to my left, the same man I'd helped off the ground earlier in the day, began laughing hysterically. I turned toward him and noticed his eyes were wild — wide and darting everywhere at once. His lips, blackened with soot, were pulled back from his yellowed teeth. He tipped back his head and howled. Beyond this lunatic, I could see a disruption along the far end of the line where it disappeared over the rise. An officer was tramping behind the men with his sword raised shouting something I couldn't hear. Men dropped to the ground and rolled to their backs with their muskets clutched to their chests and bellies as the officer passed them. I was about to follow suit and had dropped to one knee when Andy grabbed my arm and shook his head.

"Not our regiment! Wait for Colonel Matthews!"

I straightened back up and almost immediately heard a bellow from the right side of the line. "Get down, all of you! Get down!" I snapped my head to the right at the familiar voice and saw a tall officer with a heavy dark beard marching with great confidence behind the line of men. He had his sword raised over his head to get our attention and was using his free hand to gesture. I felt immediately relieved. It was Neil. We were in good hands and would be picking peaches before the day was done. Men quickly dropped to the ground and rolled to their backs as Neil strode down the line. "Artillery is too hot, boys! Keep your places and lie down!" As Neil passed behind Andy, I couldn't help glancing back with a big grin on my face. Neil gave me a quick nod and was passing behind me when the cannon far up on the hill boomed once again. I dropped to my belly and rolled onto my back with my musket clenched to my chest. The gentle thud of the cannon ball let me know that it had found flesh, either human or horse. I slid my right elbow back and used it to partially raise up. Above me, Neil executed a strange pirouette and turned back my way. I noticed first the surprised expression on his face and next that his legs had not turned with the rest of his body. His upraised arm went slack, bending limply at the wrist, then the elbow, and finally the shoulder. The sword that arm had so resolutely raised slipped silently to the ground. As Neil's knees buckled, his upper body continued to rotate and his head drooped lazily until he was looking me right in the eye. His left leg fell away from his body then, dragging a long string of bloody gray intestine with it. Something warm, heavy, and wet hit my legs, but I didn't look down.

Neil never spoke again, but collapsed forward and fell across my chest with a choked sign. His weight dropped me flat back and crushed my musket into my body, pinching my fingers painfully. Using my legs, I rolled to my right, freeing a little space between us. I pushed against my musket for all I was worth with my forearms and shoulders and used it like a lever to pry Neil away from me as I rolled to my right. He slid to the ground on his left side with his face pressed mostly into the ground and lay still with his right leg twisted tightly at the hip like a wrung-out washrag stuck out from his body at a grotesque angle that my mind was unwilling to comprehend. I rolled farther to my right and was about to scramble away from Neil's body when I noticed he was still there. He was watching me through his right eye, which was still alert and alive. I dropped back down next to him and put my face close to his so he could more easily see me. I found his hand and held it tight as I looked deeply into his bright blue eye and said goodbye.

"You done good, Colonel Matthews," I said. "You done good. Your war is over now but you led us well and made us soldiers. You never once let us down. We'd of followed you to the ends of the Earth and back, I hope you know, and never of once questioned your devotion to us. And we'll get you back home now, Colonel Matthews. We'll get you back home to your wife and your little girl." A faint smile played over Neil's lips and he gave me a slight nod. Then the light went out of his eye and he was gone. "You was like a father to me," I added softly. "I won't ever forget you."

"Oh, Lord, Colonel Matthews! Oh, Lord!" Andy was up and standing over me then, helping me untangle myself from Neil's body. I slid away from Neil but stayed on the ground, feeling too shaken to stand as the whiskey I'd just gulped rose up in my throat on a wave of nausea. The man on the other side of me was now back to his senses and was unfastening the blanket roll that he wore in a loop over one shoulder.

Captain Jones appeared out of the smoke, looked down at Neil's body, and was visibly shaken. "Oh, Samuel," the captain said as he squatted next to Neil and tenderly patted his shoulder. "I'll miss you, dear friend." Captain Jones lifted his head to see the cluster of men staring down at him and rose to his feet.

"Men, let's get Colonel Matthews to the rear. Has anyone gathered his effects?"

"No, sir."

"Fetch me his hat."

Sergeant Carson appeared with Neil's hat, which Captain Jones sat next to his body like a bucket. The captain squatted down, rolled Neil to his back, and gently went through his pockets. He gathered the folding knife with the ivory case that I'd seen so often in Neil's hands as he sat whittling by the fire of a night, the lucky gold dollar that he'd worked so heavily between his thumb and forefinger that Lady Liberty's head was about rubbed away, and a small copper anti-slavery token. Captain Jones unbuttoned Neil's frock coat, removed his watch and fob, and went through his interior pockets, finding his diary, the stub of a pencil, his Bible, a packet of letters, his wallet, and a tiny framed portrait of a little girl with golden curls in the pocket closest to his heart.

"Alright, then," Captain Jones said as he wiped tears off his face. "Roll him on the blanket. Someone fetch his leg and his sword." I helped roll Neil back onto his side as the blanket was spread on the ground behind him. Several of us rolled him to his back and worked the blanket under him. Andy reached over and carefully closed Neil's eyes.

"Here, then," Andy said and pointed at my pants. "Here, then, Eli."

I looked down at the large piece of beef steak across my thigh and couldn't for the life of me figure out where it had come from. When realization hit, my hands began to tremble again, but not so badly that I couldn't peel the slab of Neil's flesh from my pants and add it to the wreckage on the blanket. Two men appeared from the smoke carrying Neil's mangled left leg with a portion of his lower body still attached and trailing intestine. Ignoring the gore, they placed the leg reverently with the rest of Neil's body. Sergeant Carson handed Neil's sword to Captain Jones.

"Let's get him to the house there behind us. It's being used as a field hospital," said Captain Jones. I squatted next to Neil's head and gathered up one corner of the blanket. The man who had been in line next to me took the corner across from me, Andy gathered one corner at Neil's feet, and Sergeant Carson gathered the other.

"At the count of three," Sergeant Carson instructed. "One, two, three." We all lifted in unison. Neil's body lay heavily in the sling as if he were asleep in a hammock enjoying the late afternoon breeze. To distract myself, I imagined him that way with a cool glass of lemonade in one hand and an interesting book in the other.

Captain Jones looked over at Davey, who had dropped his musket and was standing at Neil's side silently sobbing. "Private, pick up your musket and take Colonel Matthew's personals and his sword along with the men. Pass them to Sergeant Carson when his hands are free."

"Yes, sir." Davey scrambled after his gun and held it in his left hand as Captain Jones tucked Neil's hat into the crook of the boy's arm and handed him the sword.

"Alright, men. Colonel Matthews was a gallant officer and a loyal friend to us all. His war is done now. May God bless him and keep him. For-ward, de-taillll!"

Captain Jones saluted Neil's body as we moved as a single man to carry our leader quickly to the rear. Sergeant Carson set the pace and led us back toward the copse of oak trees, beyond which stood the orchard and house. I was focused on staying in step and affording Neil the respect he deserved, so I didn't hear the boom of the cannon this time, only the shriek of the shell when it was already upon us. Sergeant Carson had always told us not to flinch when we heard the shells shriek like that because they were already past and there was no sense in showing fear. So my head was up when I saw the gaping hole open in the back of Andy's blouse and his body fly forward into the large oak tree under which we were passing. My eyes were open when the trunk of the tree exploded into a shower of splinters. My mind was clear when Davey dropped his load and ran away in the smoke. By the time the acorns began to pelt me, though, I'd fallen to my knees with my palms raised before me and was screaming.

"Noooooooooooo!"

I was sobbing with my head tipped to the heavens when the little rectangle of heavy paper drifted back to Earth, spoiled now with a smear of blood but still bearing the likeness of a stoic young woman and a little girl of about two years with tight curls and a handkerchief pinned to her little dress.

CHAPTER 36

COMING HOME: THE WALLS COME DOWN AND ONE LAST THING

Everything went dark and a tight cocoon pressed around my body, but I wanted to run. I struggled to escape from whatever was holding me so tightly to this horrible place, but my knees were pressed against my chest and my arms were pinned tightly to my sides. *Let me go. Oh, please, let me go.* My heart pounded and my breath came in short, shallow puffs. I took a deep breath and strained with all I had against the force that was holding me still. My head, rather than the cocoon, ripped open and a little crack of light entered my consciousness. I was angry now and focused my rage on that crack of light, willing it to explode into a thousand jagged shards. The light, however, didn't cooperate and, instead, glowed gently as cousin Isaiah's face, followed by his shoulders and upper body, popped though the crack. He seemed to be peering cautiously around a heavy door that had been pushed open just a bit. Isaiah's face dissolved into a grin as he made eye contact with me. I scowled back at him. Isaiah turned then and looked back over his shoulder, nodding and speaking to someone else behind the door. The crack of light widened and there was Neil, standing beside Isaiah with the most loving and patient look on his face. Both of them smiled wider and then broke into laughter. Andy had come up from behind and was attempting to worm his way between them. Neil and Isaiah made room for Andy's grinning mug and draped their arms over his shoulders.

My body was racked by agonized sobs again. I tried to shoo them all out of my mind's eye, but they wouldn't go. My eyes darted around in a panic looking for anything, anything at all that I could use to wall them out.

"Mick! Help me!"

"Ah, my pleasure — I've been waiting for you to ask. You were strong and brave, you know. You held the hands of the cousin you adored and the man who was as much a father to you as your own while they slipped away and left you. You accompanied your beloved brother's body home, comforted three young widows, and held their children. You reassured your sisters that your brother had not suffered, stood silently with your father as he stared out over the hills, kissed your mother's tears. You offered tender strength and unwavering compassion at three funerals that emptied every house and hollow in the county. You never once broke down back then, did you? Even as your hometown fell to its knees. You stayed steady and made things easier for everyone else. What a heavy load for a boy of only seventeen."

"Stop it, Mick! Why are you doing this to me?"

"And you went back to the war, didn't you? Some marveled at your bravery and sense of duty, but that was never it, was it? You knew it was the easy way out — so much easier to be back among brothers who likewise held their grief behind a wall of resolve and could take their anger out against a sanctioned enemy. Much more comfortable than being enveloped in the open wound of your family and that of your entire town. And there was always the hope, of course, that death would find you, too, out there in some farmer's field far from home. But that didn't happen for you, did it? You returned home at the end of the war a hero with pain and anger so deeply ingrained across your heart that you never again felt fully alive."

I moaned, too broken down to resist the pain. "They left me, Mick. I loved them. I needed them. And they all left me."

"Yes, they did. Feel the grief and anger of that betrayal all the way down to its core. All the way down. And when you're done with it, well, it's time for you to forgive and allow joy back into your being." Mick left me then with a soft pop.

I looked back at the three smiling faces still before me in the light. Neil's lips began to move and I heard his voice softly in my ear. "Come back to me now, come back." The darkness swept forward to blot out the light and I realized with a jolt that the cocoon wrapped so tightly around me that I could barely breathe was Neil's arms. I felt him breathing against me and didn't understand. The acorns were still pelting the side of my face. Trickles of Andy's blood were still running down my back. I'd watched Neil die, but Neil was holding me.

A fresh wave of grief filled me and I screamed again. "Noooooooooo! Don't leave me!" I sobbed and choked. Powerful pain seared through my right thigh and I suddenly realized my leg was on fire. I struggled against Neil. *What had happened to me? Was I hit?* Another wave of grief tore through me, threatening to split my heart wide open. The pain in my thigh intensified until I was sure my leg would also rip apart. I pulled a hand loose and frantically patted down my leg. I felt the hard lump of something round in my pocket and pressed my hand against it. Stonewall Jackson's acorn. *It's cursed! Dammit! Why had I trusted a Reb?* A wave of rage and grief crashed down over me. I heard the skin on my palm sizzle and pop as the acorn burned me through my jeans. *My hand! It's destroying my hand! I need that cursed thing away from me!* I slid my charred hand up my thigh and struggled to push my fingers into my pocket, but Neil held me too tightly. Rage filled me up. *Why is he letting me get hurt?* The pain ripped past my hip and up my back. I screamed with no words as the searing pain sank its red talons into my head. I wanted to push it down, push it away, refuse to own it, but, instead, this time I felt it. I felt every last bit of it and let it take its best shot at destroying me, finally not afraid of what it would do to me. My entire body, my entire existence burned and writhed and when I thought it couldn't get any worse, my mind detached and I found myself inside the pain just having a little look around.

I walk from room to room in what appears to be the second floor of an empty house, throwing back the curtains and opening the windows to a strong, refreshing breeze. Out the windows, I see green grass, trees swaying against a beautiful pink and violet sky shot through with the golden rays of the sun, and the smooth rolls of the mountains in the distance. The birds are singing all at once. I divide their chorus up into individual songs so I can visualize each bird and then allow the melody to come back together.

I find the stairs and go down to the first floor of the house. I realize that I'm in my own house. It's empty except for a few pieces of furniture. I go from room to room on the first floor and open all the windows. The house fills with the glorious light of dawn — expectant and golden. I walk into the dining room and find a red axe, like one I used to own, stuck in the dining room table. I can see that the axe is pinning a note to the table. I move over to read the note.

It's time to ride your donkey, fool!

I laugh. Of course. I walk to the front door of the house and find that it's standing wide open. I step over the threshold. The sound of the birds becomes one continuous swell of joy. I bounce off the porch and onto the lawn. A dirt trail stretches off into the distance. A herd of does and fawns stands along the trail. They are waiting for me. I turn to take one last look at my old house. The walls tremble and creak, breaking free of the foundation. Then, as if caught in a vortex, the house begins to swirl and break apart. A gentle joy sweeps me as I watch the house reduced first to rubble, then to dust, and finally to a swirling cyclone of crackling red energy that climbs my leg and deposits itself in my jeans pocket.

The scene flickered away and the searing pain in my leg was replaced by a gentle throbbing. My awareness was now full of the most beautiful indigo blue light. I stepped forward into the light, stretched out my arms, and invited the glow of awareness into every crook and cranny of my being. From behind me a man gently cleared his throat. I slowly dropped my arms and turned to find Lieutenant William Dupree smiling at me from beneath a neatly trimmed mustache. He was resplendent now in a beautiful dress uniform of gray wool with light blue collar and cuffs. His hat was crisply blocked and the silver star pinned through the crown was polished to a dazzling gleam. Gold braid decorated his sleeves and matched the pairs of gold bars on his collars and the double row of meticulously polished gold buttons that marched up his chest. Beneath the black leather belt worn over his coat, a red sash was carefully tied. A sword in a silver and gold sheath hung at his side, reaching almost to the toe of his polished boot.

"You done good, kid," Bill said. "You done good."

I moved closer and smiled up into Bill's eyes. "Thank you for guiding me, Bill."

"My pleasure entirely. But, your war is over now. It's time to get on home."

"See you around, hey?"

"Every time a crow caws, kid. Every time a crow caws." Bill snapped to rigid attention and offered me a formal salute. I bent my right elbow to return it and found Neil's hand on my forehead. I wrapped my fingers around Neil's and squeezed.

"I'm back."

"Are you sure?"

"Yeah."

The cocoon around me gently unwound. Neil continued to hold me with one arm while he stroked my head. "I'm so sorry. I knew in the portrait gallery that I didn't survive the war, but I couldn't tell you. I'm not sure why, but I just couldn't tell you."

"Oh, Neil. Do you remember what happened?"

"Yes. And I remember how distraught I was when I realized I was hit and was being called away. I struggled to stay — I wanted so desperately to stay. I remember you were there and you helped me let go. Thank you."

"You're so welcome, Neil. You're so very welcome."

Neil kissed my head and held me a while longer. "Are you ready to get out of the rain and hail? There's an open shed behind the Otto House where we can wait the rest of this storm out."

"It's raining?"

"Yes, you're soaked through and the hail pelting us is the size of golf balls. Your face is badly bruised. Let me stand you up." Neil slowly stood up, bringing me upright with him. He kept his arms around me and my head tucked under his chin, deflecting most of the hailstones that were pounding us. "You have your legs?"

"Yes, I'm ready."

Neil took my hand and led me through the downpour just a short distance to a rough, old shed tucked up under the trees. He escorted me through a narrow doorway into a dry, dusty space, which judging by the furnishings had at one time served as an outhouse.

I looked up at Neil and gave him a weak smile.

"Oh, your face. I'm so sorry I didn't find you sooner." Neil gently ran his fingertips over my face, which I realized now was throbbing in a dozen places. An angry lump over Neil's left eye indicated that he hadn't been spared by the hail, either. Otherwise, he looked whole and healthy — soaked to the skin and probably as exhausted as I was, but very much alive. I pushed the wet hair off my tender forehead and reached around to explore the numerous sore spots on my back. Pressing my saturated t-shirt gently against my skin, I caught the last annoying trickles of water still running down my back.

"Good thing we brought a change of clothes," I cracked.

Neil smiled at me with his entire being. "Yeah, good thing."

We stood silently listening to the hail drumming the wooden roof of the shed for quite some time. When the storm finally slackened enough to allow conversation, I asked my question with no preamble.

"Did you know about Andy?"

"Andy?"

"Andy was killed, too, as we were carrying your body to the rear."

"Oh, no. Oh, no. I'm so sorry." Neil teared up.

"No, no, no, no. You shouldn't be sorry. If it was going to happen, it was going to happen. And you were right there waiting when he needed your help. He loved his wife and baby so much, Neil, I don't think…" My voice trailed away imagining what it had been like for Andy to leave us all behind in 1862.

"Well, he loves you so much, too. And so do I. I know it hasn't always been easy, but…do you realize how much you've always been there for me? And now what you've done for me? I should still be crying in my beer but instead I feel like my life is suddenly a wide open adventure." Neil wrapped me up and hugged me.

"I love you guys, too, and I'm glad we've hung out together for at least a couple lifetimes," I said into Neil's chest.

Neil gently kissed my head and laughed. "At least a couple."

Neil let me go then and stuck his head outside the shed. "It's getting late and the sky is brightening to the south. Want to hoof it back to the vehicle through this last little bit of rain? We could find a hotel, shower, have a nice dinner? You up for that?"

"I am, for sure."

"Sweet."

Neil and I walked under the trees to the ravine, where I skirted around the big oak tree but paused to look one last time up the hillside at the gray monument. Neil stopped beside me.

"I'm pretty sure that's the monument to the 36th Ohio," he said. "It probably marks their farthest advance."

"Is that on our way out? Can we stop up there?"

"Sure, we can stop there, even if it's not on our way out."

Neil led the way back to the vehicle, this time making sure I was able to keep up. Instead of looping around in the soybeans, he found a different route that took us straight south on a beautiful farm lane bounded on both sides by split rail and studded with mature shade trees. We lingered for just a moment under a large maple as the rain tapered off and blew away. As the sun started to reappear through a low ceiling of thin, gray clouds, Neil pointed to a gap in the fence. "The last leg of the trail runs straight east from here and ends in the field where we parked. We cut off the southern loop of the trail and didn't see where A. P. Hill came storming across the field with his light division. Think you might like to see that some other time?"

"I'd like that, Neil. I'd like that a lot."

We started up the trail through a close-cropped field but were confronted almost immediately by two cannons set to mark a Union battery position. Neil pulled me away as I swung a hard kick in the direction of the nearest gun. "I can understand your sentiment, but we are talking government property here," he said as he dragged me down the trail by the arm. "And there's no sense in breaking a toe."

The parking area was empty by the time we reached the SUV and the sun was low in the sky. I was starting to shiver and was about to ask Neil to retrieve my suitcase out of the back so I could change into dry clothes on the spot, but he made a better suggestion. "If we hurry," he said, "we'll be able to see the sunset over the valley from the top of the hill."

"Let's hurry, then." I grabbed my fleece off the backseat and pulled it on over my wet t-shirt. Comfort could wait.

Five minutes later we were pulling into a parking space at the top of the ravine. The gray monument stood just a few hundred feet back along the road. I'd leaned over Neil trying to see it as we'd driven in but it was too far off the road to get a good look. I'd craned my head as we passed and had strained against my seatbelt to catch a glimpse out the back windows. "Be patient, we'll get there in time," Neil had assured me.

The sun was setting behind us and beginning to light up the clouds over the valley as we got out of the vehicle and walked to the edge of the bluff. I stood next to Neil where Confederate troops had been waiting for us so long ago and imagined myself as the hawk, riding the thermals over the wide valley. Just as soon as I got airborne, though, I crashed back to Earth. *My feather. Where's my feather?* I looked up at Neil panic-stricken.

"Neil..."

"Close your eyes."

"No, Neil, we have to go back..."

"Trust me and close your eyes for just a minute." Almost in tears, I closed my eyes. "Now open them."

I opened my eyes and there was my feather, twirling just beyond the tip of my nose between Neil's thumb and forefinger. "You had this in your hand when I found you. I put it in my pack for safekeeping."

I smiled up at Neil and accepted the feather from his hand. "Thank you."

"It's a hawk feather, isn't it?"

"Yeah, it is. I found it on the trail. It marked the route to...to the oak tree."

Neil put his arm over my shoulder and gave me a squeeze. "You still okay? Still want to see the monument?"

"Yes. Let's see it before the sun goes."

Neil left his arm where it was and we walked together along the crest of the hill toward the gray granite monument. As we walked, I noticed something happening in the sky. I gasped and dashed out from under Neil's arm.

"Neil, hurry!" I called back to him, pointing at the sky. "Do you see that? Hurry!"

We ran together through the wet grass and just as we reached the monument to the 36th Ohio Volunteer Infantry, a rainbow appeared across the low ceiling of gray clouds. "Whoa," Neil breathed. "It's arcing right over the monument."

"Yeah."

We watched the rainbow intensify and then fade away as the sun dropped lower. In the waning golden light, we read the inscription on the front of the monument and carefully examined the detailed muskets, swords, and other equipment that were carved in the stone. Then we walked around to the back of the monument and read the inscription there.

THIS REGIMENT ADVANCED NEAR THE BRIDGE OVER ANTIETAM CREEK ON THE MORNING OF SEPT. 17, 1862, SUPPORTING STURGIS' DIVISION. IT PARTICIPATED IN THE CHARGE BY WHICH THE BRIDGE WAS CAPTURED. LIEUT. COL. SAMUEL MATTHEWS WAS KILLED NEAR THIS SPOT.

ITS LOSS WAS 1 OFFICER AND 1 MAN KILLED; 21 MEN WOUNDED; 2 MEN MISSING. TOTAL 25.

One officer and one man killed. Two men missing. Two men, including a scared boy named Davey who'd dropped his load and run for all he was worth.

Neil and I turned and stood behind the monument for a while, silently looking out over the valley as the sun dropped below the horizon and the landscape softened. "I guess we should go," Neil finally said. "The park closes twenty minutes after sunset. And I want you to put ice on your face — your right eye is swelling shut."

"Okay, but I need to do something first."

I left Neil and walked a few yards past the monument to stand alone at the edge of the ravine where he and Andy had been killed. One last time, I scanned the beautiful rolling valley guarded by its granite and marble sentinels. Back behind the South Mountain range, the clouds were glowing pink in a violet sky. Against that backdrop, the bowl of the land offered up a magical swirl of iridescent greens and golds. Only one thing was missing. I dug into my wet jeans and worked the acorn out of my pocket. Clutching my feather in my left hand, I cocked my right arm and flung the acorn into the ravine with everything I had.

"Damn, you have an arm," Neil said. "You know, Ellie, we really could use a good center fielder for Wednesday night softball, if you'd be interested."

I looked back at Neil who was gazing at me with unabashed admiration. "I just might be."

Far off in the distance a hawk screamed. Joy filled me up and overflowed into a grin that lit up my face. "I believe we can leave this valley now, Neil."

"Alrighty, then. Follow me."

EPILOGUE

Neil and I ended up staying the rest of the week in the Sharpsburg area, reluctant to break our connection to the place and return home. We avoided the battlefield for most of the week, choosing instead to poke around nearby Shepherdstown, West Virginia, and the historic district of Harpers Ferry. By Friday, though, we were ready to finish our hike and set out before dawn so we could see the sun rise over the battlefield. I'd like to be able to tell you that the heavens split open in riotous song as the sun lifted above the fog that morning, but nothing of the sort happened. It was quiet and peaceful — an ordinary sort of start to a beautiful day.

CAST OF CHARACTERS

ANDY. I called Andy on the way back to the hotel after dinner that first night, just to hear his voice. Neil and I ended up sitting in the parking lot of the hotel for over two hours sharing the highlights of what had happened. Andy was thrilled that his personality had stayed the same for at least two lifetimes — taking that as confirmation that he was doing at least a few things right — and was proud that he was brave in battle and looked out for me. He was stunned when I told him about Ashley and Zoe and quietly introspective when I shared what I'd learned about Carla. He sobbed when I told him how he'd died. I'm glad Neil was there on speakerphone to support my brother and walk him through his grief.

When I returned home, I found a small package from Wyoming waiting in my mailbox. It contained a shiny pebble of hematite and a note from Andy suggesting I keep the stone in my pocket to ward off negative energies.

CARLA. Shortly after I returned home, Carla called and asked if I'd like to fly out to see Andy with her. I checked in with my brother, who assured me he'd be thrilled to see her, and we flew out in early October. Sitting together around a fire under an impossibly clear sky full of stars, Andy and I gently explained to Carla what we'd learned about her previous life. Carla took it all in and was relieved to finally understand her stubborn compulsion to commit to things that weren't right for her. She shared that she'd always thought it was a necessary part of growing up to put aside your true desires and stick things out, as painful as that might be.

I flew home alone two weeks later, not because Carla and Andy had reconciled, but because Andy had introduced Carla to his new friend, Jake, who just happened to be the director of a local dance troupe. When I left Carla at the studio with a key to her townhouse in my pocket and a promise to pick up Bianca and pay the pet sitter, she and Jake were sharing a green juice after a coaching session. I had never seen Carla more radiant.

ASHLEY. I wasn't exactly sure what I should share with Ashley about her past life. The window through which I'd peered into her world seemed so small, offering me only a suggestion of what she might have experienced. In the end, I invited her and Zoe to my place for lunch in late October. It was a glorious fall afternoon, the first spell of Indian summer after an early frost, so we enjoyed our quiche and fruit salad out on the deck. After lunch, while Zoe dragged around a piece of ribbon for Bianca to stalk, I asked Ashley if she'd ever felt afraid of losing Paul and being left alone to raise Zoe. Her eyes went wide and she admitted that she lived in constant, overwhelming fear of losing her husband and having to support herself, but had shared with no one what she felt was a completely irrational obsession. I told her then about Andy and the letter he'd read to me in 1862. Ashley laughed at the thought of being married to Andy, looked pained at the news of his death, and was downright shocked when I got to the part about the soap business. She'd just that weekend taken a soap-making class at the arts center, had loved it, and was playing around with the idea of a home-based business.

Right before Christmas, Ashley stopped by with a box of handmade soaps and lotions for me to test for her and the exciting news that she was pregnant. She'd shared her worry with Paul, who immediately had a complete physical, took out more life insurance, and assured Ashley he was going nowhere.

NEIL. Neil and I have been inseparable since coming back from that first trip to Antietam. We both agree that we're not exactly a couple, but are definitely best friends and confidantes. We'll let everything else play out from there. We've returned several times to the battlefield since September as Neil works on developing his leadership academy. He surprises me each trip with a new tour that focuses on the leadership styles of a fresh set of Civil War officers — both the successful and the not so much. With my permission, Neil has modified the "Zoo of Generals" for use in his lesson plan, expanding it to include the civilian folk I met at the portrait gallery. We're planning on visiting other battlefields and museums in the future where Neil feels sure we'll encounter additional casts of characters to fill out the menagerie.

And before I forget, Neil's new living history friends have tagged along several times now on our Antietam excursions and are encouraging Neil to train as a battlefield guide. He's seriously considering it as long as it won't interfere with his summers — he'll be spending those with his kids.

TERRI. Terri is still struggling to find her tribe, but I've been encouraging her not to give up. She's recently embraced the idea of jettisoning things from her life that just aren't working and has been talking about leaving the university. Through a bit of trickery, I was able to get Neil and Terri back together for drinks and appetizers, this time at my house in early November. The two of them got along tolerably well and Neil has been enthusiastic about mentoring Terri. He's met with her several times but hasn't been able so far to help her modify her approach. Neil is beginning to recognize that he's not going to be able to reach everyone. We're both wondering if Terri might just need one more lifetime, or maybe two or three, to crack this particular nut.

Neither Neil nor I have been able to broach the subject of the Civil War with Terri, but we haven't ruled it out when she seems ready.

ISAIAH. Since we were still around and avoiding the battlefield, Neil and I stopped by Isaiah's metal works shop that first week in Sharpsburg. Isaiah looked up from his work and grinned when we stepped over the threshold of the historical log cabin that served as his shop. He'd been expecting us, he said, and even had a pot of coffee on. As we sat together and sipped coffee on the little porch attached to the back of the cabin, Isaiah asked with a twinkle in his eye if the veil out there on the battlefield had been thin enough for us the other day. Isaiah wasn't at all surprised when I immediately said yes and shared my conviction that we were cousins back in the day. He grinned and nodded. That had been his impression, too, he shared. That had been his impression, too.

Since that afternoon, I've dropped in to see Isaiah numerous times. We share a quirky knack for being able to finish each other's sentences and have been making up for lost time. During my most recent visit, we rode horses and had a green apple battle in the orchard behind his farmhouse. Chances are slim, however, that we'll be slaughtering a hog together any time soon.

ME. I woke up in my own bed that first morning back home and felt completely at ease for the first time in my life. I rolled over to check the time and found staring at me from my bedside table the tiny iron snake that Isaiah had given me in the diner. I laughed and stared back, truly understanding how it felt to shed your old skin and be reborn. My deep-seated grief had completely washed away with the last drops of rain on the battlefield and months later has shown no signs of settling back into my life. My world now is bright and wide open and my sense of wonder at its beauty is limitless.

I started writing this story down as soon as I got home, sure that it didn't belong to just a few and needed to be shared with others who are searching for their own paths home. Andy and Neil keep telling me it's going to be a bestseller and I'll never have to work for a living again. That's fine with me because all I want to do now is write, explore, and write some more. According to Mick, of course, I still have more to remember and am at great risk of falling straight off track, but I'm willing to allow the rest of my life to unfold in all good time. Until then…

It's time to drop your baggage, Seeker, and climb up on that donkey.

ACKNOWLEDGMENTS

I send crows with messages of gratitude strapped on their backs to Ame Hughes, Molly Baker Halstead, Nancie Waterman, Jacob Nordby, Elmdea Adams, Barb Black, and Heidi Sherwin, who read parts or all of an early draft and provided a magical mix of invaluable feedback and encouragement to keep writing. Thank you one and all, with special thanks to Molly, who provided an especially detailed critique that helped me focus the story, and to Ame, who read every revision of every chapter and stuck with me to the very end.

I send a crow, also, to Joanne Sprott, who provided editorial services. Thank you, Joanne, for your fine assistance.

I would also like to acknowledge Melvin Clarke, abolitionist lawyer and lieutenant colonel of the 36th Ohio Volunteer Infantry, who was the real Samuel Matthews. You will find mention of Colonel Clarke, rather than my fictional Colonel Matthews, on the 36th Ohio monument at Antietam National Military Park. Thank you for your devotion and sacrifice, Colonel Clarke, and thank you for inspiring this story.

Meet the Author

Linda S. Gribko was born in Oregon and raised in semi-rural Maryland—in the middle of nowhere, but just twenty miles from the galleries and museums of downtown DC. Naturally drawn to nature, art, and writing, she chose natural resources as her initial career path while pushing art and creative writing into the hobby closet. She earned a B.S. in wildlife and fisheries at Virginia Tech and spent several years after graduation chasing field positions across the majestic and not so majestic landscapes of the West—the Cascade Range of Oregon, Prince of Wales Island off the coast of Alaska, the western slope of the Rockies, a trailer parked beside a dam in eastern Washington.

After some additional bouncing around and a few years as a restaurant manager, she landed in Morgantown, West Virginia—convinced that she needed to pursue a graduate degree. She earned a Ph.D. in forestry from West Virginia University, but never really thought out what she might like to do with such a degree. With a need to support herself, she stayed on in Morgantown and worked in numerous fields—academia, computer modeling, garden design, retail sales—and kept herself afloat while failing to feel passionate about her work. Skills in mapping and GIS eventually led her to a corporate career in market analytics, which she left in early 2014 to launch a butterfly gardening business.

Although never setting out to be a writer, Linda always wrote. As she wound her way through her unplanned life, however, her writing moved from quirky and free-flowing to staid and minimalistic. Leaving behind the animal stories of her youth and the satirical essays of her teenage years, she leaned into the production of research articles, landscape maintenance plans, and business reports. She began a butterfly gardening blog in 2014, but struggled to get excited about topics that others had already covered. She moved on to philosophical posts and enjoyed writing those well enough that she outlined a book about tree communities as analogs for human behavior. Before she'd written a complete chapter, though, fate intervened in the form of a writing prompt. The assignment was poetry. She penned *Holding Back Her Song*, a poem about stepping out of the shadows to express oneself. The outline for the tree book hit the shredder and in November 2016 she published *Giving Voice to Dawn*, her debut novel.

Passion for writing novels has now eclipsed Linda's desire to plant milkweed and New England asters in her neighbors' yards, and she's shuttered the butterfly gardening business. In addition to working on the next installment of *Ellie's Story*, Linda is also a photographer and artist, best known for her wildflower photographs and her nature mandalas—round, digital illustrations created from her photographs.

Ellie's Story Continues...

Come along as Ellie explores her passions and rides her donkey into adventure. You can find her continuing story in the second book in the series, *The Lion's Apprentice*, set on the fields of Gettysburg.

Stay up to date on all L. S. Gribko's doings and join the journey to the third book of *Ellie's Story* when you sign up to receive her newsletter (https://www. MilkweedRising.com/subscriber-page/).

And, don't forget to express your overwhelming joy at having read this story by leaving a review wherever you purchased your copy. Your support is so very much appreciated and helps others find and enjoy *Ellie's Story*.

Made in the USA
Monee, IL
09 June 2022

97762841R10187